The Ladies of Hatteras

The Ladies of Hatteras

Dorsey Butterbaugh

Copyright © 2022 Dorsey Butterbaugh
All Rights Reserved
Fenwick Island, Delaware

Cover photo and photo of Dorsey Butterbaugh by Tim Collins of TC Inspirations, Salisbury, Maryland.

Production assistance by Steve Robison, Rehoboth Beach, Delaware.

ISBN: 9798370855702

To Suzanne, the Lady in my life.

1

Tall, faded dune grasses swayed in a collective rhythm like gentle swells coming off the ocean or a crowd of people doing the wave at a stadium. Unlike the stadium crowd or the ocean water, the grasses were silent in their movement. It caused one to take a deep breath as a sense of peace permeated the scene. There were a few gusts over fifteen knots, otherwise the wind held steady between eight and ten. To the left, the double line of dunes was all that protected the road from the Atlantic Ocean, which was resting peacefully for the moment. To the right lay Albemarle Sound, a two-mile-wide body of water so shallow you could walk nearly all the way across. Its brackish waters were also calm. This stretch of sand served one main purpose in nature's long-term plan, and that was to protect the mainland of North Carolina from the Atlantic Ocean. Like many barrier islands, the Outer Banks of North Carolina were narrow yet effective in performing their duty. Challenged frequently during the winter months and throughout the hurricane seasons, the piles of sand, held together by the roots of the dune grasses, stood firm against the tantrums of Mother Nature. Today, however, there was no anger. Today, there was tranquility.

Route NC12 ran from Norfolk to the southernmost tip of Hatteras Island. Except through Nags Head, it was two lanes the entire stretch. The road's surface sported enough bumps and irregularities to keep one close to the 50 mile an hour posted speed. Dr. Robert Battlegrove looked at the speedometer and verified the cruise control was holding at 55. The fuel gauge read a touch above half and no alarm lights were flashing. A glance in the rearview mirror showed no one following. The road ahead was clear, and he worked a kink out of his neck and stretched his legs against the floorboard. It had been an uneventful seven-hour trip from Baltimore, exactly how he planned it. Except for one stop for fuel and his bladder, the miles and time passed quickly. It was the way it used to be five years before. Except for the ongoing construction of new businesses and beach houses along the way, the scene was the same. The miles ticked off, a little less than a minute a mile. Yes, it had been an uneventful trip. He planned to keep it that way the next forty minutes or so.

A mile marker flashed by. If he remembered correctly, only fifteen miles to the bridge, and then onto the island. Three more mile-markers and then he saw the sign he had been anticipating: *Oregon Inlet...12 miles*. He smiled as he saw the holes in the sign. The same sign with the same three holes had been there since he first came to the Outer Banks some ten years earlier. His smile widened. So many years had passed—so many seasons, so many storms, even a few hurricanes. Beaches eroded away, houses were damaged, and a new inlet had cut through the island a couple years earlier. Yet the sign survived it all.

"Hello, dear friend," he said, as the sign disappeared from his rearview mirror. It was the same greeting he gave each time they met.

Twelve miles to Oregon Inlet, a mile or so across the bridge and then onto Hatteras Island. Hatteras, North Carolina was some fifty miles long and a stone's throw wide most of its length. For years, the island was a remote vacation spot where people went to escape the routine of their life back in *urbania*. Housing choices were simple. You stayed at one of the old wooden motels, you camped, or you rented a cottage on the beach. Activities consisted mostly of surfing, fishing or sunbathing. In years past, while the island was busy during the summer season, it was never crowded. With a little effort, you could always find a secluded spot on the beach. Over the past couple decades, however, that all changed. The permanent population was now over four thousand, and with the real estate boom and mankind's continual migration back to the ocean, Cape Hatteras had become one of the premier vacation spots along the east coast. It was now crowded at least six months out of the year.

It had been a good excuse to stop going there five years before, thought Robert.

A good excuse maybe. However, not a truthful one.

Five years. It sounded like such a long time. Sixty months, 260 weeks, 1825 days. The sign with the three holes had weathered many storms. Yet, the time had passed quickly. He had been busy…too busy maybe. First, he had to finish medical school, then a year's internship before starting his residency in emergency medicine.

That's where he was now in his life. Finish this year, and then a year as the chief resident (announced the week before) of emergency medicine at Johns Hopkins Hospital in the heart of Baltimore—a good combination to complete a great education. It took a disciplined mind and a strong body to survive the rigors of such training. Physically, he lost a few pounds. Emotionally, he'd kept from being committed to the psych unit. Two good landmarks, two good mile-markers indicating things were going to be okay. He would survive. A lot of years under his belt. Less than two years to go.

The miles passed smoothly and quickly. The new BMW X3 took the irregularities in the road with little effort. Robert smiled. So far, the SUV was living up to its reputation. Power, performance, and comfort; all rolled into one. Jet black on the outside, black leather on the inside, sport wheels, a luggage rack, an upgraded Bose stereo system and all-wheel drive—everything he wanted. The car was a gift to himself. He initially planned on making such a purchase when he completed his residency. However, learning that he had been named chief resident moved the timetable forward. He tried telling himself that status had nothing to do with his decision. He knew, however, there was a certain amount of ego involved. After all, it was this ego, kept mostly under wraps, that allowed him to survive the grueling education and training necessary to reach a point in life where such a vehicle was affordable.

Robert chose Hatteras Island as his first road trip because the Outer Banks beaches were open to the public. So long as you didn't act crazy and knew what you were doing, you could drive on the beach anytime. He loved all sorts of outdoor activities, from skiing to hiking and camping, to long rides where few others ventured. However, his favorite was surf fishing along the Outer Banks, another reason for his return to the area. To the young doctor, there was nothing like being on the beach in the early morning and watching the sun rise from the ocean.

Robert had looked forward to this trip for a long time. Finishing his residency was the goal. The new vehicle and subsequent ride on the beaches of Hatteras were the rewards. That the timetable had been moved up was of little consequence. That just made it more exciting. And that excitement was building the further south he traveled.

When the bridge onto the island broke the horizon a few miles later, his heart started to race, his palms started to sweat. Both were unusual circumstances for him. After medical school, a year's internship and three years of residency at one of the craziest emergency rooms in Maryland, nothing much fazed him. The sight of the Oregon Inlet Bridge, however, did evoke a strong reaction. He told himself it was the excitement of finally getting back to the beaches after such a long furlough. He told himself it was the excitement of knowing his many long years of training and hard work were finally paying off. And while he still had a year as chief resident, life would be much better now. More sleep. More time to teach the younger aspiring students under his charge. More time to relax. More time to enjoy the fruits of his labor. He told himself that was why he harbored such anticipation. He knew, however, there was more to the story; reasons he had kept buried in his soul.

Until now, when the bridge onto Hatteras Island came into full view.

2

Samantha Mathews pushed open the door to the office, pausing a moment to let her eyes adjust to the inside lighting. She reached back to make sure the door closed properly. While early in the season, she had already spotted a few flying pests the day before. She loved living on Hatteras Island. She loved working at her parent's campground and resort. She loved the life on the beach. She loved wearing her tan well into the winter. She hated the insects. Bugs and hurricanes—two things that brought reality to the fantasy of living at the beach.

Checking again to make sure the door had latched; she walked up to the registration desk. "Mornin' Rhonda. Mornin' Mako."

Mako and Rhonda were the two young night clerks. They had been working at the campground since they were twelve. They were both locals, strictly defined as having been born, raised, and educated on the island since birth. They were cousins, both coming from a long line of the Green family. History claimed Wilbert Green was one of the first settlers on the island many years ago. Many of the cousins' ancestors never left the island their entire lives. The cousins were close in this claim, having only been to the mainland a couple times for field trips during school. Both girls had bubbly personalities. Both were skinny and wiry, had the Hatteras requisite dirty blond hair and bikini fitting bodies. Rhonda's hair was short and cut right below her ears. Mako's was longer and tied in a ponytail. Both had wide smiles and could flirt with the visiting boys with the best of them. They could turn on the charm towards adults as well. Their real value, however, was that they loved to work nights. Few others on the island stayed awake past ten o'clock. Unless the fish were biting at the Rodanthe pier. The cousins were hard workers and liked being the head honchos of the campground when Samantha and her parents retired for the evening to their double-wide parked on the pad behind the motel.

According to the folklore, it was locals like Mako and Rhonda who gave the island its character. Anyone else, dubbed implants, only fed off the energy of the original island residents. The problem, while the overall population of the island was increasing, the ratio of locals to implants was dropping at an alarming rate. Locals were moving out, the present generation of young adults wanting to experience something more than living in the sand their whole lives. Implants were moving in, wanting just the opposite.

While Mako and Samantha were true locals, Samantha and her family (mother, father, son, daughter, and dog) implanted to Hatteras some twenty years before when

Samantha was four years old. Their first visit was a week's vacation, made on the recommendation of a neighbor back in Ohio and to trace some genealogy lines her father had discovered. The next summer's stay was three weeks. The third summer they came and never really left, except to go home and pack up their house. Her parents bought a rundown, bankrupt campground on the edge of Avon, a small town in the middle of the island. It was a struggle for the first few years. Nearly all money went to pay the mortgage or was reinvested into the business. There were few dollars remaining for anything else. They lived off the land, or in this case the sea. Seafood was not uncommon five to six nights a week. Samantha didn't care though. She loved it. It was a gigantic playground, a gigantic sand box. In addition, until she was old enough to understand the difference, there was a giant swimming pool in her back yard. Times were tough the first few years, yet she and her family persevered. As the island grew more popular, the business grew. They now had a seventy-five-pad camp site and a thirty-five-room motel, with four cottages built by her father and brother right on the oceanfront.

In the recent past, her parents toyed with the idea of building a restaurant on the edge of the property that butted up against the main road, Highway 12. However, this idea was nixed when many of the other local restaurant owners voiced their concerns about increased competition. One man, a good friend of the Mathews and the owner of a restaurant called Avon Dunes right across the street, said he was thinking about opening a campground behind his restaurant.

The result: hands were shaken, beers were raised, friendships prevailed, and the idea of a Mathew's restaurant was dropped. The reason was simple. Regardless of whether you were a local or an implant, if you owned a business you not only depended on the tourist trade, you also relied of your fellow business owners. A compliment, a recommendation, a kind word—all served as much needed free advertisement. A harsh word or negative review could spell disaster. So, the addition of an adjoining restaurant was discussed amongst family members, talk was as far as it went. She would find out later that her father had other ideas though.

"Everything okay?" Samantha said making her way around the registration desk.

"Seventy-five and eighty-five," Mako retorted proudly. The two numbers represented the occupancy rate of the campground and motel respectively. They were the first and most important pieces of information Samantha wanted to know each morning. Occupancy rates were directly proportional to the profitability of any lodging business. They were also excellent indicators of the success of auxiliary businesses, in the Mathew's case, the general store to the left of the office. It was due to open in five minutes.

Samantha looked upward and said a silent prayer to the fish and weather gods. This spring had been exceptionally warm, and the creatures of the sea were already starting their northerly migration up the east coast. The waters right offshore were swarming with bluefish feeding off smaller sea trout and other species. The beaches were swarming with fishermen trying to feed off the fish. Of all the reasons people came to Hatteras Island, fishing was at the top of the list.

The numbers were good for this time of the year, which boded well for the rest of the season. It had been an exceptionally slow winter, attributed to the fact that the temperatures throughout the rest of the eastern United States had been mild, thus people didn't feel the urge to escape.

"Anything new?" Samantha asked.

"No, ma'am. Tide started comin' in 'bout a half hour ago so most everyone is already on the beach," Mako said.

"Well, the Avon Dunes will be glad." The restaurant across the street specialized in local seafood dishes. They were especially known for what they could do with fresh fish.

"Billy around?" Samantha asked, referring to her brother.

"No, ma'am. Ain't seen hide nor hair of him," Rhonda said.

"If you see him, tell him to come by," Mako quickly added.

Samantha smiled. She knew both girls had a crush on her younger brother, especially Mako. She had been silently stalking the boy for years. Samantha always felt there was at least a partial reciprocal feeling, yet Billy never pursued what would surely be an easy catch.

"Good work with the numbers," Samantha said as a way of keeping everyone's mind on track.

"Thank you," the cousins said simultaneously.

"Fish are doin' all the work," Mako added.

The girls were pleased with the overnight numbers for several reasons. First, the busier the front desk, the faster the night passed. The only thing the two cousins ever complained about was how slow the night went when business was slow. Second, smiles were wide because good numbers meant good bonuses. All employees of the Mathews were paid well compared to other employers on the island. However, a substantial portion of their income was based on the performance of the business, hence the importance of the occupancy numbers.

Samantha chatted a couple more minutes before heading to the store side of the complex. Her parents were both at the south end of the island checking on the *project* as they dubbed it. The job of opening the store was left to her. Additional help came in at eight, but the first two hours were all hers. A family member always opened and closed the store. It was a business practice that had served them well over the years, showing the employees the owners themselves were able and willing to work the crappy shifts. The cousins worked most of the overnights.

The coffee was already brewed. The homemade muffins supplied by Mako's mom lined the counter. Sausage biscuits supplied by Rhonda's mother sat in the warming case. Sundry, prepackaged baked goods were neatly displayed along the first aisle by the coffee. It was a good bet none of these products would move until the muffins and sausage biscuits were gone.

Samantha counted the muffins. Two dozen had been ordered. There were two rows of eleven. She let a smile cross her face. One of the perks of working the night shift, she thought. The muffins were popular and would probably be gone in the first hour, if not sooner. During the height of the season, there were times when the daily order went as high as ten dozen. The sausage biscuits ran a close race.

Samantha poured herself a cup of coffee, added a creamer and two sugars. She stared at the muffins. She resisted the urge, arguing that if she ate one, the balance of the display would be ruined. And heaven help anyone who caused a display to go unbalanced. Her father was adamant that the store be kept fully stocked, clean and in balance at all times. While Samantha fully understood the reasoning behind the first two, she never mastered the thinking behind the latter. In her mind, just the opposite was true. An imbalance of muffins meant someone had already partaken, which meant the product was good. Her smile widened. She'd let her father win this morning and leave the muffins alone. Maybe later, if there was only one remaining.

After the appropriate amount of stirring, she took a careful sip of her coffee. It was hot, yet tolerable. She never understood how people drank coffee so hot. What good did it do if it burned your mouth? Blowing across the top of the liquid, she glanced at the clock on the wall and headed for the door. One minute before six, time to open.

The time of day caused a long yawn. Why couldn't her brother have gotten up this morning? It was his turn? She chuckled as a way of hiding her anger. He wasn't doing much of anything anymore. According to the cousins, he'd even lost his passion for fishing. Her anger subsided, replaced by worry. He wasn't getting any better; if anything, he seemed to be worse lately. Quieter, more withdrawn, not interested in doing much of anything except sitting on the beach in his old truck. He didn't even take his surfboard anymore, another previous passion. She decided she would talk to her parents to see if something could be done. It was a talk they'd had before and would probably end with the same results. They could do nothing as he was an adult. He couldn't be made to do anything he didn't want.

She put all these thoughts aside as she turned the lock. As usual, there was already someone waiting at the door with a vehicle at the gas pump. She put on her *good-morning* smile and opened the door. She focused on the face standing before her. She started to add a verbal greeting to the smile. The words, however, would not come. Her eyes widened. Her mouth dropped open. Her coffee fell to the floor.

3

Except for the light from the stars bright enough to penetrate the overcast sky, darkness engulfed the area. It was even darker inside the cab of the SUV. With a strong imagination, you could see the waves basting the beach as the tide continued to ebb. In reality, all you could do was hear the sea. Robert could barely make out the shadows of his fingers moving back and forth in front of his face. Even though the temperature had dropped considerably, the windows were down, sending a chill through his body. The wind had changed, now coming out of the north. While the newness of the car's interior still permeated his sense of smell, the aroma of the ocean was able to get through. Of all the smells he had experienced in his training, including the most odoriferous infections imaginable, nothing implanted in his mind like the smell of the ocean at night. Whenever his stomach started protesting the stimulation of his nostrils, he forced his thoughts to what he was experiencing now. It was something he loved to do when he was here before; sit, listen, and smell the ocean. That desire had not changed with time.

He closed his eyes as he sucked in another breath. He remembered scenes of the past, images he had kept buried for many months. He argued he was too busy. He argued he had more important things to do rather than think about that summer. After all, he was a medical student and now a resident at one of the greatest hospitals in the world. The training had been intense, the expectations high. He had more important things to do than think about the memories of Hatteras.

Tonight, however, he was beginning to wonder. An undergraduate degree, four years of medical school, a year's internship and now residency—he should be feeling fulfilled. He had nearly reached his goal. He should feel pride; he should feel a sense of satisfaction. He thought how lucky he was to get his Beemer a year early, to be sitting on the beach enjoying the ambiance of the ocean. The peace, the tranquility, the calmness; these were all part of the experiences he grew to love and missed so much these past few years. But he was back. He was here now. So, what was missing?

He knew the answer, only he refused to acknowledge it. After all, he was soon to be a chief resident at Johns Hopkins Hospital. What could be better? Friends told him when he started medical school that ambition could be blinding and dangerous. Focus, concentration, determination were the attributes required to succeed. He hadn't reached the pinnacle of his career yet, but he could see the summit. A Hopkins chief residency was the epitome of a climb up Mt. Everest.

Today, however, about the time he crossed onto the island, his heart emptied. He felt unfulfilled, unsatisfied, like everything he had done these past grueling years was for naught. He tried telling himself these feelings were ridiculous, they were just a letdown of not having anything pressing to do; no lives to save, no first-year resident to ream out, no attending physician's ass to kiss. Yes, he had nothing to do.

Except to relax and wait.

He arrived at the designated spot thirty minutes before the time. He knew he was in the right place for two reasons. First, the mileage down the beach was correct. Second, a flash of his headlights out into the water showed the remnants of a shipwreck just beyond the breaking surf.

The shores of the Outer Banks were lined with hundreds of vessels that had battled with Mother Nature and lost. Some wrecks could only be seen during low tide. Some could be seen protruding above the surf regardless of the tide status. Others required snorkel and fins to explore. Then there were the hundreds, maybe thousands, of boats relegated to what Samantha called *the nursing homes of the sea*. These were the vessels neglected or abandoned, sinking or partially sunk, that lined the many dilapidated piers on the bay side of the island. Some saw these as eye sores. Others looked upon them as chapters in the history book of Hatteras Island.

This particular oceanside wreck was one of the few close to the shore that could be seen regardless of the tide. She was *The Lady Hatteras*, an old wooden cargo schooner that traveled up and down the east coast during the late 1800's. Robert smiled as he remembered asking why the word *The* was included in the ship's name. It was explained to him the way it was explained to generations following *The Lady Hatteras*'s demise. "She was named by her original owner who felt she was a proud ship and was majestic under full sail. The *The* captured that image."

She carried textiles from New England to Florida, fruit from Florida to New England. History claimed she made the same trip nearly a hundred times. She was on the northern leg of her trip, loaded with grapefruit when an unexpected late August storm struck from the north. Gunwales low to the water, she didn't have a chance. She went down in less than thirty minutes, or so the one survivor claimed. A hurricane several years later washed her off the bottom and brought her ashore to where she now rested. Since then, she remained fixed to her spot surviving more than a hundred years of Hatteras nor'easters, storms, and hurricanes. The spooky thing was that the boat's final resting place was less than twenty yards from where her captain's body washed ashore, or so the one survivor claimed. Whether truth, fiction, or a little of both, *The Lady Hatteras'* history was recorded in the memories of the islanders, passed on to anyone with the time and inclination to listen to the tale.

The spot was chosen not only because of the isolation it brought, but also because of the history that lay just offshore. It was a spot where Robert had spent many hours. Fond memories swept forth like waves across the sand. Surf in, surf out. Memories flowed in: memories washed away.

Time passed. Quickly? Slowly? Robert didn't really know. Nor did he care. It had been a long time since impatience was not a part of his psyche. Emergency medicine plus his underlying personality required it. If there was ever a prototype for A-type personality, he was it. He figured that was why he liked emergency medicine so well and why he succeeded. The pace of the ER kept him in stride.

Tonight, however, as the surf massaged the beach and darkness fell, a salty breeze tickled his nose. His A-type personality transformed into a B. For the first time in a long time he felt at peace, with himself and with the environment around him. The worries of Baltimore were far away. He was relaxed, a rare feeling for him. At the same time, there was a nervousness growing in the pit of his stomach as the designated time drew near. Something was about to happen. She was about to come. How much time was left? Would she even show up? These questions threatened the peace of the night. He was about to turn on the overhead light to look at his watch when he caught flashes of light from the corner of his eye. They were approaching from the south. The headlights bounced a couple of times, smoothed out, and then gradually grew in intensity.

As the lights grew brighter, his heart beat faster. His anxiety heightened. His sense of relaxation evaporated.

He noticed his sweating hands, like when he approached the island earlier in the day. He laughed nervously, wondering why he was reacting so. The last time he felt this way was right before his interview for the chief resident position. That interview had gone well. He could think of no reason this meeting would not do the same.

After all, what was the big deal? He was only meeting the great-great-granddaughter of the only survivor of the shipwrecked *The Lady Hatteras*.

4

The Jeep Wrangler pulled alongside his SUV. Lights were doused, the engine cut off. The quiet of the evening returned. If Robert remembered correctly, it was the same vehicle she used to drive—ugly green exterior, tan seats, a canvas top that was seldom up, big ass tires for the beach, and very little in the way of a muffler system. Some things never change, Robert thought. Then again…

Before he could finish the thought, the door of the Jeep opened. A moment later a figure slid into the passenger seat next to him.

"What kind of car is this?" she said.

Robert made sure he kept his ego in check. "BMW."

"Smells new."

"It is."

"Nice."

"Thanks."

A pause ensued.

"You're driving the same Jeep, I see," Robert said.

"Gets me where I need to go."

"Nice it's still running."

"No need to change," she said.

Another pause.

"So, how have you been?" Robert asked nervously.

"Fine, and you?"

"Okay."

"What you been up to?"

Again, he reminded himself to control the tone of his voice. She always accused him of having an ego big enough to cause a tsunami. "Finishing my residency."

"Still at the same place?"

"Still at Hopkins, yes."

She paused. "Shouldn't you be done?"

"I'm doing an extra year."

"Why?"

It was his turn to hesitate.

"You got a chief residency?" she guessed.

Robert was surprised she was able to put the pieces together. He nodded.

She seemed genuinely impressed. "That's wonderful."

"Thank you."

"You're welcome."

"What about you?" Robert asked. "What have you been up to?"

"Same thing, helping with the park."

"How's that doing?"

"Business has been great. We had our best season ever last year. Winter's been slow, but reservations are doing well for the summer."

Robert pushed away a piece of hair the wind blew across his face. He caught a whiff of her perfume. She smelled wonderful as always. "That's good," he said. "How 'bout your parents. How they doing?"

"They're fine."

"Your brother?"

She hesitated, turned, and looked right at him.

A couple more stars had awakened, serving as spotlights on an otherwise darkened stage. The soft light reflected off her face. She looked like an angel before. Five years of time had not changed that impression. His hands started to sweat again.

"Why are you here?" she asked. There was a drop in the pleasantness scale.

He locked into her eyes a moment, and then looked away. "Initially, I told myself I wanted to check out my new vehicle on the beach"

"And after the initial conversation with yourself?"

The eye contact returned. There was a pause followed by a slow exhale. "I came here to see you. I missed you."

5

From the moment Samantha saw him in the store some fifteen hours earlier, the same question kept scrolling across her mind: what was he doing here? Her emotions were initially mixed. First, there was surprise, almost a sense of shock; then a strange sense of happiness followed by a wave of anger. What right did he have to come back into her life, and without warning? After what they had been through, all over a three-month period of time. He appeared suddenly. He left suddenly. He reappeared the same way.

Of all the emotions she felt, anger had been the strongest. Yet, as the afternoon progressed, and the time approached for them to meet, she managed to put that feeling aside, replacing it with a large dose of curiosity.

What was he doing here?

Once the initial shock of seeing him at the store resolved, she felt a wave of panic. What if her parents walked in? They were supposedly down in Buxton, but Samantha didn't know for sure. Her parents finding Robert standing in the middle of the store would not be a good thing. And what about her brother? If he walked in, that would have been a greater disaster. She was polite, yet firm. The cousins didn't know who he was yet picked up Samantha's sudden change of behavior. They had also heard the coffee hit the floor. They knew better than to say anything. They simply watched as Samantha recovered from her shock and ushered him outside. He acted like he wanted to talk. She simply wanted to get him out of Avon as quickly as possible. She said she was busy and they could talk later. He said when. She said nine o'clock. He said where. She said same place as always. He left. She returned to the store to get her pulse under control and to clean up the coffee. Once that happened, her anger began to build. It had been five years, five *long* years. He left the Friday before Labor Day. Her life hadn't been normal since. She suspected that Robert had no clue. He was probably too busy thinking about himself to worry about her, or anyone else for that matter—including her brother, who hadn't been the same either.

At one point she stopped her thought process, refusing to let her mind wander too far into the past. She told herself to focus on the present. She was able to control her mind, but the ache in her heart proved hard to ignore. He had always been able to stir her fire, from the first time she set eyes on him, the first time he walked into the store five years before. Even when he was gone, even when she thought about him and her anger rose, the pit of her stomach still burned. It was a passion she had never experienced before him. It was a passion she had not experienced since. Instead, she focused on her work, and on her brother. Thinking about her brother fueled her anger, only now wasn't the time, she thought.

He missed her. She stared out across the water, then turned and looked at him. "You came here to see me, huh," she said. "Well, your actions over these years certainly haven't demonstrated missing anyone." She was unable to hide the sarcasm from her voice. Prior to that Friday, it was a trait foreign to her persona. Since then...

She watched his mouth open. She waited for the tirade of excuses that were sure to follow. However, his mouth closed quickly. He looked away. His shoulders slumped. Finally, he spoke softly. "No excuses. Not even a good reason."

"How about you were busy saving lives?" she mocked.

He looked at her. She could tell he wanted to rip into her, to tell her he had indeed been doing just that. After all, saving lives was important and he felt honored to be in the profession that focused on that task. She also suspected he wanted to add that the profession was lucky to have him as a member.

Again, he didn't go down that road. Instead, "Look Sam, I'm sorry if I've upset you by coming here. I'm sorry if I've disrupted your life. I mean you no harm. I just wanted to see you."

"After all this time, you just suddenly decided you wanted to see me?"

"It wasn't sudden. It's something I've been thinking about for a long time."

"Why now?"

He contemplated the question. "Like I said, no excuses."

It was Samantha's turn to think. She tried hard to understand, but her anger was still in the way. "What about Billy?" she finally said.

"What about him?" Robert asked.

"Did you come down to see what kind of damage you did to him? You're feeling guilty about that, huh?"

Robert stared hard at her. "You've lost me there, Sam."

"Bullshit." It was a rare profanity from Samantha.

"Samantha!" Robert exclaimed, partially in surprise, partially as a way of stalling for time. He was correct in his comment a moment ago. He didn't understand what she was talking about.

She watched him a long second. "You really do have a lot of nerve, don't you?"

He started to repeat her name. Instead, he took a deep breath. His training as an emergency room physician dealing with all kinds of patients in all kinds of mental states kicked in. He extracted his own emotions out of the scenario. With a calm gentle voice, he said, "Samantha, please, what's going on?"

Her eyes squinted in the darkness to better see his face. She looked away as she spoke. "You left the Friday before Labor Day weekend. You barely said goodbye to me. You said nothing to my parents, nor did you say anything to my brother. When Billy got home from the boat that night, he seemed really upset. We suspected he got crappy tips that day, although he claimed they brought home over a hundred pounds of tuna and a small sailfish. When he learned that you had left without saying goodbye…well, he became even more distraught. Then two days later, Sunday…"

She stopped and wiped her arms across her eyes. She turned and looked out the side window.

"Sunday what?" Robert encouraged.

"Captain Willey went out without Robert and never returned."

"What do you mean *never returned?*"

"Just what I said, *never returned*. They found the *Lady Hatteras II* floating out in the gulf stream about thirty miles offshore. No one was on board. His body was never recovered."

Robert collected his thoughts. He had met Captain Willey multiple times and had even tagged along with Billy on several occasions, serving as second mate. *Lady Hatteras II* was a sturdy boat. Willey was an experienced and safe captain. Born and raised on the island, he started fishing as soon as he was able to hold a pole. He started working as a mate at the age of twelve, got his first boat at nineteen, and had never done anything else since. "What happened?" Robert queried.

"No one knows."

"Did he have engine trouble or something?"

"When the Coast Guard got there, the boat started up without a problem, although both engine hatches were open."

"He just disappeared?" While Robert wasn't an expert in boating, he still found that a difficult pill to swallow.

"The Coast Guard did what they called a thorough investigation. In the end, they declared it an accidental death. They figured he got surprised by a ship's wake and fell overboard."

"Accidental? You don't sound so convincing."

"I wasn't there. I don't know what happened."

"I'm sorry. Willey was a great captain. From what Billy told me, *Lady Hatteras II* was one of the most successful boats in the region. Billy told me he was thinking about taking over the boat when the old man retired, if that ever happened. How old was he anyway?"

"Fifty-eight."

"Is that all?" Robert said a little surprised. "He looked older."

"It's a healthy life down here. Ages you quickly though."

"Wasn't too healthy for Willey." Robert mocked.

"Accidents happen." Unfortunately, it was an all-too-common phrase heard amongst people who earned their living from the sea.

Robert continued. "I understand Billy would be upset, devastated even, but Captain Willey wasn't the first person to die off Hatteras; won't be the least either." Robert remembered Billy once saying that the hungriest shark of all was the sea itself. "Why did Billy take it so hard for so long?"

"He didn't take Willey's death hard. It was that you left without saying goodbye."

"Me leaving? That bothered him that much?"

"It's also what he perceived you did to me. He hasn't been the same since."

Robert continued to ignore the peripheral questions. He still hadn't got down to the nitty-gritty of what this was all about. "Call me ignorant. Call me stupid. Call me dense. But I still don't understand. What's happened to Billy?"

"Like I said, he hasn't been the same since you left."

"You have to be a little more specific than that, Sam."

"He's lost interest in everything. He doesn't fish anymore. He doesn't surf. He hardly goes out on the beach; and when he does, he just sits in his truck, smokes like a fiend and drinks Mountain Dew."

"We all liked to do that," Robert said. He fondly remembered learning to drink Mountain Dew because beer was so expensive.

"But not alone," Samantha snapped.

"He's been this way since that weekend five years ago!?"

"Since the day you left."

"You think this change in behavior is my fault?" Robert was having a hard time understanding.

"Like I said, he came home upset that day from fishing, and he learned you up and flew the coop."

"Then two days later Captain Willey disappeared." Robert added.

"That added fuel to the fire," Samantha acknowledged. "Only that's not what started it."

"So, you blame me!"

"We all do."

"Your parents too?"

Samantha's eyes bore into him. "Robert, you came down here like a whirlwind. You captured my heart. You even made an impression on my father, which is hard to do. I thought the feeling was mutual. Evidently it wasn't." Samantha held up her hand as Robert started to respond. "It doesn't matter." She paused to get control of her emotions. "We let you into our family. That doesn't happen here on the island very often."

"I know that, and I appreciated it," Robert said. He was well aware of the tightness of the community. They liked tourists for their money and not much else. The locals, long term implants included, were friendly, but only to a point. There was always that line in the sand, and it was usually quite clear on which side you resided. Robert had been invited across the line. The Mathews befriended him even before he and Samantha started going out. For Robert, it was great. It gave him the sense of a family, erasing some of the loneliness felt by being away from his own home.

Robert came to Hatteras that summer on the recommendation of a friend who got a job with one of the local contractors building houses on the beach. His friend worked for the same man the summer before and had a great time. He said the pay sucked, but the cost of living was cheap. Only thing expensive was fishing line and beer. He also had a room for only twenty-five dollars a week and that included one meal a day. Having always loved the ocean, Robert jumped at the chance to spend a whole summer at the beach. Besides, he needed a break from the rigors of medical school, and this sounded like the perfect opportunity.

So down to Hatteras he had gone with his friend. Only his friend didn't last long, deciding he didn't want to be away from a new girlfriend. His friend packed up, leaving Robert stranded. Robert didn't care. He was already in the groove of working at the beach and wasn't about to leave prematurely. Besides, he had a lot of thinking to do and quickly learned the beach was one of the best places for that. He'd finished an especially tough year at Hopkins; each year of medical school seemed to get more difficult when he had been told to expect the opposite. He had to decide on a specialty before he graduated from medical school. He was considering several options, including general surgery, orthopedic surgery, and pediatrics. Unfortunately, he liked them all. The solution, or so claimed the director of the emergency room, was to go into emergency medicine. There you got to see it all, experience it all, do it all.

He remembered the first day of his emergency room rotation. His first patient was a nine-year-old with a broken collar bone. His second patient was a ninety-year-old with a urosepsis—blood infection from the urinary tract. The remainder of the day sported a variety of patients in between. So yes, you could see it all in the emergency room. He did a couple other elective ER rotations after that and was often down there when rotating through other services. He quickly decided that the heartbeat of the hospital was its emergency room.

"You usually don't pick up and leave the family so quickly," Samantha said, bringing his attention back to the present.

"I said goodbye," he said defensively.

"To me."

"Everyone knew I was leaving."

"Yea, but…"

"But what?" Robert said, unable to hide a hint of demand from his voice. As an afterthought, he added, "How did you all expect me to go?"

"We didn't expect anything!" Samantha said tartly. "You could have at least said goodbye to Billy."

After a pause, Robert said, "You're right."

Samantha's eyes continued to bore into him. However, her facial features softened a few degrees. "He was really disappointed."

"He knew I was leaving. We talked about it the night before."

"He was very distraught," Samantha said.

"You make it sound like he was more upset that I left than he was over Willey's death," he vocalized.

Samantha hesitated. "In some ways you're right."

"Why the meeting out here, and so secretive?" Robert asked to take the conversation in a different direction. He didn't ask why she seemed so anxious to get him away from the store this morning. She walked him back to the car, stood by him while he pumped his gas, took his cash and waited there as he pulled away. He never made it into the store to get a coffee. It was right as he got into his car that she told him to meet her here at nine o'clock tonight.

"I have my reasons."

It was obvious no further explanation was going to be offered, so he chose another direction. "I'm still confused why Billy is so distraught that I left. You, I can understand, but Billy?"

Samantha responded. "Billy was always a loner, even when he was young. He made friends easily, but he never let anyone get close to him, not even me, and I'm his sister. While he dabbled, as he liked to call it, with a girl here and there, he never had a serious relationship. I always thought, and still do, that he likes one of the girls in the office, but despite gentle nudging by me and not so gentle overtures by her, he never pursued it until you came along. You were able to bring out a side of him no one saw before. He was more outgoing, more talkative, friendlier, and overall seemed a lot happier. For the first time in his life, he seemed excited about something. His enthusiasm for fishing even increased. He always liked to fish and was very good at it."

"He's an excellent first mate," Robert injected.

"Anyway, like you said before, he started talking about buying the *Lady Hatteras II* when Willey retired. He had thrown the idea past the old man who seemed okay with it. My parents were even willing to help with the money."

"We talked about that some," Robert admitted.

"Some?"

"Okay, a lot," Robert conceded. "At times that was all we talked about. He figured the old man had about three or four years left before retiring, and then Billy would be captain of his own boat."

"He never said much about it until that summer," Samantha said. "Regardless, we were pleased he was finally excited about something."

"You're blaming my going back to school as the cause of his change in behavior?" Robert said.

"That, the perceived effect on me, and the death of Captain Willey."

Robert took in a couple of deep breaths to collect his thoughts. It still didn't add up. "Why has it gone on this long?" he thought aloud. "That's not..." He hesitated.

"Not what?" Samantha queried.

"Not normal," Robert said.

Samantha wanted to be angry at him for saying that. Yet she knew Robert was right. It wasn't normal. If anything, Billy's condition, his state of withdrawal, was worse now than before.

"What happened to the boat?" Robert asked.

"The Coast Guard towed her back. She's been up on land ever since. Word is she's for sale. Although no one around here's going to touch her."

"Why?" Robert asked.

"She's jinxed."

"Jinxed?"

"She threw her captain overboard."

"A little superstitious down here, are we?"

"More than a little," Samantha corrected. "Anyway, the boat's just sitting there wasting away."

"Why hasn't Billy offered to buy her? That's what he wanted to do before, wasn't it?"

"My folks and I have all talked to him about it on several occasions. He says he's no longer interested in fishing."

"What's he do all day?" Robert asked.

"Not much," Samantha continued. "He takes care of the grounds and works in the store occasionally. Most of the time he sits in his truck out on the beach. Some nights he doesn't even come home."

"Is he drinking?"

Samantha gave a *humph*. "I wish it was that easy an explanation."

"Has anyone talked to him about his behavior?"

"We try. He just blows us off. Then he becomes even more reclusive for a while."

"I still can't believe my leaving triggered all this."

"Believe what you want," Samantha snapped. After a pause and with only a slightly softer tone, "What are your plans?"

"Plans?" Robert said.

"You're here. What are you going to do?"

"Oh." He followed with a couple *aahs* before better organizing his thoughts. "The official reason is to come down here and check out this vehicle on the beach. The unofficial—and real—reason was to see you. Both tasks have been accomplished, and to be honest, that's as far as my plans go. This is day one, I have the rest of the week to do whatever I want."

"You haven't changed, have you?" Samantha said accusingly.

"What do you mean?" Robert challenged.

"It's always about you—what you want."

"Samantha! That's not what I meant. I have six days and no plans. My only requirement is that there be some semblance of enjoyment in them."

"Well, I hope you accomplish that goal," Samantha said. "And I'm sure you will. You've accomplished everything else in your life you set out to do." She grabbed the door handle.

"Samantha!"

She hesitated, but only a moment. The door opened and she stepped out.

"I want to see Billy," Robert said.

Her head snapped in his direction. "He doesn't want to see you."

"Shouldn't he be the one to decide that?"

"You leave him alone, understand?"

The door slammed shut. The door of her Jeep opened and closed. The engine revved up. She pulled away a moment later.

Robert watched the taillights disappear into the night. He scratched his head, wondering what the hell was going on.

6

The sun, two finger breadths off the horizon, sent an orange glow across the water. The breeze from the night before had dissipated, allowing the ocean to settle into a near mirror surface. Soft gentle swells rose a foot or less. Lazy waves slapped at the beach doing little more than getting the sand wet. *Surf's up* would not be heard on the beach today. Scattered sea gulls dove low across the water, teased by the schools of alewives just beneath the surface. Occasionally a bird would get lucky. For the most part, the birds did a lot of flying and very little swallowing. The sun was rising out of its ocean bed, but that was all that was happening. Nature had yet to yawn and stretch her legs. It was what the locals called a lazy sunrise. There certainly weren't any fish biting, exhibited by numerous vehicles lined up along the beach, each with at least two poles standing at various angles to the sand. The humans watching the poles were all inside their vehicles, waiting, hoping, drinking coffee, smoking cigarettes or simply watching the day awaken. The question on everybody's mind: when would all this change? When would the fish decide they were hungry again and come back into shore? As of yet, there was no sign of activity anywhere along the thirty mile stretch of sand. The lack of chatter over those still using the CB radio network indicated no one had done anything of significance since the tide started going out some two hours earlier.

While there was no definite road on the beach, there were two sets of treads, one just off the edge of the wet sand—faster yet more dangerous, and one set down the middle of the beach—slower and much safer. Robert followed the latter path.

He took his time, looking at each vehicle he passed. At the same time, he made sure he stayed in the ruts as this part of the beach was proving to be a lot softer than expected. It amazed him how the sand conditions could change so quickly. One moment you were cruising along on firm packed sand, the next you'd swear you were in quicksand. It was these sudden changes that caused the most problems. Some locals claimed the change was due to the wind. Some blamed it on the wave action and how high the water reached the dunes during high tide. Some said it was a combination of both. Robert, however, believed in a fourth theory which stated that the sand had a life of its own and did whatever it wanted. The joke amongst the locals was that the seagulls ate the fish while the beach ate the cars. Robert took care to ensure his vehicle didn't become the beach's next meal.

It was another mile before he broke clear of this group. Two more miles, and then he spotted a lone vehicle sitting far off the surf up against the dunes. As he drew closer, Robert saw it was an old truck. As the distance lessened, he saw it was an old Toyota Tacoma, rusty green, no tailgate with big, oversized tires. He wondered about the vehicle's mileage. It had close to a hundred fifty thousand miles five years ago. He figured it was probably over two hundred thousand now. That it was out on the beach, a figure was sitting in the cab puffing on a cigarette, indicated it still ran.

Robert wondered why the truck was parked so far from the water. He thought that to be strange. He put that thought into his *think about it later* file. He pulled up on the driver's side. He put down the window and looked toward the truck. Billy sat in the driver's seat, staring straight ahead. One hand was on the steering wheel, the other held a cigarette. A can of Mountain Dew sat on the dash. His hair was sun-bleached blond, unkempt and long. He wore an old dirty white tee shirt that had at least two holes Robert could see. Billy had always been meticulous about his appearance, even if only going out onto the fishing pier at night to fish and relax. In the past, his arms were very muscular for his rather small stature. Now, they looked wasted. The skin on his face was dusky, his eyes were sunk deep into their sockets.

Not wanting to stare too long, Robert said, "Mornin'. Beautiful day, isn't it?"

"Ain't no beauty in it till the fish start bitin'."

"Guess you're right there."

"Ain't a matter of right or wrong. All 'at matters is if the fish are bitin' or not."

Robert laughed. "Whatever you say." He started to ask his old friend if he knew who he was when the boy's head slowly turned in his direction. Robert had to keep from gasping. The young man looked worse than he first thought. He had a ghostly appearance, an ashen color, like patients Robert had cared for who were dying of some terminal disease and had given up hope.

"Why are you here, Bobby?" Billy asked.

The question and the sudden change of tone caught Robert off guard. There was something nice about the question, however. Billy was the only person who ever called him Bobby. Billy said that Robert was too formal a name for someone on Hatteras Island. Samantha called them the B and B twins. While they were miles apart in many ways, they were at times inseparable. The Hopkins doctor let a smile cross his face. It was good to hear the name Bobby again. The smile was short lived, however, as the old friend's stare brought Robert's mind back to the present. "I came down here to see Samantha, and to see you."

"Bullshit!"

This time the profanity did not come as a surprise.

"You knew I was here?" Robert said.

"I saw you at the store yesterday morning."

"Why didn't you say something?"

"My sister was obviously trying to keep you away."

Robert's eyes narrowed. "Tell me Billy, why would she want to do that?"

The Hatteras boy looked away. "Don't know. You'll have to ask her."

Much like he did when dealing with a difficult patient in the emergency room, Robert kept his voice calm. "I'm asking you, Billy. Why would she want to keep me away from you?"

Billy lit another cigarette. His hands were shaking, something Robert had never noticed before. After a long drag, Billy said, "Guess she's blaming you for the way I am."

"Just how are you, Billy?"

"Like I said, I'm here."

"That didn't answer my question," Robert noted. All the emotional switches that had been turned off during the drive down here were flipping back on. The good doctor's mind was starting to spin. Something was going on with Billy, and around Billy. And everyone seemed to be blaming him. Which would be okay if Robert knew what that was; if he knew what happened that Labor Day weekend that started this mess. He asked the question. "What happened that weekend, Billy, besides Captain Willey dying?"

"Like I said, I'm here."

"Like I said, that didn't answer the question." Robert's voice was soft yet firm.

A puff of smoke trailed out the window of the old truck. "Maybe I'm not ready to talk about it," Billy said.

Robert reminded himself of the one-step-at-a-time adage in medicine, although patience was seldom a virtue in emergency medicine. He did learn that a little patience often led to a lot of information. Robert sensed the same principles would hold true here. Something was wrong with Billy, and the answer wasn't going to come quickly, although Robert already had a couple ideas. By saying he wasn't ready to talk about it, Billy confirmed something did happen that weekend other than the death of Captain Willey.

"Patience," the young doctor mouthed softly. Louder, he said, "Well, whenever you're ready to talk, I'll be here."

"Just like before."

Robert didn't fall into the trap. "You knew I had to go back to school, Billy."

"You didn't have to. You chose to," Billy corrected.

Whatever was going on, Billy's mind was still as sharp as a fishhook. He had always come across as somewhat of a dumb islander who knew little else besides fishing and surfing. However, as the two became friends, Robert discovered the boy was quite smart and well read. While he barely graduated high school, he was wiser than most his age. The exception was Samantha, who let her guard down on occasion and demonstrated signs of brilliance. Samantha mentioned more than once that she and her brother both loved to read, and with the internet, topics were limitless. Robert was a little surprised to hear this at first. When he asked about it, Samantha replied, "Come down here in the winter sometime. You'll see why."

Robert brought his focus back to the present. "Yes, Billy, I did choose to go back to school. I finished, too. I'm a doctor. In another year, I'll be finished my residency in emergency medicine."

"Then tell me what's wrong with me," Billy challenged.

Robert let out a nervous laugh. "I'm good, but…"

"Not good 'nough, huh?" Billy mocked.

Robert forced his anger to remain under control. He noted he had to do this a lot lately. It wasn't the kind of thing he had planned for his vacation. He came here to get his mind off his work, to clear his thoughts as he prepared for his last year of residency. It was important he start the year with a fresh set of attitudes. Yes, he came to Hatteras to test out his new vehicle. Yet there were other reasons; Samantha being one, Billy another.

He silently admitted he didn't know what to expect when he drove onto the island after so many years. What he hadn't expected was what he found so far. He struggled for an appropriate word. Finally, *mess* came to mind; nonspecific, yet descriptive. *Mess*, he repeated silently.

Aloud, "I think I know what's wrong with you. I just don't know why. On the other hand, I suspect you know the why, but not the what."

Billy had always been quick at picking up word innuendos. That had not changed. "Then why don't you start with the what?" he said.

"Why not start with the why?" Robert challenged.

"Because."

"Because why?"

Billy looked in his direction. "This ain't like old times," he said. "Things've changed."

"Those changes are what I'm trying to discover."

"Maybe you're barking up the wrong tree."

"Maybe I'm barking up the right tree, only no one's listening."

Billy looked away. He took a couple drags on his cigarette before flicking it out the window.

Robert contemplated what to say next. Should he be open and let Billy know his thoughts or should he remain vague until he had more information? His inclination was the first choice. However, his thoughts along these lines, i.e., Billy's condition, were only based on a theory, which was based on a lot of instinct. There were few facts. Robert thought back over the summer he and Billy spent together. They were fun times, easy times, free of stress, very few decisions to make. There was always a morning shower. However, shaving was optional. Hair was shampooed, never combed. The uniform of the day was cutoff jeans and an old surfer tee shirt. Shoes were never worn, even though Robert didn't like the feel of sand between his toes, something he fussed about a lot and was teased about just as much. Even on the construction site, work boots were optional. There were strict rules about leaving nails on the ground or in boards. The only decision that really had to be made was whether to go to work or not, and that was predicated on whether the surf was up or the fish were biting. Surfboard and fishing rod were stowed in the back of the truck right next to one's tool belt, square, and circular saw.

Things changed. Now, many decisions were made daily. Showers were sometimes twice a day. Shaving was not an option. Hair was blown dry—a big waste of time in Robert's opinion. Dress shirts and dress pants, along with a clean lab coat were the norm. There was even time spent selecting the proper necktie, depending on which of his regulars might show up that day. Dr. Battlegrove had managed to accumulate his own group of patients who used him as their primary care physician. Naturally, each of these patients had their favorite tie.

Then came the need to make decisions about saving people's lives.

Yes, times were much simpler that summer, even with the sand between his toes. "I saw the wreck of *The Lady Hatteras* yesterday," he said. "It was dark, but she looked pretty much the same."

"She ain't changed much," Billy agreed. He lit another cigarette followed by a long swallow of Mountain Dew. "She ain't got too many storms left in her, though."

Robert didn't ask how he knew that. The doctor had little doubt that if Billy said it, it must be true. "I suspect you're right," Robert said aloud. He focused on what to tell Billy. He decided to let Billy in on what he was thinking, only to soften the blow, using general terms and phrases. It was a technique used when telling someone they had a bad disease or when talking to a family about a death. *We did everything we could* or *they never suffered* were common phrases.

Robert chose his words carefully. "You fished the Friday I left, right?"

Billy nodded. "That's why I wasn't able to say goodbye."

"Yeah, I knew that." Robert paused. "You didn't go out on Saturday like you planned because the weather was too bad. A nor'easter was starting to blow when I left."

"We figured we got in just in time that Friday," Billy said. "The inlet was pretty rough as it was. Blew hard all night and most of the next day."

Robert continued. "So, you didn't go out Saturday, but Captain Willey went out the next day, Sunday, by himself. Unfortunately…" Robert paused again. "How am I doing so far?"

"Go on," Billy prompted. He emptied the Mountain Dew.

"Actually, there isn't any further to go," Robert said. "I was hoping you could tell me the rest."

"The rest of what?"

"I know Captain Willey died on Sunday," Robert said. "But what happened that Friday to get you so upset, and to keep you upset this long?" Robert hoped upset was the right word for the conversation.

"What makes you think I'm upset?" Billy said defiantly.

Through his training, Robert had become good at reading people. Billy's denial was obvious. It was also a sign that Robert was on the track of something. The question was how not to scare Billy away. "Firm with ginger," Dr. Harold Kerrigan, the chairman of the emergency room liked to preach. So gingerly, Robert proceeded. "Something happened that Friday while you were out fishing, or maybe when you got back. Captain Willey's death was simply icing on the cake. You haven't been this upset all these years just because I didn't say goodbye. We did that the night before. Nor have you been upset all these years because of Willey's death. Dying at sea is a part of the life down here. You hope it doesn't happen, but it does. No Billy, something else triggered your reaction."

Billy looked at the ocean. Robert could tell he was struggling with his own decision over how much to say. He smoked a whole cigarette before speaking. "Captain Willey would never have gone out like he did that Sunday."

"You mean he would have never gone out alone?" Robert queried. "I thought I remember you telling me he used to do that all the time, especially before the season started. He used to go out and scout the shoals?"

"Yeah, he did that. But…"

Robert reminded himself to remember the ginger. "But what, Billy?"

"He would have never gone out on Sunday."

"Sunday?"

"Yeah, we never fished on Sunday. You never knew it by listening to his tongue, but Captain Willey was a very religious person. To him, Sunday was a day of rest."

7

Samantha pulled into the gravel parking lot and immediately recognized the only vehicle at the gas pumps. A deep scowl crossed her face. And it started out to be such a good day, too. She had slept well. The weather was clear. The NOAA weather station promised the same for the next few days. The temperature was already in the mid 60's. It all boded well for business. While reservations were brisk, they had plenty of spots to fill before they could turn on the no vacancy sign. She noticed that morning Billy was already out of the house, which was a good sign. He had been sleeping later and later and doing less and less. So yes, it had started out as a good day. Until she saw the SUV at the gas pump. Her assumption that he already left the island was obviously wrong.

Like the day before, she tussled with mixed emotions. She still *sweated* him as the cousins called it. At the same time, the sight of him, the thought of him, stirred her anger. She told herself months ago she could forgive him for leaving the way he did, but she could never forgive him for what he did to Billy.

She contemplated ignoring him and going directly into the store. She was afraid, however, he'd follow her inside. She didn't want anyone else to know he was back. The sooner he left the island, the happier she'd be.

She parked her Jeep in her usual spot off to the side and walked to where he was just finishing filling up with gas. "Morning," she said. "I thought you left yesterday."

Robert looked up and smiled. "I did, but I came back. I spent the night in Nags Head. That place has really built up."

"Tell me about it." She reminded herself not to let his charm get to her. "So, what are you going to do now?"

He tilted his head to the side. "Meaning?"

"You said you came back. For what?"

"To see you." A wide grin crossed his face.

"Bullshit!"

"I don't remember that word being so common when I was here before," Robert said. "Matter of fact..." He never got to finish the sentence.

"It isn't," Samantha snorted sharply.

"Well, I've heard it twice already today." He glanced at his watch. "And it's only seven o'clock."

"Where'd you hear it the first time?"

"From Billy."

"Billy! Where'd you hear it from him?"

"I just left him out on the beach."

"I thought I told you to leave him alone!" Samantha snapped as her anger rose.

Robert, on the other hand, kept his voice calm. "You did. I just didn't listen."

"Robert!"

Robert capped off the tank and slid the nozzle back in its sheath. The pump beeped. He hit the *no* button, indicating he didn't want a receipt. "I'm not the cause of Billy's problem."

She looked at him, blinked and replied with disdain. "Then who is?"

"I haven't gotten that far yet, but I'm making progress."

"A bold statement, don't you think?"

"Maybe."

"You wanna explain?"

"Maybe."

"Cut the crap, Robert. What are you talking about?" She hated it when he played with her.

"Sorry," he said with sincerity. "I don't have all the facts together yet."

"Might I ask where you got these facts?"

"From Billy?" Robert said. "I told you, I just left him on the beach. Far as I know, he's still there."

Samantha instinctively looked toward the east. Then her head snapped back. "You...you..." Her anger boiled over.

Robert continued with a calm voice. "Samantha, you're angry, number one. Number two, this isn't the place to talk. So, you get calmed down and tell me when and where, and I'll explain." He hesitated. "I'll make you a deal. Give me a chance to do that – explain, that is. Listen to me for five minutes. Then you decide. If you believe me, fine. If not..." He paused again as he struggled with his own emotions. "I'll leave the island and never bother you again."

Samantha's eyes widened. It was such a bold statement from someone who a moment before was toying with her. This wasn't different from the past. One minute he'd be all serious; the next, he'd be teasing her. She often had a hard time telling which side of the fence he was residing. He liked to play emotional games. At times they were fun. Mostly, they were not. She confronted him about that once late that summer. He abruptly apologized and stopped. Had he forgotten that conversation? Had he regressed into this previous behavior? Or was he sincere? She reminded herself he could turn it on and off like a light switch. It was a quirk in his personality she didn't like. But in spite of her anger, she wanted to give him the benefit of the doubt. She always gave him the benefit of the doubt. That was true with most people she dealt with. It was in her nature, a flaw in her personality perhaps.

She glanced at her watch. "Give me forty-five minutes." The cousins were always looking for extra time. Maybe they'd cover her a bit.

"Okay," he managed to say, surprised at how easily she had agreed.

She turned and headed for the store.

"Sam?"

She stopped.

"Where're we going to meet?"

She continued to walk. "Do you really have to ask?"

8

The wreck of *The Lady Hatteras* was much more visible in the daylight hours and had changed little these past five years. Gentle waves basted what remained of the hull. A pair of seagulls perched atop what was left of the main mast. Robert wondered what *The Lady Hatteras* looked like afloat and under full sail. He let his mind flow freely, but knew his imagination was probably far better than reality. Robert was correct in his assessment regarding the ship's parts atop the water. They had changed very little, but had he been able to see below the surface, he would have seen *The Lady Hatteras* was in a most precarious state. Her support beams were almost completely worn away, held up by the thinnest of timbers. Like Billy said, she didn't have many storms left in her.

Robert continued looking at the wreck before his thoughts were cut off by the sound of a motor in the distance. This time the old Jeep came at him from the north. A minute or so later, Samantha was spreading a blanket across the sand. She pulled out a basket from the back of the Jeep and laid out a plate of bagels, a container of cream cheese and a thermos of coffee. He sat down across from her and picked up a bagel, spreading cream cheese on the cut side.

"What's the occasion?" he said, biting off a piece of the bread. He wiped the excess cream cheese from his mouth.

"No occasion," Samantha replied. "I figured you haven't eaten yet, right?"

"Right."

"Okay then."

She seemed in a much better mood than when they last parted. Robert was glad. This was supposed to be his vacation, yet so far there hadn't been much fun. They ate in silence, each looking over the ocean. As the sun rose off the horizon, the breeze picked up. An occasional fish jumped, but the seagulls remained perched atop the wreck, their bellies full from early morning successes.

Robert stared at the shipwreck another minute before turning his gaze on Samantha. Such a contrast in appearance, *The Lady Hatteras,* so old, so weather beaten, so vulnerable. Samantha Mathews, the great-great-granddaughter of the only survivor of that fateful night—so young, so beautiful: tough yet vulnerable as well. She was Robert's *Lady Hatteras*. He used to tell her she was the ship that kept him afloat. At least she had in the past. Now, he wasn't sure.

"I'm listening," Samantha said, interrupting his train of thought.

Wiping his mouth again and taking a long swallow of the coffee, Robert refocused. "For starters, I think your brother is very depressed. He looks terrible. He has tremors, and he smokes like a fiend. He's also lost a lot of weight. However, I think there's more to his depression than just being depressed. I'm not a psychiatrist and I may be off the deep end here, but I think he's also suffering from what's called PTSD, or posttraumatic stress disorder."

Robert waited for the defensive attack he was sure would come. Only it didn't. Instead, "I've heard the term," Samantha said calmly through her own mouth full of bagel.

"We see it in the emergency room." Robert continued, "usually after some severe trauma. Symptoms can include nightmares, guilt, depression and anxiety. You can also see an increase in substance abuse."

"My brother doesn't do drugs; I can tell you that." The defensive reaction was resurfacing.

"Nicotine is a drug," Robert said gently.

"Nicotine?"

"Cigarettes. He used to smoke an occasional cigarette. Now…"

"He isn't anxious."

"Maybe not externally, but internally I'm willing to bet he's a mess. Like I said, he lost a lot of weight. He looks tired. He has resting tremors. He…"

"He can't be tired. He sleeps all the time," Samantha interrupted.

"Is he sleeping? Or is he just lying in bed because he's tired." Robert took another drink of coffee. "Does he have nightmares, do you know?"

Samantha looked away. "Yes," she said hesitantly. "And they seem to be getting worse."

"That's why he's so tired," Robert conjectured. "He's afraid to go to sleep. He's depressed because he has no energy because he's so tired. It's a snowball down a hill that's tough to control. You may even consider it an avalanche."

"What caused all this?" Samantha said, concern replacing her sarcasm.

"Blame it on me," Robert said. "That's exactly what he wants you to do. That way he doesn't have to face the real reason."

"If you're not to blame, then who is?"

"It doesn't have to be a *who*. It can be a *what*."

Samantha paused to digest what he was saying. "You still have my attention." Her voice softened.

"Thank you." He made sure there was sincerity in his voice. "I think something happened the Friday I left, either while they were fishing or when they got back. I think it was related to Captain Willey's death, too." Robert paused. "I acknowledge I'm stretching things, but I'm wondering if Willey's death was really an accident."

Samantha's eyes widened. "That does sound like a stretch." She had wondered the same thing many times.

"I thought the same until I put together a couple of things from my meeting with Billy. First, I noticed he was parked away from the water, about as far away as you can get to be precise. From what I recall, he always did the opposite. I remember more than once having to move our vehicles back as the tide came in. I think that means something." Robert paused for a sip of coffee. "Has he been fishing since Willey died?"

"He goes out on the beach almost every day."

"I don't mean that. I mean out on a boat. Has he mated for anyone else?"

"People have asked, but he's refused. He always has an excuse," Samantha replied.

"That's not like him," Robert said.

"Not at all," Samantha acknowledged. She took a sip of her coffee. "So, what does all this mean?"

"I think he's afraid of the water." Robert continued with a quick breath. "He also said he wasn't ready to talk about it yet. It took me a second to realize he was acknowledging something did indeed happen that day."

"Didn't push him?"

"I did not."

"Isn't that unusual for you?"

Robert ignored the barb. "A lot of times people need to get things together in their minds before they're willing or even able to verbalize their feelings. That can take time."

"That's not what I meant by unusual," Samantha said. "I was referring to your not pushing the point." Robert was one of the more persistent people she had ever met.

The doctor cocked his head to the side. "You know Sam, I'm trying really hard here."

"Trying what?" Samantha said.

He stared her in the eye a long moment. Finally, he said with exacerbation, "Forget it. Just forget it." He started rising to his feet.

"Robert!" Samantha spouted. Her voice softened. "Robert, I'm sorry. It's just been…it's been hard."

It was his turn to give the benefit of the doubt. He sat back down. They finished eating in silence.

Gathering up the trash, Samantha said, "Why did he blame you instead of talking about what happened?"

"Fear."

"Fear of what?"

"Of what happened, or maybe of what else might happen." Robert paused. His mind kicked into overdrive. Their eyes met as both came up with the same thought.

"Whatever happened is still out there!" Samantha said, looking at the ocean.

"Not an uncommon situation in posttraumatic stress. Sexual assault victims fear their attackers reattacking. People in severe car accidents will not drive or even ride in cars because of fear of getting into another accident. Whatever set him off may still be out there. The threat may be perceived versus real, but…" His mind jumped ahead. "This all reinforces what I was saying earlier about him being afraid of the water. He was never like that before. Hell, I remember being out on the pier with a big hammerhead shark on the line and him out in the water surfing. He was fearless then…Now?"

Robert had also been gazing at the water. He looked back at Samantha. His mind was distracted by memories of the past. She was beautiful then; she was even more so now. Her dark brown hair hung in a ponytail below her shoulders. The hair was pulled tight across the top of her head. Her eyes, also a deep brown, looked directly at you, appearing to delve deeper than skin's surface. Her face was round, her teeth perfectly aligned within a captivating smile. She wore a yellow polo shirt with the campground logo across the left pocket. She was well built and still very fit. Her arms were muscular, her abdomen hard, her legs long and lean.

His gaze returned to her face. That was what first attracted him to her. There was magnetism in her look. Even when she was angry, she captivated you with her eyes. He had been in love with her back then. Was the feeling still there? Was she still his *Lady Hatteras*? Had it ever really left, or had he buried it deep in his subconscious, keeping his mind focused on his education? It was what he had to do to succeed. What more could he want? He chuckled inwardly. Maybe to have his tuition loans paid off. But like his father said, that was a small investment for what his future held.

A small investment, a small price to pay. But what price was he really paying?

He looked at the ocean, wondering why Samantha had done this today. Five years before, they met during the third day Robert was on the island. While he was staying in Waves, a small town a couple miles north of Avon, the campground was the only convenience store in the area. He stopped in that day for coffee and to get a sandwich for lunch. Samantha waited on him. They talked briefly while she made him a fresh roasted turkey on rye. Eye contact was brief, but a connection was made; smiles were exchanged, heads were nodded and the hopes for another time filled each other's mind. The next three day's visits were for the same purpose, the only difference being the meat on the bread. On Friday, he was almost late for work as traffic getting down to the job site was heavy; also, because he lingered in the store longer than on previous days. He asked her if she wanted to go to the fish fry with him that night. The Waves Volunteer Fire Company held one every Friday during the tourist season to raise money for their firehouse. She declined, thanked him, and explained she had to work. However, she asked him if he wanted to join her at a bonfire on the beach her family was having for the campground on Saturday. She promised hamburgers, hotdogs, her mom's homemade potato salad, and all the iced tea he could drink. He accepted. It was here he first met her parents. It was here he first met Billy. Her parents were too busy with their guests to pay him much attention. Besides, Samantha simply introduced him as a customer from the store who was working on the island for the summer. Billy, on the other hand, immediately saw past this. While they were both adding wood to the bonfire, Billy asked Robert if he liked to fish, to which Robert replied that he really didn't know how. Fishing lessons and a friendship started the next day.

Early in the evening the following Monday, he and Samantha had a picnic on the beach. Samantha chose a secluded spot several miles south of the campground. Robert noticed an old shipwreck barely visible above the far breakers. Samantha informed him the name of the shipwreck was *The Lady Hatteras*. It was then she told him the story of the ill-fated ship, including her being related to the only survivor. Robert listened with as much interest as he could muster. After all, it was the first time they'd been alone, and he was having trouble concentrating on her words.

When she finished the story of the shipwreck, they ate. She made some sort of seafood salad. He brought a bottle of wine and a loaf of French bread. The seafood salad was delicious, the wine terrible, and the bread stale. It was a wonderful time though. They talked about their dreams, his going to medical school and becoming a successful doctor, she about staying on the island and becoming a successful businesswoman. He was well on the way to fulfilling his dream. From what he had seen so far, she had a long way to go towards hers. They talked to one another. They listened to one another. She kept looking at his face. He had a hard time keeping his eyes away from her body. She wore a red two-piece bathing suit with a thin white cover up. It was a wonderful time.

Much to Billy's objections who wanted to continue the fishing lessons, over the next few days, they had several more dates, each at the same spot, each under similar circumstances. She arrived in her old Jeep, he in a three-wheel Honda dune buggy borrowed from his landlord. She brought the food. He brought the wine and stale bread. After the fourth such rendezvous, they kissed. It was the most fantastic kiss he had ever experienced. Her lips were gentle. Her skin, despite all the exposure to the sun, was silky soft. She closed her eyes. He kept his open, afraid he might miss something. The next weekend, he was invited to her house for Sunday dinner. Nervous for one of the first times he could remember, he arrived right on time, dressed in a shirt and tie, and carrying a bottle of more expensive wine and a loaf of fresh bread. As Samantha had warned, her parents were quite inquisitive as to how this boy had captured the heart of their daughter. He later learned it was the first time for such an event.

During the meal, Billy was talkative to a fault, telling his parents how he and Robert had been fishing several evenings the week before, and how Robert had already become adept at casting in the surf. While casting such a rig might look easy to the naive observer, it was not a skill easily mastered. Under Billy's tutelage, however, Robert became at least respectable in getting the bait in the water.

Samantha's parents were cautiously happy for their daughter and ecstatic their son had found a friend. They didn't seem to mind that Billy was taking time away from the two. Samantha didn't mind either as she was glad Billy finally had someone he could drag out to the beach other than her. While she liked the beach and liked to surf, fishing was another story. She never quite saw the sport in throwing a hook the size of a watermelon out into the surf attached to a piece of piano wire for a leader and using a hunk of bloody bait fish for bait, all to catch a fish you could go down to the local market and buy a whole lot cheaper and with a whole lot less time expended. At the same time, she acknowledged the values of fishing to the island and to their campground business. Fishing was one of the many things in life that didn't make a lot of sense to her.

The dinner that Sunday went well. Samantha's parents gave their approval and Robert was set for at least one good home cooked meal a week.

Robert's eyes snapped back to her when he realized he had been out in la-la land. It took him a moment to remember what they had been talking about. "Billy's afraid of something or someone," he said.

Samantha took her time to digest his words. "What do you want to do?" She asked with concern in her voice.

Robert recalled something from the beginning of their conversation. He made sure his own tone followed hers. "Does that mean you want me to stay?"

She hesitated. "I want my brother to get better."

"Is that all?"

"Don't push your luck."

He looked at her, hoping to catch even a hint of a smile. There was none. "Okay, it's a start," he said. He drained his cup of coffee. She offered more, but he declined. "Where to start I guess is to make sure you understand what I'm talking about and to see if you have any questions," he said.

"I get the gist of what you're saying," Samantha replied.

"Do you think I'm on the right track?"

"You're the doctor."

"Samantha!" For all her beauty, her tongue could be awfully tart.

"Okay…Okay. I see where you're coming from. Like you said, it's a stretch," she said. "For now, let's give your theory the benefit of the doubt."

"Any more questions?"

She shook her head side to side.

"Good," Robert said.

"I should talk to Billy," Samantha said, hesitation in her voice.

"I'm not sure we're ready to do that yet," Robert argued.

"We!"

Robert tipped his head to the side. "You want my help or not?"

More hesitation. "I'm not sure."

"Least you're honest."

"Robert, I've always been honest with you. On the other hand…"

With much effort, Robert held his tongue. He was not about to get into a swordfight of words with Samantha. If they were going to help Billy, they needed to remain allies. Besides, a battle of words with Samantha was a suicide mission.

He examined their options and verbalized his thoughts aloud. "Yes, I think you, or I, or we should talk to Billy. However, I want to do a couple other things first. For starters, I want to see the boat."

"The boat?"

"Yeah, *Lady Hatteras II*. She's still around, isn't she?"

"I don't think she's been sold yet. If not, she's down at the inlet."

"She's for sale!?"

"Willey's widow put her up for sale the beginning of last summer. From what I've heard, there haven't been any bites though."

"That sounds odd," Robert said. "I thought a boat like that would sell fast, especially with her reputation for catching fish." Fisherman gave a lot of credit to the captain and crew of a charter boat. There was also a lot of credit given to the boat itself.

"She lost her captain overboard without a clear understanding why. People down here may be hard core. They're also superstitious as hell."

Robert remembered a similar conversation with Billy. "Anyway, I want to see the boat, then make a visit to the widow."

"Should I go with you?" Samantha asked.

Robert smiled. "I'd like you to go."

She failed to hide a small blush, but she refused to let her mind wander into the cause of the blush. "When?"

Robert pondered the question. "It's been five years. I'm not sure we need to rush."

"I'm not sure you're correct," Samantha countered.

Robert looked straight at her. "Meaning?"

"While Billy hasn't been well, he has been getting by. I'm concerned you being here may change that."

Robert frowned. "You really think I have that much impact on him?"

"Either way, you coming back may open old wounds. Isn't that part of what you're talking about?"

Robert pondered some more. "You afraid he may go off the deep end?"

Samantha shrugged. "It's possible, isn't it?"

"Possible, yes." Robert said. "Then I guess we'd better go sooner than later."

"I guess we should."

9

Entrance onto Hatteras Island was either the aforementioned bridge across Oregon Inlet from the north or a free public ferry boat from Ocracoke Island across Hatteras Inlet from the south. The two inlets were the hubs of the fishing fleet. Fisherman liked to argue which inlet was better for the boats. The debate was often heated and fierce, usually while resting elbows atop the bar at one of the local watering holes. The consensus was that Oregon Inlet was rougher but more predictable while Hatteras Inlet was smoother but tended to change more with the weather. And while the professionals didn't complain about the roughness, their paying customers did. What the captains wanted was predictability in the waterway, i.e., a low risk of running aground as changes in the channel were often found the hard way, especially after fierce storms. Few noticed that the professional fleet always let the private boats go out first after such storms—a matter of courtesy of course.

Captain Willey always listened to the debate and would add his two cents if someone bought him a beer. Then he'd go home shaking his head at the wonderment of it all. You see, the success or failure of fishing had nothing to do with which inlet you called home. What mattered was your skill as a fisherman; the when, where, and what bait to use, along with a generous portion of old man luck. Captain Willey kept his boat at Hatteras Inlet, claiming to buy into the myth that blue marlin were warm water fish, thus it only stood to reason that the more southern fishing fleet had a better chance of latching onto one of these trophies. Truth of the matter, Willey chose Hatteras Inlet because he was good friends with the owner of the marina and was given an occasional break on yard costs and hull out fees. Captain Willey's reason had nothing to do with fishing.

It was the owner of the marina that Robert and Samantha now sought. The young boy in the office, who Samantha didn't know, told them Mr. Arnold was out in the yard painting a boat bottom. That told Samantha one of two things. Either the boat owner was a very big VIP or Arnold was short of help. She guessed it was the latter as good help was getting harder and harder to find on the island. Many businesses were forced to import labor from overseas. It was a topic of conversation heard more and more when the various business owners gathered either formally or informally. Sam and her parents had talked about the possibility for the upcoming season but had yet to make that decision because of the agency cost involved.

Samantha and Robert found Arnold a short time later lying on his back beneath a fifty-foot Bertram. The boat's exterior had recently been cleaned and waxed, and showed no signs of having been exposed to the previous winter's weather. Fiberglass and stainless steel were polished. The few pieces of teak had already been treated with a fresh coat of stain. They watched the man roll on the paint a few minutes before he noticed them. They didn't want to disturb him for fear he might spill the paint, which cost over two hundred dollars a gallon.

Robert thought back over the time Billy let him help paint the bottom of *Lady Hatteras II*. It was hot. The paint smelled. It was thick, and heaven help you if it wasn't spread on evenly. It was a challenge and Captain Willey paid them generously for their efforts. It was the first time Robert learned about barnacles and their potential effect on an unpainted boat bottom.

After another minute, Arnold finally noticed the two people standing above him. He recognized Samantha as a big smile crossed his face. "Hey, Sam. How ya doin'?"

He put down his roller pan and slid out from beneath the boat. He held his arms wide. "I'd give you a big hug, but…"

Samantha smiled. "I'll take a rain check, thank you very much."

Arnold laughed. Just over 5' 7", he was a short, stocky man. His face carried a full beard that had not been near a set of clippers in months. His hair was dirty blond and pulled into a ponytail that hung well below his shoulders. He wore an old hat with the marina logo, *Hatteras Marina and Fishing Center*, barely visible. His face, hat, and beard were speckled with fresh blue bottom paint. He was shirtless, but wore an old tan set of coveralls that had obviously participated in the painting of numerous boat bottoms of various colors. His feet, without socks, were barely hanging onto a pair of old boat shoes that were easily two to three years past their rightful burial date. While he was short and stocky with a gut pushing at the buttons on his coveralls, his arms and legs were strong. For a man pushing sixty, he was very fit, minus the middrift bulge.

"Anyway," Arnold said. "Who's your friend?" He looked at Robert, his head cocking to the side.

"Sorry. Please forgive my manners," Samantha said. "This is Dr. Battlegrove. He's down here visiting a few days. I'm just showing him around."

Arnold looked at Robert, obviously trying to place the face. To break off the gaze, Robert turned away and took a few steps toward the boat. "She's a beauty," he said.

"That she is," the marina owner said, also turning his attention toward the boat. "Too bad her owner doesn't know the first thing about boating."

"It's an awful expensive toy if you don't know how to use it," Robert commented.

"Problem is he doesn't know he doesn't know."

"I see," Robert said.

"How's your ma and pa?" Arnold said, turning his attention back to Samantha.

"Fine. They're down here somewhere running around as we speak," Samantha replied.

"Still politicking, huh?"

Robert never remembered Samantha's father doing any kind of politicking. He put that thought aside for later discussion.

"Billy?" Arnold continued.

Samantha hesitated. "Same old, same old."

The marina owner let a moment of concern cross his face before the smile returned. "Tell him whenever he's ready, I got plenty of captains lookin' for mates this summer. Good crews are getting harder and harder to find."

It was a problem indicative of the island youth moving away. Robert used to go out occasionally with Billy and Captain Willey. He served as second mate. He didn't do much unless they got into a school of fish. Then two mates meant twice as many fish boated. If you didn't get any billfish, at least you'd come back with an ice box full of seafood. People always liked to have their pictures taken with a pier full of fish. By the end of the summer Willey was hinting that in another season or two, Robert might be able to mate on his own. To which Robert liked to reply that he could mate just fine now, thank you. To which Captain Willey would reply that knowing how to mate at sea made you a better mate on land. And the banter would go on and on, always clean and always in good fun.

"I'll tell him," Samantha said, forcing Robert's thoughts back to the present.

"Anyway, what brings you down this neck of the woods?" Arnold said. "Surely you're not…"

"Robert here wants to see the Willey boat. It's still for sale, isn't it?" she said quickly. That Samantha cut the marine owner off did not go unnoticed by her companion.

Arnold hesitated as if caught off guard by the question, which Robert noticed. "Yeah, it's still for sale. The widow ain't told me any different," Arnold replied.

"Can we take a look at her?" Robert asked.

"Sure." Arnold's quick recovery was also noted.

"Point us in the right direction. We'll find her," Samantha said. "I know you have to get the bottom finished before the paint starts to dry."

Arnold looked at the boat he was working on and back at the two people standing before him. Robert could tell the man was torn between which way to go. Finally, he said, "She's over at the north-west corner of the yard. Same place she's been since the day the Coast Guard brought her in." He carefully wiped a bead of sweat off his forehead with a part of his arm unpainted. His tone of voice suddenly changed into that of a salesman. "She's a beautiful vessel and takes the seas well. Always caught a lot of fish, too."

"Thanks," Samantha said, as she led Robert away.

They walked through the narrow aisle. The ground was paved with a combination of crushed stone and oyster shells. There were also several potholes filled with water. Robert wondered aloud how deep the small volcanic appearing craters were to which Samantha replied not very deep at all. She explained that the ground had to be smooth for the travel lift to pass by.

"You don't want a bumpy ride when you have tons of fiberglass in your hands," she commented.

They were surrounded by boats of all shapes and sizes, old and new, wood and fiberglass. Many had tall tuna towers that reached high above the bridge. Most had aluminum outriggers that could be spread wide to give more lines and more water covered with each mile traveled. While there were a variety of makes and models, all had one thing in common, they were all powerboats and they were all rigged to fish offshore. Samantha commented that in less than a month the yard would be empty, the boat slips full. "They work twenty-four hours a day to get the boats in the water this time of the year," she said. "If they can get the help."

"Why is that? I mean why does everyone wait until now to get their boats in the water?" Robert asked.

"Several reasons," Samantha said as they continued walking between the boats. "For one, many captains aren't back from Florida where they've been working for the winter. For another, you can't really wax the hulls or paint the bottoms until it gets around fifty-five degrees. Finally, a lot of owners only carry liability insurance for three quarters of the year. March fifteenth is often the day many policies kick in."

Robert laughed.

"What's so funny?" Samantha demanded, stopping in her tracks.

"For someone who doesn't like fishing, you know a lot about it."

She tipped her head to the side. "I don't like camping either, and I run a damn good campground." She turned and headed down the aisle.

Lady Hatteras II sat up on blocks at the end of the aisle. She was a forty-two-foot Hatteras Sportfish made of white fiberglass. Her lines were sleek, her freeboard, high, and her bow flared to an exaggerated degree. It was a design specific to deflect the rough waters off Hatteras. She sat tall and proud, although she had obviously not seen the bristle end of a scrub brush for some time. The space between the boats was narrow, so the boat hunting duo had to duck as they made their way along the port side towards the stern. The boat, as were the other boats next to her, was backed tight against the fence that bordered the northern edge of the marina property.

The other side of the fence looked to be an abandoned, overgrown parking lot. Robert thought he could make out what looked like the remains of a block foundation about a hundred feet or so from the fence. He tried to remember what was there but came up blank. There had been so many changes to the island since his last visit. New buildings up. Old buildings down. There were too many to remember. There was something about that block foundation, however, that was trying to light a spark.

He turned his attention back to the boat. The swim platform extended three feet off the stern. It was made of teak wood that had turned to the expected ugly gray color when exposed to the weather untreated. Robert remembered the swim platform always being an area of pride with Billy. He scrubbed and oiled the teak on a near daily basis. The swim platform, like the rest of the boat, looked nearly new by the beginning of each morning. It took a lot of soap, water and elbow grease, but Captain Willey was insistent that his boat look the best. Sadly, the boat was now a collection spot for the heavy salt air, the swim platform, a collection spot for bird droppings.

The platform was a good five feet off the ground. With some effort, Robert was able to pull down the two-rung ladder, cutting the distance in half. He climbed onto the swim platform, working hard at avoiding the piles of bird droppings. He knew the ducks liked to perch there when the boats were in the water. He didn't realize the habit continued in dry dock. He remembered Billy and Captain Willey always fussing about the birds. He also remembered it was Billy who discovered that as long as you fed the ducks twice a day, they seemed to leave their particular platform alone. Miss a meal, and they'd undoubtedly leave a message of displeasure.

Samantha accepted Robert's hand as she made her own way up the ladder. It was the first time they had touched since Robert returned to the island. It was the first time they had touched in over five years. The event did not go unnoticed by either party. Robert tried to prolong it. Samantha, however, gently pulled her hand away. Robert turned and slid over the top of the stern bulkhead. He put his feet gingerly down on the floor of the cockpit, anticipating more *unpleasantries* beneath his feet. Leaning against the gunwale, he gazed at the oversized fighting chair in the middle of the deck. The first thing most people noticed about any boat when walking along the piers was the fighting chair. The chair was like the hood ornament on a car; the bigger, the flashier, the better. The chairs symbolized what the boats were about, power and big game fishing. *Lady Hatteras II*'s was no different. It was a combination of white vinyl, wood, and stainless steel, and like the swim platform, was kept clean and polished on a regular basis. Six stainless steel bolts held the chair in place. There was a wide waist belt that could be used to hold a person in the chair, if necessary, especially when the seas were rough. The chair was impressive to look at and functional in its use. Robert had been in the chair several times, but never with anything bigger than a small bonito on the hook.

In its heyday, the chair stood out like its brethren on other boats. Now it sat wasting away, the continuous exposure to the elements giving it an age beyond its years. The white vinyl was speckled with mold. The arms were stained. The metal footrest and rod holder were pockmarked in response to the salt air. Like the boat in general, care for the boat's chandelier, as Billy liked to call the fighting chair, had been lacking.

Robert glanced up at the bridge but decided to go inside first. The boat's owner prior to Captain Willey had outfitted the cabin in luxury, it was said, to please his wife. However, as Willey's wife wanted nothing to do with her husband's mistress, as she liked to call the *Lady Hatteras II*, the good captain was free to do what he wanted when he took command. Willey's goal was to make *Lady Hatteras II* a sleek mean fishing machine. All the fancy furnishings and decor in the salon had been removed. All that was left were a small sofa against the starboard bulkhead and a dinette table against the port wall. Four additional chairs were folded and held against the walls by bungee cords. Not uncommon for a boat this size, the engines were beneath the salon floor. The starboard hatch was wide open. Curtains on the port side windows were closed. The starboard side curtains were open, allowing enough light for reasonable visibility. Long shadows, however, warned any intruder there was still a need for caution. The shadows gave an eerie feeling to the musty atmosphere.

Robert stepped carefully around the open hatch, pausing halfway across the floor. He peered into the starboard engine well. He pulled a small penlight from his shirt pocket. He admitted to himself he didn't know what he was looking at except one big ass engine. He also didn't know what he was looking for. From what little he did know about engines, and from what he had learned helping Billy check the various hoses, wires, and fluid levels, everything looked to be in place. Just like he remembered, the engines were shiny. All wires and tubing appeared new. There was not a speck of oil or soot anywhere to be found. The bilge, which to many professionals and boat surveyors was the true telltale sign of the boat's condition, was spotless, just like Robert remembered. He walked forward and looked toward the port engine. He knelt, leaned into the open well and smiled to himself remembering the first time he had looked into the hole. He never realized just how much boat was beneath one's feet, or how much was beneath the water's surface.

Shining the light around the edges, he saw the fishing rods lined up against the starboard bulkhead. Each was held in place by a hook and tied down with a small bungee cord. Two tackle boxes sat against the port side. There was also a large gaff hook secured against the bulkhead above the tackle boxes.

Robert leaned further into the well and looked forward. Several toolboxes and a large army footlocker holding spare parts sat against the forward bulkhead. Each was held in place by a series of bungee cords. Robert asked Billy one time what they did aboard boats before the invention of bungee cords, to which the young mate replied, "You had shit rolling all over the place."

You would never have such an occurrence aboard a Willey boat, even in the worst of seas. Everything was tied down in place. Robert smiled as he remembered that even the person in the fighting chair could be tied down.

He swept the light around the area again before rising to his feet. "Everything looks intact," he said to Samantha, who had made her own way into the cabin and was standing across from him.

"That's a good thing," she said. "Isn't it?"

The doubt in her voice reinforced his own doubt. "I think so."

Robert closed the port hatch and left the starboard side open. He turned, faced forward, and made his way down the two steps to the galley. Except for a three-quarter sized refrigerator and the faucet over the sink, the galley had also been stripped clean of amenities. The stove had even been removed. In its place were two Igloo coolers. The cabinets all had heavy duty latches added to the doors. He opened the first cabinet and then the next. Several more followed. Each was empty except the one above the sink. In it, a near-empty bottle of Jack Daniels laid on its side. Robert's eyes widened. He glanced over his shoulder. Samantha stood behind him, watching his actions. When she saw the bottle, her eyes did the same. She said nothing.

She spun on her heels and leaned through the doorway of the aft head, or bathroom. A moment later, she said with disgust, "It smells putrid in here." She immediately stepped away from the door.

Robert closed the door to the cabinet without comment and turned in her direction. "It is a bathroom," he said. He switched places with her. The fact that their bodies touched in the process did not go unnoticed.

Robert leaned in. The pungent odor attacked his olfactory nerve with vengeance. He snapped his head back out the door. "Phew," he said. It was an odor he had come across before, but at the moment he could not place it. "I'd say the holding tank needs pumping out," he said as a way of explaining the smell. He knew, however, that was probably not the case.

He closed the door to the head and moved toward the bow. The spacious forward area was designed to serve as the master stateroom. Like the rest of the vessel however, all furnishings had been removed. The only thing remaining was the queen size bed. The stateroom now served as the main storage area for the fishing gear. The equipment in the engine well was all extra. A long narrow rack sat across the top of the bed. It gave the impression of a wine rack for very long necked bottles. A multitude of rods, each holding an offshore caliber reel, sat in the various slots. Several large tackle boxes were lined up against the walls. There was even a couple on the floor. Three gaffing hooks hung from the ceiling; each was a different size; each had its own name. That was how Captain Willey called for them when they had fish on. The smallest was named *Wimpy*. It was used for small fish like Bonita and dolphin fish. *That-a-Boy* was used for larger fish such as yellowfin tuna or small sharks. The biggest gaff forward was termed *Son-of-a-Bitch* and was called for when they hooked a bill fish. *Lady Hatteras II* carried a fourth gaffing hook as well, the one Robert saw in the engine well. It was called the *Dreamer*. Its use was obvious. Billy told Robert on more than one occasion his one dream in life, besides one day owning the *Lady Hatteras II*, was for Captain Willey to call out for the *Dreamer*.

"Wow!" Samantha's voice broke Robert's train of thought. "I've never been up here before. Quite a lay out."

"Willey was a stickler for order," Robert said.

"Billy used to talk about that," Samantha acknowledged. She let out a soft chuckle. "Matter of fact, Willey's tidiness had a profound effect on Billy. While I wouldn't call my brother a total slob before he went to work for Willey, he gave the term a run for its money. One week with Willey and things started to change. My brother's room was neater, his truck, cleaner, and even his personal appearance improved." She looked around before heading back into the main salon.

Robert was about to follow when he noticed the door to the forward head ajar. Instinctively he reached over and pulled the door closed. The suspected click of the metal latch was missing. The door swung back inward. Robert grabbed the handle and started pulling the door closed again when he noticed the door frame was splintered. Closer inspection showed a piece of the molding missing. He pushed the door open and peered in. He saw the piece of molding lying on the floor against the base of the toilet. He stepped into the small room, reminding himself not to suck in a deep breath like he had done in the aft head. He wanted no more noxious surprises. He quickly realized, however, the earlier stench was missing. Resting his hand on the lid of the toilet, he bent down and started to pick up the piece of wood. Moving the wood away, his eye caught a dark stain on the floor beneath the piece of molding. He leaned in closer. He could not tell what it was. He raised the lid of the toilet. He wished he had not done that because therein lay his surprise. He was about to probe the bowl with the stick when he suddenly heard voices coming from the main salon. He quickly put the wood back on the floor, closed the lid to the toilet and rose to his feet. He was coming out of the forward cabin as Arnold was making his way past the open engine hatch.

Making sure he remained on the offensive, Robert said, "Willey certainly has an array of fishing gear. Does that all come with the boat?"

"I would think so, but I'll have to check the listing," Arnold said.

"Okay," Robert said. "She is a beauty."

"She cleans up real good," Arnold said, automatically shifting into his sales mode.

There was something about what he just said and how he said it that bothered Robert. "How 'bout the engines?" he asked.

"Ah…they ain't been run in a few years, so that might be a problem. They've been winterized though."

Robert peered into the engine well.

"That'll all come out in sea trials," Samantha said. She had been standing at the doorway listening to the conversation.

"Anyway, I certainly appreciate your time, Mr. Arnold," Robert said. "I like her a lot. Wouldn't mind seeing the specs on her if you got 'em."

"Nobody's been by to look at her in a long time. I got to dig 'em out. What say you give me a few days?"

"I may not be down here that long, but I'll call and give you my address," Robert said.

Arnold shrugged. He said nothing.

Robert turned his attention to Samantha. "Well, Sam, what say we get from underneath the man's hair so he can get back to work?"

Again, Arnold said nothing. Samantha nodded in the affirmative.

10

They were a good five miles north of the marina before either spoke. The windows of the SUV were down and the sunroof, open. The sun was about to peak, so the maximum heat of the day was nearly upon them. There was still a bite to the air as Mother Nature reminded them summer was still a few weeks away. Traffic was light so Robert set the cruise control. He sat back, his right hand on the wheel, the other resting on the door. The dunes at this end of the island were a lot shorter than those up north. To compensate, the beach was wider. The grass never seemed as thick either to Robert, who often wondered why this part of the island didn't just blow away in one of the fierce winter storms. If not then, surely one of the recent hurricanes would have taken the area as a souvenir. However, except for a hurricane a few years earlier when a temporary cut sawed through the southern portion, the barrier island held true to its duty of protecting the mainland.

Nothing was more symbolic of the island's survival than the Cape Hatteras Lighthouse which was now coming into view. It was the highest structure for miles around. On a clear day or night, its light and black and white spiral could be seen twenty miles offshore, warning mariners they were approaching shallow waters and the dangerous shoals of Hatteras. If Robert remembered the statistics correctly, it was first built in 1803 and heightened to its present level several years later. It now stood 208 feet tall. More importantly, however, was the number 268. That was the number of steps to the top. He and Billy used to go up there frequently. Besides being fun racing to the top, which Billy always won, the panoramic view of the area was spectacular. The beach could be seen for miles, so the best area to surf could be easily identified. The barber's pole, as it was nicknamed by historians, was one of the most recognizable lighthouses in the world.

Robert thought about turning into the road leading to the base when he remembered Samantha mentioning she didn't want to be gone too long. Instead, he said, "I'd like to go up there again sometime."

"I like it best at sunset," Samantha said.

"I remember that."

Samantha started to say something, surely a smart remark or thereabout, but her voice remained silent

A few more miles passed, and Robert said, "Something about this whole thing smells really fishy."

"Fishy is what we do here," Samantha said.

Robert couldn't tell if she was making a joke or was being curt. He wisely gave her the benefit of the doubt.

"There are just too many unanswered questions?" he said instead.

"Like?"

He hesitated before responding. "I don't have it all together yet. Let me think about things tonight. We'll talk tomorrow." Not talking also meant he didn't have to decide how much to tell Samantha of the little extras he saw on the boat. He wanted more time to digest things.

Samantha turned toward him. It seemed strange that he wasn't willing to spew it all out. Unlike him, she thought. She shrugged and let it go. She wasn't ready to talk herself.

They rode to the campground in silence.

11

Robert had a good appetite during the earlier picnic but lost it after the visit to the *Lady Hatteras II*. Now his stomach was telling him to get over the earlier assault on his nostrils and get about the business of feeding his gut. Robert contemplated his options, including stopping at one of the local eateries along the mid-portion of the island. He pulled into the parking lot of one, an old ice cream parlor he remembered from the past, but he left almost immediately. He decided to honor Samantha's request of minimizing the people who know he was back in the area. He wasn't sure why this was a good idea; at the moment, however, it seemed like the right thing to do. He headed north instead, with the thought of leaving the island for the night. He had a room reserved at a local motel in Nags Head. He chose the place because the motel was oceanfront and because there was a greasy spoon diner next door. He was usually very conscientious about his diet; however, tonight he felt he needed some brain food as they liked to call it in the ER at 3:00 am.

Forty-five minutes later, Robert was tucked away in a corner booth with a blank legal pad in front of him. Once a draft beer was placed within his reach and while waiting for his salad, he picked up his pen and started tapping it gently against the table. He felt like he was back in the emergency room working on a complicated case. Only instead of a living patient with obscure abdominal complaints, he was dealing with a dirty fishing boat. He believed that just like the patients who came into the emergency room dirty and disheveled, *Lady Hatteras II* would clean up real good if given the chance.

Robert focused on the blank page. He was interrupted by the arrival of his Caesar salad. The waitress was a cute young blonde from one of those eastern European countries. She was dressed in a size too small blouse and a four inch too short black skirt. She had bright blonde hair pulled in a ponytail and a wide friendly smile. She cleaned up real nice, too. Robert watched her walk away. He took a bite of the salad after dipping it in the dressing. He put down his fork, took a sip of beer, and picked up his pen. At the top of the page, he wrote: *Lady Hatteras II*. Beneath that he wrote:

Cleans up real well. Dirty now though!!

He paused and underlined the last sentence. Under that he wrote: *why?* He continued writing as his thoughts flowed quickly.

If she was for sale, why was she so dirty?

Another bite of salad, another sip of beer and:

Mr. Arnold. Good friend of Captain Willey. Doubt if he cleans up very well.

Why was the salesman of such an expensive boat so disorganized and so unenthusiastic about a prospective buyer?

Dinner arrived—a large basket of fish and chips. Like in the emergency room, unless someone was dying, his hunger won out over his eagerness to continue with his legal pads. He ate half of the fish and all the chips before his stomach told him capacity was close. His beer was refilled, a doggy bag called for, and he went back to work, but not before watching the waitress clean off his table and walk away.

He continued with his notes.

Hidden in the back of the yard.

Why was a boat for sale not on display out in front where she could be seen?

Engine hatch open, inside a mess.

Material in toilet bowl.

Bathroom smell?

Door busted!

Whiskey bottle!

His pen stopped. He suddenly realized what the smell was in the bathroom. He had experienced it many times. It was obnoxious and could hang around a long time.

He dropped the pen to work a cramp from his fingers. He had a lot of good information, but nothing to tie it all together. Something was missing. He contemplated his options. An idea came to mind, a bit off the wall, but an idea nonetheless. He argued it through by reminding himself that when he was in the emergency room and got stuck, he went back to the bedside. He always taught his medical students and residents not to be afraid to reexamine the patient. So that's what he would do.

He finished his beer, paid the bill, collected the doggy bag, and headed out the door. Now, he wished he had stayed on the island. Outside, it was a beautiful, clear sky, a beautiful night for a drive. As he crossed onto Hatteras Island a short time later another thought crossed his mind. Maybe he'd make two stops.

12

Robert sat silently, looking across the parking lot. A rusting badly-in-need-of-repair fence was all that separated him from the boatyard. The night sky remained clear, allowing the stars above to shed their light across the area. His night vision maximized, he continued scanning the area in all directions. Toward the south, tall, majestic shadows glared back at him. He felt like David looking up at a whole army of Goliaths. He figured he was safe though. After all, there was a fence. He looked into his rearview and side mirrors on a regular basis. Darkness was all that attacked him from those directions. He had been parked for over an hour. He had seen nothing or heard nothing out of the ordinary. Good or bad, it was a very calm night.

The foundation to the previous building was to the left. He was finally able to remember what had been there before. It was the site of the Bluefish Café, a popular eatery. It specialized in local fresh seafood and homemade desserts; specifically homemade berry pies topped off with freshly churned old fashioned ice cream. While he and Samantha didn't eat dinner there a lot because of Samantha's schedule, there were frequent late evening trips for dessert. It was one of the few places on the island that stayed open past sunset. Samantha's father especially liked the blueberry pie. A piece was always tucked away in the back of the Jeep for him. Robert made a mental note to ask Samantha what happened to the place, other than it had obviously burned down.

His gaze moved back in the direction of the fence. He could barely make out the stern of the *Lady Hatteras II*. Earlier in the day she looked so ordinary mixed in with the rest of the boats. A sixth sense, however, told Robert she was far from ordinary. There was something about her, a mystery, a story trying to be told. Like a depressed patient in the emergency room crying out to him, what was she trying to tell him? What had he yet to discover? He waited another five minutes before opening the car door, telling himself now was as good a time as any to find the answers.

13

Samantha lay on her back facing the ceiling, her arms folded behind her head. Her body commanded sleep. She closed her eyes. A few moments later they were again wide open. The action was repeated several times. A cool breeze snuck in through the partially open window. The curtains swayed slowly back and forth in response, casting soft gentle shadows across the room. She laid still, pulling in her breath slowly, exhaling softly. She listened to the silence around her. She had heard her brother moving about in his room a few minutes earlier. That noise was gone. While both her mother and father snored loudly, the door to their room at the end of the hall was closed so all sounds from there were filtered. The ocean was even quiet tonight, an unusual occurrence of late. She tried blaming the silence that engulfed her as an excuse for her insomnia. She knew, however, that her sleeplessness was caused by something else, or rather someone else.

Ever since she saw Robert at the store two days before, her mind spun like the tires of a vehicle stuck in the sand. There had been a whirlwind of emotions.

Vacillations between joy and anger started immediately. Mixed in were good doses of curiosity and concern. She was curious as to why he was here. She was concerned about the impact his visit might have on Billy. Her brother didn't seem a whole lot different that evening at dinner, although he did seem to eat faster than his usual scarfing of food. At first Samantha took this as a sign that he had something he wanted to do, like when he was a kid and couldn't wait to get back outside to play. A good sign, she thought. Then the negativism in her personality made her think his eating fast was an excuse to get away from the table quickly so he wouldn't have to talk, something he wasn't fond of doing anyway of late. A bad sign, she thought. She tried to pay close attention to her brother's state of mind, although he was so withdrawn most of the time, any fluctuations in his behavior were difficult to pick up. He did seem more jittery than normal; although she acknowledged she might simply be picking up her own state of anxiety.

State of anxiety—there was no denying that was how she felt at the moment. There was little doubt of its cause either. She focused on that. Was she anxious because Robert was back on the island, or was she anxious because of her own reaction to seeing him again?

She rolled onto her side and looked out the window. Her heart pounded in her chest. She could even hear her pulse in her ears. She told herself her blood pressure was probably up and that she should have it checked. Then she laughed aloud, her hand clapping across her mouth to keep the noise in. Her blood pressure wasn't the problem. It was her broken heart. While the scar had healed, Robert had ripped it wide open with his return. The emotions she was feeling now were the same she experienced when he left five years before. She thought she was over him. She thought the scar was stronger. She was wrong. She loved him then. She had little doubt she still loved him now. But before she could begin to focus on that feeling, she had to get through all the negative crap his return brought with it.

Her eyes filled with tears. Of the many emotions, anger took over for the moment. Why did he have to come back? Why was he doing this to her? Why didn't he just stay in Baltimore and finish his training so he could become the great doctor he always dreamed about, always talked about? Why didn't he just stay there? After all, he hadn't changed, had he? He was still the same self-centered bastard as when he left. Sure, he could turn on the charm with the best of them. Sure, he wowed her off her feet. Sure, he was good in…

She cut the thought off. She refused to allow her mind to remember the good times they had. She was not ready to go there.

She rolled over, turning her back to the window, turning her back to the memories. She told herself nothing would change until Billy was better. Robert claimed there was more to the cause of Billy's condition than him leaving that Friday and Captain Willey's death that Sunday. She didn't know whether to believe Robert or not. She reminded herself about his ability to charm, his ability to hurt. Still, he seemed sincere. Then again, he seemed sincere before when talking about their future together.

And then he up and left.

Still...

Was she so desperate for Billy she was willing to believe Robert again? Was she so desperate for Billy she would let this man back into her life?

She laughed again, softer this time. He was already back in her life, having returned two days ago. He came into the store the first time five years earlier with the usual early crowd of men seeking their first coffee of the morning. The men did one of two things when they left the store. They either went fishing or they went to work. The preferable choice was the first, although the second alternative was more common. She knew she had never seen him before. She never forgot a face. She could also tell he had never been in the store before. The regulars knew what they wanted and where everything was located. Newbies, as the regulars liked to call them, wandered around, just like they did on the island in general. There were other things that gave his newness away as well. For one, he had a fresh haircut and no sunburn or suntan. For another, his tee shirt, a surfer's shirt, was not faded and was free of holes. His work shorts were also without signs of the usual wear and tear. Finally, he was hatless. She remembered thinking to herself while he might not want to mess up his freshly cropped hair, that attitude would change quickly. The Hatteras sun was quite unforgiving, even on overcast days. He failed to worry about all this as he made his way up and down the several aisles of the store. He found the coffee, was shown the cups by one of the locals and selected a muffin with little hesitation. A sandwich was made, he paid in cash, said thank you, and left with a smile.

His hair, again freshly cut, was jet black, medium length and combed off his forehead. His face was long and thin, his eyes a deep blue. He had near perfect teeth shown off by a wide smile that was punctuated on each end by a deep dimple. His neck was long and attached his head to a tall torso. While he wasn't all that muscular, he was thin and well built. His arms were long, his fingers the same. His nails were clean and well maintained. She remembered thinking that wouldn't last long either. Overall, he was quite good looking, even to the point of deserving the word handsome. Or as the cousins liked to say, he was a hot cross bun.

"Enough," she mouthed softly. She turned and looked at the clock. It was 2:16 am. She let out a long sigh. She had to get up early and open the store. She contemplated adding ten minutes to the alarm, but it was already set for 5:30, the hour for maximum sleep and minimum ready time. She let out another sigh followed by a groan. She closed her eyes, slowed her breathing and ignored the heartbeat pounding in her ears. It was time to go to sleep. She listened a moment. All was quiet. She reached back, fluffed her pillow and pulled the blanket up to her chin. While her room wasn't cold, it had cooled down nicely from the heat of day. It would be a good night for sleep, all be it short. Another deep breath followed by a long exhale.

Then the silence was broken. Her eyes snapped open. Her senses perked up as a shot of adrenaline rushed through her blood stream. Shadows flowed across the ceiling like waves across the beach. A long moment passed. There it was again. It was a sound, a noise, one she had heard before, many times before. It was a moment before she recognized it. It was the sound of Billy's truck door opening. The truck was old, the door hinges rusty. They made a distinct *screech* when disturbed. Someone was getting into the truck which was parked right in front of the house. She started to jump up to go after him. After all, it was the middle of the night and where was he going? Then she remembered Billy was in the next room asleep. She had not heard him go out.

She jumped to her feet and went to the window. She pulled aside the curtain. It took a moment for her eyes to adjust before she could make out the silhouette of the truck. It was parked right next to her Jeep. She made sure she stayed back from the window so she wouldn't be seen. A dog barked in the distance. She figured it was one of the camper's pets. Another dog barked, and then another. She didn't know much about animals, but she knew barking dogs at night when all was quiet the moment before probably meant something. She leaned forward. She saw nothing move. She heard nothing. The barking stopped.

She stepped closer to the window. The driver's side of Billy's truck was open. She immediately thought someone was trying to steel his truck. Then she realized that was absurd. Who would want the truck anyway? Still, someone was in it. She slipped on her robe. As she left the house, she grabbed an aluminum bat off the porch. It was the only weapon they had, and it wasn't for prowlers. Crime on the island was almost nonexistent. There hadn't been a major crime in several years. They kept the bat handy for the occasional dog that got loose from a campsite and needed encouragement to go home.

She stopped at the bottom of the steps, trying to decide how she was going to make it across the gravel parking lot without giving herself away. Though it was only a few feet, she decided speed was of the essence. The bat raised above her head, she traversed the distance swiftly. Her feet, calloused by years of going barefoot, ignored the sharpness of the stones.

As she suspected, the driver's door was open. A figure was leaning across the seat. She guessed the person was trying to hot-wire the truck. Again, she thought, why steal such a truck? It had to be some kid from the campground. Getting to the door, she lowered the bat. She decided because it was probably a kid, she'd speak first before swinging. Otherwise, she would have just given the person a wallop.

She pushed the bat hard into the back of the figure. "If you move so much as an inch, I swear to God, I'll shatter your brains all over the place," she said without a hint of politeness.

The figure made a noise as the pain of her poke took effect. The head started to turn.

"I said don't move!"

The head movement stopped. There was a moment's silence. "Samantha, is that you?"

More silence followed as the voice registered. "Robert?"

The head turned again, this time more quickly. Luckily for him, there was enough light coming from the campground that Samantha could make out the face. She lowered the bat. She forgot to do the same with her voice. "What in the hell are you doing here, and this time of the night? And why would you be stealing Billy's truck?"

Robert put his finger to his lips. "Shh!"

Samantha raised the bat. "I'd be careful who you were shushing."

"Samantha! I'm not trying to steal Billy's truck."

"Then what are you doing?"

"Let me out of here and I'll tell you."

Samantha hesitated. Finally, the bat was lowered, and she stepped back. Robert sat up and slid to the ground. Nodding toward the bat and one hand reaching back to his spine, he said, "You could hurt somebody with that thing, you know."

"You're lucky I thought you were a kid from the campground or else I would have whacked you a good one."

"Do you always shoot and ask questions later?"

"We don't take kindly to car thieves down here. We usually hang 'em."

Robert wasn't sure if she was kidding or being serious. He knew it was not the time to inquire.

"So, what are you doing?" Samantha pressed. She noticed his free hand held a small plastic bag.

The dogs started barking again. "Can we go somewhere and talk?" Robert pleaded.

Samantha hesitated. She felt like whacking him across the head, not so much as to hurt him but to knock some sense into him. How dare he come to their house this time of the night? She told herself he was lucky she wasn't a violent person. "You'd better have a damn good explanation," she said.

"I do," Robert said, continuing to rub the small of his back.

"Where you parked?" Samantha said. By now her voice was quieter.

"At the end of the road," Robert replied.

"Go on down there. Let me change and I'll be there in a minute."

"You're okay the way you are," Robert said. A smile finally crossed his face.

Samantha raised the bat above her head.

"Just kidding," Robert said.

The Ladies of Hatteras

"Go!"

The doctor caught-red-handed-truck-thief did as he was told.

14

Five minutes later, they were headed south on the main road. Robert turned into the first access road to the beach. He parked so they were facing the road. Shutting the engine off, he said, "You warm enough?"

"Yeah, thanks." Samantha had snuck back into the house to put on a pair of jeans and sweatshirt. There was a moment's silence. "So, let's have it, what were you doing back there?" Samantha's voice was still agitated, only not as loud.

"I was collecting DNA samples," Robert said.

"You were *what?*"

"Collecting DNA samples." He paused. Samantha remained silent, so he continued. "I'm going to tell you some things that may lead you to believe I've gone off the deep end, but let me get through the whole thing before you say anything or pass judgment. Okay?"

She nodded in the darkness.

The doctor turned detective continued. "When we were on the boat this afternoon, I saw several things that alone didn't mean much, but as I thought about it later, I realized things just didn't add up. To start with, for being a boat salesman, Mr. Arnold wasn't very knowledgeable about the *Lady Hatteras II*, nor did he seem all that interested in selling her. On top of that, the boat's a mess, and she's stuck back in the corner of the marina where no one can see her. Now, I'm not a salesman, but I don't think that's how you sell a boat, especially when all the other boats he had listed were right out front. I didn't think about that until later, but I noticed it when we first drove through the gates."

Robert took a breath. "Arnold did have his moments where his salesman gene kicked in, but they were short lived. For the most part, he seemed uninterested in making a sale. Matter of fact, I'm wondering if he was purposely trying not to sell the boat."

"Why would he do that?" Samantha inquired.

"That's one of many questions," Robert admitted. "But there's more." He paused to organize his thoughts. "I found a couple other things you didn't see. First, the boat doesn't look like it has had anything done to it since it was pulled five years ago. Now that's a guess, but it certainly appears that way. The one engine hatch was still open, almost like Willey was having engine trouble or something when he allegedly fell overboard."

"Allegedly?"

"I'll get to that," Robert promised. "Yet, if he was having engine trouble, why were there no tools out, or any signs of trouble? The engines were as clean as the day they were first installed—exactly how I remembered them. Second, there was a half-empty bottle of Jack

Daniels in one of the galley cabinets—you saw that too, didn't you?"

Samantha nodded in acknowledgment.

Robert continued quickly. "You're going to ask what's so unusual about that and my response is that Captain Willey was very strict about drinking aboard his boat. Beer was fine, but hard liquor was a definite no-no. Guests were told that even before they left the dock."

"Maybe it was there for when he got back," Samantha suggested.

"Maybe, except for one simple fact, Captain Willey didn't drink whiskey."

"You suggesting it was left there by Billy?"

"He would never do something like that."

"Thank you." Samantha said. "Then who?"

"Another unanswered question," Robert replied. "However, there's more. Do you remember that awful odor in the one bathroom, or head if you please."

"How could you forget that?"

"Well, I knew I recognized it, only I couldn't place it at first. Then, fortunately or unfortunately, it hit me later. It's what we call drunken puke, or what a drunk vomits up. Now it sounds gross, but it has a very specific and very lasting odor."

"Lasting meaning it stays around for that long a time?" Samantha queried.

"Lasting in that it's a smell you don't easily forget. As far as how long it lasts, that's yet another valid question. However, what's really of interest was that the empty bottle and the vomit in the head were still there to begin with."

"You lost me there," Samantha said.

"Why did Billy leave the boat dirty like that?" Robert threw out.

"Maybe he didn't," Samantha defended.

"Exactly!"

"Then how…?"

Robert paused, toying with what to say next. He decided that since he had been caught red handed, why not fess up all the way. "There's more."

"More?"

"The door frame in the forward head was broken. It wouldn't latch or close. While that may sound simple on land, on a boat, you don't want something like that banging around. Again, if the boat's really for sale, why wasn't it repaired?"

"You tell me," Samantha said.

"I don't know." Again, he paused, contemplating whether to continue. Finally, "There's more."

"Robert!"

"I'm not making this stuff up, Samantha. It's all there for you to see."

"I'm sorry. Go on."

"There's a stain in the forward head, right under the commode that looked like blood to me. And…" He hesitated.

"If you're going to gross me out again, it can't be any worse than—what did you call it—drunken puke," Samantha said.

"It's worse," Robert said. Samantha stared at him, her eyelids rising high. Robert continued. "Stuffed down in the commode was what looked like a pair of boy's underwear."

Her eyes widened. She looked away. "Maybe you have gone off the deep end," she huffed.

"Maybe I have," Robert acknowledged. "That's why I went back and took a closer look tonight."

"You went back to *Lady Hatteras II* tonight?"

Robert nodded.

"What did you do there?"

"Like I said earlier, I was collecting DNA samples."

"Okay smart ass, what does that mean?"

Robert explained. "I collected the stuff I found and I'm going to send it to a friend of mine who's a pathology resident at Hopkins. He has a special interest in forensics. He wants to work for the FBI when he's finished his training. Anyway, I'm going to have him look to see what he finds."

"What if he doesn't want to help you?"

"I've already talked to him."

"You called him tonight, in the middle of the night?"

"I called him at the hospital to see if he was still there and sure enough, he was."

"Should I ask what he was doing up this time of the night?"

"Like I said, he's a forensic buff. They work better when it's dark out."

"What if he doesn't find anything?"

"Oh, he'll find something. The question is will it be of any value?"

"Value for what?"

"Hopefully to answer some of the questions that keep popping up."

Samantha looked out the window a moment before turning back to Robert. "You still haven't told me what you were doing in Billy's truck?"

"Collecting DNA." He didn't wait for her to ask for further explanation. "I want to see if Billy is connected to the stuff I found in the boat."

"Boy's underwear! You think…"

Robert immediately recognized where she was headed and cut her off. "No, I do not. What I expect to find is that he's not connected to any of that. That'll help with the timeline, meaning everything we found happened after that Friday when they came back."

"Then presumably that Sunday when Willey went out by himself," Samantha added.

"Allegedly by himself," Robert pointed out.

"What did you actually find in Billy's truck?" Samantha asked, after a moment of silence.

"A few strands of hair and a couple cigarette butts."

"DNA can be found on that sort of stuff?"

"Any part of your body that sheds can be tested for DNA. Some areas are better than others. I'm not sure which are which. I collected what I was told."

"By your friend?"

"Yeah. Like I said, I called him before I went back to the marina. I wanted to make sure I wasn't barking up the wrong tree."

"Does he think you were nuts like I do?"

"He wouldn't be able to process that notion."

"Why's that?"

"Cause he's crazy just like me."

Samantha snorted. "I guess anyone who stays up working this time of night when they could be in bed is a little off center."

"Including those who break into other people's trucks?" Robert questioned.

Samantha started to agree before catching herself. "The truck was unlocked. You didn't break into anything."

"Tell that to my back," Robert said.

Samantha didn't offer any sympathy or apology. Instead, "Where's all this *stuff* you collected?"

Robert pointed toward the back of the vehicle.

"Back there!"

Robert nodded. Even though it was dark, Robert swore Samantha turned pale. "Don't worry, it's all packaged up."

"I would hope so." Samantha squirmed in her seat. "When or how long will this testing take?"

"I'm going to overnight it to him in the morning. He'll start working on it right away. From that point on, it'll take at least a few days."

"You'll be gone by then!"

Robert hadn't really considered that part of the timeline. "Yeah." His voice softened. "Only this time I don't suspect I'll stay away as long."

He saw Samantha start to make a smart comment. However, as she had done several times recently, she bit her tongue. She was trying, he thought. He spoke aloud. "The next question is what to do next. The presumptive answer is for one of us to talk to Billy. However, the more I think about that, the more I want to wait for the test results. I want to have some hard data to confront him with: less likely to scare him off, I think." He paused. "What do you think?"

She looked hard at him. "You actually went back down to the boat tonight and took things off of it?"

"I certainly didn't take anything that will reduce the sales price," he mocked with a soft laugh.

"I didn't mean that," Samantha responded. She leaned toward him, hesitated, and then kissed him gently on the cheek. Sitting up straight, she continued. "I feel a lot of things, a lot of conflicting emotions right now. I don't know what you being back here means. I'm not even sure why you're here. But so far I guess I should say thank you, thank you for trying to help Billy."

"I came here for more reasons than Billy," Robert said.

Samantha leaned over and kissed him again, this time on the lips. "That may be true, but let's leave it at that for now." She again straightened up.

Robert wanted to say more. He wanted to do more. Experience, common sense, or a combination of both told him to keep still and keep quiet. There was hope, he told himself. He wasn't sure exactly what hope meant. He also knew he wasn't going to get the answer to that question tonight. "Okay," he said reluctantly.

"Thank you," she repeated.

"You're welcome."

15

Of no surprise to Samantha, the sun seemed to rise a lot earlier than usual. Light made its way through the window, erasing the earlier gray shadows across the ceiling.

The breeze had picked up, yet there was already an increased warmth to the air. While her body was exhausted, her mind continued to race through an array of emotions. Unlike earlier when anger dominated her feelings, she found her attitude was softening. While Robert's basic personality hadn't changed, he was more mature, more caring, more willing to listen. His voice was softer; like his touch, his kiss…

A wave of electricity shot through her spine. "Jesus," she said aloud, realizing what almost just happened. Pulling the covers up to her neck, she rolled away from the window and buried her face in her pillow. She was so confused. She kept asking herself why. Why did he have to come back into her life? Was it to confuse her? To complicate matters? Hell, her life was already chaotic enough. And this was supposed to be peaceful Hatteras Island. At the same time there was something else she had not felt before, and that was hope. She felt hope for Billy, and for herself. When Robert returned, he brought a bag full of feelings with him. Buried deep in that bag was a small canister of hope. Samantha told herself it was this emotion she had to hold onto. Still, there were a lot of other issues, issues Robert knew nothing about. "More conflicts," she muttered.

Insomnia won the battle as her body pleaded for sleep. After a few more minutes, she got up, dressed and went to the store. The cousins were there, one working on a crossword puzzle, the other watching the small TV in the back room. Samantha laughed internally as she thought about her earlier comments concerning people who worked nights. The cousins, while they certainly had their young adult issues, were normal enough.

Greetings were exchanged. Numbers for the night were reported. Samantha could tell by their expressions that they wanted to say something about her appearance, i.e., how tired she looked. They knew by the look on her face, however, to keep their thoughts to themselves. While the three were relatively close, Samantha was still their boss.

When Samantha opened the store a few minutes early, there were already several regulars waiting for their morning coffee and muffins. Despite her fatigue, the time went by quickly. Ten o'clock came and her mother arrived to relieve her for an early lunch. As things in the office were slow, Samantha said she'd be back later in the afternoon—not an unusual routine. Samantha left a few minutes later and headed south towards Buxton. She was scheduled to meet Robert at the lighthouse at eleven. She pulled into the parking lot twenty minutes before the hour. Robert was already there, his SUV parked in the far corner. As she approached, she could see the driver's seat was in the reclining position and Robert was sound asleep. She was glad at least one of them got some rest.

He woke up as she closed the door to her Jeep. She handed him a cup of coffee and a paper bag. "Blueberry," she said.

He pulled his seat into the upright position as he pushed his hair back. "Thanks." He tested the temperature of the coffee. Finding it wasn't too hot, he took a long gulp. "You know how to get there?" he asked.

"Yeah."

"Then hop in. I'll drive if you want."

She didn't argue and slid into the passenger's side. She chased away the memories of the past few hours. Other than a word or two for directions, she remained silent. Robert did the same, content with enjoying the scene while eating his muffin and sipping his coffee.

Except for being the home of the famous Hatteras Lighthouse, Buxton was not a whole lot different than the other small towns on the island. The same single two-lane route NC12 ran through the middle. Road front properties on either side were mainly commercial, usually either restaurants or small shops geared toward the tourists. Ocean side properties off the main road consisted of two to four-story houses built on wooden pilings. The design was practical in that there was some protection from flooding. Aesthetically, in that the view of the ocean over the dunes was much better. Most of these homes were owned by individual families. A few were for private use only; the bulk of the houses were on the rental market. Buxton, because of the lighthouse and wide beach, was one of the more popular sites for vacationers.

It was a different story on the Albemarle Sound side of the road. Here the houses were mostly small single-story cottages that sat directly on the ground. Most were occupied by locals. Many had been in the same family for generations, although that pattern was showing signs of weakness as more and more of the younger generation moved off the island.

Samantha directed Robert to turn right just on the southern edge of Buxton. The side road was narrow and ended less than fifty yards at the sound. The sun, nearing its peak, sent long fingers of bright sunlight across the mirror top water. Tall dune grasses were all that separated the road from the water. There wasn't even a guard rail. The widow's cottage was on the left. It was small and appeared well kept. While there was hardly a lawn, there was a small garden in front that sported a variety of spring flowers. The house itself was white with red shutters. The exterior looked weathered, but generally the house looked in good condition. It presented a pleasant view. Robert slowed to a crawl so they could enjoy the moment.

It was short lived, however, as Samantha said, "Why's the sheriff here?"

"Sheriff? Where?"

Samantha pointed to the car sitting in the oyster shell driveway. "That's Alex Smith's car." The vehicle was a several year-old Dodge Durango. Its official capacity was marked only by several antennas on the back and a local government license plate.

Robert pulled up to the curb. Just as he and Samantha got out, the front door of the house opened A short pudgy man came out onto the porch. He wore the standard grayish law enforcement uniform, wide brim hat included. His weathered face made him look to be in his late sixties. In reality, he was just over fifty. He had short muscular arms. His fingers matched. He had a bulging gut that pressed against the wide gun belt. He pulled the door shut as he headed down the steps. He looked up and saw the two visitors. A friendly smile crossed his face. "Samantha Mathews! How's the prettiest girl on the island doing?"

Samantha returned the smile. It was the same thing the sheriff said to every girl he met, including her mother. She accepted the compliment without question. "Fine, thanks. And you?"

"Oh, I've been better. But seeing you will add some sunshine to what has started out as a dreary day. I am surprised you got here so quickly. Why, the widow is still warm."

"What are you talking about?" Samantha asked.

"You being down here so fast to check out the property."

"We're not down here for that," Samantha defended. "Robert here is interested in the old man's boat." She started to make a more formal introduction when something the sheriff said crossed her mind. "What do you mean she's still warm?"

The sheriff's face turned somber. "The widow...she passed."

"Passed! You mean she's dead?"

The sheriff nodded.

"What happened?" Samantha inquired with sadness in her voice.

The sheriff explained. "A friend stopped by this morning to pick her up for church. When Mrs. Willey didn't answer the door, she let herself in with an extra key. She found her dead in her bed. We figured she died in her sleep, most likely from a heart attack. She did have a bad ticker you know."

"She had a mild heart attack last year," Samantha recalled.

"They took her away about half an hour ago. I was closing up when you showed up." The sheriff paused. "She was a staunch woman. Even after Old Man Willey died, she remained active, especially in her church. She liked to play bingo, too, if I recall correctly."

"Yeah, my mother used to see her there once in a while," Samantha said.

"Anyway, I gotta get back to the station to finish the paperwork. First though, over to Doc Robins's office. He said he'd sign the death certificate if I brought it by. I'll imagine you'll be in touch."

Samantha was staring at the house. "Yeah, I guess so." She turned to Robert. "There isn't anything we can do here so we'd better go, too." She led a stunned Robert back to the car.

16

Johns Hopkins Hospital was world renowned for many aspects of medical care, from its School of Public Health, to cutting edge research, to the education of physicians and other professionals, to children's diseases, to cancer care, to world famous brain surgeons. The list was long and distinguished. The famous dome atop the original building rose high above the skyline of Baltimore like an emperor with outstretched arms admiring his kingdom. Beneath the dome standing some twenty-feet tall in the main lobby was a marble statue of Jesus with his arms outstretched in a similar fashion. He was welcoming in the sick and feeble people of the land.

Even though Robert had been through this lobby hundreds of times over the years, he always slowed his pace. He mouthed a short prayer asking for the strength and guidance to survive yet another day at the Johns. While Jesus was the king of Christianity, Johns Hopkins was the king of medicine, or so his professors liked to preach. Even with his own ego teetering on the edge, Robert was able to see the exaggeration of that idealism. Johns Hopkins Hospital was one of the highest rated hospitals in the world. It was not, however, the savior of all. The hospital had its problems just like anywhere else.

As always, Robert paused and gazed at the statue. Eye contact was made with a prayer for guidance. The young doctor nodded. Jesus seemingly nodded back. The moment over, Robert continued his journey through the lobby. He passed the line of old wooden telephone booths that were said to be as old as the building itself. While the actual equipment had been upgraded over the years, the oak structures hadn't changed. The world of Hopkins medicine was full of history. Robert often wondered how much history was made in these booths during their days.

He exited the historical lobby, passing beneath heavy black wooden arches. Suddenly, the atmosphere changed. History moved forward to the modern age as he entered the main corridor of the hospital. The quiet of the lobby was gone. Here, people were moving in all directions. Many wore white lab coats, their eyes fixed forward, already knowing their destination, already late. Others in more casual attire walked slowly, looking up at the sometimes confusing signs hanging from the ceiling, no clue where they were going, and already late. Robert stared at the signs a moment just to make sure nothing had changed during the week he was gone, no buildings torn down, no new buildings added. It amazed Robert that the hospital could never get its construction projects completed at the same time. There was always something being torn down or something being built. This just added to the chaos of the environment, the opposite of what he left a few hours earlier.

Johns Hopkins Hospital was a large complex of many buildings, all connected by an array of corridors on the main floor. The entire campus took up several city blocks. Robert had been lost among the many hallways, staircases and elevators more times than he cared to remember. He had little doubt that situation would continue before his training ended. Institutions such as this took on a personality of their own. They had organs—various buildings. They had veins—hallways, staircases, and elevators. They had a heartbeat—the massive heating and air conditioning system buried somewhere in the bowels. And they had blood flow that kept the whole place alive - the people moving among these various innate structures. Like the historical lobby he just left, the hallways of Hopkins still amazed Robert, even after all these years. He was proud to be a part of it. He was proud to be one of the cells carrying oxygen through its body.

The institution was unique for other reasons as well. It had its own subway station located in the basement next to the main parking garage. It was reported to be one of the busiest stations in Baltimore. Hopkins also had its own Subway Sandwich franchise in the main cafeteria and was reportedly the number one Subway franchise on the entire east coast.

It was to the latter of the two subway stations Robert was headed, his stomach telling him to hurry as it had not been fed since somewhere between Norfolk and

Richmond, Virginia. He had been anxious to return to Baltimore, not because he was in a rush to leave Hatteras Island, nor was he all that anxious to return to work. A part of him did miss the excitement of the ER; other parts reminded him what he was leaving behind. His feelings for Samantha today were stronger than they had ever been. He was sure of that. He was also convinced Samantha felt the same, or at least close to it. They said goodbye at their favorite spot on the beach, the shipwreck of *The Lady Hatteras* watching over them. Their kiss goodbye had been long, their bodies held tightly together. She added that he had better not do to her what he did before. He promised to be in touch soon. She threatened the aluminum bat if he did not keep his word. He reached back and felt the sore spot on his spine and smiled. He whispered softly in her ear, "A second bruise I will never seek."

They kissed again. She stood beside her Jeep and watched as Robert made his way down the soft sand. Both Hatteras ladies grew smaller in his rearview mirror. It was hard to keep his foot on the gas pedal. It was hard not to jam the SUV in reverse and speed back over the treads he had just made. He knew, however, that if he had any hope of recapturing the past, he had to first solve the dilemma of the present. He had to find the *why* of Billy. Samantha placed the blame on him in spite of the doubts he raised this past week. That hovering cloud would continue until he could remove it. There were many questions to answer. There was a mystery begging to be solved. He believed the bowels of Hopkins was the best place to start.

He continued his journey toward the cafeteria.

17

Dr. Dennis Tucker was sitting in the far corner of the area roped off for Subway customers only. He was sucking on a straw jammed into a cup of Mountain Dew. It was the only soda Robert ever saw him drink, claiming it wasn't the taste so much as the need for caffeine. Coffee, Dennis said, was too hard on his stomach. Robert never argued the point, always making sure he had an ample supply in his apartment if his friend stopped by.

Dr. Tucker was medium height, stocky, with a receding hairline that would make most men cringe. A pair of wire rimmed glasses teetered on the tip of his nose. His arms were short and pudgy. His fingers matched. He wore a clean yet wrinkled lab coat, opened except for a button near the middle. Around his neck was a yellow tie, loose with the top button of his shirt wide open. He was studying a pile of papers spread across the table, oblivious to the activity going on around him. He initially failed to notice that someone had entered his space, defined as two arm lengths or closer. He was a friendly sort of chap once you got to know him, but he was a hard nut to crack. He had long ago built a wall around himself, he claimed out of deference to his profession. He loved what he did and defended his specialty of pathology to anyone who would listen, or to anyone who dared mock his chosen field. The study of pathology was not high on the esteem pole of medicine, and because he was often put on the defense, his friendship was hard to win. It was said that Dennis Tucker could piss off a new acquaintance faster than anyone. It was a skill he practiced frequently. It was also a skill Robert recommended he modify if he had any hopes of getting into the FBI, his ultimate career goal.

For whatever reason, Robert didn't piss Dr. Tucker off the first time they met. Matter of fact, they hit it off rather quickly. Robert found the man not only unique in his personality, but unique in his love for what he did. Robert wouldn't go so far as saying Dennis Tucker was obsessed with his chosen field, but the description was close. Robert learned the way to deal with his new friend was to shut up and listen; the same technique he used in the emergency room when dealing with an agitated patient.

Dennis looked up from his papers, a scowl on his face secondary to having been disturbed. Seeing Robert, however, his expression quickly changed. "Robert! Welcome back to the God-awful, putrid, smog- ridden air of the city. How the hell are you? How was your trip? Did you see her? How was she? Did she even talk to you? How was the ole' Beemer on the beach? You didn't get stuck, did you? Did you get laid?"

Another thing that turned people off from Dennis Tucker was that he spoke in loud, fast spurts, and had a habit of asking a series of questions, all in one breath, all without giving anyone a chance to respond. Robert, on the other hand, listened and waited for the tirade of questions to finish. "Thanks. I'm fine. The trip was great. Yes, several times actually. She's fine. Yes. The car did great on the beach, and no asshole, I didn't get stuck!"

And..."

"And what?"

The pathologist grinned. "You missed one."

The ER doctor frowned. "No, I did not get laid."

"Too bad." Dr. Tucker turned his head to the side and stared at his friend. Then he broke into a hearty laugh. "She talked to you, huh?"

"Yeah." Robert sat down across from Dennis.

"You'll have to give me the details sometime."

"Yeah, we'll have a beer later."

"That'd be great. Have a seat."

Even though Robert was already sitting, he followed with a "Thanks." He motioned to the papers spread out across the table and said, "What are you working on?"

"Income taxes."

"For this year?"

"No, I always give the bastards in Washington my money a couple years in advance." He took a sip of his Mountain Dew. "Yes, this year."

"You're a little late, aren't you?"

"I took an extension."

"You took an extension, or you filed for one?"

"Same thing, isn't it?"

"Dennis!"

"Don't sweat it. We don't make enough as residents for Uncle Sam to worry about anyway."

"You're right there." Robert had calculated the salary he earned divided by the hours he worked and discovered he was making less than minimum wages for saving people's lives. "Anyway, what do you want to eat?"

"You buyin'?"

Robert laughed. "I'll put it on your account…with an extension."

Dr. Tucker smiled. "I'll have the usual."

Robert returned a few minutes later with a pair of Italian cold cuts, another Mountain Dew for Dennis and a bottle of water for himself. As he set the two trays down, he noticed there was a new set of papers spread across the table. Contrary to the previous display, these were neat and orderly. There were a couple pages containing nothing but columns of numbers. There was a page of graphs. Another page had the words "Connect the Dots" across the top in bold letters.

Dennis unwrapped his sandwich and took a couple bites. Unlike in the ER where food was devoured like tree branches through one of those high-powered, noisy wood shredders, pathology people ate in a more civilized manner. To those working in the emergency room waiting for lab tests, a civilized manner was often mocked as how slow can you go? Robert knew that trying to rush his friend here would be wasted energy, the same as pushing the lab. Dennis once told him that lab techs were like turtles. They were steady and very methodical, which in reality is what you wanted from such a profession, especially since major decisions concerning a patient's care were often made on *the numbers from the lab*. So instead of saying anything, Robert turned his attention to his own barking stomach.

With half his sandwich gone, the other half wrapped for a later snack, Dr. Tucker pushed the tray aside. "You know Robert, one of the smallest particles of matter known to man is a very small dot known as the electron. Now, the number of electrons in the universe is unimaginable. However, they all have one thing in common. They are all connected in one way or the other. Even in space where there is supposedly a vacuum, there are still particles floating around connected to one another by an electromagnetic field, otherwise known as gravity. The whole universe is held together in a similar fashion. Everything is a dot. Everything is connected."

He pushed the paper titled *Connect the Dots* towards Robert. "The problem I have with the material you sent me is that there are both dots and connections missing." He picked up a pencil, pointing to the numbers on the paper. "I know you emergency room types want to keep everything simple and frown upon the esoteric, so let me go over what I got. I'll keep it simple. First, the liquor bottle had no material I could analyze for DNA. There were a couple of fingerprints, but these were smudged too much to be of any value. The material labeled aft head looked like vomit. It contained food particles and digestive juices. There were also traces of alcohol. We were able to DNA test this. I'll get back to these results in a moment." He paused for a sip of Mountain Dew. "There were several items in one plastic bag labeled bridge. For the most part, that was all junk, i.e., non-human material. However, there were a few strands of hair mixed in with the stuff. I tested this and came up with two different sets of DNA. One set I guess to be from an older person as there were signs of graying and did not match anything else you sent me. There were a couple other strands of blonder hair that matched with the material labeled truck."

"That would be Billy," Robert said. "The gray hair is probably from Captain Willey, the owner of the boat and the one who disappeared overboard." Robert had briefed Dennis on what he had learned upon his return to Hatteras Island.

"Well, I didn't find anything else on Captain Willey from what you gave me," Dennis said. "As for the material labeled forward head floor, that was blood like you suspected. That also matched the DNA from the shorts in the forward head, which also by the way matched some hair and blood that was stuck in the piece of wood you gave me."

"So, nothing from the bridge or truck matched anything inside the boat itself," Robert interrupted.

"That's correct," Dennis said. "But this is where the plot thickens. The underwear was indeed a boy's small. I assume that would not fit anyone you know about being on the boat that day?"

Robert nodded in agreement and said, "I wasn't there that day, but Captain Willey didn't take small children out with him."

Dennis continued after a moment's pause. "Then secondly, a very curious thing that I almost missed, the tag on the underwear was in Spanish. Now, I called a friend in the FBI who did a little research. Turns out, this brand of underclothing is not available in the United States. It's made in Mexico and can only be purchased there and in other South American countries."

Robert started to interrupt again, but Dennis raised his hand. "Let me finish." Robert paused. The pathology resident continued. "Like I said, DNA material in the underwear matched the blood on the floor, and blood and hair on the wood, which you said was from the door frame. Correct?"

Robert again nodded in agreement.

"However!" Dennis paused for effect. "There was additional DNA material in the shorts that did not match this."

"From whom?" Robert asked.

"That's one of the dots that's missing," Dennis said.

"What kind of material?" Robert asked.

Dennis hesitated. "DNA testing is still reliable after all this time. However, specific material identification can be tough. But I think it's semen."

Robert sat back in his chair and tried to digest what Dennis had just told him. "Let me make sure I have it straight," he said after a full minute of silence. "The dots are the liquor bottle, the vomit in the aft head, the two sets of hair samples on the bridge, the stuff from Billy's truck, the blood on the floor of the forward head, blood and hair on the piece of broken wood, and the boy's underwear."

"Which actually contain two different DNA materials, or two dots," Dennis clarified.

"Right," Robert acknowledged. He took a sip of his water. "The connection between the dots is the blonde hair on the bridge and stuff in Billy's truck. We can assume that's Billy. And the vomit in the aft bathroom and DNA matched is the forward head, including the boy's underwear."

"So far so good," Dennis encouraged.

Robert paused. "But the semen doesn't match anything we found so far and…" He paused again.

Dennis completed the difficult thought for them both. "What was semen of a different DNA doing in a young boy's underwear?" He took a drink of his soda. "Two dots, one missing, with an unknown connection," he added.

"I think we both know the connection," Dennis suggested. "What we don't know is the *who*."

Dorsey Butterbaugh

Robert had been hungry when he first sat down. His appetite, however, disappeared as potential answers emerged.

18

Samantha lay in bed gazing upward. There wasn't any breeze. The curtains were still. There were no shadows dancing across the ceiling. The house was quiet. Her parents and Billy went to bed early. She was the most tired of the bunch, at least it seemed that way at dinner. Yet, she was unable to fall asleep. Her mind refused to cooperate and listen to her body, which by now was starting to ache. Closing her eyes, she turned her head to the side. She had a big day ahead of her. Besides opening the store, she had several appointments in the afternoon of which one looked promising. She knew she'd need to be at her best for that one. A well-rested body and a well-rested mind would be the requisite of the day. She took a couple deep breaths and tried to settle down.

She was about to doze off when she heard a sharp sound followed by music. She rolled over, sat up, and reached for her cell phone sitting on the bedside table. She was too sleepy to wonder who might be calling her this time of night. She was too sleepy to curse the caller, but made a mental note to do that in the morning. "Hello," she said without a lot of conviction.

"Sam?"

She thought she recognized the voice. "Robert?"

"Yes, it's me."

"What time is it?"

There was a pause. "Twelve-thirty. Did I wake you?"

"This is Hatteras, sweetheart. We go to bed with the sun."

"Sorry."

Samantha sat up on the side of the bed. "What's up?"

"You told me to call you when I knew anything," Robert said.

Samantha stood up and shook the circulation back into her legs. She told herself to be nice. After all, he was calling, something he hadn't done in five years. "Okay."

"Are you where we can talk?"

"I was in bed." There was a pause on the other end. Samantha had no doubt where Robert's mind went. A smile crossed her face as she forced her mind to stay focused. "Give me a minute. I'll walk outside."

As she walked across the parking lot she looked towards the campground. Things were quiet. There were a few lights on inside the various trailers and tents, otherwise the place had settled down nicely for the night. As she approached the store she contemplated going in and saying hey to the cousins. She decided, however, she didn't want anyone to know she was up and about. She turned ninety degrees and headed toward the ocean. She walked up to the top of the sand dunes, using the beach passageway behind their home. She faced east toward the water. She could hear it more than she could see it. She pulled in a deep breath. There was something about the smell of the ocean at night. She closed her eyes before looking upward. It was a beautiful night. The sky was perfectly clear. Stars she had not seen in ages were shining through the darkness. Here there was a gentle yet cool breeze. She pulled her bathrobe tighter around her waist. She did a quick scan of the area.

Except for a vehicle parked a mile or so to the south, the beach was empty. "You still there?" she said.

"Yeah. Where are you now?"

"On the beach."

"That was fast."

"It's right behind our house. Remember?"

"Oh yeah."

There was a pause. She heard what sounded like papers rustling. "Where are you?" she asked.

"In my office."

"You have an office?"

"Well, it's not officially mine yet. It will be in a few weeks."

"Impressive."

"Don't be. It's not much more than a closet."

"Whatever," Samantha said. "So talk." She contemplated sitting down, but decided against getting sandy. She loved the ocean. She loved living and working on the island. And she loved the beach. She hated the sand, however, when it got into her clothes or in her bed.

A thin smile crossed her face as she remembered that Robert didn't even like the feel of sand between his toes.

"I can give you more details later if you want," Robert was saying. "For now, I'll be as brief as possible in case we get cut off or something." He paused briefly. "I met this evening with the pathology resident I told you about, Dennis Tucker. As I imagined, he was very enthusiastic and very helpful. He was able to do testing on almost everything I sent him. To begin with, I'm convinced something bad happened on the boat that day. However, the DNA testing shows that neither Billy nor Captain Willey were involved. Yet, based on Billy's reaction, I'm willing to bet he knows what happened, but is afraid to talk. Now, is Willey's death two days later a coincidence? No one knows, but according to Dennis, probability theory says there is a connection. He likes to say that everything that happens in the universe is represented by a dot, and all dots are connected one way or the other."

"What about the death of Mrs. Willey the other day?" Samantha questioned.

Robert paused. "You know, I never thought about that, nor did I say anything to Dennis about that, although I know what he'd say."

Samantha finished the thought. "That her death wasn't a coincidence."

"There's a connection somehow," Robert said.

There was a long pause. Samantha spoke next. "Does this friend of yours have any idea of what actually happened on the boat that day?" There was a sense of mocking in her voice.

As he had been doing since returning to the island the week before, Robert let the tone of her voice roll off his back. He made sure his own tone remained non-condescending. "He has a theory, yes."

"Then what are you waiting for?"

Robert's discipline eroded somewhat as he was unable to avoid going for the shock value. "Someone sexually assaulted a young boy, a Mexican or Hispanic boy to be more precise."

"What?" Samantha was unable to respond further.

"It's just a theory," Robert said.

Samantha forced herself to recover quickly. "What do you think?" Her tone had lost its bite.

"If you buy into the connect-the-dot theory, it makes sense."

"If you don't buy into the theory?" Samantha challenged.

"I wouldn't know," Robert admitted.

"You think the theory has merit?"

"There are too many dots with strong connections."

"Connections being the DNA testing?"

"The DNA testing shows there is a connection. It doesn't define the connection."

"Sounds like splitting hairs to me," Samantha said. "But regardless, if the theory is correct, then…" She hesitated.

"There are still both dots and connections missing," Robert interjected.

Samantha continued "Specifically, who was the boy, and who…?" She didn't know how to finish the query.

"Exactly," Robert said.

Suddenly, the air felt chillier. Samantha pulled the collar up on her robe. "What do we do now?" She asked.

"Try and find the dots, and then hopefully the connections will become evident."

"How do we do that?"

"I think it's time to talk to Billy."

19

In most professions, returning from vacation was at least a semi-event for the person involved. Questions flowed freely. Statements of jealously were bestowed. Photos were sought. In emergency medicine, especially in an environment as busy as Hopkins, the opposite tended to occur. Few staff members even knew Robert had been gone for the week. Those that did had little time to dwell on the fact. The Monday morning of his return was typical for the day of the week and time of year. To be polite, it was a zoo. When he walked in to begin his seven am shift, there were already twenty patients in the waiting room with the wait over four hours. It always amazed Robert that people would wait so long for stupid stuff, or more professionally defined as non-emergent complaints. But wait they did. Little did they know that ninety percent of the time they were being cared for by a medical student, an intern, or a resident in training. It was the upper residents' job to ensure that these medical students and green doctors received the appropriate training, and at the same time didn't harm anyone in the process. To Robert, echoed by most of the other senior residents and attending physicians, taking care of the patients was the easy part. Supervising the *greens*, as they were called, was where the stress developed.

It was all taken in stride, however. Teaching others was payback for those that did the same for you. Robert always considered himself fortunate in that, except for a few isolated instances, those that taught him went out of their way to ensure he not only learned the science of medicine, but how to act as well. Even in the bowels of the emergency room, patients were cared for with respect and dignity. During the learning process, mistakes were made. It was an expected occurrence. Mistakes, however, had better be limited to clinical aspects of patient care. Mistakes were not tolerated regarding other aspects of treating patients, i.e., respect and dignity. This held true for other staff members as well. The old days of doctors yelling at nurses and acting like fools was a thing of the past.

This is what Robert faced his first day back from vacation. No questions were asked about his trip. Statements of jealousy were non-existent. There was no time for questions about where you went or what you did. There was no time for pictures. Robert just said hello and took report. The first order of business was to deal with a first-year resident who had reamed out a nurse for taking too long to collect a urine sample from a patient awaiting an emergency appendectomy. Counseling was provided in the chief resident's office which consisted of a senior resident to junior resident reaming, the threat of yanking out the junior resident's own appendix without anesthesia and the demand of an apology to the nurse involved. Out of the office and pleased with how he handled the situation, Robert dug right in and started seeing patients. He had to get the numbers in the waiting room down before he could focus on the other areas of his responsibility, mainly teaching.

The one advantage of all this, and one of the draws to emergency medicine in general, was that time flew by. Before he realized it, it was time for noon conference and lunch. It was also the first time he had a chance to empty his bladder. Courtesy of a drug rep, he had just finished piling his plate with Caesar salad and lasagna when his cell phone started buzzing. He set his food down and pulled the device from his pocket. Because they were in a small conference room, and because the food on this particular day was good, the place was packed, and thus very noisy. He excused himself, threatened bodily harm to anyone who messed with either his food or seat and stepped into the hallway.

Away from the noise, he raised the phone to his ear. "Hello," he said.

"Robert?"

"Speaking."

"It's Sam... Samantha Mathews."

"Oh, hi."

There was a pause. "Can you talk a minute?"

Robert thought about the plate of food sitting on the chair in the conference room. His stomach told him the answer was no. Other parts of his body encouraged a different response. His stomach lost. "Sure. What's up?"

"It's Billy. I'm worried about him."

"You've *been* worried about him."

"Yeah, but I'm afraid he's getting worse."

Robert loved it when patients described their problems in such vague terms, such as *I feel bad all over*, or *I have this pain I can't describe*. *Worse* was one of those terms. His responsibility was to ratchet down the description into a cleared response. "Tell me exactly what's going on."

"Like I told you, and I guess you saw for yourself, he has been very withdrawn and depressed. He has his good days and bad days, but lately he seems to have regressed even more. He's quieter. He's around the house less. He seems to be sleeping a lot more, too. I felt he might be doing better, and then..."

"And then what, Samantha?" Robert encouraged.

"You showed up."

Robert leaned against the wall. He pushed the phone tighter to his ear. "You mean to say I'm the blame again?"

"I'm not blaming anyone," Samantha barked. "I'm just telling you." Her voice softened. "You did tell me to call, didn't you, if anything changed?"

"Yes, I did," Robert acknowledged. He paused as a thought crossed his mind. "Connect the dots," he told himself. Aloud, "Maybe I am the cause. The question is why?" He continued to work the idea. "Maybe it isn't me as much as it's me being down there...showing up, like you said. My presence stimulated something, most probably whatever set him off the first time."

"Well, Captain Willey died two days after you left five years ago," Samantha said.

Robert felt his face pale. "Samantha..." He heard her suck in a deep breath as both verbalized what both were thinking at this very moment. "Willey's widow died while I was there last week."

There was a period of silence during which time Robert cursed himself for letting Samantha talk him into waiting awhile before talking to Billy. Robert thought it a good idea; that it was time. Samantha vetoed the idea, arguing that opening up such a line of discussion might only make her brother worse.

He cursed again. "Listen Sam, I just got back from vacation so I can't get any time off right now. I have to work all this week, including the weekend, but I'm off next Monday and Tuesday. I don't have to be back till Wednesday night. I can leave here Sunday when I get off and be there by Monday morning."

There was another pause. "What do I do in the meantime?" Samantha said.

"Do you think he's a danger to himself?"

"What do you mean?"

"Is he a suicide risk?"

Samantha hesitated. "I don't think so. He's never said anything like that before."

"How about a danger to other people?"

"I don't think so." She quickly added, "What did you think when you saw him?"

"I only spent a little time with him, but I didn't see anything to indicate either harming himself or someone else. Besides, this has been going on for a long time. I would think..." Robert cut the thought off when he realized what he was about to say would have been incorrect. Suicidal behavior can crop up in someone anytime during a depressive episode. "You just have to watch him, that's all."

"And do what?"

"If there's a concern, take him to get him evaluated."

"Take him where?"

"The emergency room."

"We don't have an emergency room here," Samantha pointed out. "The closest hospital is in Nags Head. This is Hatteras, Robert. We're lucky we have a doctor who comes down here once a month."

"All I can suggest is to keep a close eye on him and if you're concerned, then take him to Nags Head," Robert said.

"Okay. You'll be here when?"

"Early Monday morning, Monday noon the latest."

"I'll see you then."

"Sam."

"Yes."

"Call me if you need to...or if you want to."

There was a moment's hesitation. "I will."

The line disconnected. Robert knew that no matter what happened next in the emergency room, time would no longer pass quickly.

20

Monday morning quarterbacking was easy. This was true whether pertaining to sports, taking a test, caring for a patient or making some other unrelated decision. Robert began to wonder whether he should have gone to Hatteras on his vacation. And if he did, should he have made contact with Samantha. For the most part, he felt good about his decision, in spite of the problems discovered with Billy and Captain Willey, and in spite of the missing dots and connections now confronting him. It was also good to see Samantha. Once she got over her anger and all the negative stuff about blaming him for her brother's condition, she seemed genuinely pleased to see him. He and Samantha were certainly two dots still connected. The bond may not be as strong as in the past, but there was hope.

An old caution flag appeared, warning of the threat to his education. He only had a year to go and then he could let some of those defense barriers down. For now, he had to stay focused. Maybe he should have waited before going back to Hatteras Island.

Robert let out an audible laugh. "Bullshit," he mouthed. There was already something interfering. That's why he was headed back to Hatteras now. Five hours under his belt with two or so remaining. If traffic remained light, he figured he'd be on the island by sunrise, just like the trip a couple weeks before. Whether he wanted it or not, whether the caution flags were flying or lay limp, he had something else going on in his life other than his education. It was an annoying feeling. It was a scary feeling.

He let the thought linger. How did he really feel? What were his true emotions? Was he doing the right thing? Was this really going to interfere with his training? He suddenly felt like Dennis Tucker with all the questions spurting forth without a break for an answer. He cleared his mind. A smile crossed his face. "Horny, in love, yes, probably," he said aloud.

There was also another force hidden among all these thoughts. That was Billy. It didn't really bother him that he was being blamed for Billy's condition. He knew that wasn't true so there were no guilty feelings. He was bothered by the fact that Billy was in such a condition, regardless of who or what was to blame. They were friends. While they had only known each other for a short period of time, they had become close. For Robert, Billy was a breath of fresh air, a bright young man who was way underutilizing his abilities. He had been one of the happiest people Robert had ever met. It was this sense of satisfaction with life that drew Robert to the boy that first

Sunday at dinner. It was this continued sense that kept Robert coming back for more. Billy taught him how to relax and how to have fun. He said that's what made surf fishing so special. The fishing itself wasn't all that big of a deal because hours went by with nothing happening. It wasn't the anticipation of catching the big one. It was just the fact that they were there, on the beach, feet buried in the sand, a beer or a Dew in hand, and most importantly, no worries in the world. Billy said more than once that you couldn't be happy in life if you were carrying barrels full of shit on your shoulders.

Robert's thoughts stopped. "Barrels full of shit," he said aloud. That's exactly what Billy was doing, carrying a lot of barrels. That's why he was depressed. That's why he was no longer happy. It reinforced Robert's theory that something happened that Friday before Labor Day. Now, more than ever, Robert was convinced he was on the right track. The question: where was that track going to lead? He thought back over his series of questions from a moment ago. None of the answers mattered except that he was doing the right thing. He needed to help Billy empty those barrels. No need to Monday morning quarterback any longer. Coming to Hatteras on vacation had been the right decision.

Another flag fluttered its warning. It took him a moment to realize this one wasn't urging caution. This one was promoting the opposite. An inner voice was telling him to hurry.

Then his cell phone rang. He reached over where he had tossed it on the passenger seat. He looked at the caller ID. "Well, hello, sweet thing. What are you doing up so early?" he said.

"Robert?"

"It's me."

"Robert, Billy's missing."

The flag from a moment ago started fluttering faster.

21

Samantha was a person who feared little. She took things in life as they came, analyzed them, did what she could for the better and moved on. Sure, she was sad at times. She felt pain, and she worried. Yet fear itself was not one of the major factors that made up her psyche.

That was until tonight when Billy didn't show up for dinner. Her parents initially showed concern. However, Samantha blew it off as Billy simply staying on the beach to fish. They had heard the blues were running good with the evening tide. After dinner and making sure things were okay in the office and store, Samantha went to check out her theory. Billy was nowhere on the beach. Samantha asked a couple people she knew. No one had seen him all day. His truck was not easily missed. She went back to the campground, saw that the lights were out in the house indicating her parents had gone to bed. She thought about going in to see if they heard anything. She decided not to disturb them. If he was home, his truck would be, too. Like many of the locals, even if he could walk, Billy drove his truck—the argument being you never knew when there was going to be an emergency on the beach—an emergency defined by a sudden improvement in the surfing conditions or fish swarming in the breakwaters. Fishing gear and surf boards were nearby at all times. At least that's the way it used to be. Lately however...

Samantha gathered her thoughts. She made a couple calls to see if he was with anyone they knew. She even drove to a few of the restaurants where her family dined on occasion. No one had seen him. No one had seen his truck. She contemplated contacting the sheriff but decided against that. She didn't want to overreact, causing her brother any embarrassment or bring any undue attention to him. His psyche was fragile enough. She drove up and down the middle portion of the island trying to figure out what might have happened. She ruled out the truck breaking down. He would have called. Same thing if he had been in an accident, except if...

She refused to let her mind go there. Besides, the sheriff would have already been in contact.

Her level of concern rose with each passing hour. When the clock in her Jeep passed midnight, concern turned to a high state of anxiety. At three am fear took over. This was unfamiliar territory for her. Her fear rose quickly. She lost her ability to maintain control of her emotions. That's when she called Robert.

He started off real bubbly and cheerful, just like he usually did. When she told him the reason for her call, his demeanor changed. His concern only added fuel to her concern. He asked her a couple questions about his most recent behavior. When she assured him she had noticed no significant change, he reassured her Billy would be okay, concluding that the truck was probably the issue. After all, it was old with high mileage.

She tried telling herself this was probably true. However, once fear grabbed hold of you, it was hard to get the teeth to release. All she could do was wait for Robert. Per his suggestion, they met at the Rodanthe fishing pier. Samantha left her Jeep there and the two headed south. On the way she told Robert all the places she had checked. While Robert seemed interested, he also seemed more relaxed than she would have thought. As they passed the campground, she said, "You don't seem too worried."

"I am," he said defensively.

"You sounded a lot more concerned on the phone."

"That was before I had time to think."

"Think about what?"

Robert ignored the question. Instead, he asked, "Did Billy know I was coming down here today?"

"I don't believe so."

"You didn't talk about it with anyone where he could have overheard you?"

"The only person I talked to was you."

"Where were you when we talked?"

Samantha pondered the question. "We've talked three times since you left. The first was when you called to tell me about the DNA stuff. I went out to the beach, remember? Then you called the other night to verify you were coming. And I called you a few hours ago."

"Where were you when I called the other night?"

"In bed."

"Oh, yeah." Robert remembered well because he had trouble keeping his mind focused on the conversation. "Was Billy home then?"

"He was in bed, too."

"His bedroom's next to yours?"

"Yes."

"He must have heard us talking."

"Okay," Samantha acknowledged. "What's that have to do with him being missing now?"

Robert ignored the question, instead asking, "When was the last time you saw him?"

Samantha thought a moment. "Sometime yesterday afternoon. He stopped in the store to get a Mountain Dew and a sandwich."

"How has he been acting?"

"His normal withdrawn self."

"Did he say anything unusual?"

"Not that I recall." A few seconds passed. "He did say he wanted to get a haircut. That was strange, something he hadn't said or done in a long time. His hair is pretty long."

"I noticed that," Robert said. It was his turn to pause. Then a smile crossed his face.

"Robert!"

"I don't think he's actually missing," Robert said.

Dorsey Butterbaugh

"Then where is he?"
"He's waiting for me."

22

Robert had noticed the fog building as he was coming through Nags Head. It thickened as he crossed the Oregon Inlet Bridge onto Hatteras Island. Conditions were no better the further south he went. He could barely see the sign for the entrance to the campground as they passed by. He slowed down. Thank goodness traffic was almost non-existent. The trip though seemed to take forever, especially with Samantha sitting beside him in a withdrawn, quiet mood. It was obvious she was worried more than usual about her brother. Robert's reassurance didn't seem to help. The fog only made her emotional state worse.

Finally, after about thirty minutes, she spoke. "Are you going to tell me where we're going?"

"Down the road a bit."

"Well, the road ends in a bit, so how 'bout being more specific."

Robert hesitated. He didn't want to say too much in case his intuition was wrong. At the same time, he decided to share his thoughts. There had to be a sense of trust. There had to be a willingness to be open. "He's at the lighthouse. More specifically, he's up at the top."

"Hatteras Light?"

"Yes."

"Why there?"

Robert explained. "We used to sneak into the lighthouse after hours. We called it our tree fort. As you know, the view is fantastic." He paused. "Billy was always more willing to talk up there, to open up so to speak. He said it was like being in heaven. He said it was the only place on the island where he really felt safe. I kidded him about that once when he promptly pointed out that the lighthouse has withstood more hurricanes than any other structure on the island."

"How did you get in?" Samantha asked. "Don't they lock the place up at night?"

"The main entrance, yes. But there's a small door around the backside that most people don't know is there. It looks more like a covering over a window. We used to squeeze in through that." A smile crossed Robert's face. "He told you he needed to get a haircut. That message was meant for me."

"Huh?"

"You see," Robert explained, "when it was originally built, the lighthouse was never supposed to be a black and white spiral. It was supposed to be diagonals like a barber's pole. Anyway, it got painted by mistake the way it is today so they just kept it that way. Besides being one of the tallest lighthouses in the world, it's also dubbed the tallest barber's pole. It was an inside joke between your brother and me. If one of us said that we were going to get a haircut after work, it meant we were going to meet there later that night. Sometimes we were only there for a short period of time. Sometimes we'd stay for hours."

"You think he's there now?" Samantha said with new hope in her voice.

"If I was a betting man." Robert looked at her, smiled and winked.

"You better bet on keeping your eyes on the road," Samantha said, pointing forward, "otherwise we won't even make it there."

Robert slowed down in deference to his passenger. He was glad Samantha seemed to be perking up. A car passed them going way too fast for the conditions. Robert checked to make sure he had his fog lights on. They were, only they didn't seem to be doing much good. "It's getting thicker," he commented.

"Symbolic," Samantha replied.

Robert again glanced at her. Like in the past, she occasionally came out with something that totally amazed him. She was a transplanted island girl, but very smart and very insightful. He refocused on the road. He contemplated what he would or should do if Billy wasn't at the lighthouse. He tried making a list of options. Billy never wandered very far from home. He claimed to have only been off the island a few times since his family moved here. He went to Ocracoke occasionally to fish and surf, but that was a ferry ride to another island. When

Robert was here for the summer, Billy said he hadn't been to the mainland in years. Robert doubted that had changed in the five years since. Billy touted there was no need to leave Hatteras. The island had everything he needed. At the time, Robert was in no position to argue, in many ways having to agree. *"What more could you want?"* was a frequently heard comment. Robert had even considered throwing in the education towel at the end of that summer and staying on the island. He was offered a full-time job with the same construction gang. The foreman said he was good and showed a lot of potential. However, his ego won out. He returned to Hopkins to finish his education. While he knew that was the right decision, there were some trying days in the ER that caused him to second guess his decision.

Yes, Robert doubted if Billy had left the island. The closer they got to Buxton and the lighthouse, the more confident he was in his theory.

If only there wasn't so much fog!

23

Robert turned into the road leading to the lighthouse some thirty minutes later. Traffic remained light. The fog remained heavy. Otherwise, they reached their destination without incident. Robert could barely see the base of the brick structure. He looked up and watched as the light flashed toward the east, the rays of light reflecting off the droplets of water. He wondered just how effective the old lighthouse was today. His guess was that if you were out on the water and could see the light, you were already in trouble. He figured the boats that were in port stayed there and those that were out at sea stayed there. There would be little inlet traffic this day. Hardcore seamen tolerated a lot regarding the weather. The fog, however, tended to bring everything to a halt.

Hearing the gravel from the change in road surface beneath the tires, Robert steered to the far end of the parking lot. Visibility was worse the closer to the water. He put the windows down and inched the vehicle forward. It was as if they were in total darkness, except the darkness was gray. Robert could not remember the last time he had been in fog so thick. He said as much aloud.

"I've never seen it this bad either," Samantha agreed. She was staring hard ahead.

Both saw Billy's truck at the same time. Samantha had her door open and one foot on the ground before the BMW came to a complete stop. Running to the truck, she ignored Robert when he said, "He's not in there."

She had to verify this for herself. Looking at the lighthouse, she said, "You say there's a door on the other side?"

"Yes," Robert answered. There was obvious hesitation in his voice.

"Come on, let's go," Samantha directed. It was obvious she was anxious to get in.

Robert hesitated.

"What's the matter?" Samantha said, stopping a few feet away. Robert didn't say anything. She continued. "You don't want me to go with you, do you?"

Robert's mind spun rapidly looking for a solution to the dilemma. His training taught him to make important decisions quickly. Sometimes they were directly from a textbook. Other times improvisation was necessary. "Tell you what," he said. "Let me go up first and talk to him. I'll ask him if it's okay if you join us. Either way, I'll call you as soon as I get up there. Okay?"

Disappointment flashed across Samantha's face. It disappeared quickly, however, as she realized Robert was right. It was their tree house, not hers. She nodded her approval. "Call me right away."

"I will, I promise."

Samantha went back and waited in the SUV, her cell phone in hand. Robert headed across the parking lot toward the lighthouse. The minutes ticked by. The cell phone remained silent. How long did it take to climb the steps? Thinking about that, she realized she had never been to the top. Again, how long did it take? Just like the trip through the fog, time seemed to crawl along. She was still worried about her brother, although her anxiety was lessened somewhat by finding his truck. A phone call from Robert would help.

She stared at her phone. She was about to call Robert when she sensed someone was nearby. She looked up and saw Robert and Billy coming out of the fog. She leaped out of the car and ran toward her brother. She gave him a hug which he returned in kind. She started to speak but stopped when she realized her oration was going to be a tongue lashing, something he didn't need at the moment. She stepped back, forced a smile and said, "You okay?"

Billy nodded.

"Good." Samantha looked at Robert who motioned that she should back get into the SUV. She did, but only after a long hesitation.

Robert turned his attention to Billy. He spoke gently, yet loud enough for Samantha to hear. "We'll see you later, Billy. You be careful driving home, okay?"

Billy shrugged. Eye contact was made, but his expression remained flat. He turned his attention to his sister. A worried look crossed his face. "You be careful, too," he said.

Samantha's mouth dropped open. A chill ran through her spine. It was the first such thing he said to her in many months. He used to be a very caring, almost overprotective, brother. Since that Labor Day weekend, however, all his focus seemed inward. He wasn't mean. He wasn't nasty. There were no verbal assaults. There definitely was no physical threat. He had simply lost his sense of compassion. His comment, while subtle in nature, was a massive turnabout. She was ecstatic. However, a cautionary glance from Robert warned her not to show too much emotion. Billy was obviously still in a very fragile state. Along with that, Samantha's enthusiasm was quickly drained when she realized she and Robert were going to leave Billy there. She wasn't too keen on that. After all, they just found him after he had been missing all night. Robert's actions prevented any further response. He was already in the SUV. She climbed in the passenger's side, the engine was started and they pulled away, leaving Billy standing beside his truck. Samantha looked in the side view mirror and saw her brother pull out a cigarette. The flash of a lighter followed. The rest was lost in the fog.

Robert inched across the parking lot and found the entrance to the beach without much trouble. He rode over the dunes with caution and headed south. While he could hear the ocean, he could barely see it. Luckily the tide was out so there was plenty of room between them and the water. He drove about a half a mile and stopped. He shut off the engine. Turning toward Samantha, he said, "First off, if you're wondering why I didn't call you when I got to the top of the lighthouse, I didn't have cell phone service. The only thing I can figure, it had something to do with the heavy electric motors that run the light. They probably put off an electromagnetic field that blocks the signal or something like that. I didn't get service back until we were halfway down. By then I figured we'd be out in a minute or two."

A concerned expression crossed his face. "Fortunately or unfortunately, I was right about your brother. Something did happen that Friday while they were out fishing. He acknowledged that his being up in the lighthouse was his way of letting me know he was ready to talk. He did overhear our conversation the other night, so he knew I was coming down today. He knew I'd look for him there. Like I told you, we used to hang out there a lot."

"Why not just meet somewhere down on the ground and talk? And why did he have to run away?" Samantha said.

"He felt safe up there and he didn't run away. He was just there waiting for me."

"Why would he feel unsafe somewhere else?" Samantha asked.

"It's a little convoluted, but he's not worried about his own safety. He's worried about the safety of others." Robert paused. "Specifically, you."

"Me!"

"That's what he said."

Confusion crossed Samantha's face. "Why me?"

"He wouldn't say. He just said that what happened that day involves you. He's been afraid for you ever since. That's why he's been so depressed, so withdrawn. He's afraid, just like I said. Only I thought he was afraid of the water when in fact he fears something else."

"Afraid of what?" Samantha asked anxiously.

"He wouldn't say."

"Then what did he say? You two were up there long enough."

"He didn't say a whole lot at first except that he was okay and was glad that I came to see him. I asked him if he was ready to talk. He suggested I talk first. When I asked him what I should talk about, he said that something obviously brought me back so why didn't I tell him what that was all about."

Robert paused as he looked toward the ocean. The fog seemed to be lifting, but he could still barely make out the water line. As he was a give-me-the-facts kind of a guy, he didn't give a lot of credence to symbolisms. He did wonder if there was a message in the fog, symbolic of things going on around him.

He continued. "I debated what to tell him and at what level of detail. I wanted to be honest with the thought of building some trust. At the same time, I didn't want to make things worse for him, since he had come forward and said he wanted to talk. I decided to lay the cards out on the table, to give it to him straight. It's kind-a-like talking to a patient who has a bad diagnosis, there's no way to sugar coat the news."

"What did he say?" Samantha asked.

"That's the funny thing…or maybe it wasn't. He listened intently, seeming to focus on my every word. In the end, he didn't say anything for a long time. Then when he talked, he said he was afraid to say too much because of you. He must have referenced that at least a half-dozen times. I didn't press him because he was conversing. I think we opened the door a crack today. I didn't want him to clam back up. I did ask him to give me a hint. He told me to just look around. He said there were clues all over the island. I asked if he could be a little more specific. He did just the opposite. He said I should look on Ocracoke, too."

Samantha gave him a dumbfounded look.

"You obviously don't have any idea what he's talking about," Robert noted.

"Correct," she said. "Did he say anything else?"

"He just kept saying he was worried about you," Robert said.

"Anything else?"

"No…yes. Just as we left the lighthouse, he grabbed my arm and looked me straight in the eye with kind of a haunting look. Then he said very softly, 'The boy never left the boat.'"

"What does that mean?"

"I haven't a clue. I was hoping you might have an idea."

"You're the doctor. You should be able to figure it out."

Robert ignored her sarcasm. "I should be able to, but I can't. There are too many pieces of the puzzle missing."

"Where do we go from here?" Samantha asked.

"Not very far in the fog."

Samantha opened and closed her mouth. "I guess I deserved that."

"I was trying to help before. That's all I'm trying to do now," Robert reiterated.

"That's all you're trying to do?"

Their eyes locked together. "One step at a time," Robert said.

"Good answer." Eyes unlocked, both sets focused on the water. After a few moments, Samantha repeated. "Where *do* we go from here?"

Robert continued. "I want some time to digest what he said. And you're right, I should be able to figure it out."

"Maybe I can help," Samantha offered, her tone softer.

Robert looked at her. "That would be nice. First, however, I need to figure out what he was talking about regarding your safety." As an afterthought, he added,

"Have you noticed anything that would make you think you were in danger?"

"No," she said immediately.

"You sure?"

"Yes," she insisted.

They sat in silence; their gazes again toward the east. The fog slowly burned off as the sun rose off the horizon. Robert placed his hand on the middle armrest. With only a moment's hesitation, Samantha laid her hand atop his. Their fingers interlocked. She slid down in her seat and closed her eyes.

"He made me promise that I wouldn't let anything happen to you," Robert said.

"Thank you."

"You're welcome."

Minutes passed in silence. The edge of the water came into focus. Soon the sun itself could be seen poking through the mist. As the heat of the day intensified, the fog dissipated further. In less than thirty minutes, it was totally gone. The sky was clear. Visibility was all the way to the horizon. A light breeze kicked up across the sand. A school of porpoise could be seen a mile offshore heading north. Robert straightened up, rubbing his eyes with his free hand. While it started out crappy, it was going to be a glorious day.

Very symbolic, Robert hoped.

24

They pulled into the campground parking lot long enough to see Billy's truck parked up near the house. Making a sharp U-turn and heading back toward the main road, Robert asked Samantha if she wanted to stop to get a bite to eat. She declined, saying that she had to get back to the store. Besides, she wanted to make sure Billy was alright,

The ride to Rodanthe to retrieve Samantha's Jeep was mostly in silence. They held hands. Samantha stared out her window. Robert diverted his time between looking at the road and looking at his passenger. On the surface, he downplayed what Billy said about making sure Samantha was safe, but his stomach was in knots as his mind spun in overdrive trying to figure out what it all meant. Billy said there were clues all over the island. All Robert had to do was drive around to find them. There was the Ocracoke connection as well. And what about the comment about a boy never leaving the boat?

"What boy?" Robert wondered aloud.

He tried to map out a plan. The main problem was time. It was now eight-fifteen Monday morning. He had to be back in the ER Wednesday at seven pm. There was also this thing called sleep. So far, he was doing okay, even after driving all night. He knew, however, he could hit the wall at any moment. If he could at least get a short nap, that would take the edge off. The question was where to fit that into the day.

A plan formed. Maybe he should start on Ocracoke and work his way north. That way he could catch a nap on the ferry ride over to the island. After dropping Samantha off, he stopped for a donut, a bottle of water, and fuel. Then he headed south again. The fog remained in hibernation. As he drove along the main road, he kept an eye out for anything that might answer the question of what Billy was talking about, and why he didn't simply tell him. Robert was afraid to press the point on either issue. Billy said to look around. So far, Robert saw nothing that gave him a clue to the above.

The ferry was already boarding when he arrived, so he pulled onto the heavy steel deck almost immediately. He was asleep before the boat left the dock. Except for a couple bounces and rolls as they crossed Hatteras Inlet, he slept soundly. The next thing he remembered was the car behind him honking, encouraging him to wake up and move.

Misty rain had replaced the sunshine, bringing a dreariness back to the day. Robert turned into the visitor's center parking lot to stretch his legs. The coolness of the rain felt good as it helped bring life back to his body. He realized that except for the climb up the steps to the lighthouse, he had been sitting pretty steadily for the past twenty-four hours. He took a brisk walk around the parking lot, ignoring the rain that intensified. He went into the visitor's center building, accepted a cup of free coffee and a map of the island. By the time he got back on the road, the traffic from the ferry had dispersed. He noticed the wait for the return trip was light; a good sign, he thought. He remembered waiting with Samantha for over an hour to go back and forth. But the wait then was just additional time they got to spend together. Today, he was alone with a timetable to keep. On the main road heading south, he set the cruise control on fifty. He sat back to enjoy the ride, although that task was proving difficult as the rain intensity increased.

The majority of the island was under the control of the National Park Service; thus it was protected from development. Like Hatteras, Ocracoke's natural function was as a barrier island for the mainland of South and North Carolina. As such, the landscape looked similar. The only difference Robert ever noticed was that the dunes seemed a little shorter than on Hatteras, thus making Ocracoke even more susceptible to the ire of Mother Nature.

He passed a sign telling him twenty-two miles to Ocracoke City; the main population on the island was located at the southern tip. He let his seat back a notch, adjusted his backside and tried to find a more comfortable position. He knew he needed to get some exercise. One of the tricks to surviving the rigors of residency was to ensure plenty of exercise along with maintaining a healthy diet. Both were difficult tasks. He adjusted his position again and willed himself to relax. It was another difficult task as his mind continued to spin with answerless questions.

"Get control," he mouthed aloud. "Get control."

The town of Ocracoke was a small quaint town with heavy dependence on the fishing and tourist trades. The road into town was lined with numerous shops and eateries. The sidewalks were now basically empty but would soon be filled with tourists from all over searching for the best hat, tee shirt, or other souvenir, along with the best places to eat.

Robert drove slowly through town, looking side to side, trying to see if he could discern what Billy was talking about in the way of clues. Except for the inevitable turnover of store fronts, the place looked exactly as he remembered. He drove around the harbor circle, stopping for a couple pedestrians. He wondered about the nearest hospital in the event someone was struck, or if there was some other medical emergency. Was it still Nags Head? That was a long way off in an emergency. As an afterthought, he wondered where people in general got their health care. He saw no blue sign with a big white H in the middle. He saw no offices indicating the presence of doctors, or even dentists for that matter. Places to shop, places to eat, and a couple motels. That was about it. That was Ocracoke.

He pulled into an empty parking lot that overlooked the harbor. A couple sailboats were anchored out in the middle, otherwise the anchorage was empty. About half the slips at the city dock were full, some covered with plastic shrink wrap, the rest exposed to the elements. He saw no activity around these boats. That was no surprise considering the earliness of the season plus the rain.

He continued scanning the area looking for clues. Billy insisted they were there. He was about to back out of the parking space when something caught his attention. He leaned forward and turned the windshield wipers on full speed. Off to the left at the edge of the harbor was a tall structure. A closer look showed it to be a building under construction. While the idea of a building under construction was of no particular interest, the structure was several stories tall. Somewhere in the back of his mind, Robert remembered Samantha telling him about height restrictions on both islands. So, either he was looking at a mirage or the height restriction had been changed.

He backed out of the parking space and headed toward the project. The building was right on the edge of town and overlooked the harbor. As he drew closer, he saw there were several other buildings in various phases of construction. He noticed the beginning of a long pier partially completed along the waterfront.

He pulled up to the fence that surrounded the complex. There were various signs hanging on the fence indicating who was doing the electrical work, the mechanical work, etc. In the middle of all this was a large sign that read:

Goldberg's Ocracoke Plaza

Luxury Hotel and Condominiums

Luxury Shops and Five Star Restaurant

Opening in the Fall

Preview by Appointment Only

For Information Call...

That's where Robert's eyes froze. In the bottom right-hand corner was a picture of Samantha with her name and number below the photograph. She was staring right at him, wearing her captivating smile. Robert closed his eyes, reopening them a few seconds later, just to make sure he wasn't imagining things.

He was not.

25

Robert couldn't nap during the ferry ride back to Hatteras. His mind was way too active to relax. He went over to Ocracoke hoping to find clues, connections for the dots. Instead, he found more dots without connections. The bottom line, he was now more confused than ever. To start, why hadn't Samantha told him she was a real estate agent? What was the big secret? Robert assumed this was the clue Billy was referring to. What did that have to do with the Friday before Labor Day, and how was Samantha selling real estate related to that? And where was the danger? Robert racked his mind trying to put the pieces together. There were a lot of dots to connect. He sensed there was one main piece of information, one big dot, he had yet to discover. Dennis Tucker liked to call this dot the sun; the one that pulled all the rest together. Robert let out a nervous chuckle. It was hard to find the sun when it was raining. He thought about the weather earlier in the morning.

"Had the fog really cleared?" he wondered aloud.

He was awake when it was his turn to exit the ferry. He pulled off to the side to look around. The shopping center that had been built since his last visit was open for business. He thought about walking through, but it was still raining. Instead, he drove over to the marina entrance. He contemplated checking out the *Lady Hatteras II* again, in case there was something he had missed. He was about to drive through the gates when the entrance sign he hadn't noticed before caught his eye. It told the name of the marina, mentioned big game fishing and gave a number to call for reservations. It was the word reservation that caught his attention. There was a clue there, he was sure. He jerked the SUV into reverse, looked at his watch and jammed his foot on the accelerator.

He was at the Coast Guard station in less than five minutes. The officer on duty, a short thin young man in his early twenties, was behind the desk. He wore the standard white shirt sleeve uniform. He had one stripe on his arm and no ribbons on his shirt. That meant he was new and green like an intern.

The young sailor was polite, but with a firm, official voice. Robert smiled. He explained what he wanted and why. The lack of expression on the young man's face indicated that he knew nothing of the *Lady Hatteras II* and the fate of her captain, or why such requests for a copy of the official accident report might be made. He turned his back on Robert and focused on the computer terminal behind the counter. A few keystrokes were punched A moment later, the screen filled with information. The Coast Guardsman turned around. "Says here I'm supposed to get authorization to release this information."

"Authorization from whom?" Robert inquired cautiously.

"The commanding officer here."

"How do we go about doing that?" Robert said.

"We won't for at least several days," the young man said. "He won't be back till the end of the week."

Robert's mind spun rapidly. "That's too bad," he said. "I'm only going to be here until tomorrow. I was planning to make an offer on the boat later this evening, but I have to give the insurance company all the information first. That's why I need the report. It's them asking for it, not me." Robert reflected upon what he had just said. He figured if he was going to lie, he might as well tell a big one. "The owner's going to be disappointed. Word is she's in a mighty need of the money to help pay her mortgage. Seems the insurance money has all dried up. I'm going to make her a fair offer, but I've got my own insurance company to deal with first." He forced a disappointed look across his face.

The young seaman looked wide-eyed as he weighed his options. Regulations were regulations. He had been told that many times throughout his training. At the same time, it had been impressed upon him that the Coast Guard was also into community service. They were much more than simply a search and rescue organization. He was wrestling with the dilemma. There was no one around for advice. He had to make a decision, a somewhat new phenomenon for him. Since arriving at the Hatteras station some eight months prior, he basically stood behind the desk, answered the phone, and did what he was told. Activity at the station had been relatively quiet since his arrival, rescuing idiot boaters being the exception. He was up for promotion in several weeks. He didn't want to do anything to jeopardize that. He contemplated his options, deciding it was better to err on the side of community service. He pushed the appropriate buttons to print the report. He took the several pages, stuck them beneath an electric stapler and handed them to Robert. "Here you go, sir. You have nice day."

"Thank you," Robert said. "I'm sure the widow will be very pleased." He forced himself not to look at the report as he headed for the door. He also forced himself not to run to the car. He sucked in a deep breath and showed an external calm.

He pulled out of the compound onto the highway. He turned into the first pullover. He lifted the official Coast Guard report of the *Lady Hatteras II*. The first page contained the name and file number of the report, the name of the officer who took the original call for the missing vessel as well as the officer who wrote the final report. Page two gave a more narrative description of events. The original call came into the Coast Guard station at 2145 (9:45 pm) that Sunday evening. It was from Captain Willey's wife who reported that her husband had not returned from a day out on the water. She had already called the marina. The security guard there verified the *Lady Hatteras II* had yet to return. There was also a note indicating there were no distress calls from anyone in the region. The report went on to say that the security guard knew Captain Willey well and insisted this was very unusual. With this, the official alarm was sounded, and a search and rescue operation put into effect. A helicopter was dispatched from Beaufort, North Carolina and arrived at the Hatteras station an hour or so later. However, because it was already dark with no moon to help with visibility, it was decided to wait until morning to begin the official search. The helicopter took off the next morning with the first break of light. The entire fishing fleet went out as well to help.

Lady Hatteras II was spotted by the helicopter just after ten am on Monday. The boat was some fifty miles offshore; thirty miles south of the island. A rescue swimmer was dropped. The boat was empty. The report also noted that the swimmer commented there appeared to be no mechanical trouble and no signs of foul play. The station's thirty-two-foot cutter arrived on scene a short time later. The vessel was towed back to the station's dock. The investigation was completed. The boat was taken over to the marina where she was pulled. She had been there ever since. The conclusion was that Captain Willey fell overboard and drowned. It was noted that seas were two to three feet that day with winds out of the south.

Robert read through the report again. While the pages provided a lot of additional information, more dots to connect, the specific question of who reserved the boat the Friday before was missing. He continued to believe there was a connection between the Friday fishing trip and the unexplained trip that Sunday. He quoted Dr. Tucker aloud. "All things are connected."

Robert tossed the report on the passenger seat and headed north. By now, the rain had subsided. Clouds were starting to break apart; the sun was again peeking through. The weather on Hatteras could change from one extreme to another rather quickly. He reviewed the information he just read. Two things that stood out were the lack of mechanical problems and no signs of foul play. Now, he was no expert in this sort of investigation, but he had developed a well-trained eye over the course of his own training. He thought it strange the report claimed no signs of foul play when he was able to find the things he found without a great deal of difficulty.

"More dots without connections," he said aloud. And still no big dot. He continued to sense he was missing something, that he had seen the big dot, only failed to recognize it.

He drove past the entrance to Hatteras Lighthouse and was about to speed up when a thought crossed his mind. He made a sharp right-hand turn onto the last road at the edge of town. Both sides were lined with the standard three to four story homes built on wooden pilings. The design of each dwelling was different, yet there was still a similarity about them based on the builder. This development was one of the older communities in the area. They looked more weathered than most but had obviously withstood the sands of time. He saw no signs of damage on any of the buildings. Then again, he didn't expect to. Whenever a building like this was damaged, it was imperative the repairs be done quickly; otherwise the next storm might prove even more disastrous. He did a lot of this repair work the summer he was there.

Robert took his time driving through the area. He thought he recognized some of the houses he had worked on but wasn't sure. He was about to turn around and head back to the main road when a couple signs in the yards of the last two homes caught his eye. He drove up to the end of the cul-de-sac and stopped. He stared at two identical signs to the one on Ocracoke from Goldberg Realty with a picture of the listing agent below the red lettering.

Samantha again smiled at him.

He continued looking at one sign and then the other. He knew he had found the clues. Now, what were they telling him? He stared harder. Samantha was staring back. The above question was repeated. What was she trying to tell him? Then he saw the answer. He had found the sun. Only it wasn't Samantha giving him the message. It was someone else.

The other dots suddenly became connected.

26

In medicine, a patient comes in with a set of symptoms, be it in a clinic, a private office or an emergency room. The clinician then searches for a cause or causes. Tests are run, x-rays taken, a physical exam performed; and then *voila,* you have an answer. Oftentimes, the dilemma becomes what to do with these results. This was the predicament Robert found himself in.

He was at what was becoming his favorite diner in Nags Head, sitting at a corner table near the back of the room. He was staring at his legal pad. He now had a lot of dots, a lot of information. He even had some of them connected. He also believed he had the big dot as well, the sun that brought all the rest together. While there were many more connections to find, more questions to answer, Robert believed he had answered the top two. First, what did Billy mean when he said: the boy never left the boat? Secondly, why was Samantha in danger? He had a theory about it all. The problem, there was only one person who could verify this theory, and that was potentially a very risky venture.

He was distracted as his turkey club and a beer arrived. A short time later as he collected his change from the cashier, he decided the best approach was to take the data to the patient and lay the cards on the table, letting the pieces fall where they may.

Now all he had to do was find the patient.

27

Robert didn't know what he was dreaming about. He did know it was good. He also knew he had been sound asleep and would still be in that state if it wasn't for the noisy truck that pulled up beside him. He sat up, pushed a strand of hair from his eyes and did a big stretch. He arched his back against the seat and looked out through the windshield. Except for a few stars that were rising off the horizon, it was pitch black. The moon was nowhere to be seen. He sensed a few clouds overhead, but they were hard to discern without any significant night light. He could hear the waves pounding against the beach, and while he couldn't see her, he knew the wreck of *The Lady Hatteras* was close by. It was low tide, so he had nothing to worry about there. He still had a fear of falling asleep only to wake up surrounded by water, the tide having come in and washed him out to sea. He smiled at the thought. There were recent days where that might not be such a bad thing.

He took a deep breath, shook his head and rubbed his eyes. He got out of his BMW and walked to Billy's truck. "Maybe it won't be so foggy tonight," he said.

"Won't start till after midnight when the dew point gets right," Billy said.

"Think it'll be as bad as yesterday?"

Billy hesitated. "Hard to tell." The boy lit a cigarette and took a deep drag. "Want a beer?"

"Na, but thanks anyway. I had a couple with lunch this afternoon. Put me right to sleep."

A can of beer materialized and was handed to him. "Have one anyway," Billy directed. "It'll help you relax and make it easier for you to tell me what you have to tell me."

"What makes you think I have anything to tell you?" Robert said defensively. Pulling the tab on the can, he took a long swig.

Billy chuckled. It was the first time Robert had seen such an emotion since returning to the island. "Why else would you have left a note on the windshield of my truck telling me to meet you here tonight?"

"To get a free beer?" Robert smiled. "I was really hoping for Mountain Dew."

"Bullshit." The humorous voice was gone.

They each drank in silence. Billy sucked on his cigarette. Robert stared out across the water. He often wondered what it would have been like to be on *The Lady Hatteras* just before she sank. He didn't imagine it would be too pleasant, not like his dream from a moment ago. It had to be surreal, knowing what was happening yet having no control over the outcome. You knew the ship was going down, but there was nothing you could do. He compared it to watching a patient die right before your eyes. Despite your best efforts…

He turned his attention to Billy. "Why didn't you just tell me what happened, instead of my having to find out for myself?"

Billy reached into the cooler sitting on the passenger seat and pulled out two more beers. He handed one to Robert. Pulling the tab on his own, he said, "For one, you wouldn't have believed me. For another, you wouldn't have spent so much time down here."

"Time down here doing what?" Robert asked.

"Doing your little investigation thing, and…" His voice trailed off. He took another deep drag from his cigarette.

"And spending time with your sister?" Robert offered.

"You said it, not me."

Robert smiled. Billy was always a conniver. He was always meddling in Robert's and Samantha's time together. If the fish weren't biting, the surf was up. Now, he seemed to be doing the opposite.

The conversation got serious. "How much danger is Samantha in?" Robert asked.

"People don't fall overboard if the boat don't rock," Billy replied. "Seas were calm that day."

"I see."

"Do you?"

"I think so."

"Then let's hear what you got," Billy directed.

Robert paused. "Did you know the boy on the boat was sexually assaulted?"

Billy took a sip of beer. "I suspected as much."

"Did you see or hear anything?"

"No. Once we got done fishing for the afternoon, I curled up on the floor of the bridge like I always do. I slept the whole way in. Sometimes Cap would wake me up and we'd swap out. This particular day, he took the boat the whole way in. I didn't wake up till we hit the inlet."

"Then what happened?" Robert queried.

"Same thing as always. We pulled up to the scales and unloaded our catch. We had a mess of blues and dolphin, but we didn't have any bill fish. We fueled up, then went over to our slip...same routine every day. The captain settled up, I got my tip, and away they went." Billy hesitated. "The boy never left the boat."

"Are you sure?"

Billy nodded in the affirmative.

"Then what happened?" Robert coaxed. He added a moment later, "You're sure you're okay talking about this?"

Billy glared at his friend. "It would have been nice if we had this conversation a lot sooner."

Robert swallowed hard. "I deserve that, and you're right."

Billy continued without further comment. That was one thing Robert liked about the boy. He always said his piece and then moved on. "As you know, most captains like their boats cleaned up before the end of the night. Willey was different. He didn't care when I cleaned 'er up, so long as it was before the next trip, which for us was Monday morning. Because of the weather, our booking for Saturday got canceled. Cap told me to just come down Monday morning early. I usually didn't like doing that cause I didn't like leaving a dirty boat, but that particular Friday..."

"It's okay if you want a break," Robert said.

"I've had a break for five *freakin'* years," Billy said firmly with a hint of anger.

"Then go on," Robert said softly.

Billy did as he was told. "I knew you were leaving that Friday. We said our goodbyes the night before, remember?"

Robert nodded. He didn't bring up the fact that he drank more beer than he ever had that Thursday, slept very little because he was up every hour peeing the beer away, and then woke up the next morning with a terrible headache that he carried the whole way back to Baltimore.

"I left the boat in a hurry that Friday, not because of you, but because I was upset about the boy; also, because I was worried about Sam. I wanted to get home to her as soon as possible," Billy said.

"You really do care about your sister, don't you?" Robert said.

"Obviously more than..." The boy stopped in mid-sentence.

"I could try and explain," Robert said. "But you'd consider it all bullshit anyway."

"You're right there."

Robert told himself maybe another time. He was about to say something to that effect when Billy interrupted him. "How do you know there was definitely a... what did you call it... a sexual assault?"

Robert hesitated as he questioned how much detail to provide. Deciding to stick to his all cards on the table theory, he said, "I was aboard the *Lady Hatteras II* and collected some stuff I doubt you knew was there."

"What kind of stuff?"

All cards on the table, Robert reminded himself. He spent the next five minutes explaining about his and Samantha's visit to the boat and his subsequent collection of material later that night.

"You broke into the boat?" Billy said with surprise.

"There wasn't really anything to break into. She was wide open," Robert defended.

"Still." As an afterthought, Billy added, "How do you know I'm not involved?"

"None of the DNA I found in the cabin matched your DNA," Robert explained.

"How the hell'd you do that?"

Robert reached over and tapped the cigarette in Billy's mouth. "Pretty good sample right here."

"Where'd you get...?" Billy paused. "You broke into my truck, too, right? I thought somebody was..."

"Bullshit," Robert snapped. "Your truck's so messy, I could take it to Jersey and back, and you wouldn't know the difference."

"Would too!"

Robert smiled. That Billy was being argumentative was a good sign, a sign there was some life coming back. "Anyway, the DNA testing showed you had nothing to do with what went on in the cabin."

"What about Capt. Willey?"

"Same thing."

Billy lit another cigarette and finished his beer.

"Who all was on the boat that day?" Robert said carefully. This was the piece of information he was seeking. This was the big dot, the sun. He was pretty sure he knew the answer; he just needed it verified.

Billy provided the verification a moment later. "Arthur Goldberg chartered the boat."

"Who else?"

"There were two other men, both real business looking like," Billy said. "Neither came dressed for fishing, that's for sure. Neither seemed all that interested in fishing either. I thought that a little strange, but we get those kinds of parties once in a while where only one or two of the people actually *wanna* fish. The rest just go along for the ride."

"Or go along for something else?" Robert said.

"Huh?"

"Who brought the boy?"

"They all came in a big black Mercedes."

"Tell me about the boy."

"He came on board all bubbly and all excited. He didn't speak hardly any English. I think he spoke Spanish. But it was obvious he had never been on a boat before."

"How old was he?"

"Eleven...maybe twelve. It's hard to say because I ain't been around too many...you know."

"Hispanics," Robert offered.

Billy nodded. "Or kids," he added.

"Did anybody say who he was or where he came from?" Robert inquired.

"No, and Captain Willey didn't ask. You learn real quick in this business to do what you're paid to do, which is go *fishin'*. The less said the better."

"What about the other two men?"

"Again, they didn't seem all that interested in fishing. They stayed in the back chairs and didn't want their turn in the fighting chair. They did seem to enjoy the ride though." Billy opened another beer, offered one to Robert who declined. He continued. "If you're going to ask what they said, they didn't say much."

"You didn't pick up on anything?"

"Like I said, you learn to keep your nose out of where it don't belong. Somebody thinks you're listening in on their conversation, good tips go right out the door. Stay focused on catching fish, and catching fish only, a good tip is assured."

"Did you get a good tip that day?"

"Always."

"Always? You've been out with these guys before?"

"Arthur Goldberg, yes. He usually charters with us two or three times a year."

"The other two men?"

"Never saw them before."

"The boy?"

"Same thing."

Robert paused to organize his thoughts. "I thought Willey didn't take children out."

"Normally, he didn't," Billy replied. "He told me on the way out he had no choice. Goldberg threatened to cancel the charter if we didn't take the kid."

"That seems odd," Robert said.

"Money talks," Billy injected. "Remember, our Saturday charter had already cancelled, and the chances of us picking up another on such short notice was slim."

"I see." Robert paused. "Who did Goldberg bring with him the other times?"

"Same kind of people…business associates he called them. The last I think was two or three weeks prior."

"What's he been doing since…" Robert had difficulty finishing the sentence.

"I haven't a clue."

"Samantha ever go with you."

"No."

Robert paused as he contemplated how to ask the next series of questions. He remained concerned about pushing the envelope with Billy, yet the boy seemed to be holding up under the stress. Then Robert realized his friend wasn't holding up under the stress. He was unloading it. After all these years, he finally had someone to talk to. Robert struggled to remember the facts about post-traumatic stress disorder. Oftentimes people inflicted with this condition simply needed someone to listen with compassion and believe what they were saying. That wasn't the cure-all, but it was often a beginning. He hoped that was the case with Billy.

Before a wave of guilt could capture Robert's mind, he continued. "What do you think happened to Captain Willey?"

"Coast Guard said he fell overboard," Billy said.

"That's not what I asked you," Robert reminded.

Billy hesitated. "I think I agree with the Coast Guard. He probably fell overboard. The question is who pushed him?"

"And why?" Robert added.

"Yeah...and why?"

"Do we have any way of knowing if anybody was with him that Sunday?" Robert asked.

"He didn't have a charter, I know that."

"Because he didn't work on Sunday?"

"Right."

"Did he ever take the boat out on a Sunday just for a ride?"

"No. That was the day he spent with his wife."

"It must have been something important...something unusual to get him to go out on the water that particular day?"

"I doubt he went out willingly," Billy said.

"Why do you say that?" Robert asked.

"The boat wasn't clean, remember?" Billy replied. "Besides, if he was going to go out, he would have at least called and asked if I wanted to go along. He used to go out by himself once in a while before I started mating for him, just to check things out and all that. But once I signed on, he always called to see if I wanted to go. He said he always felt more comfortable as he got older if I was with him. You know, if something happened and all that. Besides..."

"Besides what?" Robert encouraged.

"Capt. Willey didn't know how to swim."

"For real?"

"For real."

Robert paused. "Have you been to the boat since?"

"Ain't been anywhere near the marina."

Robert walked to the water's edge. He slid off his shoes and kicked at a small wave. He took a few more steps, stopping as a wave crashed above his knees. The water felt cool. He looked toward the shipwreck. He could hear the waves crashing across the top of the exposed wood, but it was too dark to make out the structure. Besides, the beer was fuzzing up his eyes. *Fuzzy eyes* was what Billy used to say when they drank too much. Their vision never got blurry, it got fuzzy. Robert never quite understood the difference, but he never argued either. It was one of the quirks that made Billy, Billy.

He was about to turn around when he heard a noise behind him. A moment later, Billy was beside him.

"Water's cold," Billy said. The soft glow from a cigarette lit up his face.

"It'll warm up soon enough," Robert said.

"That it will."

"Why you afraid of the water?" Robert asked gingerly.

"I'm not afraid of the water," Billy said defensively.

"Then?"

"I'm afraid of what the water might wash ashore," Billy added.

"It's been five years."

"You never know."

Robert started to kick at another wave but stopped before his foot hit its target. Billy was always good at telling stories and putting images in people's minds. Robert remembered what Billy said earlier about making him find out the information himself because he would never believe Billy otherwise. The boy was smart. "I realize this is a big step for you tonight," Robert said aloud.

"Ain't a big step so long as it don't rock the boat."

Robert started to again kick at the water. Again, he hesitated. Like Billy said, you never knew what might wash ashore.

28

It was four-fifteen Friday morning. Except for the maternity unit which had three women in active labor, the various units around the hospital were quiet. This included the emergency room where only four patients were left in the waiting room, two of which were regulars sleeping off their drunken state. The hallways were eerie in that, like a major highway, they were bustling with activity a few hours before, but were now empty.

Because everything else in the hospital was quiet, the cafeteria was booming with activity. To no one's surprise, there was a sizable line at the Subway Sandwich counter.

Robert waited patiently, glad to get out of the hustle-bustle of the emergency room. Even when the ER wasn't busy, there was a buzz in the air, a sense of urgency. The cafeteria had a buzz about it, too; only it had nothing to do with medicine. Here, the conversation focused on family, friends, weekend plans, unit gossip, and who was sleeping with whom. It was like a light switch on the door. Walk into the cafeteria, forget about all the chaos behind you. Walk out, the urgency of medical care returned. Robert was no different. While talking to

Dennis Tucker, medicine seemed like a faraway dream. It was like the ER was on another planet, which in many people's opinion, it was.

When his order was ready, Robert paid and took the two trays over to the familiar corner table. He sat one in front of Dr. Tucker, the other in front of his own seat. "This place is busier now then it is during the day," he said looking around. There were only a few empty tables in the whole cafeteria.

"This place is always busy at night," Dennis Tucker said.

"Well, I don't get to come up here this time of night. It's a fluke I'm here now."

"You should stop by more often. It's a happening place." Dennis unwrapped his sandwich and took a bite.

"I see." Robert watched two young residents at a nearby table, oblivious to anyone else around them, as they held hands and looked dreamily into each other's eyes. "Love is in the air," he muttered.

"If those two put any more love in the air, her belly's going to get big," Dennis said.

"More power to them," Robert said. His mind wondered to someone who might help with his version of love. Taking a bite of food, he glanced at the papers spread across the table. "Still trying to get your taxes straightened out?" Robert asked.

"Nah, they're done."

"You're still here, so I guess the IRS didn't get you."

"I'm safe as long as I stay within the walls of the Johns."

"You think so, huh?" Both men laughed. "Anyway," Robert said. "What have you got?"

Taking a swallow of Mountain Dew, Dr. Tucker gathered the papers on the table, stuffed them in a briefcase sitting on the floor and pulled out a manila folder. Another sip of soda, a glance at the folder. "Your boy Arthur Goldberg is quite a character. Seems he owns half the property along the mid-Atlantic seaboard. He has holdings as far north as Atlantic City, as far south as Myrtle Beach. I don't know if I'd go as far as calling him another Donald Trump, but he's at least the Trump of the beach. He has a small casino in Atlantic City, three hotels in Myrtle Beach and over two hundred other properties in between. And he's still building. The property in Ocracoke is his latest project."

"You say he owns how many houses?" Robert asked.

"A couple hundred at any one time," Dennis responded. "He's what's called a flipper. He buys properties and puts them right back on the market after sometimes fixing them up. Sometimes he doesn't even do that."

"He fixes them up himself?" Robert asked, a little confused.

Dennis laughed. "I doubt if he even sets foot in most of the houses he buys."

"Then how does he get them fixed up so fast?"

"Part of his empire is a construction company," Tucker explained. "I suspect he has men from these crews do the fix 'em up stuff on the side."

"And floats the cost back to the main project," Robert said as an afterthought.

"Now, you're thinking like one of us," Dennis said, referring to the forensic side of the pathology business.

"Lucky guess," Robert argued.

Dennis continued. "I have a friend of mine in the FBI..."

"You have friends in the FBI?" Robert interrupted.

"Yes, Mr. Hot Shot ER Doctor, in spite of what you may think, I do have friends, lots of them actually. I even got laid the other night."

Robert laughed. "How much did it cost you?"

Dennis threw a paper napkin across the table. "She paid me, smart ass."

Robert laughed again. "Anyway, go ahead. You have a friend in the FBI..."

"Who did a quick look up on your buddy here," Dennis said. "Seems his record is clean, although there have been a few preliminary probes into his financial doings. Nothing ever came of these, however."

"What's a *preliminary probe*?" Robert inquired.

"One where the party in question doesn't know they're being investigated."

"Sounds sneaky."

"It's all sneaky," Dennis said. With a mouth full of food, he continued. "If Goldberg is good at flipping houses and other projects, why Ocracoke? That seems like a very unlikely place to put up such a large project. Seems risky to me."

"Maybe the potential for return is high," Robert suggested.

"I've never been down there, but isn't Ocracoke rather desolate?"

"That's being polite."

"Egress is by ferry only, correct?"

"There aren't any bridges," Robert acknowledged.

"Then, again, why?"

Robert pondered the point and made a mental note to ask Samantha, after he confronted her about not telling him she sold real estate. The question was how to do it and do it correctly. "All dots are connected in one way or another," he said aloud.

Dr. Tucker broke into a wide grin. "There's hope for you yet, boy."

They finished eating in silence.

29

It amazed Robert how much information Dennis Tucker was able to gather in such a short period of time. When confronted about this, Dennis said it was because of who he knew, his friends so to speak. He reiterated the fact that, despite what some might believe, he had other friends besides Robert. He also claimed he knew where and how to look. A vast amount of information could be obtained right off the internet. With a few select passwords, even more information was available. He explained that forensic pathology was a lot more than cutting up dead bodies.

Robert reviewed some of what he knew. Billy verified that Arthur Goldberg had chartered the boat that Friday. Goldberg, a young Hispanic boy, and two other men went out that day. Robert didn't want to think about what happened during the trip. From the evidence found aboard the *Lady Hatteras II*, a lot more went on than fishing. Billy never heard anything on the trip home, when the assault presumably took place, because he was up on the fly bridge asleep. Any sounds were drowned out by the noise of the engines and action of the ocean against the hull. At the end of the day, Billy claimed the boy never left the boat. When confronted about this, Billy said he was sure. While Robert continued to keep all doors of possibilities open, he suspected Billy was right. That would explain the trauma in post-traumatic stress disorder. It would also explain Billy's concern for Samantha's safety by her working for Arthur Goldberg.

So, the big dot had been discovered in one Arthur Goldberg. Some connections were made, but there was more work to be done. The question now was where to go next? Then Robert decided that wasn't it either. The question was whether he should even continue with the investigation? After all, he was a barking dog in a quiet community. Sooner or later, he was going to wake up the neighbors. Sooner or later, he was going to rock the boat. A shiver went up his spine as he thought about the potential consequences related to that. Arthur Goldberg was a successful and powerful man. Robert had no doubt some of his success came the old fashion way, hard work mixed with a bit of luck. However, it seemed there were other causes of his success, including murder.

And not of just one person either!

Another chill flew up the doctor's spine.

He was sitting at the small, cluttered desk in his soon-to-be chief resident's closet, or CRC as it was better known. The room was big enough for a bed, a desk, a chair, plus the extra folding chair that was reserved for those getting called into the office for an official tongue lashing. The chair was as famous as the office itself. To the *greens* in the emergency room, it was not a comfortable seat. You knew if summoned to the CRC and invited to take a seat, what followed would not be pleasant. Robert stared at the chair a long moment. He had been invited to take a seat twice in his first year of residency and once the next. He had avoided the chair since.

Robert moved his eyes to the computer screen. The waiting room was now totally empty. Larry Dawson was doing a good job of keeping things running smoothly. As a second-year resident, he was already proving himself capable of not only providing excellent clinical care, he was also good at managing the flow of patients, a significant requirement for a chief resident. Dr. Dawson was already on Robert's watch list for such a position.

Robert was always glad when he and Dawson worked together. It made for a much smoother shift. He checked his email, deleted those of no interest, and saved the rest for review later. He thought about a short nap, but quickly decided against it. While he was behind on his sleep, he knew a nap would only make him feel worse when he awoke.

Leaning his head back and closing his eyes, Robert contemplated the two earlier questions. First, should he continue probing into this *thing,* for want of a better word? He reminded himself the dangers of transgressing into the jungle. Second, if the answer to the first question was yes, then what approach should he take? He definitely didn't want to do anything that caused trouble for Samantha. At the same time, he was concerned she was already in some sort of unknown danger. Then there was the thing about the boy not getting off the boat. What was that all about, and what did it mean? Was it what Robert imagined? And what about Captain Willey's death? It certainly looked like a lot of dots with very strong connections, all circling around this Arthur Goldberg fellow. Again, the word *murder* emerged. Robert had learned not to pass judgment on people too quickly. At the same time, Arthur Goldberg sounded like a scary man. If Robert's assumptions were wrong, then fine. On the other hand, if he was right...

Robert didn't remember anything in the Hippocratic Oath about murder investigations.

What to do? He kept repeating the question over and over. Billy said not to rock the boat. Dennis Tucker smelled a good mystery and wanted Robert to pursue it with no holds barred. He even offered to go down to Hatteras with Robert to have a look around. He especially wanted to see the boat.

Robert glanced at the computer screen followed by the shelves full of books overhead. The problem with this dilemma was the lack of anyone to talk to or anywhere to go for additional information. Unlike a problem in the emergency room where there were ample resources, both human and otherwise, he was on his own with this one. A faint smile crossed his face as he surmised what one of his favorite attending physicians would say. "When out in the wilderness, you just have to practice wilderness medicine." Which meant you had to make do with what you had. In this case, Robert felt he didn't have a whole lot of anything except a lot of dots with few connections.

Robert thought again about the phrase, "Practice wilderness medicine."

"Okay, then," he said aloud. "Just what do I have?" As an afterthought, he added, "What else do I need?" With additional thought, the answer slowly came into focus.

He was about to pull out his yellow pad and write it down when his beeper went off. He glanced at the small screen. "Ambo 492. Cardiac arrest."

He jumped to his feet and headed out the door. On the way, he called the pathology department. By the time Robert reached the trauma room, Dr. Tucker was on the line. "Hey Tuck, I need you to do something for me, some more investigative stuff."

He then told the pathology resident what he wanted.

30

When Robert came to Ocean City as a child, he never paid much attention to the landscape around him. He knew there were condominiums with hotels and motels mixed in. He recognized there were buildings of different shapes and sizes. Focusing on anything more specific, however, was not on his agenda. The important things during those early years dealt with the water temperature—pool and ocean—ice cream, pizza, the boardwalk. When he reached puberty, all focus was on girls. Real estate was simply where he slept at night. So long as there wasn't too much sand in his bed, he didn't really care.

Now, as he drove north on Costal Highway, having entered Ocean City at the southernmost point on Route 50, he found himself paying attention to the buildings surrounding him, while ignoring the things that were once important, the exception being a couple bikini clad girls that crossed the street in front of him.

The southern end of the city contained an array of old wooden structures that had been around for generations. Each building contained several apartments, and each apartment could house an unmentionable number of people on any given night. Robert remembered staying at one place many years ago where the only sleeping space was beneath the TV stand. But the rent was cheap, and the landlords never seemed to mind as long as the place wasn't too trashed and the beer cans taken to the dumpster in the morning. Like Billy said, money was money.

As Robert drove north the buildings increased in size and quality. He recognized old traditional names that had been around for years like the Commodore Hotel and Phillips Seafood House. There were newer names with national chains integrated into the mix. There was a Quality Inn, a Best Western, and a Hilton. They were new, all big, and he was sure a lot more expensive than when he was a teenager.

Continuing on Costal Highway, he passed Dumser's. He was tempted to stop for a milkshake, his favorite food when he was younger. "Maybe later," he said aloud. He was here to work, not play.

Condo row came into view. This was a ten plus block of high-rise condos. Some were relatively new; one was just being built. Others had been there for years, clothed in the expected weathered look. For the most part, they looked in good shape. Not a surprise however, as this was the high end of the real estate market in the city. No groups of intoxicated teenagers hanging over balconies here.

Past condo row, the buildings changed to a variety of three- and four-story condos with an occasional taller one thrown in for good measure. Robert continued on Costal Highway until he crossed Route 54. He was now in Delaware. The architecture decor changed once again. Here, they were lower-level structures, mostly one or two-story houses with an occasional standalone business or small strip mall. Traffic also seemed to suddenly die down. The atmosphere was calmer. People walking along the streets did so at a slower pace. It was like he'd entered a different world.

Robert slowed down as the speed limit dropped to thirty-five. A yellow warning sign announced strict enforcement of the same. He smiled as he saw an unmarked police car sitting in the median less than a hundred feet past the sign. "Strictly enforced with little time to adjust," he muttered under his breath. He had no problem with this, however. A slower speed meant he had more time to look around. Dennis told him the Goldberg corporate office was on Route 1 in Fenwick Island. Route 1 was an extension of Costal Highway as it crossed into Delaware. Traffic was light and there was no one behind him, so he slowed even further. He didn't want to miss it.

A few blocks later, he saw a tall structure built in an A-framed shape. While the letter A itself consisted of the support structures for the building, the spaces in between were all glass. The sign in front, large metal letters built into a stone wall, read: Goldberg Realty.

He drove past, continuing to glance at the building. It was impressive alright. It was also ornate as hell. Then again, from all the other real estate signs he had seen driving through Ocean City, he imagined the business was very competitive; and booming from what Dennis had told him. There were literally thousands of condos and other associated properties listed just in Ocean City alone. Dennis didn't even look into the Delaware market.

Robert pulled to the side of the road to contemplate his next move. According to Dennis, Goldberg drove a red Cadillac Escalade. The vehicle's license plate read: BEACH. Making sure the coast was clear, Robert made a U-turn and drove past the building again. This time he focused on the parking lot. He saw no such vehicle. He turned down the side street to check behind the building. There were a few cars, but again, no red Escalade. He knew it was a long shot coming to the area, but he figured it was worth the chance. He learned in medicine that you never knew when something bad in life was going to happen, oftentimes suddenly and without warning. He extrapolated the thought that you never knew when something lucky might happen either. For whatever reason, at the moment he felt lucky.

Robert saw several people come out of the building, each staring at their cell phone. He guessed they were looking at listings of properties available in the area. One woman was so focused on her phone, she tripped, almost falling down the steps. As she recovered her footing, a thought crossed Robert's mind. He pulled into the parking lot. A sign warned of the towing of unauthorized vehicles with a cost of $250. He smiled to himself. He might be authorized to park here, but his intentions were not.

Tall. tinted glass windows led into the main lobby. The front walls were glass, the side and rear walls were lined with various photographs of condos, homes, and businesses for sale. In the middle of the rear wall was a replica of the sign in the front of the building. A short petite Hispanic woman sat at the front desk. She was on the phone, but immediately hung up as Robert approached. "Good afternoon and welcome to Goldberg Realty. Do you have an appointment with someone?" she said with a strong accented, pleasant voice.

Robert took a step closer, continuing to scan the photographs on the wall as a way of stalling for time. He had not planned his entrance well. "Ah, yes, I'd like to see what properties are available in the area." As an afterthought, he added, "Is Mr. Goldberg in?"

The receptionist smiled. "No sir, he is not. Besides, he usually doesn't work with individual customers. We have other agents for that. Would you like me to see who's available? They'd be happy to answer any questions and show you what we have."

"I was hoping to speak to Mr. Goldberg." Another afterthought. "He was actually recommended to me by a friend."

The smile continued. The voice remained just as pleasant. "I'm sorry, sir, but he's not available." She looked down at a calendar on her desk. "He should be back later this evening. He usually stops in before heading home when he's in town. If you give me your name, I'll let him know you were here. Can I have your number?"

Robert hesitated as he realized he was getting in over his head. He forced a smile as he said, "Actually, I left my cell phone in the car. I can never remember the number." He paused. "I'll tell you what. I'm going to be in the area for a while. I'll stop back later, if that's okay?"

"I'd be happy to have someone else talk to you," the receptionist said.

Robert was about to respond with a no thank you when something caught the corner of his eye. Instinctively, he leaned forward and looked at a picture of a young Hispanic boy sitting on the far corner of the receptionist's desk. The boy looked to be around ten or eleven. He had short dark hair, round cheeks, and a wide smile. His eyes were lit up like sparklers. The photograph was in a wide silver frame. What really caught Robert's attention was the engraving at the bottom. There were two lines of letters. One was in Spanish, the other English. Robert felt his face pale as he read the English version. It read: *In Memory Of.*

Robert collected his wits and forced empathy across his face. He nodded toward the picture. "I'm so sorry," he said.

The receptionist looked at the picture. Her eyes stayed fixed on the frame a long moment. Her smile disappeared. Her voice softened. "Thank you."

"Your son?" Robert asked.

She looked back at her visitor. "My brother...younger brother."

"He looks so happy there."

"He was. That picture was actually taken right in this chair." She paused. "He would have been sixteen this month."

"How old was he when he passed?" Robert asked.

"Eleven."

Robert leaned in for a closer look. "Mind if I ask...?"

Tears formed in the receptionist's eyes. "He drowned."

Robert felt himself turning pale again. "I'm so sorry," he repeated. He looked away, wondering about the definition of luck.

Their eyes met again. She wiped the tears away. "I'm sorry. Please excuse me."

"I understand. It's okay." He pulled a tissue from a box sitting on the desk. Handing it to her, he said, "It's never easy losing someone you love, especially someone so young." The receptionist blew her nose and wiped her eyes gently. Laying the tissue on the counter, she started to say something when the phone rang. "Excuse me, please," she said, turning her attention to the call.

Robert leaned over the counter and gave her a sympathetic pat on the shoulder. "I'll be back later," he said. As he straightened up, he gathered the tissue in his hand. He turned and stepped toward the doors.

The Ladies of Hatteras

The receptionist seemed to be back to her perky self as she answered the phone.

31

Robert stood on the balcony, surveying the view which overlooked Costal Highway. His room was on the third floor, providing a good view of the Goldberg office building and parking lot a half a block away. When the receptionist said that Goldberg might be back later in the day, Robert decided to hang around a little longer. He checked into the motel because his legs were aching from being in the SUV too long. Plus, he didn't want to sit in the car for fear of drawing attention to himself.

He thought back to earlier in the afternoon in the lobby of the building. The image of the boy kept coming back to him; only the boy's image was obstructed by the letters: *In Memory Of.* Robert kept trying to block the thought, only it kept reappearing. Like a song you couldn't get out of your mind, the image kept playing over and over. He had already checked three times to make sure the Kleenex was secure in the baggy hidden deep in his backpack. He had a very strong suspicion the tissue was a big dot connector.

After he left the Goldberg building, he did go to *Dumser's* for a milkshake along with a burger and fries. He drove back to Fenwick and searched for a spot to await the return of the red Escalade. It was then he decided to check into the motel. He was glad he did as the hour was getting late and he was starting to fade. He was not an undercover cop and not used to surveillance work. He found it just as boring as it was tiring. Traffic along the highway picked up between the six and seven o'clock hours. Then it died off with only an occasional car or truck. Pedestrian traffic had also dissipated. As the sun set, lights came on in the various structures around him. Lights in the Goldberg building, however, started to diminish. Robert feared the man of the hour would never show up. If he did, Robert would have little time to accomplish his task. He looked at his watch. It was a quarter past eight. He'd wait until eight-thirty before calling it a night. It looked like the building would be closed by then anyway.

Time passed. Eight-thirty came. The building went dark. Two people exited with one locking the door behind them. Robert waited another ten minutes before leaving the balcony. He pulled the screen door closed along with the curtain. He plopped down on the bed and popped a beer. Grabbing the TV remote, he flipped through the channels. He found nothing of interest. The HBO movie didn't catch his interest, one of the Smokey and the Bandit movies he had already seen several times. He yawned as he finished his beer, deciding it was a good time to catch up on his sleep.

He had just come out of the bathroom when he heard a strange noise outside. Then he realized it wasn't something strange, but a sound he had yet to hear this evening. He hurriedly pulled on a pair of shorts and made his way to the patio door. Making sure he had turned off the lights, he pulled aside the curtain. Sliding open the screen, he stooped low and stepped onto the patio. Peering through the railing, he allowed his eyes to adjust to the dark. He looked across the street. A red Escalade sat in the Goldberg parking lot. The noise he heard were the electronic doors locking with a honk of the horn. He knelt behind the balcony's barrier. Peering through the break in the two vertical panels, he squinted to focus on the license plate. Unfortunately, there were too many shadows to make it out. He noticed there were a couple lights on in the building. He sat in a squatting position and waited.

He was about to doze off when the lights in the building went out. A moment later, the front door opened. Two people walked out. At the same time, the headlights of the Escalade flashed as the doors were unlocked. One figure was a tall middle-aged man dressed in a black tuxedo. Robert couldn't tell much more about him as he turned his back when the doors unlocked. The other figure, however, stayed facing forward. While the flash of the headlight was short, it was enough for Robert to see that the figure was female dressed in a long red evening gown, and she was drop dead gorgeous. The light flash was also long enough for Robert to get a short glimpse of her face, causing him to almost faint.

He had never seen Samantha dressed up. He had never even seen Samantha in a dress. He had never seen Samantha look better.

Like pop-ups on a computer screen, a whole slew of questions filled his mind. Before he could focus on any of them, something else caught his attention. The man turned slightly, a lit cigarette sticking out of his mouth. Robert's mind raced as quick prayers were said. These prayers were answered as the man held the door for Samantha before making his way around to the driver's side. Opening his own door, he flicked the cigarette onto the ground.

A minute later, Robert was across the street. The taillights of the Escalade could be seen several blocks away. While there were several cigarette butts strewn around the parking lot, there was only one still lit. Robert picked it up, put it out against the asphalt and placed it in a baggie he had in his pocket. Questions continued to buzz around his head concerning possible explanations for what he had just witnessed. These were set aside as he realized he now had an item that might connect all the dots.

He put the bagged cigarette butt in his pocket as he hurried across the street. He planned to store it right next to the baggie with the earlier collected Kleenex.

32

For the first time Robert could remember, Dr. Tucker didn't have the cafeteria table covered with papers. On the contrary, the pathology resident was staring down at a single page. He looked up as Robert sat down with two trays of subs and sodas. Greetings were exchanged, food distributed, a few bites taken in silence. It was obvious neither resident had eaten in many hours as getting food into their respective stomachs took precedent over everything else.

Following a swig of Mountain Dew, Dr. Tucker said, "Well, Robert, you did good. You may make it in the investigative business yet."

"Thank you, but as I've said before, that's not my goal in life. That's yours." A couple more bites were taken. "Anyway, what have you got?"

"We've got one match and one near match."

Robert let the words sink in. "A match for what?" he said.

"Looks like your man Goldberg is a pedophile. The salvia on the cigarette butt is the same DNA as the semen in the boy's underwear."

Robert's stomach turned. At the same time, it amazed him how nonchalant Dr. Tucker could talk about such matters, even if this was all in a night's work for a forensic pathologist. "You sure?"

"A 97% DNA probability."

"Damn."

"That's putting it mildly."

Robert took a sip of soda. "What about the near match?"

Dennis swallowed a mouthful of food. "Statistically speaking, the receptionist at the real estate office is a relative of the boy on the boat."

"So the boy in the picture who drowned five years ago could be the same boy."

"Statistically speaking, yes."

"What about your gut speaking?"

"One and the same," the pathologist said without hesitation. "Remember, Goldberg was the one who evidently took the boy along."

Robert's sixth sense with the receptionist's Kleenex was reinforced. "What do we do now?"

Dennis hesitated. "Are you sure the man you saw smoking the cigarette was Arthur Goldberg?"

"Good question. I didn't get a good look at his face, but I do have this." Robert pulled a folded newspaper from his back pocket. It was a copy of the *Ocean City Times*. The front page showed a man and a woman at a fund-raising gala. The girl in the red dress was not identified. The man was Arthur Goldberg. The fundraiser was for the new cancer wing planned for the local hospital. According to the write-up, the gala was a huge success, a big part due to the generous efforts of Mr. Goldberg himself.

Dr. Tucker read the caption and the short article that followed. Sliding the paper across the table, he said, "Who's the babe?"

"Samantha Mathews."

Dennis's eyes widened. "Samantha, as in your Sam?"

Robert nodded.

"Holy shit. When you connect the dots, you connect the dots."

"They weren't connections I was looking for."

"I guess not," Dennis said. "What are you going to do?"

"Any ideas?"

The pathologist studied the Goldberg picture. "I'll tell you what I'd like to do, only it's illegal, unethical, unprofessional and a whole slew of other *uns*."

"I agree," Robert said. As an afterthought, he added, "How much of what we've already done is illegal?"

"I'm just running some tests for a friend." Dennis smiled as he took a big bite if sub.

"My ass."

The pathology resident chuckled through a mouthful of food. The smile disappeared. "Truth of the matter is nothing we've done so far is illegal. The stuff you took off the boat didn't really belong to the boat. At the same time, none of it would be admissible in court because of the way the evidence was collected and handled."

"So, everything has been for naught?" Robert questioned with surprise.

"I wouldn't say for naught. But you're not going to make it on CSI collecting evidence like this."

"Then what do we do?"

Dennis smiled. "Believe it or not, that part I've actually thought about."

"I might have guessed," Robert mocked. Then realizing his friend was serious, he said, "I'm listening."

Dr. Tucker responded.

33

There was a definite change in the weather in the two weeks since Robert had been to Hatteras. It was fifteen degrees warmer. The humidity had risen. The gradient temperature between night and day was narrowing as well; all signs that summer was on its way. Robert had noticed a few No Vacancy signs as he drove through Nags Head. There was also an increase in traffic. The Hatteras Lighthouse parking lot was nearly empty, however. He had driven out on the beach earlier, right at sunset and saw only a few vehicles. He suspected that activity would pick up once the tide changed. Surf fisherman didn't care whether it was day or night. All that mattered was if the tide was right and the fish were biting.

Robert glanced at his watch. He illuminated the face and saw it was almost eleven pm. If he remembered correctly, high tide was due around three. Activity in the area would pick up. By then, however, he planned to have his business taken care of. Until then, he planned to take a nap. He checked to make sure his cell phone alarm was set for one o'clock. He reclined the seat as far back as it would go and laid his arm across his face. He took in a couple deep breaths and tried to sleep.

He suspected this wasn't going to happen. He was too keyed up, his mind in mental overdrive. He'd been that way since leaving Baltimore some ten hours earlier. He continued to question what to do with all the information. He made one decision, and then he made another. By the time he crossed Oregon Inlet, he still had no definitive plan. He didn't know what approach to take with Billy. He didn't know what to say to Samantha. The only thing he knew for sure was that he had to make a delivery; a package that was wrapped in a plastic bag in the back of his SUV. The idea came from Dennis. Implementation, however, was far from simple. There were too many options and variables to consider. Plus, he was way out of his realm of training. He was an emergency room doctor, not a federal agent. "Maybe I should switch places with Dennis," he mouthed softly.

The more he tried to force the issue, the more frustrated he became. He had no mentor to turn to. There were no reference books. There was no world-famous library. There were no internet sites to browse. He was on his own. Then he realized that was not the case. There was Billy. What would he say to do now?

Billy's words came to mind. "When in doubt, go fishing." And therein lay, maybe not the solution, but at least a path to follow.

But first, Robert had a package to deliver.

34

"Why didn't you tell me you were coming down?" Samantha said, jumping out of her Jeep and stepping through the sand to Robert. She gave him a hug and a kiss on the cheek. Neither was exceptionally long, neither was especially emotional.

"I thought I'd surprise you,' Robert said. "Besides, it was kind of short notice on my end. One of my residents wanted to do a *switch-a-roo*, so I ended up with a couple days off in the middle of the week." He pulled her towards him for another hug. She responded, this time with a bit more warmth. "Are you glad to see me?" he said into her ear.

She gently pushed away. "In some ways, yes."

"In other ways?"

"Robert, you can't just pop in and out of my life like this."

Robert gazed across the water. It was a perfectly clear day. It was an hour short of high noon, but the temperature was already above eighty. A gentle breeze blew from the south. The ocean was flat, the surf, almost nil. The wreck of *The Lady Hatteras* rose above the water as if looking to bake in the sun. The inevitable seagull sat perched atop the weathered mast. A couple other birds circled the area looking for fish that rose too close to the surface. There were a few scattered vehicles to the south, one to the north. No one seemed to be catching anything, but high tide was still a couple hours away.

Robert turned and faced Samantha. She was dressed in a blue sport shirt, the campground logo printed across her left breast. She wore tan khaki shorts; her hair pulled into a ponytail. She wore no makeup. As usual, she was barefooted.

Quite the contrast to what he saw in the parking lot of the Goldberg building a couple weeks before.

Refocusing on his mission, he said. "I'm thinking about buying a piece of property down here."

"Why?" Samantha said instantly.

"I like it down here. I hear it's a good investment."

"What's stopping you?"

"Nothing really, except..."

"Except what, Robert?"

He smiled. "I guess I need a good agent."

She forced a smile. "I can help you there if you want."

"I'd like that."

Samantha tipped her head to the side. "What's this about, Robert? And don't tell me it's about buying property."

His mouth opened and closed. "Well, I have been thinking about it."

"Bullshit."

His mouth opened. It closed again. He looked away, obviously struggling with what to say next. Finally, he leaned through his side window and pulled the newspaper from the passenger's seat. Holding it out for Samantha to see, he said, "Why didn't you tell me you had a boyfriend?"

She glared straight at him, not even bothering to look down at the picture. The veins in her neck threatened to explode. "You're a real bastard, you know that?" She turned and jumped into her Jeep.

Robert watched as she sped away, throwing a contrail of sand into the air. He shook his head side to side. "So much for going fishing," he muttered.

The Jeep shrank into the horizon.

35

Robert didn't know how long he had zoned out, or if he had even fallen asleep. When he brought his eyes into focus, however, there were several vehicles on each side of him. Each showed their occupants rigging up lines, placing rod holders into the sand and cutting up bait, all in preparation for the next high tide. There was little conversation between the participants – not an unusual occurrence. Surf fisherman tended to keep to themselves. Many admitted that their time on the beach was a time to think, a time to clear the mind. It was not a time to talk.

He stretched his neck and rolled his shoulders to bring some life back into his body. He took a sip of water, swished it around in his mouth before spitting it out the window. The next mouthful he swallowed. His stomach growled. He ignored the hunger pains and took another swallow. Being hungry was something he learned to deal with during his residency. Long stretches of time without food was common. Besides, being hungry always seemed to energize him, especially at night. Fatigue usually started after a meal, such as a trip to the cafeteria with Dr. Tucker.

Neither the passage of time nor the nap helped direct him to the next step. But before any of that, he had to get past the urge to screw it all, go back to Baltimore and forget about everything. He didn't want to dig any deeper without Samantha's support. After all, this was for her.

"Wasn't it?" he said aloud.

The only response was a slight gust of wind.

His thoughts returned to the earlier theme of needing someone to talk to. He needed someone he could trust, someone who would not run at the first sign of uncomfortableness. He flipped through the names in his mental card-ex. Dennis Tucker came up first. Robert quickly eliminated him, however. For one, he was a long way away. For another, he was probably asleep this time of day.

The names continued to flip by. Another thirty seconds passed, and then it came to him. "Really?" he said aloud.

Another gust of wind gave the reply.

36

The pick-up was parked along the beach a mile north of the Rodanthe pier. The truck was old, the paint faded. Rust spots had invaded the body. But it still ran, and on the island of Hatteras, that's all that mattered. It took Robert a moment to figure out what was different. After a long stare, he realized the truck was down by the water, not up against the sand dunes. As Robert drew closer, he saw a figure off to the side tending to a fishing pole. Closer yet, Billy came into view.

Robert pulled up beside the truck, shut off the engine and climbed out of his SUV. Not, however, before reaching across the passenger's seat to grab a plastic bag. Closing the door, he made his way to the water's edge where Billy was baiting a hook. He noticed the hook was large and the bait was a whole croaker. "You expect to catch a shark or something?" he said, pulling a couple Mountain Dews out of the bag. He popped both tabs, handing one to Billy.

"Sharks should be nice and fat," Billy said, accepting the beverage.

"Why's that?"

"Cause I ain't fished for them in a long time."

Robert didn't say anything. It was a simple joke, yet such a change in Billy's attitude. The truck was close to the water and Billy was fishing, his feet awash in the surf. What a change, Robert thought. Aloud, "I brought you a sandwich."

"What kind?"

Robert cocked his head to the side. "When's the last time you had anything to eat?"

Billy thought a moment. "I guess last night at dinner." He took a gulp of soda and set the can in the sand.

"Then what difference does it make what kind of sandwich I brought you?"

"Because I'm a picky eater."

Robert laughed. He remembered just the opposite being true. "Bologna and Swiss." The emergency room physician, who averaged caring for at least two heart attack victims a night, didn't say there was an extra dose of mayonnaise added to the bread.

"Extra mayo?" Billy inquired.

Robert nodded.

"You remembered!"

Robert nodded again. "I remember a lot." It was his turn to make a point.

When the line was cast and the pole dropped into the rod holder stuck in the sand, Billy took the sandwich. Unwrapping it, he leaned against the truck. The tide was high and the surf a little rough. The waves came to within a few feet of the vehicles. Billy didn't seem to mind. He ate in silence with a swallow of Dew thrown in every so often for good measure.

"Ain't had one of these in a long time," he said, stuffing the paper back into the bag. He pulled out two more sodas. Handing one to Robert, he said, "So what brought you out here this afternoon?"

"Wanted to see you."

"Bullshit."

Robert put his own trash away. Taking a swallow of his second drink, "Maybe it wasn't as much to see you as it was to talk."

"That's better."

For as dumb as he acted at times, the boy was smart as a whip. "I need some advice," Robert said.

Billy looked at his friend, this time his head cocked to the side. "Like I said earlier, if you leave the fish alone, they get big and fat. They also get a lot older and a lot smarter."

"You're saying let sleeping dogs lie?" Robert said.

Billy nodded.

"I think it's more complicated than that," Robert said.

Billy drained his can and lit a cigarette. "Then I'm listening."

And so he did.

37

Robert was only three weeks into his chief residency and was already having doubts about his decision to do the extra year. If he had declined the offer, he would already be somewhere functioning as an attending, working forty or less hours a week while earning a shit pile of money. Instead, he had been lured by the aura of Johns Hopkins Hospital, still a resident, working sixty plus hours a week, earning shit for pay and constantly swallowing Tylenol because of the near-constant headache.

What a life, he thought. He always loved medicine and still loved the thrill of taking care of sick people, but he was finding he disliked the administrative responsibilities that went along with being the chief. There were schedules to arrange, conferences to coordinate, *greens* to teach, meetings to attend, attending physicians' asses to kiss, plus a whole slew of other political and administrative functions to accomplish, all the while doing his share of clinical shifts. Clinical medicine was great. The administrative duties sucked. No one warned him of the level of responsibility, nor the time involved regarding the latter. There never seemed to be enough hours in the day, even when he was on-site twenty-four hours a day, which was becoming an all too frequent habit. The result, his fatigue was at an all-time high, his patience was short. His temper...

Well, he didn't even want to think about that. He had always been known for his calm demeanor, even in the midst of the most arduous crisis. Lately, however!

It wasn't something to dwell on. It was just something he had to fix, which he planned to do during the upcoming weekend off, his first since taking over as chief the beginning of July. He didn't have any specific plans except that he was leaving Baltimore, and it didn't matter in which direction he headed. He was getting out of Dodge, and getting out quickly.

That is, as soon as he finished next week's schedule and went through a few remaining emails.

That was the other thing. Why did becoming chief resident automatically mean he went from three to four emails a day to an average of thirty? He easily spent an hour each day just dealing with these!

But that was the job. He had signed on for this of his own free will. He was determined that regardless of what they threw at him, regardless of the unexpected responsibilities, he'd complete the task, and do it in the expected fashion of high class and high professionalism.

First though, he had to re-length his patience and erase the word temper from his personality. That was first on his list. Second was to catch up on his sleep. He had a third goal too, only he doubted he'd be able to accomplish that. You needed a partner of the opposite sex for that.

He glanced at the clock on the wall. 3:30 pm. A few more minutes and he'd be done just in time to beat the rush hour traffic. He refocused on the schedule. He chanced a glance at the computer which was set on the emergency room census. Surprisingly, the place was relatively quiet for a Friday afternoon. All the rooms were full with only five people waiting, The longest wait was barely an hour. "Not bad," he muttered aloud.

He turned his attention back to the schedule. His eyes had just refocused when there was a knock at the office door. His temper kicked in and he started to snap for the intruder to enter. He caught himself. "Come in," he said with a much softer tone.

The door opened. One of the security guards stuck his head through the opening. Robert recognized him as one of the day shift guards who was relatively new. "Yes?" the doctor said, making sure to keep his voice pleasant.

"Sorry to bother you sir, but you've got a visitor."

"A visitor. Where?"

The door swung open all the way. "Right here. They warned me you didn't want to be disturbed, but I told 'em they were full of crap. I told them your bark was worse than your bite." Billy stepped into the office.

Robert's mouth dropped open. He saw his idea of a relaxing weekend suddenly disappear. He rose to his feet, thanked the security guard and closed the door. He turned toward Billy who was spinning around looking over the office, and said, "What the hell are you doing here?"

Continuing his inspection, Billy said, "I came to see you."

"Came to see me! What the..." Robert reminded himself about his temper. "What for?" he said with restraint.

Billy turned and faced Robert, a wide grin on his face. "You said to keep you posted."

Robert's thoughts flashed back several weeks before. It was the day he and Billy were on the beach trying to decide what to do. They drank Mountain Dews with a couple beers thrown in at the end. They kicked at the waves, buried their feet in the sand, and fished for several hours, catching nothing; all the while trying to decide what to do with the information Robert had uncovered about Arthur Goldberg. Billy expressed concern for his sister's safety. He and Robert agreed, however, present danger was probably only perceived. They agreed it was better to do nothing. They parted at sunset with that agreement, with Billy promising to let Robert know if anything changed.

Robert brought his thoughts back to the present. "How did you get here? I hope not in your truck."

"Nah, the old truck would never make it over the inlet bridge," Billy responded.

"Then...?"

Billy stuck out his right thumb.

"You hitchhiked?"

"Why not? We used to do it all the time."

"Used to," Robert emphasized. He didn't go into the differences between hitchhiking in Hatteras versus Baltimore. The words would only land on deaf ears anyway. Billy had already arrived.

Before Robert could add any additional worries to his thoughts, Billy added, "I did good, too. It only took three rides."

Robert didn't ask for details. He'd rather not know. Instead, he returned to the original question. "What are you doing here, Billy?"

The wide smile on his friend's face disappeared. "You told me to let you know if anything changed."

"I did," Robert acknowledged.

"Well, it has."

"You have my undivided attention," Robert said.

Just as Billy started to respond, Robert's attention was diverted to his cell phone that started to vibrate. He hit the appropriate button without looking at the screen. "Battlegrove here."

"Robert?"

He recognized her voice immediately. "Samantha!" At the same time, he looked at Billy. "What a surprise."

There was a brief hesitation. "No need to be sarcastic," Samantha said.

Robert frowned. "Sorry. That wasn't my intention. Actually, it's good to hear your voice." He started to say that he missed her, but didn't.

"What was your intention?" Samantha pressed.

Robert wisely avoided the question. Instead, "If you're calling to tell me Billy's missing again, I can emphatically tell you he is not. He's just misplaced a bit."

"Just what do you mean by that?" Samantha said, with both a hint of demand as well as surprise in her voice.

"He's standing right here in front of me."

There was a short pause. "Robert, you are so full of..."

Robert cut her off before she could go any further. "Stop!" he said, almost shouting.

She wisely complied.

Robert sucked in a deep breath as he again thought about the weekend rapidly drifting away. He held out the phone to Billy in such a way, the boy knew not to refuse.

Forcing a smile, Billy said, "Hey Sis, what's up?"

This time the pause was longer. "Billy? What are you doing there?"

"I thought I'd visit my old friend. Didn't you say I needed to get out more?"

There was silence on the other end. Billy took that to mean his sister didn't want to talk to him anymore, so he handed the phone back to its owner.

Robert took it and spoke immediately. "Listen Samantha, he's here, and he's okay. Matter of fact, he just got here. To be honest, I don't know any more than you. Soon as I do, I'll call. I promise." He disconnected the call, taking away Samantha's opportunity to reply. He stared back at Billy. "You didn't tell her you were coming here, did you?"

Billy shrugged. "I'm a big boy."

"She's a big girl, but if she disappeared like that, you'd be worried as hell."

Billy's shoulders slumped down. "You're right."

Robert wisely did not pursue the point. Realizing there was an important reason for the visit, he said instead, "So tell me, what has changed?"

Billy's expression turned even more somber. "Samantha's getting married."

"Married! To whom?"

"Nothing's official yet. She just happened to mention it to me the other night."

"Casually mentioned that she was getting married?"

"That's what I said."

"To whom?" Robert repeated.

Billy hesitated. "Arthur Goldberg."

Robert's mouth dropped opened. Recovering, he said, "Please tell me there's more than one Arthur Goldberg on Hatteras Island."

"Afraid not, pal."

"Shit."

"Double shit."

Robert looked past Billy out the small window in the office. The view was across Madison Street towards one of the many nondescript buildings that made up the Hopkins medical campus. Traffic was heavy as rush hour was beginning. Off to the side, an ambo, its siren off but lights still flashing, was backing into the ambo bay. Robert couldn't tell anything about the wind as there were no trees in view. More importantly, however, the sun was out and the sky was clear. Yes, it would have been a beautiful weekend.

38

In most places, they would have been looked upon as a rather odd threesome. Robert was dressed in a shirt and tie with khaki pants covered by a freshly laundered lab coat. Dennis Tucker wore wrinkled scrubs with an old, tattered lab coat. Billy was dressed in a well-worn surfer's tee shirt, jeans and no lab coat. In the bowels of Hopkins, however, they didn't warrant a second glance.

They ate in near-silence, Robert and Dennis focusing on their food. Billy, on the other hand, remained wide eyed, continuing to look around as he chewed slowly. He was having trouble comprehending the size of the hospital and the number of people roaming around. He found it especially awesome, to use his words, that the place had its own Subway franchise right in the middle.

"The place is huge," he said on more than one occasion. Finishing his sandwich and taking a swig of Mountain Dew, he repeated the statement and then added, "One thing I don't understand, Bobby, if you're such a big wig in such a big place, how come your office is so small?"

Robert turned beet red as he looked at Dennis. Dennis, in turn, started choking on his food as he fought hard not to laugh. Robert picked up a plastic knife and waved it at his pathologist friend. "If you so much as say a word, Dr. Tucker, I'll demonstrate to Billy here, how to do an autopsy on a living person."

Dennis regained control. Wiping his mouth. "I didn't say a thing."

Billy smiled at having hit a sore spot with Robert.

When they started working on their cookies, Robert said, "What are we going to do?"

"What do you mean *we*?" Dennis said.

Robert smiled. "Okay, buddy... friend... sleuth-wannabe. What do you suggest Billy and I do?"

Dennis returned the facial gesture. "I think the first thing you gotta do is get ole Billy here home."

"I can get home myself," Billy injected.

The two doctors glared at the boy from Hatteras. "You may have thumbed your way up here easily," Robert explained, "Heading the opposite direction is a lot tougher."

"Dangerous, too," Dennis added.

"Well..."

"No wells," Robert interrupted. "I'll take you home."

Billy smiled. "You'd do that for me?"

"No, I'm not doing it for you. I'm doing it to protect my own hide. Your sister'll kill me if you didn't get back safely."

"Asshole."

"Don't you forget that either," Robert laughed.

"In the meantime," Dennis said. "I'll see what else I can find out about this Arthur Goldberg fellow." He looked directly at Robert. "Seems it's no longer an option to let sleeping dogs lie."

"I agree," Robert said.

39

The miles passed in relative silence. The radio was on a country western station Billy found before he fell asleep. The volume was low, so all it really did was provide background noise. While not fond of country western music, Robert left the radio alone so as not to awaken his passenger. He needed time to think without interruption. He had a lot of information to digest, a lot of dots to assimilate. The main question, as it had been several months ago, was what to do? The decision then was to do nothing. Now, however, action was needed. Robert often thought about what might force a change of direction, but never in his wildest dream did he imagine it would be the marriage of Samantha to the scumbag Goldberg.

Again, what to do? He was confronted with a set of symptoms without a diagnosis. It was like nothing he had ever seen or read about; almost as if he was on the verge of discovering a new disease. The concept of the next AIDS epidemic crossed his mind, except there was only one victim involved, Samantha. He reminded himself that wasn't actually the case either. There was the missing boy,

Captain Willey, and Willey's widow. And look at what this whole mess had done to Billy.

Now the scumbag wanted to marry Samantha.

What to do? It was a question that loomed larger and appeared more frightening the closer they got to Hatteras. He reviewed the conversation they had with Dennis Tucker a few hours earlier. Tucker's advice was to do the same as Robert would do if faced with a similar scenario in the emergency room, which was to confront the patient with the information collected, and then see if there was any additional information forthcoming. They had collected a lot of dots. Many had been connected. They had even identified the big dot; the sun of the galaxy, as Dennis called Arthur Goldberg. But what was the unseen force holding everything together? What was the missing clue or clues that would explain the connections. Dennis sensed there was still something missing. It all sounded like a good idea, but Robert was unsure how Samantha would react to being questioned again. After all, the last time...

Why the hell was she marrying this guy? She was a devoted daughter, a devoted sister, and hovered over the campground like it was her child. So what if she was dabbling in a bit of real estate. Not a bad way to earn a little extra money, Robert thought. So why the need to marry Goldberg? Robert just couldn't imagine it was because of love. He was not her type.

A shudder went up his spine. Robert wasn't the jealous type, but damn.

A passing eighteen-wheeler broke his train of thought. He slid to the right to give the truck plenty of room. There had been little traffic once they cleared the Washington Beltway. The weather remained clear; the temperature hot. The A/C in the SUV kept up nicely. All signs pointed to an uneventful trip to Hatteras, a necessity if he was going to figure out what to do before they arrived on the island.

Robert swallowed a chuckle as he looked at a sound sleeping Billy. His doctoring instincts kicked in as he watched the boy's rhythmic breathing. Seeing his chest rise and fall, Robert refocused on the road. The truck was now back in the right-hand lane, but already a good hundred yards ahead. He glanced at his own speedometer. He had the cruise control set at seventy. What was the truck doing, he wondered? Regardless, he had no doubt that contrary to previous trips, the miles were going to tick off way too quickly.

40

The moon was full, yet partially hidden by a high layer of clouds. A few stars poked through but added little illumination to the beach. There were several vehicles to the north clustered together, probably waiting for the 1:05 am high tide. There was a single vehicle off in the distance to the south. A bonfire sent sparks into the night sky. The sea was calm. The wreck of *The Lady Hatteras* slept quietly, the waves gently massaging her old bones.

Samantha rubbed her arms in response to the images of the old boat getting a massage. The temperature had dropped at least fifteen degrees, yet it was still hot and sticky. There was no breeze coming off the ocean which usually helped cool things down. She felt the sweat roll down the back of her neck. She resisted the urge to reach back and wipe away the droplets. She didn't want Robert to know how she was responding. He might take it the wrong way. While he was a gentleman in most ways, it didn't take much for his mind to turn to romance. While that may have been okay in the past, it wasn't okay now. Besides, she wasn't sweating him. She was sweating the heat.

Or so she told herself.

She handed Robert half a sandwich. He was standing next to her, but not too close. In the past, he would have been right on top of her; in her space, she liked to tease. Shared space, he liked to respond. Tonight, however, was different. She wasn't in the mood for anyone to be in her space. He didn't seem to be in the mood either.

"Thanks," he said, accepting the food.

"I figured you two hadn't eaten since you left Baltimore," she said.

"You're right," Robert replied, taking a bite of the freshly made chicken salad. He put his hand up to his mouth to catch a piece of meat that was threatening to drop into the sand.

Samantha handed him a napkin. "Thanks for bringing Billy home."

"No problem. Besides, it's a lot easier to hitchhike from Hatteras to Baltimore than the other way around."

"I still can't believe he did that. Did he tell you why?"

Robert hesitated. "Said you were getting married and he was worried about you."

"He worries about me every time I get into a car."

"The feeling's mutual, isn't it?"

"That's different."

Robert ate a couple bites in silence. Then, "Well, are you?"

"Am I what?"

"Getting married."

It was Samantha's turn to hesitate. Once she got her wits about her and learned that Billy was okay and that Robert was going to bring him home, she suspected the real reason Billy went to Baltimore was to tell Robert that. What she didn't understand was why he just didn't call him. "Maybe."

"Maybe?"

"Okay then, yes."

Robert swallowed hard. "Who's the lucky guy?" he asked with caution.

Surprised at his tone, Samantha cocked her head to the side. "Arthur Goldberg."

"The real estate guy?"

"Yes."

"Don't you work for him?"

"I am one of his agents, yes, one of his top agents to be precise. Anyway, what difference does that make?"

Robert weighed his options before responding. He knew he had to be cautious as he had chased her away once with his tongue. He didn't want to do it again. "Well, I'm happy for you, if that's what you want."

"No, you're not," she said smartly.

He looked at her. "I said I was happy for you. I didn't say I was happy for me."

Her mouth opened and closed just as quickly. It was her turn to show caution, a task just as difficult for her as it was for Robert.

"Do you love him?" Robert asked.

"That's a little personal, don't you think?"

"You didn't answer the question."

"I'm not going to, either."

Additional caution flags warned Robert not to push too hard. "Then will you answer the question of why you're marrying him?"

She looked at him. "You're the doctor. You figure it out." For a moment, there was a strange look on her face. Robert couldn't tell if it was real or if it was a mirage because of the way the light was shining across her complexion. He had seen the look before, more than once, too. But where?"

He didn't have time to ponder the question as the expression disappeared as quickly as it appeared.

A forced smile took its place. Samantha went back to eating her sandwich without further comment. She looked to the east trying to focus on *The Lady Hatteras*. The shipwreck looked so lonely, so old, so sad in the moonlight. Her mast reached out of the water as if asking for help. Samantha's research showed that the ship was fast for her time. Built for speed, she carried more square feet of sail than most ships her size. While the cargo she ferried may not have been all that impressive—coal north to south, fresh fruit south to north—it was said she was a sight to see under full sail. Samantha would have loved to have seen her in her glory days; sails full, gunwales in the water, her bow bursting through the waves like a hot knife through butter; boat against sea, man against nature. That was the shipping industry back then. While the technology may have evolved over the years, there was really little difference today. She looked up and down the beach and tried to imagine other shipwrecks that lined the shores of the Outer Banks. She knew *The Lady Hatteras* was just one of hundreds of such unfortunate vessels swallowed by the sea. She also knew that didn't count the many vessels tied to the docks on the sound side that had been abandoned, left to be slowly devoured by Mother Nature.

Samantha continued her gaze across the water. The waves were breaking just past the wreck. She squinted to see if there was a bird perched atop the mast but found no look out. She peered further into the darkness and again tried to imagine the ship in full regalia. She imagined the lady looked so strong, so proud, so majestic. And then, in a matter of an hour, nature decided she would sail no more, and *The Lady Hatteras* was fed to the sea.

The great-great-granddaughter of the lone survivor turned her head to the side. How things could change so quickly. Smooth seas one minute; gale force winds the next. Samantha glanced at Robert. He, too, was looking at the water. A storm from the past. A shipwrecked relationship. Feelings...emotions...hopes...dreams...buried at sea so many months ago. Then like *The Lady Hatteras*, suddenly one day everything washed ashore. It was the day he showed up at the store. And the emotional seas were churned up again. If only he knew what was going on beneath the surface. She let out a slow sigh.

Robert heard the sound. Turning in her direction, "So?"

"So?" she repeated.

"Are you going to tell me the *why* behind this adventure of yours?"

She tried forcing the seas to calm, tried to erase the memories of the past. In spite of the efforts over many years, mankind had yet to discover a way to control time. Her evolving emotions were part of the ongoing process. She knew she had no control over them. The question, however, was what to do now. A wave of sadness engulfed her as she fought back the tears. She had no control of the past. She had no control of the future either.

As a defense mechanism, she quickly converted her sadness to anger. "Like I said, you'll have to figure that out for yourself." The anger was short lived, however. She looked back toward the shipwreck. Again, if Robert could only see below the surface.

They finished eating in silence. They parted ways a few minutes later. A nervous hug was exchanged. There was no tight squeeze. There was no kiss. There was no passion. Samantha got into her Jeep and headed north. Robert got into his BMW and headed south.

Samantha again fought back the tears. This time she failed.

The wreck of *The Lady Hatteras* glowed brightly as the moon watched over her, but only for an instant. Soon,

Dorsey Butterbaugh

the moon buried itself in the clouds and the beach was blanketed in darkness.

41

"How's everything going?" Robert said, half-dropping, half-setting the tray of food on the table.

"Same ole', same ole'," Dennis Tucker said, grabbing one of the two sandwiches. "You stab 'em, we slab 'em," he added with a grunt.

"We don't stab 'em," Robert protested. "They come in that way."

"Whatever. You still get the credit."

A couple minutes of silence passed as the two famished doctors ate. Wiping his mouth and washing down his food with a swallow of Mountain Dew, Robert said, "You finished the post on the guy from last night?" He was referring to the autopsy on a fifteen-year-old boy who had been shot in the chest at near point-blank range. The issue wasn't that he had been shot. That was a nightly occurrence in the emergency room. The issue was that he had been successfully resuscitated in the ER only to code on the way to the operating room. One minute his vital signs were stable with things looking up, the next minute he was dead.

It was a tough loss, especially with so young a patient.

"Yeah," Dennis said though a mouthful of food. "The bullet, a .22 caliber, entered the mid-chest between the left 5th and 6th ribs. As .22's tend to do, it bounced around before ending up against the left ventricle of the heart. In its travels, it just barely nicked the aorta, causing a large hematoma to form. When that hematoma ruptured, he bled out."

"But..."

Dennis held up his hand. "You're going to ask how come he didn't bleed out right away?"

Robert nodded.

"We'll know for sure once we get the pathology slides finished, but I suspect the initial impact caused his blood pressure to drop suddenly, so the hematoma was stable. However, once you guys got his blood pressure back up...bam! Out he bled." Dennis chuckled. It always amazed him that one of the first things doctors wanted to know if they were the cause of their patient's demise. He couldn't blame them. The fear of causing the death of another human being was a strong motivator for being careful. While he never discussed it with anyone, not even his good pal Robert, one of the reasons he chose pathology was because he could never be the cause of someone's death. By the time he got them, they were already in that state. Aloud, he said, "The rise in blood pressure probably caused the hematoma to rupture, but, he would have been just as dead, only a few minutes earlier had you not saved him when he first came in."

Robert stopped chewing. "Then we didn't have a chance?"

Dennis looked hard at his colleague. "The patient didn't have a chance. You and your staff are still alive."

"Whatever," Robert said, ignoring the error in his grammar. It was a common defense mechanism to turn the focus from the patient to the care providers. It was a way to distance themselves from the reality of death. You could hide behind the smoke and mirrors of being a medical provider. Behind the illusion, however, was the truth that someone under your care had died. Contrary to popular belief, it didn't get easier with experience. You just got better at hiding it.

Just like Robert was doing a pretty good job of hiding his feelings towards Arthur Goldberg and what he did to that boy, and now what he was going to do to Samantha. The question, as Robert seemed to be facing so often lately: what should he do? As a side bar, he wondered if he should even do anything. Was it really his business to get involved? Did he even want to get involved? He took the last bite of his sandwich as he pondered the question.

Leaning back in his chair, Dr. Tucker watched his friend a moment before speaking. "You want to tell me where you've been?"

"Where I've been?" Robert said.

"You were obviously out in la-la land thinking about something."

Robert adjusted his position. "I'm trying to figure out if I'm doing the right thing."

"Meaning?"

"For one, should I even be messing in this mess? For another, am I just going to cause more trouble for Samantha?"

"What's your gut say?" Dennis responded.

"My gut says Goldberg's a low life of the worst kind. He's also a..." Robert hesitated. He told himself to be careful with his words.

"A pervert and a murderer." Dennis Tucker wasn't known for being careful with his tongue. There was a short pause before he added, "Sounds like a real catch twenty-two to me."

"It's a bitch all right," Robert agreed. "I don't think I'd have as much trouble dropping the whole thing if it wasn't for two things. One is Billy."

"I thought you said he was better."

"He seems to be, at least on the surface. But that doesn't mean he can't fall off the edge again."

"What does he think of this Goldberg guy?" Dennis asked.

Robert thought a moment. "He's only actually met him a couple times on the boat."

"You think Goldberg knows who he is?"

"According to Billy, no."

"What does Billy think you should do?" Dennis asked.

"At first, he felt we should let sleeping dogs lie, as he put it. Now, I don't think he really knows. He's torn, just like me. Despite everything, Billy insists Goldberg seems like a real nice guy. He says Samantha praises the man all the time for being kind and courteous, a real gentleman.

"Tell that to the boy on the boat," Dennis said with a sneer.

"Yeah."

"What about Sam?"

"What about her?"

"You know what I mean," Dennis smiled.

"I can get over her," Robert insisted.

"You can, but you're not." Dennis looked away a second and then looked back. "You said there were two things in your way. Billy was one. What's the other?"

Robert pondered the question. "Her eyes. There was this look in her eyes. I know I've seen it before. I just can't place it. I asked her why she was marrying Goldberg and she gave me the look. And then she told me to figure it out myself.

Dennis leaned back and folded his arms behind his head. "Figure out the look and you'll have the answer."

"Yeah," Robert sighed.

Dennis rose to his feet. "In the meantime, stop down later. We should have the slides done on the boy by then. If you want, I'll pull the body and show you what we found." He paused as he gathered up his trash. "It's amazing, they're so tough out on the street, but when we get them in here, they're just kids like anyone else."

Robert started to agree, but stopped short. "What did you just say?"

Tucker rewound his thoughts. "Tough on the street and just kids in here."

"That's it!" Robert said excitedly.

"That's what?"

"That's the answer...that's the look."

"You wanna explain?"

And so he did.

42

"Morning guys," Samantha said, walking through the screen door. She let the door go to make sure it didn't slam like it was doing the day before. It closed partway and then the air chamber caught hold. The door closed softly. She smiled. Billy had done a good job fixing it like she'd asked. He was doing a good job of fixing a lot of things around the campground lately. At times, he seemed eager for work. Just yesterday, he came to her on two occasions asking if there was anything else he could do. She had to admit, she was somewhat taken aback by this change. She was pleased. Ever since Billy came back from Baltimore... "Don't go there," she mouthed silently.

"Morning, Samantha," Rhonda chirped.

"Morning, Samantha," Mako echoed.

Samantha walked over and laid her hands on the counter. "How are things?" she asked, looking at the registration book.

Both girls couldn't help but stare at the ring on their boss's finger. They stared at it every chance they got since it appeared three weeks earlier. It was a huge solitaire diamond poised on a high setting with several smaller diamonds surrounding the gem. The goddess of all engagement rings, as Mako dubbed it.

The sight of such a diamond would normally bring a smile to even the shyest of the female gender. In this case, however, while there were indeed smiles on the two cousins, they were forced. It was the same reaction from others in the community. In most places, when someone got engaged, it was deemed a happy event. When someone became engaged and received a diamond such as Samantha's, it became even bigger news. The community of Avon, Cape Hatteras was no different. Because it was a small community and the local residents were a close-knit bunch, it could easily be expected that such news would cause a great excitement. However, as with the Green cousins, the community's reaction was reserved. There were the normal congratulatory remarks with hugs and demands to see the ring. There was also a noticeable reservation about the whole thing. No one said anything specific, at least not in public, but there were the looks, looks that asked: what the hell was going on here? It was also obvious that Samantha was not thrilled about getting married. Sure, she played it up when she had to, especially around her parents, but the other women in the community could see through the facade, Samantha's cousins included.

Samantha saw the downward gaze of the two girls, realized the target of their eyes, and pulled her hands off the counter in an embarrassing fashion. "Numbers look good for today?" she said.

Glad the subject was being changed, Rhonda said, "All full all around." That meant that both the campground and motel were at 100% capacity.

"Very good," Samantha said, nodding her approval. She hoped the trend continued. They needed a good season. To avoid additional conversation, she added, "I'll check the store."

The cousins looked at one another. They knew they'd get no more information. It had been that way for a couple of weeks now. Samantha was getting more and more withdrawn with each passing day. She asked fewer questions each morning. She made less small talk. Her smile seemed forced. Her posture had curves where there shouldn't be curves.

They were worried.

Samantha made her way into the store. She flipped on the lights as she crossed the archway. She stopped and looked at the display of biscuits and muffins. The order of both had been doubled of late, yet they still ran out by nine am. She shrugged. That would just have to do for now. She went behind the counter and turned toward the cash register. It was one of the old-fashion, antique types, but it still worked.

Since its invention, the cash register symbolized a business's success. Money in the drawer meant money in the bank. And money in the bank was good. Samantha's father always preached that the three most important aspects of starting any new business was location, location, location. The three most important aspects of keeping a business afloat was cash flow, cash flow, cash flow. She liked to tell her father that in a business such as theirs, reservations were an important factor also. Reservations symbolized future cash flow, something as important as what was going on today. She made a mental note to check the reservation book when she went back into the office. She hadn't done that in a few days.

The cousins remained behind the counter, looking through the daily paper. They exchanged glances nervously. They said nothing. There was no need. They were worried about their boss, yet there was nothing they could do. Samantha's behavior was so unlike what one would expect from a newly engaged lady.

43

Billy watched his sister from the archway that separated the store from the office. She was staring down at the reservation book, a distraught look on her face. He wasn't sure why the expression. Things had been going well. The campground was nearly full all the time and so was the motel. His sister was a worry wart, regardless how things were going. So were his parents. He, on the other hand, worried, but not about trivial things like reservations. He had bigger things on his mind, things he had not thought about lately, that is until Asshole showed up.

He continued to watch Samantha, who had yet to notice him. She was the biggest thing on his mind, always had been, always would be. Why did Robert have to show up? Sure, it was good to see his old friend, but...

He cut the thought off.

He watched in silence. Even with the morning just starting to break, there was plenty of light coming from the office, so it wasn't as if he was hiding in the darkness. He didn't sneak in the front door either. The two cousins greeted him with their usual playful enthusiasm, Mako leading the way as usual. He didn't stay around to chat as he usually did. He went directly into the store for a Mountain Dew and Nutty Buddy ice cream. He really wanted a biscuit, but was not about to mess up the display before the store officially opened. After dropping a couple dollars on the counter, he came back to the archway.

He turned his attention to the two cousins. Mako especially looked nice today, but she always looked good. Of the two, she was the prettier although not by much. He knew he was biased. He liked her the best. She liked him, too, or so he wanted to think.

He let his mind wander. A thin smile crossed his face. His eyes rolled out of focus. Why wasn't he more interested in them? Mako especially. After all, they were young, both were cute, both were unattached. They were easy ducks to hunt. His smile widened. Two birds with one shot. Wasn't that every man's fantasy? It had been a long time since he shot his gun, and he certainly had never shot two birds at once!

He continued standing in silence, slowly sipping his soda. The ice cream had been inhaled even before he came out from the store. The two cousins had turned their attention back to the newspaper spread out across the counter. Both were leaning forward, allowing their breasts to fall away from their chest walls. "God damn," he almost said aloud. There was a rumbling below his belt. It was a sensation he had not felt in a long time. Yes, it had been a long time since he'd been duck hunting.

He was about to consider the options in more detail when his sister suddenly sensed his presence. "Billy! How long have you been standing there?" she demanded.

His train of thought was broken. Hunting season was over, at least for the moment. He felt blood rushing to his face. "I stopped in to get a soda and an ice cream," he answered. "I put the money on the counter."

Samantha smiled. They used to tease each other about taking things from the store without paying for them. Per their father, no one got anything for free, their father included.

"How you doing?" he quickly added. He watched Samantha hesitate and look at the two cousins who were listening to the conversation.

"He came in when you were in the bathroom," Rhonda said quickly.

Her eyes returned to her brother. "Fine," Samantha answered.

"Everything okay?" Billy took a step into the office. "You look upset."

"Everything's okay," Samantha said. "We're booked for the next month, but reservations after that are coming in slower than I would have liked."

Worry wart, Billy said silently. Aloud, "I see."

Samantha tipped her head to the side. "If you just came in for a soda and ice cream, why are you still here?" She didn't say it, but it was unusual for him to hang around like this. She took it as a good sign.

"Uh..." Billy struggled to find something to say. It was his turn to look at the cousins.

They were both looking at him with their inevitable smiles. Mako innocently slid her chest across the counter as she straightened up. Making him suffer a little longer, she finally said, "He came in to ask me out on a date."

Billy's eyes widened.

"Bullshit," his sister said, using uncharacteristic language. Then catching a look from Mako, she smiled and said, "Okay then, where you two going?"

"He asked me out to dinner," Mako said.

"Yeah, and he said I could come too," Rhonda quickly injected. She too snapped into an upright position. The two cousins started to giggle.

"Is that right?" Samantha said, looking at her brother. "Where you taking 'em Billy?"

Billy was astonished at the sudden turn of events. One minute he was duck hunting. The next minute, the ducks were hunting him. At the same time, he was smart enough to know when he was trapped. After all, it was three to one. He smiled widely. "Wherever they want, I guess."

The giggles continued. Samantha gave her brother a nod of approval as well as a wink for good luck. Billy almost blushed at the gesture.

"Fuckin' A," he muttered.

44

"Tell me what's so important you had to pull me out of bed so damn early in the morning," Robert said, putting the BMW into reverse and backing out of the parking space.

Dennis Tucker had been waiting outside his apartment like he said when Robert showed up at seven am sharp. He had called Robert an hour earlier, waking him from a dead sleep, the first sound sleep Robert had in several days. Dennis refused to give details, telling Robert he had something hot and to pick him up in an hour. He also told the emergency room doc to be prepared to travel. He hung up the phone without saying anything more.

At first, Robert thought it was a prank call. Dennis was probably just getting home after working in the lab all night. The pathology resident did have a morbid sense of humor, but he wasn't a jokester. He also knew the payback for such a prank would be hell. So, Robert took the bait, got up, dressed, and did as he was told.

"You got gas?" Dennis said, hooking his seat belt.

Robert looked at the gas gauge. "I filled up yesterday."

"Good."

"Good? Where we going? This is my day off you know."

"You're the chief. You never get a day off," Dennis reminded.

"Isn't that the truth?" Robert stopped at the entrance to the apartment complex. The complex was one of the more upscale developments on the north-east side of Baltimore, a mile inside the city line. It catered to an affluent clientele, boasting many amenities such as a swimming pool, recreation room, and tennis courts. Robert wondered how a pathology resident could afford such a place, but never asked. Dennis did tell him once that he wasn't studying medicine for the money.

Robert did ask why he drove an old beat-up Volkswagen Beetle, to which Dennis responded, "Got her cheap, doors are already dented, good gas mileage, low insurance, and I don't have to worry about anyone stealing her."

"You still haven't told me where we're going," Robert said, turning out of the apartment complex.

"Ocean City," Tucker said nonchalantly.

"Ocean City! What the hell for?"

"We're going to look at some property."

"Property...for what?"

"To buy."

"Who to buy?"

Dennis looked at his chauffeur. "You certainly ask a lot of questions."

Robert met the gaze a second before snapping his eyes back on the road. "You certainly aren't providing much information."

"In due time, my friend. In due time."

Robert knew that pressing Dennis was pointless. They stopped at a nearby 7-11 for coffee and a sugar fix before heading north on Charles Street. Traffic was heavy as one might expect for a summer Saturday morning and the radio warned of a thirty-minute wait at the Chesapeake Bay Bridge. Hearing that just as they pulled onto the Beltway, Robert announced his intentions of taking the northern route via Delaware.

Dennis had no objection as he didn't know any difference. He was from the Midwest and all he knew about Baltimore was how to get from his apartment to the hospital and back. This would be his first time seeing the Atlantic Ocean. He didn't tell Robert this, however. The focus was not going to be on the water, but rather various buildings in the area. He had a list of specific places he wanted to look at tucked away in his bag in the back seat. He had a theory, and like most hypotheses, field work was required to prove or disprove the theory.

In the meantime, he pulled his seat back and closed his eyes. He was asleep in less than a minute.

45

The trip North on Interstate 95, onto Route 1 and into Delaware was uneventful. Traffic was heavy but, as expected those on the highway were anxious to get to the beach, so for the most part, traffic moved at or above the posted speed. This let Robert set the cruise control and relax while Dennis slept. That was fine with Robert as he wasn't interested in making a lot of small talk anyway. He had too much on his mind. Besides, he was sure the pathologist wasn't going to let Robert in on what this trip was about until they reached their destination, so he tried to enjoy the peace and quiet, and to think.

Not wanting to put the time to waste, he made a mental list of topics and started at the top. He wished Dennis was driving so he could get out his legal pad. Then he remembered that Dennis driving would not be conducive for thinking, but holding on for dear life. As meticulous and careful as his pathology friend was in the lab, Dennis was just the opposite behind the wheel of a motor vehicle.

Robert looked over at his passenger and let the thought pass.

He focused on the number one item on his list. How did he really feel about Samantha? He started with an answer immediately but told himself to take his time, to think the answer through. While he couldn't claim he fell in love the first time he saw her five years ago, he certainly was infatuated. It wasn't long, however, before infatuation changed to a stronger, more powerful descriptor. He figured that within a couple weeks the L word started to come into play. Once the spark was lit, the fire grew quickly. It was new. It was exciting. It was wonderful. He had no doubt in his mind he was in love. And while she never said the word, her behavior betrayed her.

Then the summer was over. He returned to Baltimore, to school, to his training. It was something he had to do. He knew it. She tried to understand and remained supportive. Their last night together was difficult. There was a tension. Both felt it. Neither spoke about it. The issue was their future. It had yet to be addressed. Yes, all summer long, the topic of their future was never broached. Nor was it discussed that night.

The next day they said their goodbyes and Robert left to go back to school.

Now, five years later, he was back. Buried emotions had resurfaced. Like the shipwrecked *The Lady Hatteras*, feelings had been washed ashore and lay exposed. The question: had his feelings changed? Finding the answer was proving difficult. Except for the progression of his training, his life had changed little. Other than an occasional one-night stand with a nurse or fellow resident, the social in social life was non-existent. He told himself he did not have time for it. He told himself he had to stay focused on completing his training, completing his residency. He told himself a lot of things. Now, he knew they were basically all lies. And if not actual lies, then damn good excuses. Now that he had returned to Hatteras, he realized his feelings toward Samantha had only grown stronger. But while his life had not changed much, Samantha's certainly had. And therein lay the conflict. Could he still love her considering these events?

He chuckled aloud, swallowing the noise quickly so as not to disturb his passenger. The question wasn't could he still love her, but rather did she still love him? The answer to that came rather quickly as well: obviously not. She was marrying someone else.

He cut the thought off, telling himself not to go with that assumption. While most people married because they were in love, Sam did not answer the question that way. She didn't even hint at any sort of emotional attraction between herself and Goldberg. On the contrary, when questioned about why she was marrying the man, she responded with a sharpness in her voice, telling Robert to figure it out. Which raised the additional question of what did she mean? Robert continued to sense there was more to it than a smartass response. Robert continued to feel she was pleading for help, that she did indeed want him to find the answer of why she was getting married.

There was something else about her voice when they were talking; something that had been bothering him awhile now, yet he had been unable to grasp. He had heard it before, specifically when she was talking about Billy. She said she was fearful of his mental status.

Miles passed. EZ-Pass tolls paid. Dennis remained sound asleep, not snoring but breathing heavily.

Robert wondered when his friend last had such a good sound sleep. He guessed it had been awhile. Robert had no doubt if their roles were reversed and Dennis wasn't a crazy driver, the emergency room resident would be doing the same. He sucked in a couple deep breaths and tried to ignore his own fatigue. The last thing he wanted was to fall asleep at the wheel. One of the things he feared most about working the hours he did in the ER was...

Something suddenly crossed his mind—*one of the things he feared most*. There was that word again, *fear*. "Jesus Christ," he muttered aloud. Samantha was not only fearful for Billy, she was also afraid for herself. But afraid of what? Or who?

"Let lying dogs sleep," Billy had said, and everything would be okay. Only, the dogs were waking up, so now there was a problem. Using Dennis's analogy, there were a lot of questions, a lot of dots floating around, but they could be connected by answering the basic core question of why was Samantha really marrying Arthur Goldberg?

Traffic ahead started to slow. Robert tapped the brake pedal to disengage the cruise control. The action was enough to bring Dennis out of his sleep. He sat up, rubbed his eyes and looked at his watch. "We making good time?" he asked.

"Yes, *we* are," Robert jested.

"I offered to drive," Dennis reminded.

"That you did."

Dennis looked out the side window. A sign announced a rest stop two miles ahead. "Pull in there if you don't mind. I gotta take a leak."

"If I do mind?"

The pathology resident smiled. "Consider the alternative, my friend. Consider the alternative."

It would prove to be a profound piece of advice.

46

The detective team was back on the road fifteen minutes later, Robert a cup of coffee in hand, Dennis a Mountain Dew. Once the cruise control was reset, Robert looked over at his partner. "When are you going to tell me what this is all about?"

Dennis didn't hesitate. "When I'm convinced I know what I'm talking about."

Again, pushing the point would be useless. Just like in the hospital waiting for lab results, they weren't released until they were checked, and oftentimes rechecked. In the meantime, Robert would have to be patient, something difficult for an A-type personality to do.

An hour later, they passed through Lewes, Delaware and entered Rehoboth. Dennis reached into the backseat and pulled a piece of paper from his bag. Glancing at it, he said, "There are three properties in Rehoboth I want to check out, two in Dewey Beach, two in Bethany and three in Fenwick. Then if we have time, I have a pile in Ocean City. I suspect though, we won't have to go that far to prove my theory." The towns cited were all close to one another, separated at the most by a several miles of preserved duned beaches.

Robert told himself to keep his curiosity under control. He simply said, "Just tell me where to go."

Dennis did.

The middle of the afternoon found the two residents perched at a bar in West Fenwick. After each downed half a beer and Robert ordered a basket of wings, Dennis spread a couple sheets of paper across the bar. They were basically real estate listings that Dennis had made various notes on. Aloud, he said, "We looked at what, ten…eleven properties so far today, and what did they all have in common?"

Robert took another sip of beer. "They were all for sale."

"More specifically," Dennis coached.

"They were all listed by Goldberg Reality," Robert answered. The properties in question included a five-store strip mall, a couple standalone businesses, a house, and the rest were condos in various buildings.

"Correct," Dennis said. "But what you don't know is that every one of them is in or near foreclosure." He paused as the bartender, as a middle-aged chap with a ponytail named Bobby served their wings. Beers were refilled and Dennis continued, but not before several wings were devoured. "Each property we looked at was financed by a mortgage company called Resort Mortgage Corporation."

"Let me guess," Robert injected, wiping sauce from his lips and dousing the burning in his mouth with a swallow of beer. "Resort Mortgage Corporation is owned and operated by one Arthur Goldberg."

Dennis nodded affirmatively.

Robert continued. "Are you suggesting some sort of a scam?

"Maybe not an illegal one, but a scam nonetheless."

"You have my attention," Robert said, daring for another wing. He wished he had ordered them mild instead of hot.

Dennis, on the other hand, didn't seem to be reacting the same way. No fire in his mouth. No sweat on his brow. He ate as he talked. "I don't know all the details, nor do I think they're all that important, least for now." He stopped for another wing and to organize his thoughts. "I think it works something like this, Goldberg Realty goes about its daily business just like any other real estate agency. They list, they show, they sell; and like a lot of real estate companies down here at the beach, they also handle rental properties. They've been doing it quite successfully for many years. However, through all this, they keep their eyes out for what I'll call those special clients, defined as people who really want to buy something they really can't afford. Under normal circumstances, real estate agents and or the mortgage company simply tell the prospective client they won't qualify for that amount of money. Advice is provided to look at something less expensive. Goldberg Realty, however, doesn't always do that, at least that's what I suspect. When they get one of those special clients who are underqualified but are intent on a particular property, they offer to look for alternative financing opportunities."

"Let me guess," Robert interrupted. "Resort Mortgage Corporation just happens to be one such alternative."

"RMC, as it's called, sells normal mortgages for want of a better word. They also have an arm that specializes in what is known in the industry as a special needs client."

"Handicapped financially," Robert mocked.

"Exactly!" Dennis emptied his beer.

Silence fell as they finished of the wings and another beer each. Robert looked up at one of the many TV screens hung around the bar. A meteorologist on the weather channel was pointing to the national map, describing a cold front over the Midwest headed toward the east coast. The TV next to this sported ESPN. An outdoor channel was next. The two flat screens in the other direction from where the two residents were sitting showed a trivia game and a poker game respectively. Robert scanned the screens again and realized an interesting phenomenon. You couldn't hear any of them. There was music playing in the background, a Bon Jovi song. Robert just shook his head side to side. As if reading his mind, Dennis, who had also been scanning the surroundings, said, "Things have certainly changed since we were running around like loose chickens."

"Certainly have," Robert acknowledged. Symbolic of a lot of things in his life, he added to himself. After the bartender cleared the dishes and refilled their beers, Robert focused back on his drinking partner. "But why?" he questioned.

Dennis wiped the foam from his mouth. "I'm assuming you're asking why Goldberg finances such risky ventures. Again, I'm speculating, but I suspect a high return on his investment. For what may appear to be a risky venture, I don't really think it is. He only does this with rental properties and second homes, no primary residence." Robert tipped his head to the side indicating the need for further explanation. Dennis continued. "People aren't as apt to go out on a limb financially if it is the home they are going to live in. When investing in a second home, a rental property or even a business, however, they're more willing to take the risk."

"In other words, an easier sell," Robert commented.

Dennis smiled. "You're catching on my friend."

"I still don't understand the *why* behind it all."

The pathologist continued. "They sell the house, make the commission on the sale and make the money on the settlement. They're also making the interest on the mortgage itself, which is at a higher than normal rate because of the risk. Then, when the buyer falls behind, they lower the boom, otherwise known as foreclosure."

"I assume the contracts are written that way to make it easy for Goldberg to foreclose," Robert said.

"I assume that, too."

As Robert digested the information, he had a small epiphany. A combination of a smile and disgust crossed his face. "He sells a property today, makes money off it and then forecloses in a number of months or years, then he can sell the same property again."

"In the real estate business, it's called flipping," Dennis explained, "only instead of buying and selling properties, which is what most people do, Goldberg buys and sells mortgages."

"Is what he does legal?"

"Again, we're making assumptions, but I suspect it is all very legal, made so by how the contract is written."

"Which nobody fully reads," Robert injected.

"When you're hot-to-trot to buy something at the beach, you don't always read the fine print," Dennis said. "How many forms does a patient have to sign when they get registered in the emergency room?"

"I don't know," Robert answered. "Three or four probably."

"How many patients read those forms?"

"Point well taken," Robert acknowledged. "What happens if Goldberg doesn't get a chance to foreclose? What if the buyers keep up with the payments on the property?"

"No big deal. He still made real estate fees, money on the settlement and is holding papers with an above average interest rate. If he gets enough of these, he can bundle and sell them to someone else. There are mortgage companies in this country that do nothing but buy, bundle, and resell mortgages."

Beers were downed and glasses refilled before Robert spoke again. "What does all this have to do with Sam marrying Goldberg?"

"I'm not sure," Dennis said.

"But you have a theory, right?"

Dennis nodded and explained.

47

The door opened, causing bells to jingle which announced yet another customer entering the store. Samantha forced herself to be positive. It had been busy all afternoon. The early evening wasn't proving to be any better. Then she corrected her line of thinking. Busy was good. It was when the doorbells stopped ringing that she should worry.

Samantha forced a smile and spun around from where she was filling out an order form for next week's delivery. "Hello. Welcome to..." She stopped as she saw Robert standing at the counter. "What are you doing here?" She quickly looked around to make sure no one else was in the store.

"I'm so glad to see you, too," Robert said, failing to hide his sarcasm.

Her mouth opened, and then closed. "I guess I deserve that...but you could have told me you were coming."

"I didn't know until this afternoon." Before she could query him further, he quickly added. "I'll explain later. What time do you get off?"

"The cousins usually get here around 9:00."

"Can we talk then?"

She sensed a level of stress in his voice she had not noticed before. "Sure."

"I'll see you then."

She hesitated. "Is there something wrong?"

"I'm not sure," he admitted.

48

The sky was clear, the moon, full. A bright glow of light fanned out across the water. The seas were calm. Gentle two-foot swells caressed the sand, carrying broken shells up, washing others away. There was a faint southerly breeze that helped cool the summer air and keep the mosquitos and other bloodthirsty insects at bay. Samantha stood at the breakwater; her body silhouetted by the moonlit sky. She wore a plain pale blue tee shirt and hip hugging white shorts. Her hair, teased by the breeze, swayed north and south as the waves moved east and west. While there had been many changes in their lives, one thing had not. She was as beautiful as ever. Watching a few feet away, Robert realized he was in love with her as much today as he had been five years earlier. That was the good part. The bad was that he could do nothing about it, at least for the time being.

Samantha waited until a wave cleared from the beach and then slowly turned in his direction. She looked at him, his facial expression hard to read in the dim light. Finally, she spoke, "What's this all about, Robert? I have a strong suspicion there's something you're not telling me."

Robert had debated all afternoon and into the early evening what he was going to say. He knew this was the moment, the moment he had been looking forward to and dreading at the same time. Ironically enough, for all the thinking he had done, he had yet to make a decision as to which direction to go with the conversation. Also, ironically, it was Samantha who made the decision for him as she said, "And I don't want a bunch of bullshit, either. I want to know what's going on and I want to know now. There's a reason you and your friend Dennis are down here and it's not just to catch some sun. Let's have it!"

It was interesting that her mood and the tone of her voice were in such contrast to the serenity of the visual scene before him. Robert looked away to clear his mind, to gain some confidence. Looking back, he said, "Alright, I'll lay it on the line as simply as I can, and without any sugar coating." He paused briefly. "Your boyfriend, Arthur Goldberg is a pedophile. On top of that, he's also a murderer and possibly a repeat one at that. And that doesn't even begin to talk about the way he runs his real estate business. That's a story in itself."

Robert anticipated that if he chose the lay it all on the line approach, Samantha would immediately deny the accusations. He also anticipated she would get angry and even call him crazy. What he did not anticipate was the level at which the fury would flow. He anticipated a storm. What he got was a hurricane. She ranted. She raved. She used words he had never heard her use before. He stood still, his feet embedded in the sand, taking the storm like one of those reporters who stood in a hurricane to tell everyone what they could see. Yet through it all, there was something missing in her rage. It was like an actor on stage who spoke the words correctly yet didn't convey the meaning the way they were intended.

The abrupt end of the storm broke his concentration. Even in the dim light he could see her neck veins bulging and the sweat on her brow. Suddenly her voice was calm. There was a high-pitched hissing sound as she said, "Tell me Robert, how did you come to this conclusion?"

He hesitated, telling himself things really couldn't get any worse. "Evidence," he said matter-of-factly.

"Evidence! What kind of evidence?"

"DNA." Before she could question him further, he quickly summarized everything he knew. He told her of Bobby's claim about the boy on the boat that day; that the boy never left the boat when they returned to the dock. He told her that Arthur Goldberg was one of the passengers on the boat that day. He told her that there were a lot of unanswered questions surrounding Captain Willey's death and of the weirdness of the marina owner's behavior the time he and Samantha visited *Lady Hatteras II*. Then he told her what he found on the boat and how he went back later at night to collect samples, and how he also checked out Bobby's truck the same night Samantha poked him with the bat. He explained how he then took all the samples he collected to Baltimore and had his friend Dennis examine them in his lab.

Sam stood quietly, her breathing still hard; the veins in her neck, however, much less prominent. She was obviously trying to digest the information. She was obviously trying to do it in an objective non-emotional manner. She was struggling with both tasks. Finally, she said, "Just how did you link Arthur to all this? I know you said DNA."

Robert understood the question clearly. "I assume you have no problem with the fact that he was aboard the boat that day?"

"I guess that's a given," Sam said."

Robert continued. "Then it was the saliva from a cigarette butt. That DNA matched the DNA found in the boy's underwear."

Samantha's eyes widened. "A cigarette butt? And how, pray tell, did you get that?"

This was the area Robert struggled with the most when trying to decide how much to reveal if the opportunity arose. Deciding that since the storm was over, he'd keep with the no-holds-barred strategy. He said, "From the parking lot outside his office in Fenwick Island."

Her widened eyes turned to a squint. Before she could ask the next obvious question, he continued, "I was across the street the night you and he stopped in the office a few minutes. To be specific, it was the night of that hospital fundraiser. When you two came out, he was smoking a cigarette. Just as he got into the car, he flipped it onto the ground. I recovered it a short time later."

The eye squinting worsened. The bulging neck veins returned. Robert suddenly realized that what he thought was the end of the storm was only the eye of the hurricane. The second half of the fury was about to begin.

His meteorological skills were right on. An instant later, the winds again increased, starting with, "How dare you spy on me, you son-of-a-bitch?" It only got worse after that. The back side of the storm lasted for a full sixty seconds. It ended with Samantha totally out of breath as she spouted, "And now, Robert, I want you off this island, and I don't ever want to see you here again. Do...you...understand?!"

Robert looked at her a few seconds before he turned and walked away. Again, he expected a reaction, but this was ridiculous. He had had enough. He climbed into his SUV and started the engine. He was about to shift the vehicle into gear when he glanced up and saw Samantha's face peering through the side window. She still had that look of anger. Her neck veins were still bulging as sweat poured down her brow. Her voice was softer this time, although with just as much venom. "For the record, Robert, Arthur does not smoke." With that, she turned and walked away.

Robert looked out the front windshield toward the ocean. The moon was still bright, the sky was clear. Two-foot swells gently basted the wreckage of *The Lady Hatteras*. The storm was finally over.

Or rather *this* storm was over. Hurricane season had just begun.

49

Dennis looked across the table in silence, chewing slowly on a slice of pizza. His right hand held a pen with which he had been taking notes. His left hand twirled the straw in his cup of Mountain Dew. Obviously trying to hide a smile, he spoke. "She really said all that stuff to you?"

Robert nodded. "I didn't even get to the part of why she was marrying the scumbag." They were in a pizza shop in Nags Head where Robert had just finished telling Dennis the story of the hurricane named Samantha. "It was quite a speech."

Dennis tipped his head to the side.

Noticing the change in expression, Robert said, "What's the matter?"

"Nothing..." the pathology resident said defensively. "It's just that..." He glanced down at the notes on his paper. "You said something about this before, and just now that makes me wonder."

"Wonder what?" Robert asked.

"About people being hard on the surface, but soft underneath. I think it was when we were talking about that kid that got shot. Remember that?"

Robert nodded.

"I think there's a similarity with Samantha. You said something was missing when she was yelling at you; something about her eyes. Now you just said it was a good speech. It makes me wonder. It may have been a good speech, but was it a good performance? Hard on the surface, soft underneath."

"I'm not sure I follow you?" Robert said.

Dennis sat up straight. He looked around the diner which was emptying out rapidly from the late dinner crowd. He took a gulp of soda. "If a professional actor gave the same speech as Sam, you wouldn't be wondering what was missing. That's because his or her facial expressions, including the eyes, would be a part of the presentation, the performance so to speak. An amateur, on the other hand, might leave some of these nuances out. It's a subtle line between professional and amateur, but I think it was there."

"Huh?"

"She gave a good speech, but her performance wasn't at the same level," Dennis explained.

"So?" Robert queried.

"So, you didn't buy everything she was saying."

"Or..." Robert hesitated as he struggled to put the ideas together.

Dennis smiled. "I think you got it, buddy. Go ahead."

Robert continued. "Maybe she gave a great speech, but her performance was telling me something else."

Dennis's smiled dissipated. He leaned forward across the table. "If that isn't the case, why did she even bother telling you that Goldberg didn't smoke? It was like she was throwing you a bone, a clue, something to keep you interested, maybe even to make you go back."

Robert ignored that line of thinking and went directly to the next question that popped into his mind. "If Arthur Goldberg doesn't smoke, then it couldn't have been him I saw with Samantha that night."

"You said you identified him when he got out of the Escalade."

"I may have been wrong."

"Perhaps you made a fatal mistake in the investigative business," Dennis said. "You assumed when you should have only presumed. Another way of looking at it, you decided definitively it was him when you should have concluded it was possibly, even probably him. I suspect seeing Sam seriously distracted your attention."

"Then who the fuck was she with?" Robert spouted. He quickly looked around to make sure no one heard his outburst.

Dennis ignored the verbal snafu. "Someone who looks like Goldberg, someone who smokes, someone Goldberg would trust with his Escalade. Finally, someone Samantha would get in a vehicle with."

The two residents' eyes met. They both had the same thought at the same time. Robert did the honors vocally, "It was Goldberg, all right; only not Arthur Goldberg."

"Bingo," Dennis said, this time without his usual smile.

50

It was decided in case Samantha was nearby or had access to Billy's cell phone, Dennis would make the call to Billy. It was answered on the fourth ring. "Yeah," the voice on the other end said. It was obviously not Samantha.

"Billy, this is Dennis, Dennis Tucker. I'm the friend of Robert's you met a few days ago, remember. We both like Mountain Dew?"

"Yeah, Doc. I remember. You're the one with the big ass office. How you doing?"

Dennis laughed while looking at Robert, who was sitting on the other side of the pathologist's desk. "Fine, and you?"

There was a moment's silence. "I'm okay, but I don't know what the hell you guys did to my sister. She's been a real bear lately."

"Actually, we didn't do anything to your sister," Dennis said. "I'm afraid she's done it all herself."

There was a soft chuckle. "I can believe that."

Dennis continued quickly. "Billy, are you somewhere we can talk?"

"I'm out on the beach fishing."

Dennis again glanced at Robert. Who nodded. Dennis continued. "Billy, I'm in my office. Robert's here with me. Is it okay if I put you on the speaker?"

"You mean like one of those conference calls?"

"Sort of."

"Cool."

A moment later, "Hey Billy, Robert here. How you doing?"

"What the fuck did you do to my sister?" Billy spouted with a tease in his voice.

"Robert here's upset enough Billy," Dennis said. "Let's not make it any worse."

There was a pause followed by a chuckle. "Whatever. Hey Bobby, fish are biting real good tonight. Why don't you come on down?"

"You on the beach?" Robert asked.

"Fishing, too!"

"Good for you."

"Bad for the fish."

Robert looked at Dennis with a smile. Aloud, he said. "Listen, we need to ask you about the people that were on the boat that day. You acknowledged Arthur Goldberg was there. Who else was on board?"

There was a short pause. "Initially, there was Goldberg, another older guy who I never saw before and ain't seen since, and the guy Goldberg always refers to as his banker. I didn't remember it when I talked to you before, but now that I think about it, he's been out with us a couple times with Goldberg."

"His banker. That's all he says?" Dennis asked.

"That's the only way he's ever been introduced."

"What's he look like?"

Another pause ensured. "Actually, sort of like Goldberg himself, only a couple years older, more gray hair, less of it, too."

"Like an older brother."

"Could be, but I don't think so."

"Why do you say that?"

"Goldberg may be a schmuck, but he's always courteous and polite. This guy is rude, condescending and anything else you want to throw his way, a real asshole if you know what I mean."

"I see," Robert said.

Forcing the excitement from his voice, Dennis said, "Anything else in particular about this guy?"

"No, not really. Like I said, he's a real asshole. On top of that, he smokes like a fiend, which really irritated Captain Willey. But he didn't seem to give a shit."

The two residents' eyes again met. "Bingo again," Dennis mouthed silently.

51

It was the first time Robert could remember ever beating Dennis to the cafeteria. Usually when the call was made and the time was set, it was all Robert could do to make it even close. Tonight, however, the ER was uncommonly quiet. Robert knew, however, that the non-busyness was simply the calm before the storm. This was Baltimore and it was Friday night.

He looked around to make sure his friend wasn't sitting at a different table. Still no Dennis, Robert got in line for their food. There was no need to ask Dennis what he wanted. He was quite the creature of habit. When the food was ready, Robert went over to their usual table which had just been vacated. Wiping some crumbs onto the floor, he sat down and started to eat. He knew better than to wait because the second he did, his beeper would go off. The long-awaited lunch would have to go in the trash.

He chewed quickly, his mind abuzz with thoughts, mostly in the form of questions. The problem, every time a question was answered, a new one developed. The overriding question of late, however, was where should he go from here? Especially with the plot having thickened with the discovery, surmised and then verified by Dennis Tucker's investigation that Arthur Goldberg had a brother. All fingers pointed to this brother being the person who assaulted the boy on the boat, but what role did Arthur Goldberg play? What about the mysterious death of Captain Willey, and his wife for that matter? As the plot thickened, where did Samantha fit in all this? And was he overreacting to her supposed plea for help? Was he reading more into her facial expressions as an excuse to stay involved in the case, to stay involved in her life? Or was he just kidding himself? After all, Samantha made it quite clear she never wanted to see him again.

"How dare you spy on me?" she had said.

"I wasn't spying on you," he tried to explain. She was an accessary finding; quite a surprising one, but not the main target of his sleuthing. She refused to listen.

So back to the question of where to go from here? There was a part of him that wanted to continue the journey, even though he recognized he had little insight as to where the journey would lead and what dangers lurked in the shadows along the way. The other side said it was time to throw in the towel and move on with his life. It was like performing CPR. There came a point in every resuscitation when it was time to stop. To use the medical jargon, it was time to *call it*. You can't squeeze blood out of a turnip. You can't squeeze life out of a heart that didn't want to beat any longer. Was that the case with

Samantha? Was she a thing of the past? She had resurfaced for a brief period. Now she was gone again. Was it time to call it?

He was beginning to think so.

And then Dennis showed up with some very interesting information about Samantha's parents.

52

While past images were still embedded in his mind, it had been a long time since Robert had seen the real thing. As he remembered, the view from the top of Hatteras Light was spectacular. He was still trying to catch his breath from the walk skyward, but he ignored that as he spun around to take in the sights. The sun, an hour off the western horizon, set out vast rays of amber light across the entire area. Hatteras Inlet leading out to the ocean was churned up as always. The ocean itself sported a few swells, but overall was calm. Robert could see a couple boats coming off the eastern horizon heading toward the inlet. They were too far away to see if they had any flags flying, indicating fish on board or fish that had been tagged and released. There were a few stragglers on the beach, unwilling to call it a day. They would no doubt be there until darkness descended entirely. A few beach vehicles could also be seen at the point. They would no doubt be there all night as they waited for the tide to change.

"Pretty cool, ain't it?" Billy said, slowing turning in a circle.

"It's been a long time," Robert said. "Last time I was up here a couple months ago, we couldn't see a damn thing."

"It was really foggy that day," Billy remembered.

"Yes, it was."

The two continued to look around. Finally, Billy said, "So what's up that you needed a haircut so bad?" Dennis called Billy on his cell phone to tell him Robert needed an emergency haircut.

Robert struggled during the whole trip from Baltimore to Hatteras with what to say and how to say it. After all, he had the same self-debate regarding his last conversation with Samantha and had chosen the *all cards on the table approach*, only to have the approach blow up in his face. He was much more cautious now. "How's your sister?" he started.

Billy lit a cigarette. "Still acting weird."

"How so?"

"She's become very quiet…almost withdrawn."

"A role reversal there, don't you think?" Robert ventured cautiously.

Billy shrugged his shoulders. "Whatever."

"You'd think she'd be excited about the wedding," Robert suggested.

"She really hasn't said much about it."

"No date?"

Billy again gave a shrug. "Not yet."

Robert continued. "I would think…"

Billy gave Robert a hard look. "You would think a lot of things," he interrupted. "But they just ain't happening." He took a long drag on his cigarette. "My parents don't even seem excited. I always thought it would be a big deal the day my sister got married, but it's almost like they don't even approve, although nobody has said anything."

Robert contemplated the next step. He decided to share what Dennis had recently discovered. "Are you aware your parents are trying to develop a big resort down at the south end of the island?"

"They've been talking about doing something for years, but all it's ever been is talk."

Robert decided to continue giving information. "Evidently, for the past year or so it has been more than talk. About fourteen months ago they purchased several acres of land on the northern edge of Buxton." Robert pointed out one of the small windows to the area in question. To the unknowing eye, it was simply another piece of sand. To a more trained observer, small stakes with little red flags could be seen scattered around the area. They were surveyor stakes, meaning construction activity was on the horizon.

"They've mentioned it…not anything specific though."

"Evidently, they've applied for permits to build a pretty good-sized hotel and shopping complex. There's even a couple restaurants planned."

Billy continued to look down at the piece of land. "It can't be too big a hotel, there're height restrictions down here."

"They've applied for a variance. They want to do four stories."

Billy shrugged. "It's only a matter of time before something like that happens anyway. There's only so much building outward you can do before you have to start going up." Billy again looked at Robert. "You still haven't told me..."

It was Robert's turn to interrupt. "Your parents are in financial trouble, Billy." From all indications, they are very close to being bankrupt."

Billy's interest suddenly perked up. "Bankrupt...meaning they could lose the property."

"And more."

"The campground, too?"

"It's possible, yes."

"How?"

Robert explained. "They evidently took out a hefty second mortgage on the campground to purchase the land down here. That note came due a couple months ago. The idea was to be building by now, using the construction loan to cover their expenses. Only, as so often happens I guess, they've run into a lot of red tape regarding the permits needed to even begin the construction, much less dealing with the height restrictions."

Billy was now no longer interested in the sights. He was focused on Robert. "Why...the red tape, that is?"

"I don't know, but I have my suspicions."

"Who'd they buy the property from?"

Robert hesitated. "Arthur Goldberg."

"And he's holding the...what do you call it...the note?"

Robert nodded.

"I don't understand. He can't be doing that to my parents. He's marrying my sister. He's..." The now totally confused brother of Samantha stopped in mid-sentence. "What the hell's going on, Billy?"

"I'm not sure. I was hoping you could shed some light on it."

After a long period of silence, Billy spoke, "What's it called when one family gives something to another family when two people are planning to get married?"

"You're talking about a dowry?"

"Yeah, that's it." Billy paused again. "I did overhear Samantha talking about that to my parents once. She didn't say anything specific, but I think that was the gist of the conversation."

"Goldberg's going to give your parents the property for their daughter's hand?"

"Something like that, if that's how it works," Billy said. After a pause, he added, "You think he's forcing my sister to marry him?"

"I'm not sure if force is the right word. I'm willing to bet though, it's close."

"Blackmailing her maybe?"

Robert considered the possibility. "I've never thought about it in those terms, but you may be right, Billy."

"If my sister doesn't marry him, Arthur Goldberg is going to take my parent's property, down here and the campground."

"He could foreclose on the mortgage, yes."

"Isn't that illegal?"

"Blackmail is illegal, but knowing Goldberg, I suspect he has it all laid out nice and neat in the contract. I suspect if you confronted him, he'd simply say he was making your family a good offer."

"One they can't refuse," Billy added.

"They can, but..."

"Maybe he is a scumbag like you said."

"Of the worst kind," Robert added.

"One thing I don't understand," Billy continued. "Why does he want to marry my sister, anyway? He obviously doesn't love her, or he wouldn't act like this. I seriously doubt whether she has serious feelings for him, otherwise she'd be excited about getting married. There's gotta be something going on we don't know about."

"I agree. It's just another missing piece of the puzzle," Robert said. "Anyway, what do you think we should do?"

"Fuck if I know. You're the doctor," Billy replied. "By the way, Bobby, how'd you get all this information...you know, about the property and all that?"

"Actually, Dennis dug it up. Most of it is public record," Robert said.

"My parents being in financial trouble is in the public record!"

"No, that took a little more digging, but I wouldn't put anything past Dennis. If he wants to find out something, he'll find it."

"Smart guy?"

"Very smart."

The sun was fading into the western horizon. The last beachgoers were packing up. The vehicles out on the point were bedded down for the night. Flames could be seen from charcoal grills being lit for dinner. The boats that were offshore were navigating their way through the inlet. Robert saw no fish flags on any of them. "Was that an omen?" he almost said aloud.

The two decided it was time to part ways. Robert made Billy promise not to say a word to Samantha about the visit or anything that was discussed. Billy assured him there was no problem there, verbalizing that he valued Samantha's life too much. They shook hands in the parking lot, both agreeing to stay in touch. Robert watched as Billy got in his truck and drove out onto the beach. He said he might go down to the point and fish awhile. When the vehicle was out of sight over the dunes, Robert climbed into his Beemer. It had been a long trip down to Hatteras. It was going to be a longer trip home.

He turned on the radio in hopes of making the time pass quicker. It did little good though as his mind was far away from the country music, the only station he could find at the present. He chuckled as a self-defense mechanism. The more he was getting involved, the more complicated, the more confusing, the whole scenario became. Then that inevitable question of should he even be involved kept popping up. Samantha's harsh words scrolled across his mind. At the same time, another word, bigger and bolder, also flowed by. *Blackmail* sounded so harsh.

Questions continued without answers. The miles passed slowly. A popular Kenny Rogers tune started to play. The lyrics of *The Gambler* poured out of the SUV's speakers.

"You gotta know when to hold 'em, know when to fold 'em..."

Was it time to stop doing CPR on a broken heart?

53

The final weeks of the summer passed quickly. Baltimore's murder rate was threatening to break the record set the year before. This number was well publicized, making the local news on a near daily basis. What was often overlooked were the other traumas that went along with a high murder rate. For every person killed in the city, there were multiple attempts that failed. Thus near-fatal shootings, stabbings and other violent acts were on the rise as well. Sociologists argued there were many reasons for such behavior. Those working in inner-city emergency rooms knew there was really only one. The hotter the weather, the more restless the natives. And this was proving to be quite a hot summer.

Robert was getting so much experience in trauma, he considered applying for a trauma fellowship across town at the University of Maryland's Shock Trauma Center. The thought was short-lived as he decided enough was enough. He had been officially in school for over twenty-five straight years. It was time he started working for a living.

Besides that, he was exhausted. His year as Chief Resident was going well. However, he couldn't say the same for his underlings. There was a first-year resident he had to counsel earlier in the year about sexual harassment. The resident had been on good behavior until a new nurse started working in the ER. She was tall, thin, and built to die for. And the resident was dying. He had been trying to get her attention for a couple weeks, flirting with no reciprocation. Finally, late one night during a lull in the action, he went up and put his arm around her shoulder. She politely asked him to take it off, not once, but twice. Witnesses verified this conversation. Then she told him quite bluntly that she considered his actions a threat and asked him one last time to remove his arm. Again, verified by witnesses. By this time he had moved closer to her and tightened his grip. He laughed at her last comment, saying, "If I'm a threat, what are you going to do about it, babe?"

She showed him. Turns out if one reviewed her resume, there was mentioned under hobbies: martial arts.

Besides a broken wrist, a separated shoulder and a concussion, the resident also had his ego severely damaged. But he wasn't finished. He immediately filed criminal charges against her for assault and threatened to file a civil suit for damages as well, seeing that she caused injuries that were hindering the continuing of his training. She also filed criminal charges, only she was a bit savvier than he. She claimed attempted sexual assault. She also immediately filed a civil complaint to the tune of one million dollars, asserting she was so traumatized by the whole affair, she might never be able to work again in her chosen profession of nursing.

The whole thing was quite sticky for many weeks. Everyone was on edge. The normal pressure relieving banter that went on amongst staff was noticeably absent, which only added to the stress of the ER. Both parties were put on leave while an investigation ensued. It was finally decided by all objective parties, the resident's attorney included, that while the nurse was overzealous in her actions, she did give the resident fair warning before acting. Again, witnesses verified all this. The kicker was that the whole thing was caught on security tape. The resident's goose was cooked.

As happens many times in these cases, a quick settlement was reached, criminal charges were dropped, the resident transferred to a program somewhere in the Midwest, for personal reasons. As for nurse Kung Fu, she transferred to the ICU, and showed up a few weeks later with pictures of a new house she was building in the suburbs. It took a few days, but life slowly returned to the chaotic norm of an emergency room. The bantering between staff returned to its previous level.

The only remaining problem, Robert was now down a resident, which meant holes in the schedule, many of which he filled himself, adding to his level of fatigue.

There was something else that continued to haunt him, usually at night when he was home in bed, trying desperately to fall asleep. There was something about the whole Casanova resident / Kung Fu nurse affair. He wasn't sure if there were pieces of the puzzle missing, if there was a lesson he had failed to learn or if there was nothing at all. He tended to think it was the middle of the three options. But what was it? What was the lesson?

The answer did not come easily.

When it finally did, Robert was sitting on the edge of the bed rubbing tired eyes. He was about to turn off the light when he noticed a book sitting on the table. While he loved to read, lately he had little time, although he tried to read at least few pages each night. Currently, he was working on Tom Clancy's: *The Bear and the Dragon*. The edge of the cover served as the bookmark. The cover itself was nondescript. Then it struck him, that was the answer he was looking for. Simply put, never judge a book by its cover.

And man, did a lot of people misjudge nurse Kung Fu!

54

The summer ended. The weather cooled. Baltimore's murder rate did not. So much for the natives-restless-in-the-heat theory. There seemed to be more traumas than ever. There was also the influx of homeless patients who appeared as soon as the weather cooled. Colder weather also meant a cadre of school-aged children ending up in the ER as psych patients. This didn't count the normal population of patients, those with genuine problems and those who used the emergency room as their private physician.

The busyness helped the time go by quickly. It also helped Robert keep his mind on his work and off other things. They were able to juggle the resident schedule around so he didn't have to work quite as many hours, but the challenges of being chief were omnipresent. There were no more martial art demonstrations, although discrete hook ups between resident doctors and nurses continued. He had eight months left as chief resident and he expected it to go smoothly. He even threatened his subordinates that if anyone did anything to rock the boat, he'd personally toss them overboard. His words, mixed with the memories of Dr. Casanova, as the unfortunate resident came to be known, and all remained calm. Robert didn't get to see much of Dennis during this time. Because the ER was busy, the rest of the hospital was hopping, including the lab. If he and Dennis ate a late-night lunch together once a week, it was a lot.

Robert also started thinking about what he was going to do after his year as chief was over. He had been dreaming for years about being a real doctor earning a real paycheck. However, details of exactly how to do this remained vague. Until one day when Dr. Kerrigan, the emergency room's chairman, buttonholed him in his office and asked him that exact question. Kerrigan was middle aged, moderate height, and above average in waist size. His hair was long and greying, usually pulled into a ponytail. He never wore street clothes, electing instead to go with the surgical scrub attire. Contrary to many in the medical field, he had yet to kick his nicotine habit. One Hopkins tradition he did sport was to wear a starched white lab coat. "What are you going to do in July?" he asked on the day in question.

"In July, sir?" Robert said.

"Yes, when your year is up. You know, that'll be here before you know it."

"Oh, that July," Robert laughed. "I think I'll go to Disney World."

The medical director smiled. He had a good sense of humor. "Florida's a tough market to break into," he countered.

"I didn't know that, sir."

"Neither did I. I just made it up." A smile was shared. "Anyway, I was just wondering." Dr. Kerrigan gave his chief resident a long look. "You know Robert, there's going to be an attending position opening in July. Dr. Swarthmore is leaving to take over a new contract in Virginia."

As had other big institutions, Johns Hopkins Hospital had dived into the emergency room management business, where they took over and ran smaller non-university emergency rooms. It was a good source of business for the institution, it spread the Hopkins name, it added additional resident slots, and it served as a source of employment for the residents that completed the training program, residents such as Robert.

Robert was taken aback by the offer. The epitome for a resident at Hopkins was to be offered a faculty position at the end of your training. It was quite an honor, and yet it was being done in such a casual manner. Typical for Kerrigan, Robert thought.

"I certainly appreciate the offer, sir, and I will definitely think about it."

"You do that, Robert."

He did, too. There would be many advantages to staying at Hopkins. He wouldn't have to move, he already knew the system and the people, and while the work was indeed challenging, for an actual attending physician, it was less hours compared to that of the resident staff. Dennis told him the week before that he had been offered a similar position in the Department of Pathology, and was giving it serious consideration, although his first choice was to work for the FBI. He confided in Robert that he had already applied to the agency. Robert laughed. If he and Dennis stayed at Hopkins, Robert would have someone to eat late-night lunches with. Robert did wonder if they would be able to keep their same table.

The thought was short lived as his pager went off a few steps later. "Speaking of the devil," he muttered as he saw Dennis's number pop up on the display. He pulled his phone from his lab coat and dialed the number. "What's up?" he said as the familiar voice answered the phone.

"What are you doing?" Dennis asked.

"Walking back to the ER. I just left Kerrigan's office. He offered me a faculty position."

"That's great...but a little dangerous, don't you think?"

Robert took the bait. "In what way?"

"You and I, attending staff at the same hospital."

Robert laughed. "What's up?"

There was a definitive change in Dennis's voice. "You got time to talk?"

Robert looked at his watch. He had thirty minutes before his shift started. "Sure."

"See you in a couple."

"Dennis?!"

There was a moment's hesitation on the other end. "I just got off the phone with the IRS."

"Oh, shit."

55

Robert slid a tray towards Dennis. "The IRS finally caught up with you, huh?" he said, sitting down.

"Thanks," Dennis said, quickly unwrapping his sub. A couple bites later followed by a swig of Mountain Dew, he said. "They may be close on my heels, but as long as I stay in here, I'm okay."

"But you said..."

"There you go again, making assumptions. I said I just got off the phone with the IRS. I didn't say it was about me."

"Then what's this about?"

The pathology doctor looked his friend hard in the eye. "Did you know your girlfriend, Samantha, is a millionaire?"

Robert broke out in a laugh. "You know Dennis, sometimes you are really full of shit."

"That may be true," Dennis said. "Then again, sometimes I'm not."

Robert paused. "And this is one of those times you're not?"

"Sorry, pal."

"Sorry, why are you sorry?"

"It throws another wrench into the equation we have yet to solve."

"More unconnected dots," Robert said.

"Same thing."

"How much is she worth?"

"I don't know exactly. I do know she paid over three quarter million dollars in income taxes last year."

"Jesus Christ. How'd she do that?"

"Certainly not by selling muffins in her parent's store."

Silence ensued as the need to eat won out over Robert's curiosity. It also gave him time to think. The only problem, the more thinking he did, the more confused he became. "I really don't understand," he finally said. "We're way off track."

"I thought that at first, too," Dennis responded. "Then the more I got to thinking about it, the more I realized we weren't off track. We just weren't down the track far enough. You see, I think there's a whole lot more involved than just a few acres of property down in...What's the town called? Buxton. I think this thing goes a whole lot deeper than that. I think it's about Samantha continuing as a highly successful real estate agent. You said she was the listing agent for that property on that other island...Ocracoke, right?"

Robert nodded in the affirmative. He had discovered this through his own investigation.

"I did some research on that development myself," Dennis said. "The minimum condo in there is going for a million dollars. And there are only a couple of those. The rest run between a million and two. When all is said and done, there's going to be over seventy units in the complex. You do the math on the commission."

"So what you're saying is that it's blackmail, only a whole lot broader than we originally thought," Robert said.

"That's my guess."

"Goldberg must be pretty desperate." Robert took a sip of soda and glanced at his watch. Eight minutes before he was due in the ER. "Let's go back to the original question. Why is he doing this?"

"I was thinking of that," Dennis replied. "But I don't know what it would be."

"You've come up with all this other shit," Robert laughed. "Maybe you can come up with the answer to that one, too." Robert stood and started gathering his trash. He'd have to hurry, but if he took the stairs, he'd be okay. He started to walk away but stopped. "Speaking of coming up with shit, how the hell did you get the information about Samantha's taxes?"

Dennis smiled. "Like I said, the IRS called me."

Robert looked at his watch. Further discussion on that matter would have to wait for another time.

56

Samantha shut the door of her Jeep and headed toward the house. She wrapped her arms across her chest. The light sweater she wore wasn't enough protection against the early May wind. The temperature was above freezing, but the wind chill factor made if feel below. Staring to shiver, she increased her pace. She glanced around the parking lot. Her mother's old Cadillac was sitting in its unofficial designated spot, closest to the door of the house. Her father's Honda Pilot sat next to it, but not too close as to bang any doors. Her mother was very picky about her Caddy, even after all these years. Samantha scanned the area again. She didn't see Billy's truck. It was not all that unusual as he tended to stay out on the beach or at the fishing pier at Rodanthe until late. She headed for the campground office. Pushing the doors open, she gave a cheery hello. Mako and Rhonda were at the desk, bent over the daily paper. They looked up as they heard her enter.

"Hey Sam," Rhonda chirped. "It's a little late for you to be out isn't it?"

Samantha shrugged. "It took a while to get off Ocracoke. The ferry wasn't running on time tonight."

"Never does," Mako said.

"That's not true. It always runs on time," Rhonda argued.

"Does not."

"Anyway," Samantha injected. "Have you guys seen Billy?"

"No, but we'd certainly like to?" Rhonda teased. "I could go for another nice dinner."

Billy held true to his promise to take the girls out to dinner several months before. They said they had a good time and the food was really good. They ate at a new place in Nags Head called *The Blue Tuna*. Other than that, Samantha couldn't get a whole lot of information out of any of them about the evening. She suspected they planned it that way just to tease her curiosity. She also suspected it was a onetime dinner as Billy converted back to his old avoid-the-cousins-as-much-as-possible routine. They in turn continued to drool over him whenever they could. Samantha could also tell that while Rhonda liked her brother, Mako *really* liked him. There were times when Samantha thought the feeling might be mutual, but Billy never pursued the point.

"I'm being serious," Samantha said, bringing her focus back to the present.

The cousins followed suit. "Haven't seen him all day."

Concern formed in Samantha's mind, but she said nothing. "Okay, thanks guys. You have a good night."

"You too," the cousins said in unison.

Samantha left the office and headed for the house. She reached for her cell phone. She realized she had left it in the Jeep where she retrieved it. She checked to make sure she hadn't missed any calls. She wasn't expecting any, but in the real estate business, a missed call could translate into a lost sale. She started to shut it down when the screen told her she had one voice mail. She looked at the clock at the bottom right corner. It was almost midnight. She cursed under her breath, wondering who would be calling her this time of night. Probably someone wanted to make an appointment for the morning. Not paying attention to the number, she opened the voice mail. She pressed the phone to her ear. It took a second to recognize the voice. It was her brother and he sounded odd, almost like he was in a distant fog. But that wasn't the worst part. It was what he said that caused her legs to crumble, nearly dropping her to the ground.

57

Robert lay in bed, exhausted after working six straight twelve-hour shifts. That didn't include the additional hours he put in before and after the clinical hours dealing with the forever pile of administrative crap. The year was rapidly winding to an end. July 1st was rapidly approaching. There was still much to do as he was preparing to leave. He had to write a formal letter of recommendation for his replacement, although that was not going to be a burden in that Larry Dawson was ripe and ready for the job. He had progressed nicely just as Robert expected. Then there were the other final evaluations to do of his junior residents. Some would be moving on to other institutions. Some would remain at the Johns. In any case, the letter from the chief resident was vital to ensure a smooth transition to the next phase of their training. A good letter meant positive progress. A bad letter could be devastating. He had two first year residents who, in his opinion, just weren't ready to move on. He had discussed the two with Dr. Kerrigan a couple days earlier, and as the department head tended to do, he refused to make decisions his subordinates were hired to make. He said, "You work with them a lot more than I do, Robert. It's your call. I'll support whatever decision you make." Was it a cop out on the chairman's part, or did he have that much faith in Robert's decision-making ability? Robert laughed as he rolled over in bed. The true question, did Robert have enough confidence in himself?

He pulled a pillow over his head. It was time to sleep. He'd worry about that later.

Only, as happened often, sleep failed him. His mind raced through many areas of his life. What was he going to do after his year was up? If he accepted the faculty position offered by Dr. Kerrigan, would he stay in the same apartment, or would he move to a more upscale neighborhood? If he decided to leave Baltimore, where would he go? He had received several inquiries from people he had met throughout his years. He even had a couple recruiters call. There were options in every area of the country. He knew that decision had to be made fast because those doors would close over the next few weeks, including, he suspected, the faculty position at Hopkins.

"Stop it," he mouthed aloud. "It's time for sleep." But his brain had a mind of its own. Next topic…

Her vision came into focus. She was standing on the beach at the edge of the water. Waves splashed around her legs, leaving tattoos of sand on her ankles. She wore the plain pink bikini he liked so much. The pink offset the deepness of her tan. It did other things for her as well. It did things for him, too.

She stood silently, looking over the water, her hair pulled in a ponytail, dark sunglasses covering her eyes. She wore a thin strand of gold around her neck. Small matching dangling earrings hung form her earlobes. She was the beach's *Mona Lisa*. She was his *Lady Hatteras*. Today, except for a few birds, they were alone. She turned and looked at him. Her smile widened. She held out her hand. He moved forward and stood close to her. Their fingers interlocked. It was the first time such action had occurred. She leaned into him. Their bodies touched. Again, a first. She leaned in closer. He braced himself as her weight pressed against him. His arm went around her waist. She turned and faced him, skin and bathing suit rubbing across his bare chest. His grip tightened. She did not resist. She leaned in. He did the same. Their lips met for their first kiss. It was short, salty, but very sweet. Her hands went around his neck. They kissed again, this time longer, deeper. Tongues pried open lips. The exploration began. She pressed her chest into him. Then she took half a step closer and other parts of their bodies were pressed together. He felt things begin to happen. He told himself he should be embarrassed. He was too busy to worry about that as other fireworks were going off in his body.

They kissed some more. She pressed in harder. "You feel good," she said.

He could only utter a deep groan.

"Do you want me as much as I want you?" she said.

Another deep groan.

A hand slid down his chest, across his abdomen and onto the waist band of his bathing suit. A moment's hesitation to allow an objection, and then her hand was upon him. She rubbed him at first, and then gripped him through the material of his suit. He dug his feet in the sand and locked his knees as they began to buckle. They kissed again and then his lips went to her neck. Slowly, gently, he licked the salt off her skin. Sweat from the sun and other causes rolled down to her shoulder. He chased one droplet with his tongue. She cooed and grabbed him tighter. He touched her breast. She pulled away so he would have better access. First his hand was on the outside of the material, then his fingers climbed over the top and slid inside.

Her skin was so soft yet so firm. Her nipple was erect, telling him what he was doing was okay. He caressed her as she caressed him. He removed his hand and laid it across her abdomen. Like she did for him, he hesitated a moment. Like he did for her, there was no objection. His hand moved downward, stopping at the waist band of her bottoms. She rose to her toes and his hand was on her. She felt warm, soft, inviting. His olfactory senses kicked in. He could smell her aroma causing other senses to heighten. Her hand moved away. She undid the draw string to his suit. Her hand slid inside. She again gripped him and began to move up and down. She pressed her groin into him harder. His fingers went to the edge of the material and slid it aside. His fingers directly on her, she was softer yet. He gently circled the outside of her cave, and then as she pressed into him, his finger entered her. A hand still around her waist, he felt her begin to crumple. He held on tightly.

Time passed. How much, he did not know. Was it long? Was it short? Was it even the same day? One thing he knew, he wished time would stand still. But naturally, it didn't. He felt the heat in her rise. She wrapped her arms around his waist. Her knees started to shake and weaken. Her pelvis quivered. Her breathing became short and rapid, almost as if she were gasping for air. And then...

And then the phone rang, totally disrupting the moment. Robert jerked to a sitting position. Had he fallen asleep? Was he dreaming? He rubbed his eyes. He looked around. He was alone. The ring of the phone persisted. He grabbed the device off the bedside table. "Hello," he said, telling himself to be polite.

"Robert?"

He recognized the voice, the same voice as a moment ago, the same voice in his dream. "Samantha! I was just thinking about you."

"I bet you were." The all too familiar sarcasm had returned, only gentler than normal.

"What's up?" he said, ignoring the barb.

This time the pause was longer. "Is Billy with you?" Her tone added add: Oh, please make it be yes.

"No, he's not," Robert said cautiously. Silence ensued. "What's the matter, Sam?"

He heard her start to choke up. "I'm sorry to bother you then."

"Samantha, don't hang up...please!"

Another period of silence. "Billy's disappeared again."

58

Robert decided early during the trip south that this was it. This was do or die. There was not going to be any more bullshitting. Samantha would have to come clean with him, or he was going to wash his hands of Cape Hatteras, just like she had wanted him to do the last time they were together. Now, things had changed, and she was calling, asking for his help. Only this time, it wasn't her eyes. It was her words. She even used the word please. He initially contemplated telling her to go screw herself, but the tone of her voice reminded him of the look in her eyes; as Dennis said, the amateur actor look. He couldn't get it out of his mind that maybe she was in trouble and needed his help. He had weighed his options. If he didn't go and something happened to her or Billy, he would never forgive himself. If he went, the worst that could happen would be another hurricane tongue lashing. Not really all that hard a choice he decided. "What a convoluted relationship," he muttered aloud.

He reviewed the last conversation with Samantha. When he asked her not to hang up, she hesitated and then broke into tears. It was nearly a minute before she could get herself together. She said Billy left her a message on her cell phone saying that he was going to be away on vacation until after the wedding. That didn't make sense until Samantha told him she'd been thinking about calling off the wedding, which confused the situation even more because Robert didn't think Samantha had a choice in the matter. Robert was sure there were more details than that, but he would find out in a few hours.

He passed the road sign announcing 150 miles to Richmond. He shook his head side to side. Maybe convoluted wasn't the right word to describe just how crazy this whole thing had become. Maybe he needed something stronger.

59

Robert wasn't sure what kind of greeting to expect from Samantha when he arrived. He was prepared for the worst but received the opposite. She was waiting for him in the Rodanthe pier parking lot. As soon as he got out of his car, she stepped to him and gave him a big hug. He noticed how much she was trembling. He didn't know if she was that glad to see him or if she was that shook up. She broke away, thanked him for coming and then motioned for him to get in her Jeep. He did as he was told.

Inside her vehicle, she faced him. "Robert, I think Billy's been kidnaped."

He forced his facial features to remain neutral. "What makes you think that?"

She turned forward. He reached over, grabbed her shoulder firmly and turned her towards him. "Listen Samantha, I don't know what's going on. I don't know what's going down, but I'll tell you this, I did not drive all the way down here to get anything but the truth. Understand?" She didn't hesitate as she nodded in the affirmative. He quickly continued. "And let's set the record straight before we go any further. I was never spying on you in Ocean City. I was spying on your buddy Goldberg. You were just a byproduct of that whole thing." He paused to make sure he had his voice under control. "Only, it wasn't Arthur Goldberg I saw you with that night, was it? It was his brother?" Another affirmative nod followed. Again, Robert continued. "The last time we were together, and you were giving me one of the worst tongue lashings of my life, you had a look in your eyes that said something other than the words coming out your mouth. At the same time you were telling me you never wanted to see me again, you were asking for my help." He paused. "If I'm on target so far, here I am. Tell me what you know...everything you know." His hand dropped.

She didn't turn away as he might have expected. Nor did she give him any kind of a sarcastic comment. Instead, she said, "I know I've said a lot of mean things. And you're right. I didn't really want to chase you away. If anything, I was trying to protect you."

"Protect me from what?"

"From getting hurt and from everything that's going on down here."

"What exactly is going on?" Robert coaxed.

She looked at him, her eyes asking the question of whether he really wanted to know. He held her stare as a way of answering the question. She looked away. "It all started I guess the winter after the summer we were together. While that summer wasn't one of our bests, that winter proved dismal. The weather was cold. The fish weren't biting and the tourist trade in general went to pot. Everybody was having trouble. So I started looking for ways to make a little extra money. Arthur used to stop in the store once in a while to get gas and sometimes a cup of coffee and a muffin. While he was never overly friendly, he was friendly enough. Anyway, one day I jokingly asked him if he needed any real estate agents. He gave me one of his smiles and said it just so happened he did. He asked me if I was interested. I said maybe. He gave me his card and told me to call him once I got my licenses. I thought about it a few days, finally deciding what the hell, it wasn't going to do any harm. Again, things were slow. I took the course online, took the test and called him that spring. For whatever reason, he took a liking to me, and I to him. I had my first listing within the week, my first sale within the month. When I went to my first settlement and had the commission check in my hand, I was hooked. For reasons people down here still don't understand, that summer turned out to be a boom for real estate. I became so busy I had a hard time balancing my responsibilities at the campground with my so-called part-time job. But with a lot of schedule juggling and a lack of sleep, I made it through. I made a shit pile of money that summer and have done very well since." She tipped her head to the side. "Somehow, I have a sneaking suspicion you already know that, don't you?"

"I don't have details, but I know you've been very successful with whatever you've been doing." He held up his hand in case there was going to be a verbal attack. "Again, it was information Dennis discovered while looking into Goldberg Realty."

She contemplated his response before moving on. "Again, I've done well, and while I've done the brunt of the work, the opportunity I owe all to Arthur. He gave me a start. He's encouraged and taught me along the way. He continues to do the same."

"You've made a lot of money for him in return," Robert pointed out.

"True, but that's the way business works. Don't forget he didn't have to give me the start to begin with. He could have easily taken someone else under his wing."

"He obviously saw something special in you," Robert said. The ER resident gained a faint smile for his compliment, so he continued. "You have a good set of attributes for down here. You're local, you're smart, you're proven in the business world and you have the look. You're beautiful yet you don't flaunt it...except maybe the night of the fundraiser. You looked really good that night."

Samantha's smile widened and then her facial expression turned serious again. "Be that as it may," she continued, "I dove in with both feet and have been rewarded nicely for my efforts. Now the ever-inquisitive Robert Battlegrove may ask why would a local girl like me who loves her leisure time, get involved with a business that requires so much of her time? I've asked myself that on more than one occasion, and the answer isn't all about the money. For one..." She looked out the window. "When you left that summer, I thought my life was over. Then what you did to Billy, or rather what I perceived you did to Billy only made matters worse. I don't know if I was depressed because I don't know what depression really is, but I suspect I was at least in the ballpark. The real estate business helped me take my mind off Billy, and in some ways you. As for the money side of the coin, I always had the dream of buying the campground from my parents when they were ready to retire. Sure, I'm their daughter and they could just give it to me and Billy, but they wouldn't have anything to live on. I wanted to make sure they were comfortable. So I've been saving." She stopped and gave Robert another one of her inquisitive looks. "Just how much about my finances do you know?"

"Basic IRS information," Robert said.

This time she couldn't resist the instinctive follow up question. "How?"

"Let's just say that Dennis has connections."

Again, she failed to attack as Robert would have anticipated. Instead, "Anyway, during this time, my parents began to look at expanding the business. While the campground does well, it's very cyclical. The down times can be brutal. They were looking at developing a small strip mall, restaurant, and hotel. They bought a piece of property in Buxton with that in mind. Things were going along well, and then they hit an unexpected barrier regarding permits to build higher than the code. Without the hotel, the project would be a bust.

Unbeknownst to my brother and me, my parents refinanced the campground to buy this property. Many felt they way overpaid, but it is a prime piece of real estate, probably one of the best undeveloped areas left on that end of the island. The preliminary numbers justified it though, but only with the hotel. My parents were assured there would be no problem with getting a waiver with the height restriction, but once the process was started..." She paused and looked at Robert. "We are very close to losing everything, Robert. Everything! And while yes, I have some money saved, that won't go far if I become the sole supporter of my family." Tears started to form in her eyes. "I may also lose my part-time job."

A long silence followed during which time a sense of nervousness intertwined with Samantha's other set of emotions. "You hungry?" she finally said.

"Yes."

"Let's get out of here. Your car will be okay here awhile."

Samantha started the Jeep and headed south on the main road. She regained her composure after a few miles. "Before we go any further, why don't you tell me what you know. It may save a lot of time."

Robert hesitated. "Are you taking me somewhere where you can chop my head off again?"

She looked over at him. "What's it called in the legal system?"

"Immunity," Robert suggested.

"Okay, you got immunity."

"Dennis and I have put together a theory of what's going on. A lot of it seems farfetched, but Dennis seems to think we may be close to the truth; and the truth, whether you want to believe it or not, ain't pretty." Robert paused. When he received no objection, he continued. "Your parents are way over their heads financially. Like you said, even with the money you may have in the bank, it probably isn't enough to bail them out. The financial note on the property in Buxton is coming due. Without the permits to start developing the project, the mortgage company will foreclose, which means they'll get both the property in Buxton as well as the campground. We're referring to a company called Resort Mortgage Corporation, which by the way just happens to be owned by the Goldberg Brothers.

"Now, before you start defending your boyfriend, Arthur, he's wrapped up in this as much as his brother, but we think it's his brother who's really the brains behind the company, and if not the brains, at least the muscle. From what Dennis could find out, it's the brother who has the money. Arthur is just a pawn...a lot like you."

Samantha had been keeping her eyes on the road as she drove. The last comment, however, caused her head to snap to the right. "What do you mean by that?"

"Immunity, remember?"

"Just answer the question." Her eyes returned to the road.

"Dennis thinks you may have been set up from the very beginning with all this."

"Set up! Why?"

Robert made sure his thoughts were organized before he continued. "For one, the campground is a huge piece of undeveloped real estate. If someone had the money and went in there to develop it with housing, who knows what they could do."

"My parents have discussed that," Samantha acknowledged. "But they felt the opportunity in Buxton was less risky."

Robert didn't ask for an explanation of that. Instead, "The Goldberg brothers have probably had their eye on the property for some time. They may have even talked to your parents about selling the place. But I suspect your parents said no, the place wasn't for sale. So they had to devise a plan of how to get it, just like they've devised other plans to get what they want."

"You think taking me under his wing and setting me up in the real estate business was all preplanned."

"I said it was farfetched," Robert conceded. "I bet though, he didn't think you were going to be as successful as you were, which only added more feathers to his cap and money in their bank."

"What about the property in Buxton. How does that come into play?"

"Real estate transactions are public knowledge. When the Goldbergs found out your parents were buying the property, they quickly jumped on the bandwagon and somehow ended up with the mortgage."

Samantha turned into a restaurant parking lot; one Robert did not remember from the past. She pulled to one of the far spaces. "If anyone asks, you're a client looking at property, remember?"

Robert nodded.

Samantha undid her seat belt but didn't open the door. "Okay, so they got the mortgage on the Buxton property. They had no way of knowing there'd be trouble with the permits."

"Ah, but Samantha dear, that is where I think you're wrong." Robert paused as she looked at him. One of the things that always attracted him to her was her sense of poise, her inner strength, her resolve. She conveyed confidence in everything she did. At times a sharp tongue came with it, but it was an attracting trait nonetheless. Now, however, that armor was being threatened. The confidence was gone. She continued to have periods of trembling, sometimes in her lips, other times through her entire body. It was the first time she had been vulnerable. Then he corrected that. She had been vulnerable the first time Goldberg set eyes on her several years before. He cursed the man under his breath.

Aloud, he said, "The Buxton town council controls most of what happens in the area, including the building code issues. Now, the townspeople have always been adamant about not building high, and the town council has always supported the issue. When your father approached them about the plans for the hotel, they were reluctant, but were swayed by the amount of business it would bring to their community. I don't have to tell you the Outer Banks competes for the tourist dollars with many other beach communities on the east coast. The communities within Hatteras have to be competitive amongst themselves as well. The project your parents were proposing would go a long way to help that. The town council was probably okay with the idea, until they received either a call or a visit from their strongest political supporter."

"The Goldberg brothers," Samantha half-shouted.

"Political contributions are open for public review," Robert continued.

Samantha brushed a piece of hair from her face. "You think the town council reversed their decision because of a threat from Arthur and his brother?"

"Remember Sam, this is all speculation on my and Dennis's part."

"Okay, go on."

Robert did. "Here's where it gets really speculative; or as Dennis likes to say, the plot thickens. Through all this, you suddenly announce you're marrying the very man who's threatening to destroy your family. Why? If you remember, I asked you this already. Your answer was for me to figure it out. Now that's a very interesting response to the question of why someone is getting married, don't you think?" Robert didn't wait for a response. "It told me there was something more than that four-letter word called love. It also told me it had to be something significant for you to agree to such a thing. Dennis and I then had to find the something significant. Our assumption is that he is blackmailing you. Marry him, and the foreclosure will be dropped. Say no, and bye-bye to the property in Buxton, and bye-bye to the campground and your real estate business." Making sure he kept the cockiness from his voice, he said, "How am I doing so far?"

"Keep going."

Robert did. "The final question, why is he marrying you? Not that you aren't a wonderful person, and you would make a wonderful wife, but..."

A pause followed. Samantha spoke, unable to keep a hint of tartness from her voice. "What's your and Dennis's theory on that?"

Robert sucked in a deep breath. "We don't have an answer to that one," he said in a soft voice. "Except if the brothers think one of them needs a trophy wife, maybe as a way to cover their indiscretions."

"Why me?"

Robert smiled. "Best trophy on the island."

Samantha's mouth opened and then closed. Eventually, "Thank you."

"You're welcome." Robert took in another breath. "Again, ideas only and certainly farfetched."

"Maybe not," Samantha conceded. "I've heard both brothers talk about needing a woman on their team."

"Why does it have to be a wife?" Robert asked.

"Marvin's a control freak," Samantha said. "A wife would be family, easy to control."

"Why doesn't he get married?" Robert said.

Samantha half-laughed, half-choked. "He's too busy playing mobster to care about anyone else."

"I've never had the privilege of meeting the man, but I suspect you're right on," Robert said. "Besides, he's also too busy being a pervert, a pedophile, and I suspect a murderer...and more than once, too." He paused. "You just said Marvin Goldberg was playing mobster. How are they connected to the mob?"

"I've heard them mention getting help with financing from people in Atlantic City," Samantha said. "I suspect that's the connection. I don't think they're involved in any other way. Arthur would never go for that regardless of his brother's interest."

"That could explain why such an extensive project in such a desolate location," Robert said.

"Huh?"

Robert explained his theory. "A good way to launder money without drawing a lot of attention to yourself. It would be interesting to see the list of buyers."

"I know most of them," Samantha said. "They all seem like normal people to me."

Robert remained silent on that point. He also didn't comment on Marvin Goldberg's probable connection to the underworld, even if his brother wasn't. It was additional information discovered by Dennis Tucker.

Samantha's body started to shake. Tears flowed down her cheek. Wiping them away with her hand, she said, "I think everything you've said is probably true, except for one thing. Arthur really is a wonderful kindhearted man."

Robert contemplated the point. "Then is Arthur Goldberg being blackmailed, too?"

Samantha wiped away another tear. "Listen, Robert, the last thing Arthur Goldberg wants to do is marry me, but neither one of us have a choice."

"You always have a choice," Robert pointed out.

"We did. But that's gone now."

Robert cocked his head to the side. "Billy's on vacation until after the wedding. He's been kidnaped?"

"Arthur and I were talking about calling off the whole thing and taking our chances with his brother. He felt that with money he had stashed away and the money I saved, maybe we could survive, not as a couple, but as business partners. Arthur was willing to break all ties with his brother if he had to."

"And then Billy went on vacation."

"Yes." The tears started again. "Arthur would never do anything that caused harm to Billy." The tears increased in intensity. "Oh, Robert, I've made such a mess of things."

Robert reached over and touched her cheek. "Samantha, you have unequivocally done nothing wrong. Do you understand?"

She tried to force a smile but failed.

"Understand!"

Samantha nodded and said, "I was afraid you wouldn't come back. I don't know what I would have done." She paused. "Thank you."

"You're welcome."

"What do we do now?" Samantha asked, recovering somewhat.

"I think the first thing we have to do is find Billy."

"How do we do that?"

"Where's his truck?"

"Missing with him. I even went down to the lighthouse. It's not there."

"Then our only other option is to go to your boy Goldberg and demand he find Billy."

"That won't work," Samantha said. "He's already confronted his brother and his brother laughed in his face. He said that Billy would be on vacation until after the wedding. He also said Billy didn't have a lot of money with him so he couldn't last all that long on vacation either."

"That's the timeline threat," Robert said. "Did he say anything more precise?"

"No, but Arthur thinks it needs to happen within a week or so."

"That gives us more time than I would have guessed," Robert said. As an afterthought, he added. "What do your parents say about all this?"

"They're well aware of the threat of foreclosure. They don't, however, know the connection between Resort Mortgage and Arthur. They also think that Billy has gone on vacation like he said. He left them a message saying he was going to find some mountains somewhere to explore."

"Mountains! Billy hates the mountains," Robert said. He remembered more than one conversation with his old friend dealing with the concept of trees. Trees, Billy used to say, had only one purpose in life, and that was to shade a house. Otherwise, they were useless. Robert pointed out that every house on the island was built of wood which came from trees, to which Billy would shrug and say nothing more. As far as mountains, the only mountain he ever cared to cross were the dunes leading to the beach. Then he used to complain about them. No, the only real mountains Billy liked were...

Robert's eyes widened and he looked hard at Samantha. "Sam, what did his message to you say?"

"I have it right here," she said. "I saved it." She reached into her pocket and retrieved her cell phone.

A couple buttons later, Billy's voice could be heard. "Hey, Sam. It's Billy. Just wanted to call and tell you I've decided to take a little vacation till after the wedding. Thought I'd go out and explore the mountains awhile. Take care of yourself and tell the lady and Asshole I'll see them when I get back."

Robert played it two more times, making sure he heard it correctly. Handing the phone back to Samantha, he said, "What did your parent's message say?"

"Basically the same thing, although he left out the asshole part."

"That would be expected."

"Huh?"

"I would never hear the message left on your parent's phone. Yours however..."

"I don't understand, Robert?"

"The message is for me, at least the last part. The first sentence is to you...that's basically telling you, you have to get married for him to return. On the surface, the part about the mountains simply tells you where he's going, put in there so your parents won't worry, at least too much. However, when he mentions *asshole*, that brings a whole different meaning to the message. He's telling *me* he went out to explore the mountains. I may be splitting hairs, but you don't go *out* to the mountains, you go *up* to them. Unless..." He paused. "Besides sand dunes, the only mountains Billy ever said he liked to explore were the ones out on the water. He always referred to waves as mountains. The bigger the better too?"

Still perplexed, Samantha said, "So where is he?"

"He's on a boat somewhere?"

"A boat!"

"That's my guess."

Samantha paused. "Why would he leave a message for you on my phone? Why wouldn't he call you?"

"He was probably only allowed two calls—one to your parents, one to you. He just hoped you did what you did when you got the message."

"Which was?'

"To call me. He was betting you had no one else to turn to."

"I really didn't," Samantha admitted. "What do we do now? How do we find him? He could be anywhere. God, if anything happens to him!"

"He's going to be okay, Samantha. We'll find him. I promise."

"How?"

"That part I haven't figured out yet."

"What do we do first?"

His growling stomach answered the question for them. "We eat."

Samantha hesitated. "I'm not really hungry now."

"Maybe not, but you still need to eat."

They got out of the Jeep and headed across the parking lot. She reached over and grabbed his hand. It was a small gesture, but one with a huge meaning.

60

They ate quickly and in relative silence. Robert was glad he insisted they eat. Not only was he himself famished, he noticed Samantha guzzled her meal down as well. He suspected she had not consumed any food for many hours; and like he said, they both needed their strength. As he finished his salad, he reviewed the telephone message in his mind. It was short, sweet, and presented with what Robert felt was a bit too joyous occasion for someone having been just kidnaped. Maybe there was a message there too. The lady he assumed was Samantha. The asshole was himself. Out to the mountains meant out to sea, or at least somewhere on a boat. While Robert was confident about the last two parts, the first was still bothersome. There was something wrong there. It wasn't until they were walking across the parking lot with Samantha a few steps ahead that it struck him. The lady wasn't Samantha. After all, he was already talking to his sister. He told her to tell the lady. The lady was someone else. Or...

Back in the Jeep, Robert buckled his seat belt quickly and said, "Head south."

Samantha looked at him with a quizzical eye but did as she was told. A few miles passed in silence before she finally said, "You going to tell me where we're headed?"

Robert hesitated. "I have a theory, but I'm not..."

"Robert! We're supposed to be open with each other, remember?"

Robert nodded and started explaining. "At first I thought the lady in the phone message was you. But that doesn't make any sense because he was already talking to you. I started thinking about who else it could be. Then I realized he wasn't referring to a *who*, but a *what*. If my theory is correct, the *what* is the *Lady Hatteras II*, and that's where he is."

"At Arnold's marina?"

"Remember, the boat's hidden back in the corner out of the way. You can see it from the parking lot of the old Blue Parrot, but that's about it."

"Why there?" Samantha asked.

"Good question. We'll just have to ask Arthur Goldberg's brother that, won't we?"

A few more miles passed. Samantha was ignoring the speed limit, which was fine with Robert. Unlike Dennis, she knew how to drive. As they passed the entrance to the lighthouse, she said, "You know Robert, I always thought Marvin was strange. He was always quiet and sort of kept to himself. Sure, he could be friendly when he had to be, but he never went out of his way to do so. But it wasn't his lack of speech that was so bothersome, it was his eyes. They never seemed to be still, always darting around, like he was looking for something or someone."

"My psychiatric buddies would say that's a sign of paranoia," Robert said.

"That certainly is descriptive," Sam concurred.

"Speaking of Marvin Goldberg," Robert said. "I've been meaning to ask, why were you with him at the office the night I saw you?"

"It was the end of the fundraiser Arthur took me to. Marvin was there as well, but remained in the background as usual. When it was over, the photographer the organizers hired wanted to take a bunch of formal pictures of Arthur and the other supporters. A couple local newspaper people were there, too. You'd have thought it was a wedding or something. Anyway, after a few pictures, one I guess you saw in the paper, Marvin said he wanted to check his mail. He uses the main office in Fenwick Island as his official address."

"He doesn't have a home anywhere?" Robert said.

"Not that I know of. Arthur told me he's kind of a vagabond. He never stays in one place for very long."

"Another sign of paranoia," Robert commented. "So why did you go with him, to the office?"

"Arthur asked me to go to keep an eye on him, to make sure he didn't mess with anything."

"What would be there that he'd mess with?"

"Beats me, unless he has a safe there or something. I suspect if Marvin found that, he'd demand to see what was inside."

"I see," Robert said. "I take it Marvin didn't find anything?"

"As you know, we were in and out in a couple minutes."

"And then you went back to the fundraiser?"

Samantha looked hard at her passenger. "No, Robert, we went out on the beach and..." She stopped in mid-sentence. Her eyes went back to the road. "Sorry, I'm trying to be good."

"That's okay. I understand."

"Yes, when we left the office, we went back to the fundraiser. Marvin wanted to stop for a drink, but I argued against it, saying that we both already had a bit too much, and any more might cause a problem with the police if we were stopped. They were out in force that night too, as we passed several on the way to the office."

"Smart girl."

"Thank you."

Robert watched the houses pass as they went through Buxton. Soon they were again protected by dunes. Almost as if an afterthought, he said. "What does your boy...I mean Arthur drink, anyway?"

"He actually drinks very little. When he does, it's usually only a glass of wine, two at the most."

"How about Marvin?"

"He makes up for the both of them whenever he gets a chance."

"Wine?"

"No," Samantha explained. "He drinks bourbon...the stuff that comes in a square bottle."

"A square bottle? With a black label on it?"

"Yeah, what's it called?"

"Jack Daniels?"

"That's it."

Both sets of eyes snapped towards one another as they remembered the whiskey bottle on the *Lady Hatteras II*.

61

Robert told Samantha to slow down as they approached the marina entrance and pulled into the parking lot of the burnt-out *Blue Parrot*. He scanned the area and looked out the back window to make sure no one was around. Traffic remained light on the trip south. Still, Robert had a high sense of caution about him, even feeling somewhat anxious. "Now who's being paranoid?" he mouthed silently. They pulled into the north corner of the lot to be as far away from the marina as possible. With the building gone, they still had a good view of the fence that separated the two properties.

With the Jeep parked and the engine running, Samantha asked, "Now what?"

Robert glanced in the direction of the marina. "I'm not..." His words were cut off. There was something wrong. He squinted against the glare of the sun and inched forward. His head tipped to the side. There was something different, something wrong with the picture in front of him. "Shit," he said when he realized what it was.

For the first time Samantha looked in the same direction. It didn't take her as long to understand. She repeated Robert's profanity.

The *Lady Hatteras II* was gone!

And then Robert's cell phone rang.

62

When the phone call from Dennis was over and Robert had briefed Samantha on its contents, they debated their next move. Several wrenches had suddenly been thrown into the mix. Dennis had come through again, with valuable information about the property on which they were presently sitting as well as the marina next door. The issue was how to use this information to get back to their main mission of finding Billy.

"How well do you know this Arnold guy?" Robert asked, referring to the owner of the marina.

"He and my father aren't necessarily close, but they've been friends for years."

"Is he the real deal?"

"What do you mean by that?"

"Does he really care about his marina?"

"I suspect he'd do anything he needed to protect it."

"Let's hope so."

"What do you have in mind?"

Robert told her.

Five minutes later they were driving through the main entrance. They stopped at the office, but Arnold's truck wasn't there. They could see the sign on the door indicating he was somewhere out in the yard. It didn't take long to find him working on one of the local charter boats. As they exited the Jeep, Robert and Samantha gave one another a look. Robert nodded in the affirmative, indicating they were doing the right thing, that everything was going to be okay.

Arnold was on a ladder waxing the hull with a buffer and didn't hear the duo until they were right on him. He seemed to jump when he realized someone was near. It was a reaction that did not go unnoticed by either visitor. Turning the buffer off, he climbed down and said, "Samantha, dear. What a pleasant surprise. What brings you to these parts?" He sat the buffer down and wiped his hands on his coveralls. There was a noticeable tremor.

Samantha motioned to her companion. "Remember Robert here? He was down a few months back looking at the *Lady Hatteras II*. He's made his decision. He's here to make an offer."

The tremors in the hand stopped a moment before resuming worse than before. "The *Lady Hatteras II*, huh. Well, sorry sir. You're a might late. Sold her just the other day."

"Sold her?" Samantha said.

"Yes, a nice couple from Florida bought her. They left one day last week, Thursday I think."

"Bought her," Samantha said. She let a disappointing look cross her face.

"So, the widow Willey's estates settled, huh?" Robert said, a perkiness to his voice.

Arnold gave him a quizzical look.

The ER doctor-turned-sleuth continued. "Well, it had to. You couldn't sell the boat until the estate settled. That's why I came down here. I heard the estate was going to be closed out the next couple months and I wanted to get a bid on the boat before someone else did. I'll call my attorney and tell him his information was wrong. He's going to be plenty pissed because the attorneys for the widow told him that the estate was still open." As planned, Robert pulled his cell phone from his pocket. "Matter of fact, I think I'll call him right now and give him a good piece of my mind. I drove all the down here from Baltimore just for this boat."

He was halfway through dialing when Arnold spoke up. "Maybe there's been a mistake. I didn't know anything about the estate still being open when I sold her. The couple was young, they were eager, and they had cash. It was a quick easy sale."

"Who signed for the widow?" Samantha asked.

The marina owner hesitated.

"Whoever did is in big trouble," Robert said. "If they didn't have proper authority from her attorneys then...a boat that size...over a half million dollars. That makes it grand larceny, twenty years minimum if I remember my law course correctly."

By now Arnold's hands were not only trembling, sweat was pouring from his brow. He looked at Robert and then at Samantha. He said nothing as she looked him hard in the eyes.

"Arnold, where's the boat?" Samantha said softly, yet with a demand to her voice.

"Why do you want to know?"

Samantha looked at Robert who nodded, giving his blessing to lay the truth on the table. She looked back at the marina owner. "My brother's been kidnaped, Arnold. We have reason to believe he's being held aboard *Lady Hatteras II*."

"Kidnaped! By who?"

"Marvin Goldberg."

Arnold went pale. He grabbed the ladder for support as his knees buckled.

"Boat theft is one thing," Robert said, the perkiness in his voice gone. "Accessary to kidnaping, that's close to life in prison."

"I didn't kidnap anybody," Arnold snapped.

Samantha glared at the old family friend. All friendliness in her glare was gone. She spoke slowly and with great conviction. "Arnold, if anything happens to my brother, so help me God..."

"Nothing has to happen to your brother," Arnold snapped. "Just marry Goldberg, and everything will be okay."

Samantha's mouth dropped open. She was speechless.

"Well, pal," Robert said. "You just confessed."

"I didn't confess to nothing. I just put two and two together like you did."

The trio glared at one another a long moment. Within that moment, there was an instant Robert thought Samantha was going to go after Arnold. He reached over and touched her arm. "Where's the boat, Arnold?" he said.

"I really shouldn't be talking about this, you know. If Goldberg finds out..."

"Listen Arnold," Robert said. He said a quick prayer, hoping the information Dennis had conveyed to him a short time ago was correct. "We know all about your relationship with Marvin Goldberg. We know he actually owns the property this marina sets on. We also know the lease is coming due in a few months. I suspect he's holding that over your head just like he's holding Billy over Sam's."

Arnold's eyes widened. Then for a moment, he seemed to regroup. "I just can't. Marvin Goldberg's too powerful a man."

"He's only as powerful as the people around him let him be," Robert pointed out.

The marina owner hesitated. Despite Robert's touch which had now become a grasp, Samantha took a step in Arnold's direction. The trembling hands came up chest high. "Okay...okay." The marina owner glanced around to make sure there were no wandering ears. His shoulders slumped. The air went out of his posture. It was almost like a large weight had been taken off his shoulders. "I got a call from Marvin a couple weeks ago. He told me to get the boat cleaned up and seaworthy. I asked him if he was going to buy it. He told me not to ask stupid questions, just to do as I was told. I asked him what he was going to do with her he didn't answer. I told him the boat wouldn't be a problem; I thought I could even get the engines running with a little effort."

"Did he say anything else?"

"No, just that he wanted it done by this past weekend."

"Did he say why?"

"No." Arnold paused. "He told me one thing I thought a little odd. He said to take the outriggers down."

"Why would he do that?" Samantha said.

"Height restrictions," Robert suggested.

"Anyway, I did as I was told, and she left here early Saturday morning. I had her looking and sounding like new, too. It's been a long time since..." He stopped and looked away. Then he looked back at Samantha. "Sam, you gotta believe me. I didn't know anything about Billy until you just said something."

Samantha stared him down a long moment before speaking. "I believe you Arnold, but if you're lying..."

"Fair enough, but I'm not."

"Where'd he take the boat?" Robert injected.

"He didn't take her anywhere. He hired one of the local captains to take her out. He went with him though."

"Do you know where they went?"

"I was here, but he didn't say where he was going."

"Any ideas?"

Arnold hesitated. "He wasn't going too far, at least before the first stop."

"Why's that?"

"When I drained the fuel tank, I only put a quarter tank of fuel back in her."

"That's not much for around here," Samantha injected.

"That was my thought, but they seemed to be in a hurry, so I didn't say anything."

"What about the captain Marvin hired. Is he around?" Robert queried.

"I doubt it. He told me when he was finished this job, he was flying down to Florida to bring a boat up for the summer."

"You saw them leave?" Samantha said.

"I watched them the whole way out the inlet. It looked good seeing her in the water again, just like the old days. *Lady Hatteras II* has one of the best set of lines on any boat I've ever seen, especially when she's up on full plane."

"You watched them leave the inlet," Robert said. "Which way did they go?"

The man hesitated. "Arnold!" Samantha snapped.

"South...They headed south."

Robert looked at Samantha and then back to Arnold. The doctor's mind was spinning. He felt he was so close. Aloud, "Sam, do any of those condos on Ocracoke have boat slips?"

"Each condo gets a slip."

"Covered slips by chance?"

Samantha nodded. "The three penthouses even have a boat garage."

"A boat garage, with height restrictions?"

Samantha nodded again.

Robert looked back at Arnold. "You left the outriggers off, right?"

It was the marina owner's turn to nod.

A smile of satisfaction formed on the doctor's face.

63

As they drove out of the marina parking lot heading north, there were several things Samantha and Robert agreed upon immediately. First, there was an increased sense of urgency. Neither named a specific reason, yet both sensed the clock was ticking and there wasn't much sand left in the hourglass. They agreed that twenty-four hours was probably the max. Secondly, with the ticking clock, came an increased level of danger, for Billy, for Samantha, and for Robert. Samantha insisted they could trust Albert not to call Marvin Goldberg. Robert wasn't as confident. However, they acknowledged they had little choice. Thirdly, while in the past they had simply reacted to whatever situation presented itself at the time, they now needed to be proactive, i.e., they needed a plan. Finally, this one being Robert's insistence, they needed reinforcements.

Luckily, Dennis was still in his office and almost done for the day. As Robert expected, he agreed to help. But before he could come to Hatteras, he needed time to think things through, get a few things together, and make a few phone calls. When queried about specifics, he said he'd let them know when he got there. He strongly suggested the sleuthing duo do nothing until the team became a trio. Robert agreed, but only to a point. He at least wanted to check out his own theory concerning Billy's location.

By now it was late afternoon. The sun was starting to drop; the temperature with it. They debated what to do until Dennis arrived. Robert insisted he at least wanted to go over to Ocracoke and look around. Samantha agreed. She pointed out one problem. They were in her Jeep, which many people knew, Marvin Goldberg included.

Some three hours later, after switching vehicles and stopping to eat, they were aboard the ferry to Ocracoke. The island had been called many things over the years, Hatteras's stepchild, isolated, often overlooked as a tourist destination, more beautiful than Hatteras and definitely much quieter. Robert hoped that any description used in the future would be a positive one, a happy one. Gloom and doom were not words he wanted to hear over the next couple days.

As the sun set, a westerly breeze picked up, adding a chill to the air. In spite of this, Samantha insisted she wanted to get out of the SUV. As the ferry load was light, they easily found a secluded spot along the port rail. Robert leaned forward and looked down. He always loved to watch the spray coming off the hull of a boat. There was something that awed him about a manmade object cutting through ancient seas. The ferry plowed through the water with ease, vibrating in response to a pair of large diesels below deck. As they approached the inlet, the water roughened. Three-foot swells rolled in from the ocean. They attacked the ferry's steel hull with a deliberate attitude. The ferry rolled gently in response, the spray coming off the sides in a well-choreographed fashion. Robert smiled. He figured it was just nature's way of reminding the manmade structure who was really the boss.

Many a vessel had challenged the *who-was-the-boss* theory over the years. Many lost. While the seas were relatively calm now, history was full of tales of sea mountains so high, it was a wonder the entire island hadn't washed away. Robert figured that while man had become a much smarter mariner, the Outer Banks was a piece of history with an unfinished ending.

His eyes lifted toward the darkening sky. He looked over his shoulder towards the west and then to the east. Just as he thought, the clouds over the ocean were much heavier and more foreboding. "Doesn't look good out there," he said.

"They're calling for a major system to pass here the next couple days," Samantha said. "One of the local forecasters says it could even be bad. Depends on how close to shore it comes."

"I'm not a meteorologist, but that looks close," Robert said, pointing east.

"That's just the beginning of the front."

"Just so long as it stays out there. Last thing we need right now is weather to deal with."

"No sense fretting about what you can't control," Samantha said.

The ferry's degree of roll increased as they crossed the middle of the inlet, the spray coming off the hull with more vigor. Robert remembered the first time Billy took him over to Ocracoke. It was an early hot summer day. There wasn't an ounce of breeze blowing. They had gotten out of Billy's truck to walk around. They got back in just as the ferry started to cross the inlet. There was no wind that day, yet the water was rough, left over from a storm the night before. As the boat started to rock, the truck did too. Robert immediately reached out and grabbed hold of the dashboard. He even started to put on his seat belt. He stopped when Billy laughed. "I'd hate to be with you if the water was rough," the islander said. Robert had never been in a vehicle that rocked so hard. It was a strange sensation.

It was a strange sensation then. It was a strange sensation now, standing next to Samantha after all these years. Samantha Mathews, the onetime love of his life, still the love of his life, who was now engaged to another man. He knew that, like himself, she was struggling with an array of emotions. Through it all, she was fighting to maintain control, control they both needed to maintain for Billy's sake. Anything else they could deal with later. Robert looked at her. He always thought she was beautiful. The passage of time only added to that impression. A yellow hat covered her head. Her hair was pulled in a ponytail. She wore a dark red sweatshirt with the campground logo embroidered across her left breast. The logo rose and fell in response to her breathing. Every so often the lettering would shake as a quiver went through her body. He knew how he felt, and Billy was only a friend. He couldn't imagine going through this with a family member. There were a lot of things he couldn't imagine. Yet, there were a lot of things he could. For one, what he was going to do to Marvin Goldberg once Billy was safe. Robert was not a violent person, but...

"Control," he mouthed silently. Samantha leaned into him. Thoughts of violence were replaced by other feelings, other emotions. He put his arm around her. She did not resist. Instead, she pressed into him, resting her head against his arm. This time he not only saw the shiver, he could also feel it. His grip tightened. "It's going to be okay," he said softly.

She looked at him. "Are you sure?"

He gave her a reassuring smile. "As sure as anything I've ever done in my life except..." Realizing what he was about to say, he stopped.

"Except what, Robert?"

He gave her a smile. "Maybe later."

"I need to hear it now, please."

Her voice was so soft, so gentle in contrast to the bite she delivered of late. He had never seen her so vulnerable. "Except how I feel about you," he said

"How do you feel, Robert?"

A sudden sense of uncomfortableness overcame him. "You're engaged, Samantha. Remember?"

"Only on paper."

"But..."

She reached up and touched his lips. "This may sound strange, Robert. As fond as I am of Arthur and he of me, the marriage was only going to be a business deal. Neither of us had any intention of it being anything else." She let out a soft chuckle. "You know, it's funny and a little strange, I guess. Arthur told me he enjoyed looking at me, just like he enjoyed looking at all beautiful women. He also liked my company. But that's all his interest ever was. He told me that once we were married, he'd stare at me till death do us part. But he wasn't interested in anything else. He said that as a way of reassuring me that if we did get married, I wouldn't have to worry about...well, you know."

Robert looked across the water so his mind wouldn't think of such things. It was hard enough imagining her getting married. Anything after that...

"So?" Samantha said, bringing his focus back to the present.

"So?"

"How do you feel?"

He pulled her into him and looked into her eyes. He repeated his earlier words. "As sure as anything I've felt in my life except..." Then he finished the sentence. "Except for how I feel about you. I love you, Samantha Mathews.

I've loved you for a long time. I've just been too career focused to realize it."

She buried her face in his chest. The earlier waves of shivers were replaced with several hard sobs. He reached down and pulled her chin up. He wiped away a couple tears with his thumb. "I hoped that would have made you happy."

She smiled. "It did. Thank you."

He leaned in. She did not resist. Their lips met. When they parted, she said, "I love you too, Robert."

They kissed again. The memories from just the night before came to mind. Like the storm brewing in the ocean, like the shipwrecks along the shore, like the boats abandoned along the sound, this history was not yet complete.

64

They held each other tightly, kissing occasionally until the ferry neared the dock. By the time it was their turn to pull off the boat, their minds were refocused on the task at hand. The ferry ride made Robert more determined than ever he was going to find Billy and bring an end to the Goldberg brothers' grasp over people. Robert didn't want to even think about Captain Willey or the little boy. The picture sitting on the receptionist's shelf haunted him.

As they headed south toward the town of Ocracoke, both recognized each other's anxiety. Robert reached over and grabbed Samantha's hand. "It's okay to be nervous," he said.

"I'm not nervous," she said. "I'm scared shitless"

Robert couldn't help but laugh. Sam's tongue was back.

"Remember, this is just a recon mission, not the real thing."

"Whatever that means," she said.

As they entered the outskirts of the town, Robert slowed to the posted speed. While they weren't exactly sure what they were looking for, each kept a sharp eye.

"What kind of vehicle does Marvin Goldberg drive?" Robert said.

"A black Mercedes."

"That shouldn't be hard to spot."

"Hopefully, he's not here," Samantha said.

"You should have called Arthur to see where he was."

"I thought of that," Samantha said. A moment later she pointed to the left. "Turn here. There's a back road into the development."

Robert turned down a side street. A partially cloud covered half-moon gave off enough light to see they were on a street from the past. The homes, while old, looked well maintained. Most were the typical cottage type designs and most had front porches, many with the old fashion wooden swings. Robert thought how much he'd like to be on one of those swings with Samantha at his side. Except for the moonlight, the street was dark. Most of the houses were unlit. He doubted there were many locked doors. This was probably perceived as a very safe neighborhood. "If they only knew," he muttered.

They made a couple of turns and then the headlights of the SUV lit up the rear entrance to the complex. Robert did a U-turn and parked on the street a few houses away. They sat silently a few minutes and then both exited at the same time. "Remember," Samantha said. "If we run into anyone, you like to take late night walks, so you wanted to see the area at night."

Robert nodded. He took her by the hand and led the way to the entrance. He could see the place was in the early phase of construction. While all the buildings were up, many didn't even have windows in place. Sam told him they were was about forty percent sold with several others waiting final finance approval. They walked slowly as if to give the impression they were indeed out for an evening stroll. Just as they entered the site, however, Robert stopped suddenly. "Shit," he said.

"What's the matter?"

"What about a night watchman?"

"Good thought, but we'll stick with the same story. Besides, this is Ocracoke."

"Yeah, Ocracoke, the refuge for a kidnaping."

"You know, Robert," Samantha said, "things aren't normally like this down here. It really is a peaceful place to live."

Peaceful on the surface, Robert thought to himself. He glanced back at the houses with the unlocked doors. Aloud, "I know."

They moved forward, using only the faint light from the moon to guide them. Samantha took the lead. She headed down one street where they turned right before heading down another. The unfinished unlit structures loomed above them on both sides. Robert felt like he was back in his childhood reading scary fairytales of haunted woods. Only instead of trees that came to life, manmade structures served as the monsters.

"The Goldbergs certainly had no trouble getting past the height restrictions down here, did they?" Robert whispered.

"Money talks," Samantha said. "And you don't have to whisper. Remember, we're here doing a normal walk around."

"Okay," he said softly. "Okay," louder the second time.

The last building sat on the southeastern tip of the property. It was where the most expensive condos were located. It was also where the boat slips were covered garages. They paused to make sure everything was quiet. They also looked around for any parked vehicles. Seeing none, they proceeded. As the building was only fifty percent completed, there was no door on the front entrance. They walked up the steps, through the large lobby and out the back to the waterfront side of the building. Robert imagined in the daytime it was a spectacular view. They headed along the pier. There were a series of boat garages in various stages of completion. Like the building itself, none had doors on them yet.

Except for the most southerly slip. This garage seemed to be complete. A finger pier ran along the side. A series of windows about twelve feet up let in light but no visibility from the outside. What Robert wouldn't give to have a peek in one of those windows. They walked to the end of the finger pier. Robert leaned around the corner. A waterside garage door blocked their view.

"How do you get in there?" Robert said.

"There should be a door here somewhere," Samantha responded. "Let's check the other side."

A similar finger pier ran the length of the garage on the starboard side as well. The same windows could be seen above. Only here, about halfway out, was a door. Robert grabbed the handle cautiously. "Alarms?"

Samantha nodded in the negative. "The electricity isn't on yet."

Robert started to turn the handle when he saw the action was going to be restricted by an eye bolt and plate held in place with a numerical padlock. He leaned in closer. "Why would anyone want to lock up such a place?" He paused. "Unless..."

He and Samantha looked at one another. "We've got to get in there," Robert said rapidly.

She grabbed his arm as he was about to pull on the door harder. "What if Marvin's on board?"

"We didn't see his car."

"Still."

Robert hesitated. "He wouldn't be inside with the door locked on the outside."

"Good point."

"I at least want to find out if the boat's there."

"How you going to do that?" Samantha asked.

The ER doctor looked around. He didn't remember a course in medical school called criminal investigation. If it existed, he wished he had taken it. He looked around again. Then he looked down. "There's only one way in," he said.

"How?"

He pointed to the water.

65

While Robert expected the water to be cold, he didn't expect it to be frigid. The term *hypothermia* came to mind followed a second later by *idiot*. He quickly put the thoughts out of his mind and refocused on the task at hand. As quietly as he could, he swam around to the back of the garage correctly deducing there would no pilings to obstruct his entry into the boat garage. He gritted his teeth as he was already starting to shiver. His ER training told him he had about fifteen minutes before he'd be in trouble. His instincts, however, told him he had less time than that. He cursed aloud at the timing of this so-called adventure. In another couple months, the water would be much warmer.

Because the piers were the floating variety, the garage doors were always a foot or so above the water's surface. Thus, he was able to get under the garage doors without completely submerging. What light the moon provided on the outside was now gone. He found himself in pitch darkness. He paused, listening for any unusual sounds. He heard nothing except the gentle lapping of the water against...

His heart rate increased. Was he hearing water lapping against the hull of a boat? He turned on his penlight, cupping his fingers over the end to lessen the amount of light. Treading water slowly, he waited for his eyes to adjust before letting out more light. He felt like he was in a cave spelunking, only instead of being confronted by a flock of bats or other cave monsters, he was looking at a giant sea creature. He had little doubt as to the name of his discovery. His heart rate increased. He was now totally ignoring the fact that his body was strongly objecting to being in the cold water. Swimming to the stern, he shone the light on the transom. This time his heart actually skipped a beat as the name *Lady Hatteras II* reflected back at him. He pulled the light down quickly and moved away. Whether he wanted to or not, he had to focus on his own situation. He knew he was already starting to enter the first stage of hypothermia. Sucking in a couple deep breaths and forcing himself to refocus, he made his way up to the bow. Robert figured if Billy was being held captive, that's where he'd most likely be. Turning the flashlight off, he gently tapped out the letters A S S H O L E in Morse code. Except for SOS, it was the only Morse code he knew. He counted to thirty and then repeated the message, this time a little louder. He counted to thirty again and was about to repeat the message for the third time when he heard footsteps inside. A short time later, the back door slid open. His heart skipped a couple more beats before starting to pound furiously as a surge of adrenalin dumped into his blood stream.

He started to move around to the front of the boat when he heard a voice. He bit his lip to keep the sound of his chattering down. The voice spoke again. It was calling his name. "Asshole...Robert...is that you?"

Robert hesitated. "Billy?" he said softly.

"Yeah, it's me, Asshole. Where are you?"

Robert heard footsteps along the gunwale. "Are you alone?"

"Yes. Where the hell are you?"

"In the water."

"Jesus Christ!"

A short time later, Robert was in the cabin of the boat wrapped in blankets crunched up in a chair while Billy was in the galley heating up a pot of water. "You're crazy, man. You know that?" the kidnaped youth said.

Accepting a cup of coffee, Robert took a couple gulps and looked around. The inside of the boat had been cleaned up and restored to her previous condition. She was as immaculate as Robert remembered from the past. Feeling the warmth come back into his body, he said. "You want to tell me what's going on, Billy?"

"Is Samantha okay?" Billy said.

"Yes, she's right outside."

"In the water!"

"No, she's on the pier. Speaking of which, I need to let her know you're okay." He started to get up, but the weakness of his legs caused him to fall back into the chair.

"Hold on there, cowboy," Billy said. "I'll let her know we're both okay. I'll tell her to get you to the car quickly when you go back."

"When I go back. You're not coming with us?"

"I can't. I'll explain in a minute." He headed for the door, grabbing his cell phone along the way. Robert heard him walk along the starboard gunwale. He heard muffled voices. While Billy was gone, Robert focused on getting his body temperature back to normal. He didn't remember ever being so cold. Then he realized in a few minutes he was going to have to do it all over again, although the return trip would be a lot quicker.

When Billy returned, he plopped down on a chair across from his friend and said, "I told Sam you were okay and to be ready when you came out of the water to get you to the car quickly. I'm going to let her know right before you go back out. She's going to pull the car up to the dock and have it warmed."

"That's too dangerous," Robert protested.

"There's nobody around. If there is, she'll say the client she was showing around fell in the water."

"Whatever."

"Anyway, how'd you find me?" Billy asked.

"Your phone message."

"Then it worked!"

"Except the boat wasn't where she was supposed to be. We had to pull that out of the marina owner, Albert."

"I'm glad you put the pieces to together," Billy said. There was an obvious sense of relief in his voice.

"You okay?"

Billy nodded.

"What's going on, Billy?"

Billy refilled Robert's coffee. "The short version is that I'm being held hostage here by Marvin Goldberg. He's threatened that if I try to leave or if anything happens to me, Sam and other members of my family will pay dearly. He says I only have to stay here until after the wedding, which he says is going to happen in a couple days. Except for cigarettes, the boat's pretty well provisioned. All the comforts of home."

"How does he know you're here?"

Billy pointed to the cell phone he had dropped back on the table. "He calls me numerous times a day in a very random pattern. Sometimes five minutes apart, sometimes an hour, sometimes several. When he calls, he asks me a question, like a scavenger hunt."

"Questions like what?"

"All kind of shit, things about the boat mostly. For example, the last one was the serial number on the microwave in the galley. Earlier today he wanted to know what word was marked in red in one of the books he left up forward. He's even asked me about words in books that aren't marked. I've looked around to try and anticipate what he may ask next, but he's too well planned. On top of that, he comes down here every couple of days to check on me himself."

"He comes here!"

"Relax," Billy directed. "He was here last night. He never comes two nights in a row."

"He's due tomorrow night?"

"If he keeps the pattern." Billy paused to light a cigarette. "I guess you don't have any of these with you, do you?" Robert nodded in the negative. Billy put the unlit cigarette back down. "I'd better save it," he said.

Robert looked around. Except for a small lamp on the table, the cabin was dark. "What do you do for power? Batteries can't stay charged too long, can they?"

"Marvin starts the engines when he's here to charge them," Billy explained. "I have an AC adapter for the cell phone which keeps that charged as well. He checks the cell phone, too, to make sure I haven't made any calls. As far as water, the tanks are full. Luckily, it hasn't been too cold. The propane bottles are full, so I can turn the stove on if I need to."

"He has everything figured out," Robert said.

"He's got me by the balls," Billy said. "There's nothing I can do."

Robert sat silently a moment. "Least not yet."

66

Fifteen minutes later, Samantha and Robert were driving through the back entrance of the development. Samantha was at the wheel because even though Robert was only in the water a short time the second time, the hypothermia quickly returned. He was shivering so hard, she talked about getting him to a doctor. He reminded her that he was a doctor arguing that he would be okay in a few minutes. He told Samantha she only had to worry if he passed out and the shivering stopped. She skeptically accepted the explanation, pointing out that the closest doctor was in Nags Head anyway. Samantha was leery about leaving Billy, but her brother reassured her he was okay. Besides, that they didn't have a choice.

Once they were out of the town limits of Ocracoke heading north towards the ferry, Samantha settled down. A few miles down the road, Robert was warm enough to talk, explaining to Samantha what was going on. He continually reassured her that Billy was okay, and they would get him out soon. When she queried him as to the how, he admitted he hadn't worked it all out yet. He didn't tell her he was hoping Dennis would arrive with a plan in place.

Robert decided in the meantime he wasn't going to let Samantha out of his sight. She protested at first, but when he insisted, she relented. She made a few phone calls to check on the campground and to make arrangement for someone to open in the morning. The cousins said they would stay if needed. Samantha also called her mother, claiming she had to go to Goldberg's main office in Ocean City for an emergency meeting. She said someone was threatening to renege on a large contract.

A couple hours later found them at the diner in Nags Head where Robert stopped the first night he returned to the island. Having changed clothes during the ferry ride, Robert was nearly back to normal with no apparent side effects from the ordeal, at least not physically. It would be a long time before he could bury the memory of just how cold he was. They ate a light dinner, Samantha opting for a salad, Robert a grilled cheese with a bowl of crab soup. Luckily, the motel had rooms left. Robert checked in under a false name and paid cash. While he got the inevitable evil eye, the young desk clerk smiled and quipped to have a good time.

The room as ordered had two double beds. There was the standard TV, microwave and small fridge. Complimentary coffee and a small coffee pot stood ready for whoever woke up first in the morning. He doubted whether it would be him.

Making sure all the doors were locked and making sure Samantha understood she was not to leave the room, Robert went into the bathroom to shower. While he was basically warm and dry, he felt a lingering deep-down chill. He was also covered in silt and salt. He turned the water up as hot as he could tolerate. He leaned forward, letting the spray hit him on the shoulders and run off his back.

Time passed. As steam started to build, his muscles began to relax. With that, a cloud of fatigue enveloped him. In all the excitement, Robert had forgotten how tired he was. He looked forward to a good night's sleep.

When he heard the door to the bathroom open, he straightened up and listened. The door closed. Silence followed. He had images of Marvin Goldberg coming at him with a knife. Oddly enough, all Robert wondered was just how big a knife?

"Robert," a voice said softly.

"Sam?"

There was a giggle. "Who else would you be expecting?"

He started to answer with the words Marvin Goldberg, but he wisely kept the response to himself. "No one."

"You've been in here awhile; I just wanted to make sure you're okay."

"I'm okay."

"Then I'll be out here."

Robert heard the door start to open. "Sam..."

"Yes?"

"Stay...please."

He sensed her hesitation. The door was reclosed. He heard her move toward him. His fatigue dissipated. His senses perked up. The shower curtain moved. Her head peeked around the corner. Even with the steam-filled air, he could see her face. "Hi," she said.

"Hi," he returned.

"You sure you're okay?"

"I could be better."

"You could?"

He reached out and grabbed her by the arm. He pulled gently. He expected some resistance. There was none. She had already undressed down to her underclothes which she easily removed. He held her arm for safety as she stepped into the shower. They faced one another. He stepped aside so she could get beneath the stream and get warm. She put her head back and wet her hair.

Water ran down her face, past her neck and across her chest. She shivered as warm water met cool skin. She straightened up and looked at him. Her eyes bore into him deeply. She wore a thin smile. Her lips parted slightly. He moved toward her. Again, she showed no resistance. Their lips met. They were salty. When he realized it was probably coming from him. He pulled away. "Sorry," he muttered, wiping an arm across his mouth.

"No need to be. You're salty because of me."

He wisely realized now was not the time to argue the point. They kissed again. Mouths were pried open. Tongues began to explore. An arm went around her neck. He pulled her into him. Their bodies pressed together, mouth to mouth, chest to chest, torso to torso. Her hands encircled his waist, locking around his lower spine. Then they unlocked and dropped lower. She grabbed the cheeks of his buttocks and pulled him into her. At the same time, she arched her pelvis towards him. Their mouths parted. She started to move gently side to side. She moaned softly.

His hands found her breasts. They were soft, just like he remembered. Her nipples were erect, just like he remembered. Like opposite charged magnets, their lips found one another again. She continued to pull him into her, her fingers gently digging into his backside. As his own excitement continued to grow, he could feel her body warm as well. Her skin turned a glowing red. His hands slid around her and pulled her closer. Their bodies pressed together. His breathing became rapid. Sweat rolled from his pours. For a fleeting moment, he remembered that just a few hours before he challenged death with hypothermia. Now he was on the verge of ecstasy. A much more pleasant way to go, he thought.

A hand freed itself from his backside and moved around and slid between them. It found its target easily, her fingers wrapping around him firmly. A shiver went up his spine. Sensing his readiness, she guided him into her. "Oh my God," he said, as her warmth surrounded him.

"You have no clue how much I've missed you," she said.

"I think there are plenty of clues that we've missed each other," he managed to say.

She giggled. Her earlier sideway motion now switched to fore and aft. Her eyes closed. Her head went back. Her lips were parted slightly as she breathed heavily through her mouth. He pushed into her harder, deeper, faster. She accepted him eagerly, arching with each motion. Their body temperatures rose together. When they reached their boiling points, they exploded as one.

67

Robert awoke the next morning to the smell of fresh brewed coffee. There was soft music coming from the radio. It took him a moment to reorient. He looked around the room. His memory cleared. He focused on the night before. He remembered being cold, colder than he'd ever been in his life. He remembered being in the shower with Samantha, no longer cold. He wondered if it was a dream. An uncontrollable shiver went through his body. His toes curled upward, threatening to cramp. Other appendages awoke. He rolled to his left. No one there. He found the same results in the opposite direction. He was about to sit up when he heard motion. Someone was in the bathroom. Samantha walked out; her hair wrapped in an oversized bath towel. Her body wrapped in another. She gave him a big smile and a good morning. No, last night was not a dream.

He managed to stammer a hello, watching her every move as she stepped toward him. She sat on the edge of the bed. She leaned forward, kissing him, gently at first, then with more vigor. She smelled so clean, so fresh. She tasted the same. She straightened up, readjusting the towel that was threatening to fall. Shucks, he thought. He forced his eyes off her body and back to her face. She continued to smile broadly. God, she was so beautiful.

"Thank you for last night," she said.

"Thank me? Thank you!" he replied. He reached up and drew a vertical line down the middle of the towel with a finger.

She laughed. "No silly. Not for that. Thanks for what you did for Billy."

"We really haven't done anything yet," he argued weakly.

"You found him and he's okay. That's a start."

"There's a lot to do yet."

"You have a plan?"

It was Robert's turn to laugh. "I suspect it'll be here soon."

"What do we do in the meantime?"

"What do you want to do?"

Samantha's expression turned serious. "You know, Robert, last night brought back a lot of memories."

"Good ones I hope."

Her hand caressed his face. "What's going to happen to us when this is all over?"

"You want the truth?"

"Please."

His eyes moved to the curtains that were partially open, letting in a few rays of the morning light. He couldn't tell if the sky was clear or cloudy, but what he remembered from the night before, it was probably the latter. "Truth is I really don't know. I'll be finished residency in a couple months, and then I'll have to find a job. It'll seem strange, I'm sure. It will be the first time I can remember not being in school. I have several leads, including an offer to stay on as faculty at Hopkins, but I haven't decided yet."

"Faculty at Hopkins! That'll be pretty prestigious, wouldn't it?"

His eyes darted back at her, his head tipping to the side. "You know, Sam, that's the first positive thing you've ever said about my training?"

She smiled softly. "I'm trying, Robert. I really am."

"Thank you."

She nodded.

Robert continued. "However, that said, I promise you this, while you and I may be apart geographically, we will never be apart again. That goes for Billy, too."

Samantha's eyes started to water. "Oh, Robert." She leaned forward and kissed him again. Robert wrapped his arms around her neck. They kissed long and hard. Then he gently licked the tears from her face. He reached up and pulled the towel off her head. Wet hair careened onto his face. He grabbed a few strands and pulled in a deep breath, again, so clean and fresh. She pulled her hair away and kissed him on the forehead. His hands went around her waist. He pulled her upward. At the same time, he scooted down in the bed. He buried his face in her chest, planting gentle kisses on the towel. He reached up and pulled the towel away. He could only stare. More gentle kisses followed.

"You know what?" Robert said.

"What?"

"If this keeps up, we may never rescue Billy."

Samantha rolled on her side and slid beneath the covers. She guided his hand between her legs. Her legs parted as he pressed a finger into her. God, she felt so good. He rubbed her softly, then more firmly. A bolt of electricity enveloped her. She grabbed the covers and threw them off. Was he going to get cold like last night, he wondered? Her hands began to explore his body, first his shoulders, and then his chest. The coolness of the air along with her touch caused him to break out in goose bumps.

Being cold was the furthest thing from his mind.

68

They were asleep in each other's arms when Robert's cell phone rang. It took him a moment to awaken and reorient. He grabbed the device off the table right before it switched over to voice mail. "Hello," he stammered.

"Robert?"

Recognizing the voice, he said, "Dennis, where are you?"

"I'm just passing those big dunes where the Wright brothers flew their airplane. Where are you?"

"We're...I'm in Nags Head. That's just a few miles down the road."

Dennis chuckled. "You're not alone, are you?"

"Dennis!"

"You'd better be with Samantha."

"I am."

The pathology's voice turned serious. "So, what's up? Did you find Billy? Where is he? Is he okay?"

Robert sat on the edge of the bed. By now Samantha was awake and listening. Robert answered the questions as best he could remember. "We found Billy. He's being held hostage aboard *Lady Hatteras II*, and he's fine."

"How do you know all that?" Dennis said.

"I was with him a little while last night?"

"You were with him? You couldn't get him away."

"It's more complicated than that," Robert replied. "I'll explain when you get here." He gave Dennis directions to the diner. When he hung up, he turned to Samantha. "I don't know what it is yet, but our plan has arrived."

Samantha smiled and kissed her bed partner. "I'm going to go take a shower," she said. "If he's at the Wright Brother's monument, he'll be here soon. Make some more coffee, will ya, please?"

Forty minutes later the trio was sitting in a booth tucked away in the back of the diner. It was early yet, and while there were customers, they had plenty of privacy. Robert filled Dennis in on the events from the night before, at least the events dealing with Billy. Dennis listened intently as he downed a plate of sausage gravy over home fries. Robert and Samantha chose the continental breakfast. When Robert was finished bringing Dennis up to date, the pathology resident sat quietly a long minute. Wiping the last glob of gravy off the plate with a biscuit, he said, "Well, guys, I think we have Marvin Goldberg right where we want him."

"Huh?" the other two participants in the conversation said simultaneously.

Dennis explained his plan.

69

As expected, the sky was cloudy. What the group didn't anticipate was the weather continuing to deteriorate throughout the day. An early morning five knot breeze quickly became ten, with gusts as high as twenty. That was before noon. The temperature fell throughout the day. The storm that was offshore to the south took a westward bend and headed directly toward the Outer Banks. Storms of this nature were common, so the locals took the weather forecast in stride, planning their day around when the worst was expected to strike; in this case, sometime after midnight. Naive to the local weather patterns, Dennis took the clouding sky as a sign it might rain later. Robert and Samantha seemed more worried, although neither said anything. Like Robert anticipated, Dennis had a plan. The pathology resident sleuth wannabe had already made the necessary phone calls and had everything lined up for the evening's *festivities*. There wasn't a whole lot to do, just wait and watch the sky become more and more ominous as the day wore on.

After breakfast, they drove to the Rodanthe pier where they transferred Dennis's gear from his old VW

Beetle to Robert's SUV. They piled into the Beemer and headed south, stopping at the campground while Samantha checked in to make sure the day was going okay. The cousins were still there from the night before, looking fresh and eager. Oh, Samantha wooed to herself, to be young again, to be so energetic with so little sleep. But money talks. When she called them the night before, she promised they'd be well rewarded for their efforts today. When she left, she asked them to tell her parents she'd be gone for most of the day. The issues in Ocean City had been resolved amicably. Now, she had a couple clients she was going to be with up in Nags Head. She didn't want anyone to even begin thinking she was heading in the opposite direction. As for Arthur Goldberg, she left a message that she had to go up to Nags Head. Only to him she claimed she had to go to the Verizon store to have her cell phone checked out. She had dropped it in the toilet again.

To kill some time, Robert and Samantha took Dennis on a tour of the island. They insisted the dunes of Hatteras were much more beautiful on a clear day. Dennis said they looked fine to him the way they were. He noted, "Sometimes sunshine is overrated for making something look beautiful." Robert looked over at Samantha who was in the front passenger seat. Dennis was right. Some things were beautiful regardless of the lighting. Dennis spent some time on his cell phone making final arrangements for the evening. Robert had to smile as his friend acted as if he was directing a play, barking out orders as he insisted on the specific timeframes he laid out. The smile faded when Robert realized this was not a play, but a real-life scenario with real life people, one of whom was deadly.

Surprisingly, time passed quickly. At five o'clock, the Beemer was parked in the parking lot of Hatteras Lighthouse. Dennis checked the schedule on his clipboard. He quoted his favorite line from one of his favorite movies, *The American President*, "Let meatloaf night begin."

And so it did.

70

Billy paced back and forth across the cabin floor. He held his cell phone in one hand. He brushed the hair out of his face with the other. When his breath became heavy, he stopped and dialed a number. Fingers on both hands were crossed, praying that the owner of the number would pick up.

He did. Only instead of the normal phone etiquette where pleasantries were exchanged at first, Marvin Goldberg lit into the caller. "What the fuck you doing calling me? I thought I told you never to do that. This had better be important."

Keeping his cool and making sure his breathing was still heavy, Billy replied. "I want to make sure you're coming down tonight."

"What the fuck does that matter?"

"I need cigarettes. I only have one left," Billy said.

"You called me because you need cigarettes?" the man yelled.

"I'm going crazy here, Mr. Goldberg. I've done everything you've told me to do. But if I don't get some cigarettes soon, I'm going to go bonkers. You smoke heavily. You know exactly how I feel. If you don't bring me some cigarettes soon, I'm going to go out and get them myself."

There was a pause on the other end as the older Goldberg assessed the situation. "You're not going anywhere! You hear me Billy? Remember, your sister?"

"I don't give a damn about my sister," Billy shouted. "I need cigarettes!" With that, he closed the cover on the cell phone, disconnecting the call.

The phone rang almost immediately. "Hello," Billy said, his voice filled with agitation.

This time the voice on the other end, while forced, was much more pleasant. "Listen, Billy. You sit tight, okay? You're right, you've done everything okay so far. Let's not blow it now, you hear?"

"But Mr. Goldberg, I need cigarettes."

"I'll be down there tonight, Billy. I'll bring you cigarettes then. I promise.

Billy hesitated. "What time will you be here?"

"I can't give you an exact time, Billy. I'll be there when I can."

"I don't know..."

"You just sit tight, you hear?"

"I'll try Mr. Goldberg. I'll try." There was such a pathetic sound to the boy's voice.

"You take it easy, Billy," Goldberg said. "I'll see you in a little while." The call disconnected again.

Dorsey Butterbaugh

Billy laid the cell phone down on the table and smiled. He then proceeded to open the fresh pack of cigarettes he held in his other hand.

71

Marvin Goldberg pulled headfirst into a parking space right on the edge of the water. He put the Mercedes in park, letting the engine run. For the umpteenth time since pulling off the ferry at the other end of Ocracoke, he took a long glance in the rearview mirror. While he had seen nothing to cause suspicion, his senses were heightened. There was an uneasy feel in the air. Goldberg took a long drag on his cigarette, the fourth since leaving the ferry. He told himself the deteriorating weather was increasing his paranoia. He told himself the opposite should be happening. The wind and the rain would serve as an additional cover. He told himself to calm down. Things were going as planned. In another couple days, his brother would be married, and all would be right with the fellows in Atlantic City. He chuckled softly. He'd heard a lot of rumors why he was forcing his brother to marry the girl, including him wanting a woman on their team. Truth be told, it wasn't as much about building the team as it was to show that he had control over his brother, which the boys in Atlantic City were starting to question. As Marvin well knew, they were all about control. He came up with this scheme to prove that he was still the boss. Once the two were married, Marvin was confident he could bring Samantha under his wing as well, If nothing else, she was a nice diversion.

Marvin finished his cigarette and grabbed the bag sitting on the passenger seat. He knew he should be livid with Billy. At the same time, Billy had been cooperative so far, far more than Goldberg had expected. And like the boy said, he knew what it was like to be out of cigarettes. It was a bitch. He told himself not to be too hard on the kid. As an old mentor once told him, sugar was often better than bullets, and a whole lot less complicated. Yes, he decided, now was the time for some sugar.

He turned off the engine, made a final check in the mirror and exited the car. He started to lock the door with the electronic key but stopped short. He didn't want to make any more noise than necessary. He pulled the collar up on his coat and headed toward the boathouse. In a minute, he would know if the boy had indeed behaved.

He walked down the south side finger pier and stopped at the side door. Holding a small flashlight, he looked at the lock. It appeared the same as when he last left. He spun the numbers to the appropriate combination. The lock popped open with a gentle tug. A hint of paranoia still present, he looked down the finger pier in both directions. A cold gust of wind cut his survey short.

Inside the cabin, he found Billy sitting on the sofa, drawing on a cigarette and slowly blowing the smoke into the air. The smell of cigarettes permeated the air. Marvin Goldberg's olfactory sense kicked in and immediately told him something was wrong. He took in another breath and recognized it as the smell of menthol. Then he remembered he had never brought Billy menthol cigarettes. His gaze turned toward the table besides the sofa. Sure enough, two packs of generic menthol cigarettes sat beside a plastic cup of water filled with ashes and cigarette butts. His earlier plan of being nice to the boy went by the wayside. "Where the fuck'd you get those, boy?" he demanded.

Billy looked at him, an innocent expression on his face. "I couldn't wait," he said.

"I asked you a question, boy." He stepped toward the youth. He pulled a pistol from his waistband and reared back to strike when a voice from the galley startled him, causing him to pause. "I brought 'em."

Goldberg spun to his left and squinted into the darkness. A figure stepped up to the main salon. "Billy called me and told me he needed cigarettes. He told me he was going to go crazy if he didn't get any. I asked him where he was. He told me. I asked him what he was doing here. He said he would tell me when I got here, which he did. Now, I'm not here to cause any problems, nor am I interested in getting wrapped up in something that's none of my business. I just brought a friend his cigarettes. So, I think I'll just take my leave, and leave you two alone." The figure moved toward the door.

Goldberg waved the gun in his direction. "You're not going anywhere. And as far as getting wrapped up in something, you did that the moment you stepped aboard this boat." He wanted to say something else, but a couple questions started rolling around in the back of his mind, questions he couldn't quite get into focus yet.

"I just..."

"Shut up!" Goldberg commanded. The arm with the gun stretched out a few inches. "Who the fuck are you, anyway?"

"Robert...Robert Battlegrove."

"How do you know Billy?"

"Old friends," Robert said. "Actually, I was on my way down here to see him when he called."

Goldberg stared at Robert and then at Billy. "How did you get in here?"

"Through the side door, just like you."

"But it was locked."

"I guessed at the combination."

"How'd you do that?"

"Billy told me you spent a lot of time in Atlantic City, so I figured you liked to gamble. I got it on the first try actually."

"The first try?"

"7777 made good sense to me."

Goldberg was impressed. He stepped toward the middle of the cabin. He motioned Robert to take a seat beside Billy, wondering what to do next. He was feeling mixed emotions; anger, confusion, paranoia, and even a speck of fear, something unusual for him. He focused on Billy. "You know boy, you've really caused a problem for yourself."

His arm again reared back for a strike. Again, a voice caused him to pause. His head snapped toward the darkness of the galley. His mouth dropped open as Samantha stepped up to the main salon. "There's no need to get violent, Marvin," she said. She stared him down. The arm dropped.

"How the fu...hell did you get in here?" he said.

"I came with Robert. He called me after Billy called him to make sure this wasn't some sort of a joke. I assured him it wasn't. When Robert said he was coming down here to bring him cigarettes, I insisted on coming along. I wanted to make sure Billy was okay."

"He was okay till you two came on board." Now, Marvin Goldberg was really at a loss for words, and at a loss for what to do. "Jesus Christ," he said aloud.

Billy started to stand up, but Goldberg motioned him to sit back down. "Listen, Mr. Goldberg, nothing has changed. I needed cigarettes, which I have. My sister wanted to make sure I was okay, which she has, and now we can continue with the plan."

"What about him?" Goldberg said, motioning to Robert.

"Robert here's a very smart man. He ain't going to do anything stupid, are you, Asshole?" Billy said.

Robert nodded in agreement.

Samantha spoke next. "Why don't you just let Robert and I get out of here and we'll continue with the plan. I don't know if you've spoken to Arthur lately, but we're getting married this weekend. Then it'll all be over."

It was obvious the older Goldberg was struggling with the dilemma confronting him. Plus, there was still an unfocused question. Little did he know that in a few seconds, the situation would worsen.

72

The ringing of his cell phone startled him, so Marvin Goldberg almost dropped the gun. He snatched the phone from his pocket. Flipping it open, he looked at the number. It wasn't one he recognized. "Hello," he said with trepidation. Questions from before continued swirling through his mind. His sense of fear rose as well.

"Marvin Goldberg?"

"Yeah. Who's this?"

"This is Agent Stackhouse, FBI. We have you surrounded Mr. Goldberg. We need you to come out with your hands up." Goldberg's face turned pale.

While the wind was really starting to howl outside, *Lady Hatteras II* was still well protected by the boat garage, allowing the occupants of the cabin to hear the phone conversation. Billy stepped toward the door of the cabin. "What the hell have you done, Mr. Goldberg?"

"What have I done?" The man of the hour glared at Robert then at Samantha. "You two..."

"They've done nothing," Billy snapped. "The FBI isn't after them. They're after you. They followed you here. You asshole!"

Before Goldberg could say anything, Samantha spoke up. "Did you drive your Mercedes here?"

"Yes, why?"

Samantha continued quickly. "Someone came into the store the other day. They first asked for Arthur. I told him he wasn't around. Then they asked for you. I told them the same. He was kind of a tall muscular looking guy. I figured he was one of your business partners. He didn't say anything else except he wanted to know what kind of car you were driving these days. I told him the last time I saw you, you were in a black Mercedes, Again, I didn't think anything of it."

"You asshole," Billy snapped. "You led them right to us."

"To us?"

"Yeah," Billy continued. "While Robert and Samantha here are innocent victims in this whole mess, I stayed here on my own accord, so I'm in trouble too." He was becoming visibly agitated.

"Settle down, Billy," Goldberg directed. "You're not in any trouble. It's me they're after."

"But..."

"I kidnaped you, remember?"

"You kidnaped my brother?" Samantha snapped.

Goldberg's stare turned in her direction. "That's what I said, isn't it?"

Samantha leaned back in her seat. "I just wanted to make sure I was hearing you correctly."

"You heard me correctly, and you're going to continue hearing me, and doing exactly what I say. Understand?"

Billy motioned to the phone that was still open in the man's hand. "What are you going to tell him?"

Goldberg looked at the phone and brought it back up to his ear. "I'm not going anywhere. You're not coming in here either. I have people in here with me. Understand?.."

"Are you saying you have hostages?" the FBI agent said.

Goldberg hesitated. A sinking feeling continued to envelop him. He knew he had to think of something fast. "Yes, I have hostages…three of them. So, stay back. If you don't..." He snapped the phone shut. His head turned and looked around the room. Robert and Samantha were now sitting on the couch. Billy was gazing out the rear door into the darkness.

Billy turned and said, "I don't know what you have in mind, Mr. Goldberg, but I know we gotta get out of here."

"We?"

"I told you, I'm in this with you."

The man with the gun didn't argue the point. For the time being, he had an ally. Billy continued. "He said we were surrounded, right?"

Goldberg nodded.

"And he said FBI, right?"

Goldberg again nodded.

"FBI's land based. They ain't got boats. That leaves us a way out." Billy motioned toward the back of the boat.

"You mean leave here in the boat?"

"It's the only way," Billy said.

Goldberg hesitated. "It's raining and blowing out there."

"That's just a small squall," Billy said. "It'll be over soon anyway."

"You sure?"

Billy shrugged. "It doesn't matter. This is the *Lady Hatteras II*. She can take anything Mother Nature can throw her way."

"How quick can we be underway?"

"Immediately."

Goldberg nodded his approval. Billy headed out the door. "Where you going?" Goldberg snapped.

Billy continued to slide the door open as he said, "I'm going up to the fly bridge to start the engines. Then I'm going to undo the dock lines. When I give the word, you put the garage door up, but only when I give the word. Okay?"

The boy was smart, Goldberg thought. Maybe he'd give him a job once this whole mess was over. He looked at him, then at Robert who was unable to hide his nervousness, and then at Samantha who for whatever reason seemed to be the calmest of them all. Then his gaze turned toward the starboard window, the side of the boat garage with the door. "Shit," he said aloud. How did he miss that? The unfocused question rolling around in his mind had suddenly become clear. If Robert and Samantha came through the door and were still here, then how did the door get relocked? The answer was a simple three letters: FBI. "Shit," he repeated. He told himself to get a grip. He'd been in tight situations before. Now was not the time to lose control. His eyes went back to Billy who was still waiting for an answer. He nodded his approval.

As Billy made his way up the fly bridge, Samantha piped up. "So now, you've not only kidnapped Billy, you're also going to kidnap us."

"Shut up!" Goldberg snapped.

"Answer the question, damn it!" Samantha snapped back.

Goldberg stared at her a second time. She was not only calm, she was also rather brazen considering there was a gun pointed her way. His eyes turned toward Robert. "I don't know how well you know Billy's sister here, but she's a real pistol." He waved the gun in her direction and let out a loud laugh. "Yes, sister-in-law to be. I'm kidnaping you two, also."

"And taking us out to sea."

Goldberg cocked his head to the side. "I don't know what difference that makes, but yes. I'm taking you out to sea."

He felt vibrations beneath his feet as the port engine came to life. The starboard engine followed suit. He reached into his pocket for the remote control to the boat-garage door. His fear was starting to subside. His panic level was dropping. Things were beginning to look up.

Or so he wanted to believe.

73

Agent Andy Stackhouse stood in the shadows of the southernmost building. Making sure not to dislodge the bilateral earpieces, he pulled his collar tightly around his neck. The building offered protection from querying eyes; it did little, however, to protect him from the wind and rain that was rolling off the ocean. He took it all in stride, however. It was part of the job. One of the main reasons he took the assignment in the Richmond office was because he liked to fish. However, you couldn't control the weather with the sport. He let a smile cross his otherwise stoic face. He was going to catch one of the biggest fish of his career tonight.

He watched as the boat passed through the last set of buoys leading from the harbor. While the weather was bad, she seemed to be riding it well. Static from his right earpiece broke his train of thought. "This is Coast Guard cutter *Avalon*. Come in Agent Stackhouse."

"Stackhouse here," he said into the mouthpiece curving around his left cheek.

"How do you read, over?"

"Loud and clear. Back to ya."

The radioman on the Coast Guard cutter failed to hide a chuckle at the response. "Were you able to hear their conversation? Over."

Stackhouse's stomach was still churning from what he heard a few moments ago. "Yes, sir, I did, loud and clear. Over."

"We copied, too," the radioman said. There was a short pause. "We have the vessel on radar. Looks like she's just leaving the harbor now."

"That's a Roger, *Avalon*. I'm losing her visibly as we speak."

"That's a 10 - 4, sir. We got her from here. Over."

"See you back at the station in a few."

"Roger that." The line went dead. Agent Stackhouse watched a moment before heading toward his car. On the way, he signed the clipboard authorizing the impounding of the black Mercedes sitting in the parking lot. Yes, like the one hostage said, the FBI didn't have boats.

But the Coast Guard did.

74

Wind gusts reached thirty knots. The seas had already built to four feet. *Lady Hatteras II*, while objecting at times to the water pounding against her hull, took the weather well. The storm was coming directly from the east, the direction she was heading. Once they cleared the harbor inlet, Billy came down from the bridge and steered from the lower helm station. He turned on the GPS and set the auto pilot to due east. When Goldberg asked where they were headed, Billy replied nowhere yet. They needed to ride out the storm first. Goldberg then asked about the possibility of running into another vessel on a night like this since there was basically no visibility. Billy replied that only idiots would be at sea on a night like this.

Billy stood easily at the helm, while Goldberg sat on one of the cushioned chairs Albert had put back on the boat. Samantha and Robert remained on the small couch that had been added as well. The wind could be heard howling outside. The engines ran smoothly below deck. Despite all this, the noise level within the cabin was such you could still hear yourself think. You could hear yourself talk.

Which is what Robert started doing. "Why is the FBI coming after you? They certainly don't know anything about you kidnapping Billy?"

Goldberg broke out in a mild smirk. "To be honest, I haven't a clue." The smile disappeared. "But you'd better believe I'm going to find out."

"It's probably about the boy," Billy said.

"What boy?" Goldberg inquired.

"You know, Mr. Goldberg, the Friday before Memorial Day weekend some five years ago. You remember the boy, don't you?" Billy said.

"What boy are you talking about?"

"Captain Willey took you and your brother fishing that day. Your brother brought a young boy with him."

Goldberg's expression turned serious. "How would you know about that?" he demanded.

"I was there. I was the mate, remember?"

Goldberg's head tipped to the side. "You know, kid, I always thought I recognized you from somewhere."

"I thought you knew."

"No."

"I was there that day," Billy said. "I don't know what happened on the way back in, but I do know the boy never left the boat after we docked."

"How did you know that? You left the boat before us. I made sure the captain shooed you off first."

"He did. I thought that a little odd, too. But it had been a long week and I was tired. Besides, when Captain Willey told you to do something, you tended to do it. But

I stayed on shore and watched. The boy never left the boat."

Goldberg didn't know whether to be angry or laugh. It seemed with every passing minute something else came up complicating the situation. He decided both reactions were appropriate. Aloud, he said, "I thought you were just some stupid kid. I didn't think you saw anything."

"Well, I did."

"That just complicates matters more, doesn't it?"

"How so?" Robert asked.

"It just does."

"What happened with the boy?" Samantha said

Goldberg's mind returned to that day those five years before. If only the boy had listened and done what he was told, nothing bad would have happened, at least nothing bad in Goldberg's mind. But the boy didn't listen. He put up a fierce fight, even after he was all drunked up. If he had only did what he was told. Goldberg felt bad for the boy. He was so young...so cute...He would have made a good...

He cut the thought off. Focusing on Samantha, "My brother wanted to bring this kid along on the trip. He was a brother of one of the secretaries in the main office in Fenwick. He said he promised the kid a boat ride as a bonus for doing a good job of cleaning the office that summer. I didn't really want any kids tagging along, but it didn't really matter to me. Besides, he was a good looking boy." He gave Samantha a wink, which sent a chill up her as well as Robert's spine. "Anyway, the captain didn't like it none either. But we fixed that with an extra hundred-dollar bill and the threat of no boy, no boat ride." He let out a soft chuckle. "You know, no matter what business you're in, money talks." He paused and lit two cigarettes. Handing one to Billy, he continued. "Anyway, as I recall, we didn't catch a whole lot of fish that day, so the trip was starting to be a little boring. On the way home Billy went up on the bridge with the captain, the boy went into the cabin to go to the bathroom. When he didn't come out for a while, I went in to check on him. Low and behold, he found my bottle of Jack and was making quite a dent in it. I gave him a bunch of crap. He told me he was sorry and would pay me back anyway I wanted. When I told him what the payment would be, he started getting really agitated like. He was drunk by then, too."

"Exactly what was the payment, Marvin?" Samantha queried.

He stared at her a moment. "You really want the details, huh?"

"Why not?" Robert chimed in. "I seriously doubt either of us is going to survive this ordeal, so if it's my time to go, then I'd at least like to know why."

"What makes you think you're not going to survive?"

"Think about it Mr. Goldberg. Can you afford to let us live?"

Goldberg's head again cocked to the side. At the same time, the gun which he had been holding in his lap was again pointed in their direction. "You're a smart man. What's your name...Robert?"

Robert nodded.

"What kind of work do you do?"

"Actually, I'm looking for work at the moment," Robert said. It was not a lie either.

Goldberg paused, glancing between the two sitting on the couch. He closed his eyes a moment as the boat rolled especially hard in response to a larger than normal wave. He then looked at Billy. The question: could he afford to allow any of them to live? His eyes refocused back on Samantha. "The payment was a little tussle in the hay, if you know what I mean."

"A tussle in the hay?" Robert said.

"I thought you were smart," Goldberg laughed. "I wanted him to, you know, to suck my dick." A hand went up to Samantha's mouth. Robert just stared. "Oh, don't tell me you haven't heard of such a thing," Goldberg snapped. "The world's full of little boys who like to make money."

"So that's what happened, huh?" Robert said, forcing his voice to remain calm.

Goldberg let out his loudest laugh, yet. "Actually, no that's not what happened. Like, I said, the boy was starting to get agitated. When I tried to collect the payment I was due, he started to attack me. I fought him off. He went into the bathroom where he puked all over the place. When he came out, he was half naked. He was crying saying his clothes were all messed up. By now I'd had a couple drinks myself and was pretty pissed. Not only was the situation getting out of control, I wasn't getting the payment I wanted. So I tried again. I thought he was going to be more cooperative this time. At the last minute, he balked again. I thought he was going to puke all over me this time, so I shoved him away. Unfortunately, I guess I pushed a little too hard. He fell back and struck his head on the door. He never woke up."

"You mean he died?" Robert said.

"It was an accident," Goldberg insisted. "I never meant to kill the boy."

"Poor boy," Samantha said.

"Poor boy?" Goldberg snapped. "All the kid had to do was do what he was told. He'd be alive today."

"What happened after that?" Robert said.

"Well, I had a mess on my hands," Goldberg said. "Instead of bloody fish all over the place, I had a bloody kid. So I threw him overboard."

"You threw him overboard?" Samantha said with disbelief.

"What the fuck else was I going to do with him? We couldn't very well take him back to shore. There'd be too many questions. I had my brother tell the family there was an accident and he slipped and fell overboard. We tried to save him, but he went down too fast. My brother, even with all his faults, is a great salesman, I'll give him that. He sold this one like a charm. I also had my brother make a nice deposit to the secretary's account to help cover any expenses that might arise."

"No one reported it to the police?" Robert said.

"That wasn't necessary. Nor would it have done any good. It was an accident. Reporting it to the police would have only stirred up a lot of cops noising around and asking a lot of dumb questions which would have uncovered a lot of things about the boy's sister and her family."

"They were illegal immigrants, weren't they?" Robert said.

"Maybe you are smart after all."

"You blackmailed them with the threat of deportation if they went to the police," Robert said.

"I don't know if I'd call it blackmail," Goldberg argued. "After all, we did give them a good hunk of change."

"What happened after that?" Robert said, trying hard to hide his disgust.

"Nothing much except that as I was throwing the body overboard, I happened to look up and see the captain staring down at me. He started to say something. I waved him quiet with my gun. I told him to come down off the bridge which he did. I asked him where the boy was...meaning Billy there. He told me Billy was asleep up on the bridge, which he did most trips back in. He assured me Billy saw or heard nothing. By now, the captain was starting to get agitated. I hushed him up, telling him that if he ever spoke a word of what he saw, I guaranteed his mate would never see another day at sea." Goldberg paused. "Your captain listened real well, Billy."

Billy said nothing.

"What happened next?" Robert continued to coax.

"Nothing. I told the captain there was a mess in the cabin. He told me to leave it. He'd clean it up later that evening. I told him to make sure Billy stayed out of the cabin. He assured me he would. He said he'd send the boy home soon as we docked, which is what he did."

"After that?" Robert coached.

"Nothing. We docked and the captain chased the boy off the boat immediately."

"Everything was okay after that, huh?" Robert said.

"Everything was okay after that."

There was a pause in the conversation as the boat rolled in response to another large wave. "We're really in the mountains now," Billy said.

"How much longer is this going to last?" Goldberg said. Quite frankly, he was getting tired of the whole ordeal and was ready to move onto the next step, whatever that was going to be. The only question he really had to decide was which country in South America he was going to go to. He always knew in the back of his mind this day may come. He was prepared financially along with the papers he'd need for such an occasion. While he was sad that the day had indeed arrived, as his colleagues in Atlantic City always said, business was business.

"I suspect it'll all be over soon," Billy said.

Goldberg had no inkling of exactly what Billy was referring to.

"What about the captain?" Robert said, anxious to get the conversation back on track.

"What about him?"

"Like you said, Mr. Goldberg, I'm not stupid. He disappeared the next day."

"Coast Guard report said he fell overboard," Goldberg said.

"Now, you and I both know that's not what happened," Robert said.

"Then, why don't you tell me what you think happened."

"I think we'd rather hear it from you," Samantha said.

Goldberg looked at her. "I was convinced the boy, Billy there, knew nothing about what happened. Turns out I was wrong, but that's what I thought at the time. As for the captain though, he couldn't be trusted. So he and I went for a boat ride the next day."

"You killed him?" Samantha nearly shouted.

Goldberg stared her down. "Don't take it personally; it's all about the business."

"But murder!"

Goldberg continued to glare at her.

"I'm curious," Robert said. "How'd you do it?"

"I figured the captain for a good man, so I made it a clean kill. One bullet to the head, and splash." The man almost seemed to snicker as he talked. "Bye-bye captain."

"You had to have someone else standing by in another boat to take you back to shore, right?"

"I certainly didn't swim back."

"What about his widow," Robert said. "Did you have anything to do with her death?"

"You are good, kid, aren't you? But no, in actuality, I had nothing to do with her death. She died of natural causes, just like the coroner's report said."

The storm began to abate, allowing everyone to relax somewhat. During this time, Robert looked at the man responsible for the death of the boy as well as *Lady Hatteras II's* captain. Keeping his emotions under control, he said, "I just have one question. How did your semen get in the boy's underwear?"

The question caught the man to whom it was addressed totally off guard. He looked long and hard before speaking. "How the hell do you know that?"

"Answer the question first, then I'll tell you," Robert said.

Still stunned, Goldberg stiffened his posture and waved the gun back and forth. Then a smile crossed his face and he relaxed. "I was a little drunk, I was horny as hell and I had just lost out on having a little boy for lunch. I guess you could say I had a party all by myself."

This time the snickering was obvious.

75

The storm let up a few minutes, and then returned with a new fury. It was as if Mother Nature was also angry at what she'd just heard. For the next ten minutes, the foursome could only focus on holding on. Having turned off the autopilot, Billy struggled to keep the bow of the boat pointed directly into the seas. While the ride was rough with water continuing to spray over the bow, *Lady Hatteras II* held her own. Billy had no doubt they'd be okay as he'd been out on her in rougher weather. Robert watched Billy's reaction, and since the local boy seemed unfazed, the Baltimore doctor felt safe, as did Samantha. Besides, she was too angry to do much other than watch Marvin Goldberg. For his part, Goldberg was holding on for dear life. While he wasn't one to get seasick, he was looking awfully peaked.

Another ten minutes and the storm subsided. This time it was over for good, just like Billy predicted. The sky cleared. A half-moon popped through a few lingering clouds. The seas, while still rough, dropped to a much more manageable three to four feet. Goldberg lit two cigarettes and handed one to Billy who accepted it with a nod. "That was an amusement park ride I don't think I want to go on any time soon," Marvin Goldberg said. He took a long drag on the cigarette. "Where we headed, Billy?"

"There's a Coast Guard cutter right up ahead of us. Maybe we'll mosey over to her and make sure she's okay."

Goldberg started to laugh and then jumped to his feet. He stepped to the helm and peered out the forward window. "What the fuck..." He glanced at Billy and then looked out ahead again. "Where did that come from?"

"She's been out here with us all along," Billy replied.

"How..."

Just then there was static on the radio. A voice came on a moment later. *"Lady Hatteras II, Lady Hatteras II, Lady Hatteras II, this is the United States Coast Guard cutter Avalon. Do you read me?"*

Before Goldberg could protest, Billy picked up the mike and said, "Cutter *Avalon*, this is *Lady Hatteras II*. We read you loud and clear."

"Is everybody on board okay?" the radioman queried.

"That's a roger. All five of us are fine."

Goldberg had had enough and was about to grab the microphone from Billy's hand when he realized what Billy just said. He looked around the cabin quickly. "Five?" Then he heard rustling from below and yet another figure appeared in the galley. "Who the fuck are you?" Goldberg demanded in surprise.

"The name's Dennis Tucker. Wish I could say it was a pleasure to meet you, then again maybe it is a pleasure." Dennis, with no apparent ill effects from the bumpy ride, took a couple steps forward. "Hey, Billy, next time I drive and you ride up forward."

Billy chuckled.

The voice on the radio interrupted any further conversation. "*Lady Hatteras II*, this is Coast Guard *Avalon*, over."

"We're still here," Billy said.

"Ask him if the transmission all went through," Dennis said.

Billy did as requested. "Cutter *Avalon*, did you receive the transmission?"

"Roger that. We have it all recorded, loud and clear. Nice work."

"Good," Dennis said. He turned his attention back to Goldberg. "I'd put that gun down if I were you, Mr. Goldberg. It's really not going to do you any good anymore."

"What makes you think that?" the man with the gun said.

"The jig's up Marvin. Everything that's been said in this cabin since you came on board has been recorded by me down below, by the Coast Guard and I also suspect by the FBI on land. That includes your confession of what you did to that little boy as well as the murder of Captain Willey."

Goldberg could only stare. He had a sick sense that things were beginning to collapse around him. But he'd been in sticky situations before and had always managed to get out of them. Why should this be any different? He still had the gun. With that thought, he stepped aside while motioning for Dennis to come up in the cabin with the others. He turned and moved back to the rear door so he could keep an eye on everyone. When he turned around, there was another surprise. Billy was now looking in his direction and was pointing something at him. It looked like a plastic pistol. Goldberg let out a laugh. "What the hell is that? A pee shooter?"

"Nah," Billy said. "It just happens to be a twelve-gauge flare gun. It may not be as powerful as the piece you're holding there, but what comes out is hot and burns like hell."

Goldberg laughed again.

"Here's how we figure it," Robert said. "It's obvious you don't value other people's lives, but I suspect you value your own. There's five of us and one of you, so here's the deal. Billy will count to three at which time you both will put your weapons down. No one will get hurt that way."

"What if I choose not to?" Goldberg hissed. He was working hard to control his growing level of agitation as well as his anger.

"I promise you this, Marvin," Samantha said, rising to her feet. "If you pull the trigger on that gun, you may very well get one of us. But, you will never leave this boat alive."

Her eyes caused a shiver to go up his spine. He quickly looked at the others. Their eyes conveyed a similar message. He looked back at Billy. The first thing he had to do was get that pistol away from the boy. "Count it down, Billy," he said. He heard several sighs of relief come from his fellow passengers. He'd be back in control soon.

"One," Billy said sharply.

Goldberg nodded. He let his arm relax.

"Two," Billy said, again sharply.

Goldberg again nodded. His arm was about to contract when he saw a flash come from the opening of the flare gun. Before he could recover, the twelve-gauge red hot flare slammed into his groin. He didn't know what he felt first, the pain from the impact or the pain from the fire that was suddenly engulfing him. He fell against the sliding door. He dropped the gun and both hands went to the point of impact. That caused burning in his hands. He screamed and slid to the floor. He looked up and Billy was standing over him. The boy had a weird look on his face, sort of like the look of morbid satisfaction. A whiff of burning flesh filled Goldberg's nostrils. He looked down at the area that was still on fire. His eyes widened and he looked back at Billy. "What happened to three?" he managed to say.

"I threw it overboard."

By now the cabin was rapidly filling with smoke and the putrid smell of burning flesh. Robert pushed Billy aside and pulled the ring on the fire extinguisher he had grabbed. A spray of white powder flew from the nozzle as the flames were quickly extinguished. The smell remained as did Goldberg's pain. He looked down and instinctively tried assessing the damage. He looked up in horror. Samantha was now standing over him. She was holding his gun in one hand, a fire extinguisher in the other. She leaned forward so that her face was only inches away from the burning man. Then she dropped the fire extinguisher directly onto the spot of the previous fire.

Goldberg struggled to stay alert, but the sudden increased pain caused him to lose the battle. As he passed out, the last thing he heard was Samantha's voice. "That's for the boy."

76

A short time later, everyone was aboard the *Avalon*. Arnold had come out with the Coast Guard. He and a Coast Guardsman were now crewing *Lady Hatteras II* back to shore.

Coffees and blankets had been passed out except to Marvin Goldberg, who was strapped to a stretcher on the deck of the Coast Guard cutter. He could still smell his own burned flesh. He could still feel the pain. And oh, what pain it was. He looked up as he heard a familiar voice. Billy was leaning over him. Samantha and the other two men were as well. Billy looked at Robert. "Well, I'd say everything went as planned tonight, don't you guys?"

Robert laughed. "Yeah, I was planning to almost die at sea."

"Me too," Dennis chirped in.

Samantha laid her arm on Robert's. "Thank you." She turned to Dennis. "Especially thank you, too. I know this was all your plan." She stepped forward and gave the pathology resident a bid hug.

"My pleasure," he was able to mumble as she squeezed the wind from his lungs.

A groggy Marvin Goldberg, fighting to ignore the smell as well as the pain, managed to say, "So this whole thing...this whole thing was a plan, a set up?"

A fourth face came into view. While Goldberg didn't know much about men in uniform, he knew enough to recognize that the man now standing over him was the captain of the ship. "Yes, Mr. Goldberg, this whole scenario tonight was the brainchild of Agent Tucker. And what a plan it was. Except for the weather, he had everything calculated down to the T." The ship's captain turned to Dennis. "Congratulations, sir. Job well done." He grabbed and shook Dennis's hand.

While the pathology resident was speechless, Samantha was not. "Captain, you just referred to him as Agent Tucker."

"That's right, ma'am. Good point, too." The captain turned his attention back to Dennis. "Sir, Agent Stackhouse was going to tell you himself when you got back to shore, but he gave me the okay to tell you here. He called the assistant director of the FBI tonight to report in. When he did, he told her about Dr. Tucker here. He also mentioned Dr. Tucker had an application in the works to get into the academy. The assistant director pulled up the application on her computer. She reviewed it quickly and approved it herself, right then and there. Now, they know you have to finish your residency, but they'll be in touch. My father retired from the FBI. I have a sister and a brother who are still in. It's a good organization. Congratulations."

Additional congratulations accompanied by some backslapping ensued. Then reality set in and all eyes returned to the figure on the floor. "It was all a plan?" Goldberg repeated.

"Pretty good one, too, huh?" Samantha said, sneering at him.

"Well, almost everything," Billy said. He was standing at the foot of the man who was spread eagle on the deck. "There is one thing that wasn't in the plan and we haven't done yet." He stepped in between Goldberg's legs. Before anyone realized what he was doing, or before anyone could stop him, he reared his right leg back and kicked the man sharply in the area of the burn. "Samantha already gave you one for the boy. That one's for Captain Willey."

Marvin Goldberg only felt the pain briefly as he again lost consciousness.

77

Robert saw the sign in the distance. A smile crossed his face. It was the first time he remembered such a reaction in several trips. Usually, he felt a sense of gloom and doom as he approached the Outer Banks. This time, however, he was much more upbeat. But why shouldn't he be? The chaos of the past few months was over. Billy was better. Robert was vindicated as the cause of Billy's issues. And the cause, one asshole named Marvin Goldberg, was in federal custody, and would probably remain so the rest of his life. As for Samantha, she was okay, too. Regarding his and Samantha's relationship, that remained to be seen. Robert was hopeful, however. They parted the last time on good terms, a novelty these past months.

As it often did, he felt his heart quicken as the sign grew closer. He loved the Outer Banks. He loved the smell of the ocean. He loved the weather. He loved the people, some even more than others. In his mind, it was a complete package. Now, all he needed to do was put a big red bow on top of Samantha and his life would be complete. Time would tell if there was such a bow.

His smile widened as he was now able to read the lettering on the sign: twelve miles to Oregon Inlet and the bridge onto Hatteras Island. He gave the sign a nod as he buzzed passed. It would be the last time he passed this sign for several weeks. An instant later, he jammed his foot on the brakes. He pulled off the road. He glanced into his rearview mirror to make sure no one was behind him. He put the SUV in reverse and backed up. He looked once, blinked a couple times. He looked again. He glanced at the sky to make sure the sun glare wasn't obstructing his view. While it was hot and sticky for the first week in July, a thin layer of clouds covered the sun.

He again looked at the sign. Sure enough, the bullet holes were gone. Then he realized it was a whole new sign. He sat in silence. How long had that sign been there? How many times had he passed it? How many times had it brought joy to other people? A sadness enveloped him. It was like he had lost an old friend. Then he had an encouraging thought. Perhaps he had gained a new one. He put the gearshift in forward and pulled back onto the road. Twelve miles to Hatteras.

78

Some thirty minutes later, Robert turned into the parking lot of the campground. He let out a chuckle. It was the first time Samantha didn't want to hide his presence. His chuckle turned to a wide smile as Samantha came bounding out the door of the store as he pulled up to the gas pump. As soon as he was out of the car, she was on him. Her arms encircled his neck. Her lips found his as she pulled him into her tightly. Then she let loose and looked at him, a wide smile on her face.

"Hi," she said.

Robert held out his hand. "Hi, I'm Robert. I'd like to buy some gas."

"I'll give you some gas," she said, jabbing him lightly in the stomach. She leaned forward to kiss him again. "But seriously, gas will have to wait. Our fuel tanks are almost empty. The fuel truck is on its way. Go on and park over to the side. I filled the Jeep up last night."

Robert got back in the SUV and was about to pull away when Samantha leaned in the window and gave him another kiss. As she did, her eyes caught the piles of boxes in the back.

"You planning on staying awhile?" she said, pointing to the back.

"Maybe," Robert said.

"Yeah, I bet."

They were on Route 12 heading south in Samantha's Jeep a minute later. As they cleared the town of Waves, Samantha shifted up to the speed limit. Her hand remained on the shift lever, covered by Robert's. All the canvas was off the vehicle so the wind blew through freely. It made conversation difficult which was fine with Robert. The only thing really on his mind was whether she would be happy to see him, and that question had already been answered. The rest of what was about to happen would be icing on the cake.

They pulled into Hatteras Marina, making good time even though they were in the middle of the tourist season. Samantha parked close to the water. As they got out, a gust of wind blew her hair across her face. She looked at the sky. The earlier thin clouds had now begun to thicken and had an ominous appearance to them. "They said we were going to get a storm this afternoon," she commented.

"I agree," Robert replied, coming around to her side of the Jeep. "You have your canvas and stuff with you?"

"It's all in the back. We'll close it up when we're done here. We've got time."

"Sounds like a plan." He grabbed her hand and led her towards the water. Because of the threat of bad weather, most of the charter fleet had already returned, although there were a few slips still empty. They headed out the longest of the piers, stopping about two-thirds of the way. *Lady Hatteras II* sat in her slip as if she was simply one of the crowd, which to most onlookers she was. To Robert, however, she was something special. There was a lot of history aboard this boat. A lot of stories she could tell; a lot of things she'd just as soon forget, too. Just like her predecessor, she had seen fair winds and calm seas. She had also weathered a lot of storms. Through it all, she lived up to her namesake. She was a true *Lady Hatteras*, proud and majestic.

The aft deck hatch was open. Billy was below leaning over the bank of batteries. Albert was standing off to the side peering in. Catching a glimpse of their visitors, Albert said. "Well, hello Sam…Robert. Fancy seeing you two here."

Billy looked toward the sound of Albert's voice. Seeing Robert and his sister, he said, "Hey sis. Hey asshole. How are you guys?"

"Billy!" Samantha said, scolding his language.

Robert laughed. "We're fine. How are you?"

"I'm cool." He climbed out of the bilge and closed the hatch. Wiping his hands on a rag, he added, "What brings you two down here?"

"We heard you were here, so we thought we'd come for a visit."

"That's cool. Come on aboard. Albert here, has her pretty well cleaned up. She still smells of smoke though.

He said someone is supposed to come down tomorrow and clean the carpet and upholstery."

"The next time you guys decide to roast marshmallows aboard a boat, do it over the side, will you? Not in the damn cabin," Arnold said.

"We'll try and remember that," Robert laughed.

Arnold held out a hand and helped Samantha aboard. Robert stepped across the gunwale behind her and went into the cabin. Billy was right, the place had been cleaned since he'd been aboard several weeks earlier. While you could still smell smoke, it wasn't as bad as he might have expected. He said so aloud.

"It isn't too bad," Billy agreed as he followed Arnold and his sister into the cabin. "Arnold called me this morning and asked me to come down and go over the boat with him. He's especially interested in the wiring."

"Not only did you roast some marshmallows in the cabin, you tried to fry up the breaker box as well," Arnold said. He pointed to the bank of circuit breakers that sat along the port wall.

"Everything seemed to be working okay that night when we left," Robert said. He was referring to the fact that when they got aboard the Coast Guard Cutter, they found Albert there waiting with one of the young Coast Guardsman to take the *Lady Hatteras II* back to port. While Billy objected, Dennis, Robert, and Samantha eagerly accepted the ride back to shore on the larger of the two vessels. Besides, Robert had a patient he had to attend to.

"You're right, but about halfway home I started having all sorts of electrical problems. Lost some of the lights and all the navigational gear went out as well. Luckily, nothing with the engine was affected."

"You got in though?" Robert said.

"Barely. But anyway, my electrician is supposed be here tomorrow as well."

They all took a seat while Billy went forward. He returned a moment later with Mountain Dews for everyone. Standing beside the helm, he said, "Speaking of fried marshmallows, how is the *real* asshole doing anyway?"

Robert took a long swallow of his soda and said, "I called the burn center before I left Baltimore. They said he was fussing and complaining of pain, but otherwise he was doing fine." Once Robert had assessed the damage done by the flare gun, Robert made arrangements for Goldberg to be flown by a Coast Guard helicopter to the Hopkin's Bayview Burn Center in Baltimore, even though what he really wanted to do was feed the scumbag to the sharks.

"Any more surgeries?" Samantha asked.

"He may need a couple more skin grafts, but that's further down the road. They expect him to make a full recovery."

"With all parts intact?" Billy inquired.

"Yes, Billy, with all parts intact."

"Shucks," Samantha said.

The other three laughed. Robert continued, "Anyway, they expect to release him by the end of next week."

"Where will he go then?" Samantha said.

"I seriously doubt whether the feds will allow him out of their sight. While I don't know how far he could get in his condition, he is considered a flight risk. They have him guarded and shackled to the bed except when he's getting treatment."

"Damn, Billy said.

"Dennis told me they plan to throw the book at him. Seems our whole plan worked just fine so they will be able to use the tape of the confession as evidence," Robert explained. "And don't forget, the other stuff we found on the boat."

"But you took all that off," Samantha pointed out.

"Seems the FBI found the liquor bottle and underwear," Arnold said.

"But..." Samantha paused. She tipped her head to the side and stared at Robert. "You put all that back, didn't you?"

"The FBI found them in a bag hidden in a forward locker."

"Isn't that like tampering with evidence?" Samantha asked.

Robert smiled. "The FBI agent that found the bag didn't suspect any tampering."

Samantha smiled back.

"Besides, they probably won't need that stuff anyway," Robert said. "The agent in charge of the case remarked on several occasions how wonderful a job you did of getting Goldberg to talk. You led him on without any semblance of entrapment. So, good work."

"Thank you," Samantha said.

"Anyway," Robert continued. "One of the reasons we wanted to have Goldberg agree to take *Lady Hatteras II* away from the dock was so then he could be not only be charged with murder, kidnaping, and all the other charges associated with those issues, he could also be officially charged with piracy on the open seas, which carries all sorts of long penalties including the death penalty if they want to push the point." Robert took another sip of his soda. "Bottom line, Marvin Goldberg will be spending the rest of his life behind bars."

"Good," Samantha quipped.

"Dennis told me something else," Robert added. "Goldberg's attorney has already thrown out feelers about a plea bargain. Seems the possibility of the death penalty has been bantered about by the feds and has old Goldberg scared. Now, I don't know the last time the feds executed anyone, but they certainly have Goldberg thinking about it. Dennis thinks Goldberg may be willing to cooperate fully with the investigation under two conditions. First, that he only receives life without the chance of parole, therefore no possibility of the death penalty. Secondly..." Robert paused and looked over at Samantha. "That all charges against his brother be dropped."

"What!" Billy said.

Samantha could be heard sucking in a deep breath.

Robert quickly continued. "It turns out Marvin Goldberg has some scruples after all. He cares about his own life; and in some form or another, he cares about his brother's."

"What are the chances of that actually happening?" Samantha asked cautiously.

"According to Dennis, pretty good. If you really think about it, the only real crime Arthur ever committed was failure to report the crimes his brother was committing. He was a victim, too. He was probably being blackmailed as well. If he ever talked, heaven only knows what his brother would have done to him or anyone around him."

"That's a scary thought," Billy said. "But now he wants to help his brother?"

"That's because the man's plum crazy," Albert piped in. "I knew that the first time I met him. One of the craziest and scariest people I ever met. Years ago he started to lean on me about various things and I told him to go take a hike. The next night the *Blue Parrot* next door burnt to the ground. I got the message loud and clear. From then on, I did whatever he wanted, which really wasn't a lot, but still..."

Robert listened to this, carefully thinking that the Goldberg brothers were certainly tough books to judge. As an afterthought he wondered: weren't most people like that?

"Anyway," he said aloud. He looked at Albert who glanced down at his watch. The marina owner also gave a subtle shrug..

Before Robert could say anything else, he heard a tapping on the side of the boat. "Permission to come aboard?" a cheery voice called out.

"Who's that?" Billy said.

"I don't know. Why don't you go find out," his sister directed.

Without realizing he should be asking *why me*, Billy slid off his seat and stepped outside. "Mako!" he spouted.

As usual, the young girl was dressed in a size too small red tee shirt and pair of khaki shorts. Also, as usual, she was barefooted. Her hair was pulled pack in a short ponytail with a pair of sunglasses sat atop her head. "Hey, Billy. How you doing?"

"I'm okay. What are you doing down this end of the island? I thought your father kept his boat up north."

"He does. I'm down here looking for a job."

By now, the others had exited the cabin. Mako was welcomed aboard. Billy watched all this in wonderment. First Robert and his sister show up, and now Mako. "What's going on here guys?" he finally said, looking at each of the others.

"Like I said, I'm down here looking for a job?" Mako said.

"A job doing what?"

"Mating."

"I thought you worked for your father when you weren't at the campground?"

"I do, but he's cut way back. He only goes out once or twice a week now, if that. He's too busy fixing boats. I still plan to work at the campground though." Her father was a part time charter boat captain who fished out of the northern inlet. He also worked full time as a diesel mechanic with a high-level reputation. Mako mated for him when she could.

"Where do you expect to find a mate job this time of year?"

Mako glanced over at Samantha for guidance. When her campground boss gave her a positive nod, she continued. "Right here."

"Right here? What do you mean?" By now Billy was totally baffled, yet he sensed something was up.

Mako continued. "You remember years ago, Billy, you made me a promise that the day you got your own boat you'd give me a big hug and a kiss, and you'd also hire me on as your mate? Remember that?"

Surprisingly enough, Billy did. "Yes."

"Well, I'm here to collect on all that."

Billy let out a nervous chuckle. "But I don't have a boat."

Robert, who had been standing off to the side next to Samantha, cleared his throat. "Um, don't mean to interrupt, Billy, but you're wrong there."

Billy looked at Robert, and then at his sister, who continued the explanation. "*Lady Hatteras II* is yours," she said choking back the tears.

"Mine!"

"Yes, Billy, she's all yours," Arnold explained. "Seems that Captain Willey put in his will that the boat was to be sold by his wife if she ever needed the money; otherwise, once she passed, if the boat was still seaworthy, *Lady Hatteras II* was to be turned over to you."

"Me! You mean this boat is mine?"

"Yes, Billy, the boat is yours," Robert said. "Congratulations."

Billy wasn't often at a loss for words, but he was now. It gave Arnold an opportunity to explain something to Samantha he'd been meaning to do. "The day of Willey's funeral, the widow came up to me and said to go ahead and put the boat on the market. Then she leaned into me and said she wouldn't be too upset if I didn't try too hard to sell her. You see, Samantha, that's why I had her buried in the back. That's also why I never cleaned her up. I didn't want her to sell. The widow told me that Captain Willey wanted Billy to have the boat someday if possible." The marina owner turned his attention to Billy. "I guess that day is today," he said.

Still at a loss for words, Billy looked first at Arnold, then at Robert, then at his sister. Finally, his eyes set on Mako. She continued to smile at him.

He stepped toward her, grabbed her in his arms and planted a gigantic kiss right on her lips. The first kiss was short. The second was not. When he finally broke away, he looked at her and said, "So you need a job, huh?"

"Not anymore," she chirped. They kissed again, oblivious to the sound of applause surrounding them.

Somewhat to Mako's objection, Billy cut the moment short. He put his arm around her and faced the others. "One thing I should tell you though," he said, a somber tone to his voice. "I am going to rename the boat. *Lady Hatteras II* will be no more." Before anyone could object, he went on to explain how he used to invite Captain Willey to come down to the Rodanthe pier and go fishing with him at night. But Willey always declined, saying he didn't need any pier to fish off of. His boat was his pier. "I promised myself that if I ever got a boat of my own, I was going to name her in honor of Captain Willey.

"What's the name going to be?" Samantha asked.

Billy looked at his sister. "*Willey's Pier.*"

79

The trip north was much more leisurely, although the wind had picked up as the sky continued to darken. Robert and Samantha didn't care. Billy was the happiest he'd been in a long time. While Robert and Samantha gave each other credit, both knew deep down it was a team effort. Another well-laid out plan.

Billy said as much when he realized he had been set up. After giving everyone a hug and handshake, Billy started babbling about all the stuff he had to do to get the boat seaworthy, especially since the little incident with roasting marshmallows. Arnold cut him off and explained that Captain Willey's will stipulated that the boat be seaworthy at the time of official transfer of ownership. Arnold went on to explain there was money set aside to do just that. So the boat was Billy's, but it wouldn't be official until Arnold was satisfied everything was in working order. He predicted about a week or so before *Willey's Pier* could make her maiden voyage under Billy's command. After everyone gave their blessing at the name change, Samantha told her brother to cool his heels and relax. "Enjoy the moment," she directed.

His excitement finally under control, Billy decided to do just that. He was going to stay on board the rest of the day, maybe even through the night. He asked Mako if she wanted to join him. She started to say that she couldn't because she was working at the campground that night. Samantha chimed in and said she already had the shift covered by one of the other summer staff.

Arnold went back to his office while Samantha and Robert bid captain and mate goodbye. As they walked up the pier towards the Jeep, Samantha glanced over her shoulder. Damn if that girl wasn't in her brother's arms again, only this time they looked like they were doing a lot more than kissing. In response, she grabbed Robert's hand, which she had seldom let go.

Slowing down and shifting gears as they entered the town of Hatteras, Samantha said, "You hungry?"

"I haven't eaten since I left Baltimore, but I can wait if you can."

"I'm in no rush. How 'bout we plan to go out to dinner somewhere nice later. My treat."

"Fine by me."

Once through the town, Samantha sped up to the speed limit. Her hand again searched out her passenger's. Both had a lot going through their minds, but with the breeze continuing to pick up, conversation was limited, which was fine. As they approached the parking lot that led to their favorite spot on the beach, Robert motioned out his side and said, "Let's go see what the surf's doing?"

"It's getting ready to storm," Samantha pointed out.

Robert looked to the west from where the storm was coming. "We have plenty of time."

Soon they were parked in their favorite spot, the wreck of *The Lady Hatteras* off to their left. Samantha slid her seat back and propped her feet up on the dash. Robert followed suit. The surf was light. The seas were calm. The ocean had not yet been forewarned of the impending change in the weather.

Robert pointed at the shipwreck and said, "You know, with Billy changing the name of the boat, there's only two of you left."

"What do you mean *two of us*?"

"Two *Lady Hatterases,* the shipwreck and you."

She looked at him and smiled. "You always did call me your *Lady Hatteras*, didn't you? I forgot about that."

"I didn't," he said softly.

"Am I still worthy of the title?" she said.

"In my book you are, and that's all that matters."

"You're so sweet."

"Thank you, *Lady Hatteras*."

Samantha leaned over and kissed him softly on the lips. "You're welcome." She then adjusted her position so her head could rest on his shoulder.

Robert continued, "I thought it was a little risky, you inviting Mako down there like that."

"It might seem that way," Samantha replied. "But those two have had the hots for one another for years. Mako told me about the promise Billy made to her the day he made it. She always said she was going to hold him to it, too."

Robert laughed. "I guess if the real estate market down here collapses, you can always open up a matchmaking service. You certainly hit the nail on the head with that one."

"Like I said, that was a match made a long time ago," Samantha argued. "It just needed a little nudging, that was all."

"Speaking of real estate," Robert said, "what's going to happen to you now?"

Samantha sat up to work a crick from her neck. "For starters, I suspect the real estate side of Goldberg Industries will survive. Arthur assured me that part had always been run on the up and up; though, I suspect the mortgage side of the business will go down the hopper. But that's no big deal. There's plenty of money out there if you know where to look for it." She paused and let out a soft laugh. "Maybe I'll now have the time to do something I've always wanted to do."

"What's that?"

"I've always wanted to be a writer. Maybe I'll write something."

"I remember you used to talk about that," Robert said. He had always filed that away along with other dreams Samantha used to talk about. "What would you write?" he asked.

"Oh, I don't know. Maybe a book or something."

Robert started to laugh before realizing she was being serious. Besides, while he may have doubted her determination to do something in the past, that feeling no longer existed. "Then go for it," he said encouragingly. He watched as a seagull dove into the water. It flew away a moment later, dinner clamped tightly in its beak. "What would you write about?"

"I haven't got that far yet."

This time Robert did laugh. "Write about us?"

"Us?"

"Yes, us."

Samantha smiled. "And what would the title of this bestselling novel be?"

Robert looked toward the ocean. "You could call it *The Ladies of Hatteras*."

"The Ladies of Hatteras, verses Ladies of Hatteras?" Samantha questioned.

Robert chuckled. "Gives it a more majestic sound."

"Not a bad idea. I'll think about it."

"You decide, it's your book," Robert said.

Samantha looked out across the water. "If Arthur gets off like you said, he'll need some support. Financially, he assured me he's okay. Emotionally, however, he'll need some help. He's officially announced the end of our engagement. He told me that even though we would have never had any sort of a physical relationship, he was looking forward to my companionship."

"Can't he still have that?" Robert said.

Samantha looked at him long and hard. "Yes, I guess he can."

"What about your parents?"

"They're going to go ahead and keep the property in Buxton but hold off any construction until this whole thing blows over. They've been assured that when they're ready to build, the permits will be available. In the meantime, they're looking at retiring and moving to Ocracoke. I found out recently that's where they wanted to be when we first came down here years ago. But they thought it was too risky a business venture back in the old days, plus it's not really conducive for raising a family. People do it, but it's hard on the kids. Hatteras is tough enough."

"Where are they going to live on Ocracoke?"

Samantha wiped a tear from her eye. "Arthur's going to give them a deal on one of his condos. He basically told them to pick out whichever one they want and he'll give it to them at cost. He wants to do that as a way of paying them back for the trouble he and his brother put them through."

"That's very generous." Robert said. As an afterthought, he added. "Tell me something, why Ocracoke? Why put such expensive condos there?"

"There aren't many places left on the east coast where you can totally escape," Samantha explained. "Arthur's vision was for that to be such a place. It's going to be totally self-contained."

"You think it'll work?"

"I had my reservations when he first told me about the project, but Arthur has the mind for such a thing." She paused. "He really is a wonderful man once you get to know him. It's just too bad he had that albatross of a brother hanging on him all these years."

"I agree Arthur Goldberg is a victim like everyone else, but he made the choice to get involved with his brother in the first place."

"He realizes that," Samantha said. "And he's not disputing his responsibility in all this. He told me he's going to do whatever it takes to make things right with the people he's hurt."

"What about the little boy's family?"

"He's already talked to the sister, the receptionist you evidently met. Surprisingly enough, she made him promise not to tell anyone else in the family what really happened. The boy's mother is still alive and lives in Ocean City where she works for Arthur as a property manager. The sister thinks it's best to let sleeping dogs lie. She was told it was an accidental death when it happened. It's still the truth, that is if you believe Arthur's brother."

"Do you believe him?"

Samantha hesitated. "For the boy's sake, I do."

"For the record, I do too," Robert said. "I watched him very carefully throughout the whole ordeal while he was confessing. I think everything he said during that time was the truth. I suspect it was the first time he ever talked about it."

"You're probably right."

"Dennis agrees," Robert said.

"Speaking of Dennis," Samantha said, "what's he going to do now? Is he really going to the FBI?"

Robert laughed. "He reports next week."

"What's so funny about that?"

"We've all been giving him a hard time about the physical conditioning he's going to have to go through. You know, he is a bit out of shape."

"A bit!"

Robert laughed. "He didn't realize it at the time, but the position he's applied for will involve field work, therefore he'll become a full-blown agent. Once he finishes with that training, he goes to Washington for a year for a fellowship in criminal pathology. Following that, he'll be assigned to one of the field offices somewhere around the country. He'd prefer to stay on the east coast, but he'll go anywhere they send him. It's a dream come true for him. As far as the physical side of it all, he's already joined a gym and is working with a trainer who is familiar with the FBI physical requirements."

"That's good," Samantha said. "I'm happy for him. He deserves it. After all, he put together a great plan."

"That he did," Robert acknowledged. "Although, I have to admit I was getting nervous with Marvin Goldberg waving that gun around the way he was."

It was Samantha's turn to laugh. "That bothered you, huh?"

"It didn't you?"

"No."

"Why not?"

"Because there were no bullets in the gun, or rather, there were bullets, but they were blanks. Taking the bullets out totally would have changed the weight and thus the feel of the gun. Marvin would have probably noticed that."

"How did you know they were blanks?"

"Arthur switched them out one night his brother was staying at his place a few days ago. Then I put the real bullets back while you all were scurrying around putting out the fire."

"I remember you did grab the gun."

"Right."

"But why keep us in the dark about something like that?"

"Two reasons. I had no way of verifying that Marvin didn't notice the change in weight and thus replace them with real bullets. Secondly, I didn't want anyone to get cocky and do something that would have jeopardized his confession. Mostly though, it's the first reason."

"You're a very smart woman."

"It wasn't my idea. It was Arthur's. He didn't know what we were planning. He was worried about Billy."

"I see." After a brief pause, Robert changed the subject. "What about the campground?"

"They don't know it yet, but the cousins are going to be promoted to co-managers. If Mako does fish with Billy, she probably won't be as involved, but that's okay. Rhonda—that's the other cousin—she's got the wherewithal to run the place on her own. Mako may not even want the job. Of the two, she seems to like the night work the best."

"Then make her the nighttime manager," Robert suggested.

Samantha cocked her head to the side as she broke into a smile. "Good idea. You're a very smart man."

Robert laughed. "Two peas in a pod we are."

Samantha's facial expression turned serious. "Are we?"

"What do you mean by that?" Robert queried.

"We've talked about everybody down here but you," Samantha said. "What are your plans? Your residency's over, right?"

"It was officially over June 30th. I counted it up the other day and I've been in school continuously for twenty-six years. That's a long time."

"Now you're a free man."

"Only for another week."

"What then?"

"I start my new job."

"Oh." There was an obvious thread of concern in Samantha's voice.

"August 2nd is my first shift as a full-fledged attending physician at Nags Head Community Hospital."

"Oh," Samantha repeated with some disappointment. Then she snapped her head in his direction. "Nags Head...as in..."

Robert broke into a smile. "Yes, Sam, Nags Head as in Nags Head, North Carolina, right up the road a few miles."

"You're joking."

"Afraid I'm not," Robert said. "But it's a little more complicated than that. You see, I told you I was offered a faculty position in the ER at Hopkins. I met with Dr. Kerrigan, that's the director, when I got back to Baltimore. We talked about various things. When I mentioned Hatteras, he told me that Hopkins ER group had recently acquired the ER contract in Nags Head."

"Emergency room services are contracted out?" Samantha said.

"Many hospitals do. It's become big business."

"I see."

"Anyway, Kerrigan made a couple phone calls and low and behold, there was an opening down here. On top of that, the director trained under Kerrigan fifteen years before me. So, I was basically hired on the spot, sight unseen, although we have talked at length over the phone. The director told me the hospital here is also looking to open a series of urgent care centers along the Outer Banks. I'll be heading up that project as well."

"You mean we're going to get health care down here on the island?"

"Definitely on Hatteras. I don't know about Ocracoke. Maybe we can do something there in the summer."

"Anything's better than what we have now," Samantha quipped.

"That's probably at least a year away. I gotta get my feet wet in the ER first. On top of that, every physician who works down here is on the faculty at Hopkins, which means I'll have to go to Baltimore every so often for meetings, to give lectures and to even work a few shifts in their ER. I want that so I won't lose my trauma skills."

"But basically, you're going to be living down here."

"That's my plan."

Samantha surveyed the area. They had the beach to themselves, as the couple vehicles that were parked nearby pulled up stakes shortly after they arrived. And yes, there was a lone seagull perched atop the mast of the shipwreck. "Why are you doing this?" she said.

"I figured I'd miss the feel of sand between my toes."

"You hate the sand," Samantha noted.

"I'll learn to love it."

Samantha smiled before her expression turned serious. "You really haven't answered the question."

"Of why I'm doing this?"

She nodded.

Robert paused. "When I met with Dr. Kerrigan, I told him my dream job would be down here, close to the beach. I even told him a little bit about Billy. I didn't go into a lot of details, but I told him the story of what happened here, and the impact it had on everybody, especially your brother. I didn't know it, but it turns out Dr. Kerrigan is an avid offshore sport fisherman, although he usually fishes out of Ocean City. When I tell him Billy's got his own boat now, I'm sure he'll want a ride.

"Anyway, I told Dr. Kerrigan that while the beach, Billy, and all that other stuff is important to me, the number one reason I wanted to be down here was because of you. And he understood. So here I am." He looked over at Samantha and placed his hand on her cheek. "The bottom line, Sam, is that I was down here some five years ago, and then I up and left. Was it the right thing to do, to go back home and finish my training? Or did I make a mistake leaving you the way I did? I think the answer to both is yes. Be that as it may, I'm here now, and it's a mistake I never want to make again." He leaned forward and kissed her gently. "You know when I was driving down here today, there's a sign up north that says twelve miles to Hatteras. I've passed that sign dozens of times in my life. It's always been the same sign, too. It's old, it's dilapidated, and it had three bullet holes in it."

"I know the sign you mean," Samantha said.

"It's been there ever since I started coming down here," Robert said, eyeing the shipwreck. "Well, today the sign was gone, replaced by a totally new one. Now, that just happened between this trip and the last.... After all these years."

"Maybe it's symbolic of a new start?" Samantha suggested.

"My thoughts exactly," Robert said.

"Then that's what it'll be."

Robert turned and looked at her. "You think that's possible?"

It was her turn to initiate the kiss. "Yes, I do." She started to lean forward and kiss him again. Then she sat upright suddenly. "Wait a minute. You're starting in a week?"

"That's right?"

"Where you going to stay?"

"I was hoping I could find a good real estate agent to help me."

Samantha showed her surprise. "You already have all your stuff with you, don't you? That's what all the boxes are in your car."

"I moved out of my apartment yesterday. I sold off a bunch of stuff, gave away a bunch more to the Goodwill. Otherwise, everything I own in the world is in the back of the Beemer."

"Then we'd better get rolling and find you a place."

"I can always stay in a hotel or motel for a short time if I need to," Robert said.

"Fat chance," Samantha said. "Did you forget this is the middle of the tourist season? It's our busiest time at the campground."

"Yes, I realized it," Robert said. "But it's a barrier I wasn't going to let stop me."

"Yeah, but..."

Robert's finger went across her mouth. "I spent many a night on the pier in Rodanthe, took a shower in the morning in the bathhouse and then went to work. Worst case scenario, that's what I'll do. I've already bought my season pass for the year. Believe it or not, you can even do that online now." He removed his finger and replaced it quickly with his own lips.

The kiss was cut short though by a clap of thunder behind them. They both looked in that direction. Large, black, ominous clouds were rapidly bearing down on them. "Shit," they said simultaneously.

They jumped out of the Jeep and scurried to the back where they worked in unison to get the top canvases and vinyl windows up on the vehicle. It would be nice to say they made it just in the nick of time, but by the time they scampered back inside, they were soaked. The storm attacked with vengeance. Rain came at them at almost a horizontal angle. The winds threatened to lift the Jeep right out of the sand. Neither passenger was worried though. They had both been through similar storms in the past, together, in the same vehicle and at the same spot on the beach. They had even driven out to the beach on purpose when they knew a storm was approaching. While some may have thought the two crazy, they relished the excitement of what was going on around them.

Robert leaned back and reached under the driver's seat. "You still keep a stash of towels?" His question was answered when his hand felt the terrycloth material. He pulled out two beach towels. He handed one to Samantha and wiped his face with the other. He watched Sam as she did the same. Her hair was matted from the rain. She had streaks on her face. The polo shirt she wore bearing the campground logo clung to her like a frightened baby to its mother. She looked a mess. To Robert though, she looked as beautiful as ever. He reached over and wiped away a drop of water that was running down her neck.

"We have plenty of time, huh?" she teased.

"I said I wanted to look at the ocean, not talk for an hour."

"You can look at the ocean now. It's a mess."

It was. Waves rolled in, striking the beach in anger, sending sheets of salt spray across the sand. They were parked about halfway between the waterline and the dunes, but the Jeep still took an occasional hit of ocean spray. They couldn't see very far past the waterline though as visibility continued to drop as the storm intensified. Flashes of lightning followed immediately by claps of thunder told the couple the bulk of the storm was directly overhead. As they used to do five years before, all they could do was hunker down and ride the storm out.

"Where do you want to go tonight for dinner?" Samantha said, rubbing the towel through her hair.

"I don't care. You choose."

"There's a new place down in Buxton that just opened up this summer. I haven't eaten there yet, but everyone says it's very good."

"Sounds okay to me. But I'll need to clean up first."

"You can shower at the campground. I'll see if we can find a spot to squeeze you in, too."

"I can sleep in the car."

"You may just have to do that."

"Or out on the pier in Rodanthe like I said earlier."

"Whatever."

Several claps of thunder ensued. "You remember when we used to ride out storms like this on purpose." Robert said between the noise.

"We were young. We were idiots," Samantha replied.

"Now we're older and still idiots," Robert said.

"You're right," Samantha agreed. She adjusted her position so she could lay her head in his lap. Robert wrapped his arms around her. He pulled her up to him so they could kiss.

Breaking away for air, Samantha said, "As I recall, we used to do more than simply ride out the storms."

"I remember."

"Well?" Samantha grabbed one of his hands and moved it to her breast. He caressed her gently. Her nipples immediately became aroused. She moaned softly. She sat up and pulled the wet shirt up over her head. Then she reached behind her and unhooked her bra. Bare from the waist up, she leaned over and kissed him on the cheek. At the same time, her hand dropped to his groin. Robert let out a soft moan that was drowned out by another clap of thunder. Sam arched her back to press her chest into his face. He kissed her, first on the left side, then on the right. "Remember how we used to make love in the back seat?" she said softly. Her words were followed by a moan of pleasure.

He didn't answer. He pushed her away, moved his seat all the way forward, and climbed into the back seat. With some effort, she followed.

The storm outside the Jeep continued another ten minutes or so. The storm inside lasted longer. By the time both were spent and they somehow managed to climb back into their wet clothes, the sky had cleared. The sun, now only an hour off the western horizon, sent horizontal rays of light across the water. The winds had died. The seas had calmed as well. Samantha and Robert climbed out of the Jeep to get some fresh air. Plus, Robert needed to get the kinks out of his legs.

They stood arm in arm, silently looking at the scene before them. No matter how many times in the past, each day watching the darkness engulf the ocean was a new and invigorating experience. A lone puff of wind passed, sending a chill through Samantha's body. Robert took her face in his hand and kissed her softly. Then then looked eastward. It was going to be a beautiful night.

The mood was suddenly broken by Samantha, as she said, "Oh my God." Her hand rose to her mouth.

"What?" Robert said, glancing at her.

Sam's free hand was pointing at the water. "Look!"

Robert's gaze followed her arm. "I don't see anything," he said watching the swells that were continuing to soften after the storm.

"That's exactly right," Samantha said. "She's gone."

"Who's...?" Robert stopped in mid-sentence. Samantha was right. She was gone. The wreck of *The Lady*

Hatteras could no longer be seen. Robert rubbed his eyes to make sure they weren't playing tricks on him. They were not. He glanced up the beach. There was no debris indicating any part had washed ashore. He looked back to the spot where the mast used to protrude out of the water. Then he turned and looked at Samantha. Her hand was still covering her mouth. Tears flowed down her cheeks.

"Your brother said she didn't have many storms left in her," Robert said. He took Samantha in his arms, squeezing her tightly. He turned her toward him and kissed her gently. Her lips were salty from the tears. He kissed her again. She responded in kind. She turned her head to look across the water. Robert did the same. "Now there's only one," he said.

"One?"

"Yes, Sam, one. You're the only *Lady Hatteras* left."

And so I was.

Dorsey Butterbaugh has his undergraduate degree from the Johns Hopkins University and a MBA from Loyola College in Maryland. He has worked as a physician assistant for over 40 years. He has also been in management and consulting in the medical field. He has been involved behind the scenes in local politics in Baltimore. He is also a political speechwriter. While his hobbies include boating and fishing, he has always been an avid reader and writer.

He has written several books. Behind Bars, with James Willey, is his first published novel. Trilogy in G Minor is the second published novel. He has several other projects in the works.

Born and raised in Baltimore, he and his wife now live full time in West Fenwick Island, Delaware, a few miles from the ocean.

Feel free to contact Dorsey at dorseybutter6@aol.com . Reviews and comments on Amazon are appreciated!

Dorsey Butterbaugh (with James Willey):

Dr. Adam Singer is a world-famous surgeon who is faced with his greatest challenge—the ability to move on with his life after facing a terrible tragedy. He meets Bobby, a local bartender in Fenwick Island, Delaware, and soon begins to experience a different culture from his norm. He learns we all have bars in our lives we have to deal with. He also learns how to love again.

A fantastic tale of humor and intrigue set in the context of your local bar. With characters reminiscent of your neighbors, you will surely not put his book down.
 - Brian Desaulniers, MD

Butterbaugh and Willey offer a plot that's an easy guide into a specialized field of medicine and into the Delmarva beach communities. Their characters are as memorable as their true to life anecdotes focusing on beach or bar life. Behind Bars is a fun book. Take it to the beach, the airport or an easy chair with your favorite refreshment. I'll take a Bud Lite.
 - Frank Minni, President, Rehoboth Beach Writers' Guild.

Mr. Butterbaugh and Mr. Willey have created a beauty of a book here about the truth of human experience. Their characters are not the shiny false placeholders we've come to accept in literature today, but people drawn so real you feel as if you'll run into them if ever you sit down at Smitty McGee's. It's a lovely story of the resilience of the human spirit and the renewal of a person's soul.

- Kerry Forrestal, MD

- Author of Club Hell and The Chronicles of the Myst-Clipper Shicaine

Dorsey Butterbaugh

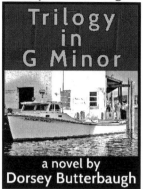

What is the power of one's dreams? April Blackstone dreams of being a concert pianist. Cliff Davidson dreams of living on his sailboat, drawing and painting, sustaining himself through his art. Jennifer Blackstone dreams of independence, of writing a novel, of romance.

Three previously unconnected lives forced by fate to come together and interconnect in a destined trilogy, a Trilogy in G Minor.

But dreams don't come easy. An untimely death. Running from the law. The perils and trials test resolve, build character, forge destiny.

Join April, Cliff, and Jennifer in an epic story of intrigue, of self-discovery, of relentlessly and tirelessly moving through their lives.

Dorsey Butterbaugh

M. R. Salisbury is the most prolific, successful author of modern-day literature, except no one knows who he (or she) is. Despite the reward offered by Salisbury University, the mystery seems secure; that is until Jamie Hopkins shows up on campus claiming to have already solved the mystery.

The sun beat down on him like a branding iron on the backside of a squealing calf. From below, sand burned his feet. The liquid within the blisters was threatening to boil. He knew the journey was about to end. Danny Warfield could sense it. It had been a long forty days and forty nights since he left the shade of the tree. His journey led him along the beach, along the water, day in, day out, night in, night out, one step at a time. He didn't know what he was going to find at the end of his journey. But he did know one thing, he was looking forward to it.

More time passed. How much, he didn't know. His ability to think clearly had significantly diminished, including the skill to count days. His focus was now solely on taking the next step. He was so hungry, so tired, and so thirsty he wasn't sure how much longer he could go on. He kept thinking, kept telling himself the journey had to be over soon.

Dorsey Butterbaugh

Turtles in the Sand, the story of Dr. Richard Baxter, a successful orthopedic surgeon who wears blinders like a horse when it comes to taking advice. A wise turtle might tell him that sometimes it is good to listen to others.

Turtles in the Sand, the story of Edward Baxter, Dr. Baxter's youngest son, who is torn between continuing his medical education or choosing another career path. A wise turtle might tell him that sometimes you have to lose yourself before you find yourself.

Turtles in the Sand, the story of Abbey O' Brian, the general manager of The Original Greene Turtle and niece of its owners, as she balances her professional responsibilities with her passion to rescue and rehabilitate turtles. A wise turtle might tell her that sometimes more than turtles need to be saved.

Turtles in the Sand, the story of these three people, whose lives intersect, beginning with a turtle lying on his back in the middle of the road.

Made in the USA
Middletown, DE
26 February 2023